A SINISTER
ESTABLISHMENT

A Regency Cozy

LYNN MESSINA

potatoworks press • greenwich village

Never miss a new release! Join Lynn's mailing list.

Beatrice Hyde-Clare Mysteries

To the dozens of awesome history buffs and Regency authors whose websites and blogs ensure that my historically adjacent cozies aren't historically embarrassing. Thank you!

Chapter One

I f *Beatrice Hyde-Clare* had realized that her refusal to consent to her betrothed's slight alteration in their marriage vows would allow his grandmother to assemble a roomful of people to witness the happy event, she would have agreed at once to his request. A promise made during one's nuptials was binding, to be sure, but she had little doubt she would have found a way to extricate herself from a pledge to cease investigating murders should the need arise—a development she deemed highly unlikely, though not impossible considering the recent spate of corpses in her life. Her confidence was owed to the fact that during her brief courtship of the Duke of Kesgrave she'd grown adept at making rhetorically persuasive arguments. If her logic did not quite meet his rigorous standards for accuracy, it was no matter, for it satisfied her own.

Alas, she had been too delighted by Kesgrave's audacity in rewriting the Book of Common Prayer—and why should he not take a liberal hand, for its lineage went back a mere three centuries while his own encompassed a full half millennium—to notice the dowager quietly scribbling messages at a table in the corner of the drawing room. It was only when the familiar trill of her aunt's strident disapproval wafted in from the entry hall that she recognized the tactical error.

"Well, no, Flora, I do not think Beatrice *chose* to have her wedding today with the *express* purpose of rousing you from your sickbed," Vera Hyde-Clare explained with just enough uncertainty in her voice to allow for the possibility, "as I believe she holds you in high esteem and would never *wish* for you to suffer a monstrous setback or have your health permanently damaged. And yet here you are, at Clarges Street, a shadow of your former self, barely able to hold your head up as you totter forward. Rather, I am merely calling attention to the misfortune of the timing, for it is so very unfortunate. It goes without saying that I would much rather you had *not* eaten a plate of spoiled oysters. But having made such an ill-advised decision—and an unusual one, too, as I would have sworn you detested the creatures—you should be allowed to bear the consequences in peace rather than summoned to attend a wedding that was not *supposed* to happen for another three days. I cannot condone the thoughtlessness. My poor dear, how terrifyingly pale you look. Do lean on me, so that you do not collapse onto the dowager's fine marble floor." She paused slightly in her speech, then added, "Oh, but it is very fine marble indeed, so elegantly veined. I wonder if it's from Italy. Livorno, perhaps. Or maybe Carrara."

As genuinely concerned as she was about her daughter's health, Vera's anxiety was no match for her instinctive admiration for quality, and Bea, noting the hushed tone with which she spoke, imagined the other woman running her fingers reverentially over the smooth marble. It was a visceral response to opulence, one Vera could no more control than the beating of her own heart, and, amused by her aunt's constancy, Bea envisioned her perched on the threshold of heaven too awed by the exquisite ornamentation of the pearly gates to enter.

'Twas an absurd picture, without question—Aunt Vera pestering poor St. Peter on the location of the seabed from which the jewels were harvested whilst he tried to find her name in the Book of Life—and Bea laughed despite her churlishness. She was further diverted when Flora, assuring her mother she felt quite sturdy, laid claim to a miraculous recovery. "Truly, I feel as though I was never sick at all, Mama. I cannot think of how to account for it save for your exceptional care. Thank you, darling, for attending to me so diligently."

As Flora's stomach ailment had been a ruse employed that morning to allow her to slip from her home at 19 Portman Square unnoticed, this assertion was decidedly false. Indeed, the whole scheme had been based on the assumption that her mother's sweeping discomfort with illness would keep her far away from the sickroom, a supposition that proved accurate when she prescribed several hours of uninterrupted rest for her daughter. Obligingly banished to her bedchamber, Flora had changed into her brother's clothes, crept out of the house through the kitchens and hailed a carriage to the Strand. There, she'd gained entry into the theater where Bea and the duke were investigating the murder of an actor and rescued them from a slow, agonizing death in the jet-black bowels of the building's cellars.

That Kesgrave had already freed them from their restraints and would have turned his attention to the door as soon as Bea had finished expressing her gratitude had no bearing on Flora's perception of herself as their heroic savior. As such, she took a sort of proprietary interest in them now as she strode into the drawing room, asserting that the only wretched thing would have been for the pair to wed without their guardian angel in attendance.

Vera, whose aversion to infirmity of any sort was so deeply ingrained even she realized there was something suspicious about her daughter's praise of her nursing skills, stared in confusion at this mention of a protective spirit and looked around the room as if expecting to see some secondary figure from the Bible standing by the fireplace, such as Noah or Job.

Fortunately, she spotted only her niece, whose customarily wan appearance reminded her why she was so cross in the first place, and she berated the girl with brusque impatience for breaking her promise to wait a full week before making her vows. "I cannot comprehend it. No, I cannot. If you were determined to ignore the wisdom of my counsel, then why do so *after* our visit to Madame Bélanger? Surely, courtesy demands that you openly rebel the day *before* a significant investment is made on your behalf? I find your behavior vexing, extremely vexing."

Since Bea resented the acquisition of the excessively lavish trousseau almost as much as her aunt, she thought this was a fair question and turned her unblinking gaze to Kesgrave for a reply, as the decision to diverge from the agreed-upon schedule had been his. Daunted by neither the presence of Vera Hyde-Clare nor the sting of her disapproval, he returned Bea's stare with unflinching calm, his own eyes, brilliantly blue and impossibly bright, glowing with a determination to see the thing done. How it might be contrived—with a modicum of dignity or amid an orgy of carping—was of no concern to him, and Bea, who knew his ability to think rationally had been corrupted by the sight of a murderous actor holding a pistol to her back earlier in the day, felt a strange sort of flutter in her belly at the implacability of his intent.

It was, in fact, much worse than a flutter, she realized, as color suffused her cheeks,

And how could she not blush, knowing all too well the

thoughts that occupied his mind? She herself shared them, and well aware of how thoroughly unsuited they were for the dowager's drawing room, she felt her face grow uncomfortably warm.

What a wholly depraved creature she must be to entertain such ideas whilst in the presence of her family!

The case was hopeless indeed when even the shrill displeasure of her steadfastly censorious aunt wasn't enough to completely quell the anticipatory shiver of delight Bea felt at the inflexibility of the duke's resolve.

Naturally, she expected everyone in the room to notice the unusual blush, but Flora drew the occupants' attention by dismissing her mother's complaint with a brisk wave of her hand. "We could not possibly allow Beatrice to marry Kesgrave with only the rags on her back, for she is not some poor orphan in a fairy story who must sweep out the soot from our fireplace or sleep in a cupboard. She is a beloved member of our family, and I know you would never want her to take a turn around Berkeley Square in a dress marred by a stain of gooseberry jam. Why, one of the neighbors might notice! 'Tis not like this tear in my own gown, which is so small I'm sure not even the dowager duchess will note it."

As if of its own volition, Aunt Vera's index finger flew to Flora's lips as she tried to stop her daughter from speaking of such terrible things as stains and tears. Although the target of her apprehension was in the hallway conferring with her butler, she could not squelch the sensation of the peeress's eagle eye hovering somewhere over her shoulder observing her family's every minor imperfection. It was a familiar feeling, as she lived with the perpetual fear of falling short of the other lady's exacting standards—a dread her daughter routinely exploited in her pursuit of a wardrobe by Madame Bélanger.

Or, if not a full wardrobe, then several new gowns by the exquisite modiste.

Having witnessed Flora's efforts on multiple occasions, Bea knew exactly what she was up to and was disconcerted to discover she felt a pang of sympathy for Aunt Vera, whose panic prevented her from realizing her daughter's dress was without defects or blemishes. Bea was saved from succumbing to the odd compulsion to offer her relative comfort by Flora, who blithely continued her speech, insisting the couple had already demonstrated incredible forbearance by waiting so long.

"Instead of offering recriminations, let us be happy for them, Mama," she exclaimed with giddy assurance. "Life is a precious gift and we must be glad they are alive and well to enjoy this wonderful event, for no one's future is assured. Why, something dreadful might have happened to them this very day had some divine force not been watching over them. *Carpe diem quam minimum credula postero!*"

Vera, whose anxiety remained acute as she frantically inspected her daughter's dress for imperfections, inhaled sharply and called for their carriage to take them back to Portman Square posthaste. "We must return my dear girl to her sickbed, for she is babbling incoherently," she said, darting an angry look at Bea. "I knew it was too soon."

The unspoken charge hung in the air for only a moment before her son strode into the room in the company of his father.

"There's no need to kick up a fuss, Mama," he said bracingly. "She's not incoherent, just speaking in Latin."

Although Russell had sought to reassure his mother with this comment, she was more unsettled than ever to discover Flora was proficient in a foreign language. For years she had despaired of her daughter's inability to learn French. If only the recalcitrant child would apply herself! The subjunctive was not *that* difficult to master.

Uncle Horace was just as astonished and stared at her as if trying to comprehend her unprecedented erudition. Finally, he said with bemused wonder, "He's right. It means 'seize the present; trust tomorrow e'en as little as you may.' It's from the *Odes*. I must confess, Flora, that I do not recall Miss Higglestone including Horace on your syllabus. And yet she must have, for your accent is uncommonly good."

Flora preened at the compliment while Vera extolled the virtues of their former governess, whose skills she had never doubted though she might have questioned them once or twice.

Unable to allow his sister to bask in the glow of filial approbation alone, Russell launched into a catalogue of the many Latin phrases he had learned during his brief yet distinguished career at Oxford: *Georgics, Eclogue, Aeneid*.

He had barely made it through the complete works of Virgil when the door opened and the Countess of Abercrombie swept into the room on a cloud of sweet-smelling perfume.

"Oh, my dear," she said with unrestrained emotion as she beheld Beatrice by the fireplace next to Kesgrave, "you are a most beautiful bride." She sighed deeply and dabbed delicately at her eyes, which may or may not have been filled with tears. Then she walked across the floor until she was mere inches from Bea, wrapped her in a gentle hug and murmured softly, "A most, *most* beautiful bride."

Familiar with her ladyship's penchant for drama, Bea submitted unprotestingly to this treatment. For her aunt, however, it was an irresistible provocation and she ceased trying to determine if her daughter had a fever to stare with wide-eyed amazement at the lovely widow.

"But...but...her cheeks are so sallow," Vera exclaimed in

confusion, "and her dress is...is...so..." But she could not come up with the right word to describe the serviceable gown of an indeterminate blue and abandoned the effort, settling on a vaguely articulate grunt of despair. "You may see for yourself how inadequate it is. One does not have to wear one's presentation gown to one's wedding but surely something better than...than..." Again, her vocabulary failed her as she waved her hand at her niece. "We must send home for something more appropriate or—and I believe this is the more auspicious plan—wait for one of Madame Bélanger's lovely creations to be ready. I am sure you agree, my lady, that Bea cannot marry the Duke of Kesgrave dressed in that... that..."—here, finally, inspiration struck and she latched onto the word her daughter had used earlier—"*rag* of a gown."

Now it was her ladyship's turn to affect astonishment, for she could not perceive anything to complain about in Bea's appearance. Indeed, pushing the young woman back so that she may inspect her properly, she noted nothing but the radiance of excitement.

"Yes, yes," Lady Abercrombie said with blissful contemplation, "a most beautiful bride."

To say that Bea wanted the whole lot of them gone, that she wished they would simply vanish from the room at the waspish snap of her fingers, would be to grossly understate the case. She'd lived a mostly quiet life—quietly reading, quietly sewing, quietly listening to her aunt grapple with her children's unerring ability to increase her anxiety with their excessive demands for money and attention—and she could scarcely comprehend how it had altered so profoundly in such a brief span. A mere six months ago she had been sitting in the Skeffingtons' dining room in the Lake District quietly eating eels *à la tartare,* and now she was in the Dowager Duchess of Kesgrave's drawing room besieged by an almost painful cacophony.

All she wanted was to be alone with the duke.

And yet it was impossible to smother the gurgle of laughter that rose in her throat at the expression of utter bewilderment on Aunt Vera's face as her relative tried to make sense of Lady Abercrombie's stunning reversal. Only five days before, her ladyship had stood in the Hyde-Clare's breakfast room—entirely uninvited, of course, for nobody was ramshackle enough to entertain guests over eggs and kippers—and insisted that Bea and the duke wait until at least May to make their vows. First, she must throw a ball to introduce Bea to society with all the pride, pomp and circumstance befitting a future duchess, a development that her relatives had failed to anticipate when they hosted their own indifferent affair seven seasons before.

Naturally, Aunt Vera had found the prospect of her niece's reintroduction to society horrifying, for it would imply to all and sundry that she'd inadequately performed the task the first time around. Nevertheless, she was grateful for the countess's support in delaying the nuptials and felt her opinion had helped convince the pair to wait a week.

But now...now she was smiling fondly at Bea and wiping maudlin tears from her eyes as if nothing would make her happier than to witness her hasty marriage to Kesgrave.

Did her ladyship not understand what was happening? Was she incapable of comprehending how the passage of time worked? Perhaps she had fallen into a fugue state and believed she'd emerged a full week later?

Although the latter would provide a plausible explanation, it seemed highly improbable, for Lady Abercrombie appeared to glow with vibrancy and health. Her eyes sparkled with satisfaction as she murmured yet again, "A beautiful bride."

Vera's brows drew impossibly closer at each repetition of the sentiment, which was truly inconceivable, and Bea imagined her ascribing some very secretive, very cunning motive to her ladyship's behavior. Clearly, the countess was playing a deeper game than anyone could imagine.

Ah, but what could it be?

While Vera applied herself to detangling the many strands of Lady Abercrombie's wily scheme, Russell continued to demonstrate his extensive knowledge of Latin. Having exhausted the works of Virgil, he had moved on to Ovid —*Heroides, Ars Amatoria, Epistulae ex Ponto*—but his sister, whose education was more complete than anyone in her family had suspected, observed that titles of books did not count as actual phrases, let alone complete sentences. Resolutely, he dug deeper into his recollection of classical studies and emerged with Emperor Augustus's last words, which he promptly mangled.

"*Acta est fabula, plaudite,*" his father corrected impatiently.

As Flora laughed at her brother's humiliation, Lady Abercrombie tsked disapprovingly and insisted she would not applaud, for the play was just beginning. Uncle Horace rushed to explain that he was merely correcting his son's Latin, not declaring the actual end of something, certainly not Bea and Kesgrave's happiness, and Russell made another attempt at demonstrating his skill, this time misquoting Seneca's maxim about great fortunes.

Bea, taking advantage of the countess's momentary distraction, extricated herself from her ladyship's firm grip and looked at Kesgrave. "Do you see what you have wrought with your wrangling, your grace? If you had not attempted to rewrite the text of the marriage ceremony in service of your own selfish ends, we would have been wed by now and far from this madness. Indeed, we would have been back in your carriage and en route to Kesgrave House."

Although Bea expected him to protest this flippant characterization of his concern for her safety, he merely laughed and noted that she was overlooking one very obvious fact. "As much as I want to be all things to you, especially a pincushion when you need a target for your surliness—how did you put it to me yesterday in the carriage: you may stick me with as many needles as you require to restore your good humor—I cannot be both bridegroom and clergyman. In fact, even if I were not the bridegroom, I could still not administer the vows, for I have not taken holy orders."

Since Bea could not argue the validity of the point, she hastily asserted the difference between waiting patiently for the minister to appear in the calm of his grandmother's elegant drawing room and Bedlam.

As if to underscore the disparity, Lady Abercrombie addressed herself to the duke for the first time, noting that *his* attire seemed a trifle underwhelming for the occasion. "I say, Kesgrave, has love made you so addled you did not notice your tailcoat is a full decade out of style? That straight cutaway and broad lapels make you look like a bailiff collecting the village rents. Could this be your valet's way of expressing displeasure of the match? If so, you must give him his notice at once—although not before securing an ensemble appropriate for the occasion. Do dash back to Berkeley Square to change. Give no thought to us, for we are happy to wait."

Aunt Vera, whose keenly discerning eye extended only to the imperfections of her family, expressed surprise at this observation and then immediately lent her support to the plan. "We can wait for his grace to change, can we not? That is to say, there is no reason why we should rush the process. Perhaps he would like the opportunity to select the new tailcoat himself, which might take a while. We would not want him to feel rushed, certainly not on our behalf, and could return to Portman Square to indicate our patience. Furthermore, we do not wish to take advantage of the dowager's hospitality. Yes, it is probably best if we leave this matter now and reconvene at a later date. I'm sure that's more convenient for everyone involved."

The hopeful note in Aunt Vera's voice, as if this propitious plan was the one that would make the couple fall in line, was more than Bea would withstand, and a peal of laughter escaped her. Truly, she could not fathom the cause of her relative's irrational persistence. The marriage would take place either now or in three days from now, and as her cousin Flora had pointed out recently, a ceremony performed in indecent haste would do little to overshadow her more outrageous behavior of goading a murderer to confess in the middle of Lord Stirling's ballroom.

The new Duchess of Kesgrave would be notorious regardless of her wedding date—and even more so when word of their newest escapade, at the Particular, began to spread, as surely it must. An august member of the peerage could not spend two days pretending to be a theater owner from Bath without causing a few dozen tongues to wag. If the actors themselves did not endlessly marvel over the dramatic revelation of a secret duke, then the Bow Street Runner who'd arrived to take custody of the villain, a confused young man who could not quite grasp the duke's interest in the matter, would discuss it at length with his associates.

It was because of their investigation that Kesgrave's tailcoat was several years behind the current mode, and while he ordinarily endeavored to turn himself out as a proper Corinthian, he did not believe his garments necessitated a postponement. Nevertheless, he thanked Mrs. Hyde-Clare for her consideration.

Naturally, the insistence that his wedding of all things did not require the first stare of fashion confounded Bea's aunt, but her uncle appreciated the practicality and assured him his coat was nothing to frown at. Lady Abercrombie, taking exception to this statement, began to specify in earnest the many details that were not au courant. Flora, who knew why the duke was dressed in an old tailcoat but was determined not to reveal the secret, hinted wildly at his being preoccupied with concerns of much greater importance than conforming to the latest rage, and Russell, in a bid to redeem himself, announced with fastidious articulation, "*Non omnia possumus omnes.*"

Bedlam, Bea thought with regret tempered by amusement, was no doubt a placid sea in comparison.

"Ah, there he is," Kesgrave murmured softly as he tilted his head, and Bea, assuming he meant the man who was to marry them, looked up gratefully. But it was not a minister who'd entered the room. No, it was Viscount Nuneaton, and she felt a frisson of alarm as she watched his lithe form stroll unhurriedly across the floor. His sudden appearance now too closely resembled his sudden appearance several days ago, and she trembled in panic at what struck her as an inauspicious omen.

It was absurd, of course, to compare the two situations, for they bore no relation to each other. On what was originally meant to be her wedding day, she'd allowed herself to be swayed from a hasty marriage by nascent familial affection and Kesgrave's evenhanded response to delay. Today, neither of those conditions prevailed. To be certain, she was fond of her family—particularly Flora, whose florid estimation of her own heroics possessed an unexpectedly endearing quality—but the affection she felt for them was but a tepid cup of tea compared with her consuming regard for Kesgrave. The duke's tractability, as well, had undergone a dramatic alteration that could be attributed only to the well-aimed double-barreled flintlock that had bedeviled their morning.

Even if Prinny himself arrived at Clarges Street to halt the proceedings, Kesgrave would briskly sweep him to the side like a flea-ridden mongrel.

Truly, she had no reason to be concerned, and as her heart resumed its normal pace, she smiled at the dandy, who was as exquisite as ever in his satin breeches and elegant cravat.

"I could not be any more delighted for you, Miss Hyde-Clare," he said warmly as he bowed over her hand. "I have never envied another man's situation, for I have always found my own to be quite complete, but I would be bending the truth if I denied feeling a tinge of jealousy at Kesgrave's good fortune. You are an original, my dear."

Naturally, Bea could not accept such a lavish compliment without demurral, and she immediately called his lordship's sincerity into question by hinting at an ulterior motive. "Still currying my favor in hopes of discovering what happened at Lakeview Hall, I see," she said with gleeful cynicism.

His interest in the matter was hardly surprising, for he had also been a guest of Lord and Lady Skeffington when Mr. Otley was murdered, and he could not figure out how a plain spinster with no consequence or conversation had managed to identify the killer. Intrigued, he had made several attempts in the months since to learn the whole story, but Bea had resisted revealing all—first because she did not trust him with information potentially damaging to her reputation and then later because she enjoyed the game. In her six and twenty years, she'd had few games with anyone, let alone handsome dandies, and she was reluctant to see this one end, even now, on the verge of her wedding to Kesgrave.

Striving for an archly satirical note, she complimented Nuneaton on his relentless determination, assuring him that all young ladies simply adored being pestered. "We consider it a very appealing trait in a gentleman."

Although the viscount was famous for his languorous affect, barely bestirring himself to wince at the *ton*'s many ill-considered sartorial choices, he laughed with full-throated appreciation and promised Bea that she would soon find him irresistible. "For I do not mean to relent until I know every-thing about your many investigations."

Bea opened her mouth to insist that five investigations did not exactly rise to the level of *many*—a remark that would have been unintentionally revealing, for even if the viscount suspected there was more to the Taunton affair than a simple accident with a torch, he could know nothing of her involve-ment in Fazeley's brutal stabbing—but Kesgrave interrupted their conversation with a pointed cough. "As much as I enjoy watching my betrothed flirt with another man, you have a more vital reason for being here, Nuneaton. I trust you secured the item?"

His grace spoke calmly, even languidly, and yet Bea could not help but detect a hint of annoyance in his tone, which baffled her. He'd objected previously to the viscount's interest in her, yes, but she'd assumed he had only been teasing, a supposition bolstered by the almost comical way he commanded their attention now. Surely, a man who possessed every advantage of wealth, privilege and breeding was immune to the coarser emotions like jealousy.

'Twas beneath him in every way.

If Nuneaton noticed anything amiss in his friend's conduct, he gave no indication as he reached into his pocket and withdrew a small silk purse. "I did, yes. It was not without its challenges, for the jeweler had yet to finish repairing the clasp and had to be induced to work more quickly. If left to himself, I suspect it would have taken several more days."

Curiously, Bea wondered what could be so important to Kesgrave that he required its delivery to his grandmother's drawing room only minutes—at least she hoped it was only minutes—before his nuptials, and then she saw the glint of gold followed by a flash of blue.

Astonished, she stared at the beloved sapphire bracelet

her mother had worn every day of her marriage until a murderer tore it from her wrist after snuffing out her life with a pillow. The last time she had seen the heirloom was barely more than a week ago, in Lord Wem's study, its delicate links tethering his lordship's watch to his waistcoat. She had paid it little heed as it shimmered in the sunlight, for she had naturally assumed it was a lovely adornment, a pretty chain with a practical purpose. But later, when she spoke to him amid the jubilant hubbub of Lord Stirling's ball, she recalled it again, the flicker of sapphire, and perceived at once its significance.

In the days since the ghastly encounter with Wem, she hadn't thought of the bracelet a single time. So many things had provided distraction: first her wedding, then the postponement of her wedding, then Mrs. Norton's missing diamond, then the murdered corpse of an unfortunate actor who had been hired to ensure her ruin.

All these events, one after another, had kept her mind too busy to return to the bracelet, and although Bea knew it was merely an object—only gold and gems—she could not squash the devastating sensation that what she had really forgotten was her mother. Having finally discovered the truth about her parents, their lives as much as their deaths, she'd turned her attention to other matters, allowing them to fade in the distance like a ship sinking below the horizon.

It was terrible, the remorse she felt at her callous disregard, and yet she could not regret anything that demonstrated so plainly Kesgrave's grace and goodness.

Incapable of speech, Bea raised her head and stared into his eyes, dazzling and blue. How could she possibly express the strange and unsettling mix of shame and pride she felt?

It was all so much more than anything she'd ever imagined.

She'd had fantasies, of course. Like any schoolroom miss on the precipice of her first season, she'd pictured her ideal suitor and conceived of something vague and benign: a kindly gentleman with even features, modest manners, and an interest in biographies and travelogues. The details of their life together were equally nebulous and consisted mostly of pleasant afternoons passed in companionable silence, each of them engrossed in their book whilst sitting shoulder to shoulder on the settee. Deeply contented, she would pause every so often in her reading to sigh happily over his quiet decency.

But this breathtaking surge of admiration, this rush of emotion, wild and overwhelming, was dizzying in its intensity, and to feel it now, again, anew, on this day of all days, when he had already awed her with his insouciant unraveling of the ropes that had bound them in that pitch-dark cellar under the Particular, was truly unbearable.

It was only luck, she knew, that placed her in the drawing room in Clarges Street with the Duke of Kesgrave, a fickle act of an indifferent god, and she felt in her bones the fragility of fate. One slight alteration in the fabric of time—if she had chosen to read the *Vicar of Wakefield* rather than seek out a biography in the Skeffingtons' library on the night Otley was killed—and she would have lived her entire life without him.

Gratitude for the capricious hand of fortune almost crushed her, and determinedly pushing it aside, she struggled to come up with the words to express her appreciation for his thoughtfulness in remembering her mother's bracelet.

Alas, when she opened her mouth to thank him, her composure deserted her completely and all she could manage was a low, distraught plea. "You must stop doing this!" she said desperately.

It was not the response Kesgrave anticipated.

Oh, no. Having been impressed by Bea's pluck and daring from the very first, even while her refusal to abide by his authority drove him mad with frustration, he'd never imagined that the presentation of a simple band could have such a disastrous effect on her self-possession.

Kesgrave's confusion, so readily apparent in the way he drew his eyebrows together and pursed his lips, helped relieve some of Bea's distress. After two decades of falling short of her aunt's unreasonable expectations, it was still revelatory to exceed his.

Taken aback by her discomfort, Kesgrave immediately complied with her request, promising never to repeat the event. "I could not even if I desired to," he assured her, "for the bracelet is the only item of your mother's in need of reclaiming."

It was perfect, Bea thought, the characteristic pedantry of his reply, and under ordinary circumstances, it would have elicited from her a fond mocking rejoinder. But everything about the moment felt remarkable, even the sunlight filtering through the window, bathing them in a golden glow, and she answered instead with terrifying honesty. "You must stop making me love you more, Damien. The feeling is already so overwhelming, I can scarcely breathe."

His features remained steady but his eyes—oh, yes, his eyes—blazed with emotion and he raised his hand as if to touch her. Mindful of their situation, however, he let it drop before he made contact, and his lips curved slightly as he shook his head to deny her request. "I fear I cannot, Bea, no. Your brief spells of breathlessness are the only advantage I have in this relationship, and I am not prepared to relinquish it."

The duke spoke softly, emphatically, and Bea waited for amusement to enter his eyes, for she knew he was teasing, but his expression remained fervent. Warmed by his gaze, she longed to move closer, to draw his lips to hers, and it was only the presence of her family that kept her firmly rooted to the spot. Vaguely, she realized Nuneaton had stepped discreetly away and was now correcting Russell's pronunciation of *vixere* ("It's a *W,* my dear chap, not a *V*"). She heard Aunt Vera thank the viscount for his attention to her son, who grumbled that he knew how to speak Latin, thank you very much. Flora laughed at her brother's embarrassment and asked Lady Abercrombie about the contents of Bea's trousseau.

Unaware that he could strike Bea dumb with a single, searing look—another advantage he had in their relationship, she thought wryly—Kesgrave held up the strand and said, "May I?"

"Yes, please," she said, offering her arm and immediately admiring the delicate band as it encircled her wrist. It was, without question, a beautiful piece of jewelry, with its heart-shaped links and marquise-cut stones, but what made it truly extraordinary was the way it traversed time and space to deliver her mother there, on her wedding day.

Oh, how you would have loved him, Mama, she thought, her throat constricting painfully as her grace entered the room with the minister in tow.

Briskly, as if she were hosting a second ceremony later in the afternoon and needed to move the first couple along, the dowager arranged the occupants of her drawing room in a half circle beside the fireplace and directed Beatrice and Kesgrave to stand in the center. She positioned the clergyman in front of them, just slightly to the left of the lavish bouquet that adorned the mantelpiece.

Bea had no idea why the dowager suddenly felt compelled to rush them to the altar—less than a week before hers had been one of the many voices urging restraint and caution—but the older woman's matter-of-fact attitude was like a balm to her heightened emotions, soothing the intensity of her feelings and allowing her to think coherently. Calmly, her gaze fixed on Kesgrave's vibrant features, she waited as the minister opened the prayer book and began the Solemnization of Matrimony. He spoke slowly, carefully, his tone earnest and somber as he explained the ordination of marriage, and Bea, who thought his solemnity was a trifle overdone, felt her heart turn over in giddy delight when the duke rolled his eyes in impatience.

Even England's most zealous pedant had his limits.

She smothered the giggle that rose in her throat and marveled again at the wonder of marrying a man whose thoughts aligned so perfectly with her own. Yielding partially to sentiment and partially to the strain of mischievousness she didn't know she possessed before confronting the Duke of Kesgrave in the Skeffingtons' darkened library, she decided to comply with his request to make a change to the ceremony. Clearly, he had not thought the matter through, for if he had paused for even a moment to consider the impact on their guests, he would never have made the suggestion.

Patiently, Bea listened to Mr. Bertram's seemingly endless litany of vows—obey, serve, love, honor, keep, forsake—and agreed to abide by them all. Then she announced she had one minor alteration to make.

The minister looked up from his prayer book and raised a quizzical brow. "An alteration?"

Bea nodded soberly. "I would like to add a vow."

Much taken aback by this presumption, the clergyman tilted his head to the side and sought to confirm that he had heard her correctly. "*You* would like to *add* a vow?"

"I would, yes," she said, her tone mildly conversational as if discussing something utterly benign like the weather. "If you would be so kind, please say, 'Wilt thou vow to cease investigating the horrible deaths that keep crossing thy path?' Then I will answer, 'I will.'"

The effect this entreaty had on the company was immediate—of course it was. To tinker with the Book of Common

Prayer was already an intolerable impertinence but to suggest such a shocking addition was the height of impudence! The temerity of inserting the wretchedness of death into a joyful event! The audacity of undermining the sanctity of marriage with irreverent humor!

Mr. Bertram glowered fiercely at the bride before directing his passionate disapproval at the dowager for allowing such disrespect to prosper in her drawing room. Her grace opened her mouth to protest the unspoken accusation but failed to say anything coherent. Flora giggled knowingly, Lady Abercrombie clucked censoriously, and Russell called out, "I say, Bea, that's not quite the thing." Nuneaton murmured, "Brava," while Uncle Horace looked around as if not entirely sure what had just happened.

But it was Aunt Vera's response—a gasp of horror so deeply felt it seemed to rise from the tips of her toes—that caused Bea to look up at her husband and grin impishly.

Chapter Two

To say that Beatrice flinched every time someone in her new home addressed her as "your grace" would be overstating the case. When, for example, Kesgrave brushed an errant lock out of her eyes, smiled down at her—his own normally kempt appearance in equal disarray from recent activities—and asked softly, "Are you happy, your grace?" she did not recoil in the slightest. No, indeed, the very opposite, for she responded by pressing her body closer to his and demonstrating the extent of her delight.

No, the first hint of a wince happened many hours later, when the housemaid who delivered her breakfast tray greeted her with an excess of deference, dropping into a deep curtsey, avoiding eye contact and punctuating every utterance with "your grace."

Good morning, your grace.

Your breakfast, your grace.

Plum cake, your grace.

Tea, your grace.

Your grace, your grace, your grace.

By the time the young woman had left the room, the

languid peace Bea had felt upon waking in Kesgrave's arms had been replaced by a fluttery agitation she could not quite squelch.

She made a determined effort, of course, smiling brightly when Kesgrave returned to the bedchamber dressed informally in breeches, a white muslin shirt and waistcoat. It helped, no doubt, that her pulse quickened at the site of his handsome figure and while he was in the room, she could think of nothing but how lovely he looked without his shirt....

Eventually, however, rationality returned and with it the keen understanding that the deference displayed by the maid had not been excessive. The very opposite, in fact: It had been exactly in line with her due as a duchess.

Assailed by the consequence, Bea had flinched.

An hour later, when another maid entered the extravagant dressing room employing her title with daunting repetition, Bea blanched visibly, a reaction the servant was too well trained to notice. To her surprise, the young woman held in her arms a gown from Bea's own wardrobe in Portman Square, and although Bea was relieved to don something worn and familiar, she was just as uneasy with the effortless way the garment had appeared in her new home. She'd imagined—naively, it seemed now—paying a call on number nineteen to pack her belongings herself while Flora peppered her with questions about the wonders of Kesgrave House and Aunt Vera bemoaned the difficulties of overseeing a very large staff.

Without question Bea was grateful to be spared the obligation of performing the chore, but she could not fully embrace the convenience of having someone else perform it for her. It was, she thought, a reasonable indication of what life would be like with the duke, and while many women would eagerly welcome the prospect of a path strewn with rose petals, she couldn't help but feel that being spared discomfort was in itself a type of discomfort.

Naturally, the utter ridiculousness of the complaint—imagine chafing at the notion of too much ease!—struck her forcefully, and as she submitted to the maid's ministrations, Bea resolved to confront her fate with unwavering stoicism. The elevation in her station warranted adjustment, to be sure, but ultimately the changes would be superficial, for it was not her innermost self that had to alter. She had earned Kesgrave's ardent regard by simply being herself, and it would be illogical of him to wish she were someone else now.

No, all he required was that she grow accustomed to the unmatched grandeur of his existence. It was an attainable goal, easily accomplished with only a small amount of effort, unlike earning her aunt's and uncle's approval, a difficult task made impossible by the prejudices the pair had borne against her and her parents for decades. For the vast majority of her life, she had striven to make herself worthy of their love, shrinking deeper and deeper into herself in the hopes of one day becoming so inoffensive she would please them.

In comparison, learning to tread lightly on rose petals was a stroll through Hyde Park on a spring afternoon.

Bea felt truly reassured by the thought, and yet when the maid finished dressing her hair and said, "I am done, your grace," she cringed.

She simply could not help it.

And when she looked at her image in the mirror—at her plain brown hair arranged in elaborate curls that framed her narrow face—she felt a wild compulsion to tear out the pins one by one and stamp on them with all her might until they were dust on the floor.

It was too much, the incongruity of her appearance, her cheeks suddenly flushed, her curls suddenly shiny, her eyes suddenly bright. It was almost as if she were staring at a stranger, and to experience that sensation on this morning, when she had woken up already feeling slightly altered, made Bea feel as though she had been supplanted by someone else: a bride, a wife, a duchess.

'Twas a dismaying sensation, as unanticipated as it was unwelcome. If anything, she had worried it would be Kesgrave who would be vaguely transformed by their union. With the obligatory courtesies of courtship behind him and the manifold privileges of a husband before him, it would not be wholly inexplicable if he began to perceive her as something of a possession, as one more thing he owned like the lavish house in Berkeley Square or the many estates that dotted the countryside.

The insidious idea had wormed its way into her consciousness late in the night after the last candle had flickered out and her eyes had fluttered shut. Reasonably, she knew the fear was unfounded, and yet her exhausted mind could find no way to reconcile feeling so possessed with not actually being possessed.

But it was morning now and Kesgrave was as familiar as ever—even the curled lock of blond hair had fallen perfectly into place on his forehead—while she looked a little bit like someone else.

Throwing a tantrum over her slightly altered appearance would do nothing to alleviate her disquiet. Indeed, it would only exacerbate it, for what a fine picture it would make, the new duchess indulging a fit of temper as her first official act. What a flurry of gossip it would cause in the servants' hall and rightly so. Poor, beleaguered Kesgrave, tethered to an irrational termagant who could not glance into a looking glass without kicking up a fuss and venting her spleen on an innocent assortment of hairpins that had been in the family for generations.

How quickly the once great name had been corrupted by an unsuitable bride.

It would never have happened if he had adhered to the original plan and brought home the beautiful and unbearably elegant Lady Victoria.

Oh, but the humiliation would not end there, with the officious and appalled chatter of the domestic staff. There would be other consequences, for the maid—Dolly, her name was Dolly—would find the exhibition deeply agitating and assume she was somehow responsible for the outburst. Determinedly, Bea would assure her that she had done nothing wrong, but the girl, trained in deference from the cradle, would be unconvinced by the truth. The housekeeper, equally unmoved, would terminate the girl's employment unceremoniously, and now Bea, on her very first morning of her very first day as a duchess, would be responsible for the penury and inevitable life of privation of one perfectly lovely young maid who had the misfortune to perform her duties with slightly more skill than her new employer could handle with equanimity.

Bea realized she was being absurd again, for if there was one advantage to her new station it was the ability to override housekeepers. As the Duchess of Kesgrave it was her prerogative to keep on her staff all the egregiously competent maids she wanted. All the same, it was a salutary reminder of how drastically her situation had changed. Miss Hyde-Clare could stamp on as many hairpins as she'd like to no effect. Not even Aunt Vera would raise an eyebrow, except perhaps to note the impropriety of a young lady jumping in response of anything other than the bidding of her betters and bemoan the frightful cost of hairpins.

Imagining her relative's familiar disapprobation soothed Bea's nerves considerably, and she managed to contain her apprehension long enough to thank Dolly for her efforts. She even congratulated the maid on her enviable proficiency without mentioning sow's ears and silk purses.

Pleased with the compliment, Dolly tilted her eyes down as she curtsied. "My pleasure, your grace."

Bea flinched.

Bristling with apprehension, she nevertheless straightened her shoulders and stiffened her spine with a resolution she was far from feeling. In the adjoining dressing room, the clock struck eleven, and although it was foolhardy to ascribe malevolence to an inanimate object, she felt quite convinced the timepiece was mocking her timidity. The morning was half gone, and she had yet to emerge from her bedchamber.

It was insupportable—the cowardly display.

Surely, she was made of sterner stuff than her poor showing would indicate. She recalled the terrifying moment in the Skeffingtons' library when she believed the Duke of Kesgrave was seconds away from bashing in her skull with a candlestick. On that occasion, she had resolved to meet death without cowering.

How, then, could she cower now while meeting the household staff?

To even compare the situations was lunacy, she knew, for a vicious murder bore no relation to a slightly awkward interaction with one's retainers. That her mind linked the two indicated a diminished ability to produce lucid thoughts.

The room itself did little to improve her mental acuity. Its sumptuous furnishings—the rosewood chaise longue with brass inlay, the tufted window seat with embroidered silk, the gilt mirror with its scrollwork top—spoke of lavish wealth and five hundred years of Empire. Everywhere she looked, she was reminded of rose petals.

She could not calmly remain there, waiting for Kesgrave to strew her path. It was the height of hypocrisy, was it not, to claim to desire discomfort and then immediately shrink at the first hint of it.

Inhaling deeply, she rose to her feet and strode purposefully to the door.

If it were done when 'tis done, she thought, then 'twere well it were done quickly.

After a moment's consideration, she settled on the servants' quarters as her destination. She would first attempt to earn the approval of the housekeeper before taking on the gargantuan challenge of ingratiating herself with the butler, Marlow, whose mien was as intimidating as his size.

If she and the duke had held true to their original wedding date, then the new mistress of Kesgrave House would have arrived in Berkeley Square to find the household staff assembled in a neat row to meet her properly.

Nothing, however, about their courtship had gone according to plan—and a good thing too, Bea thought, for the rules governing social interactions did not allow for a spinster to woo a duke. But, as always, it was the servants who suffered for the lack of conventionality and, it must be said, consideration. Having had the presence of mind to ensure Bea's mother's bracelet was present at the proceedings, the groom failed to account for other, more mundane matters and overlooked the step wherein he alerted the household staff of his immediate nuptials.

In consequence, Mrs. Wallace had turned a bright pink yesterday upon discovering that she was greeting the new Duchess of Kesgrave in her second-best apron.

Flustered, the estimable woman swiftly regained her composure, welcomed her warmly and provided a light collation in the drawing room, complete with the tea cakes she recalled Miss Hyde-Clare...er, that was, the *duchess* enjoying the last time she had visited them.

It was a minor slip, almost too small to be noticed, but

the housekeeper's color rose again, and although her expression did not reveal her thoughts, Bea was convinced the other woman held her responsible for the regrettable breach in etiquette.

And Kesgrave!

He had done absolutely nothing to improve the situation. Rather than soothe his housekeeper's nerves with banal decorum, the notoriously high-in-the-instep duke had chosen that moment to become irreverent and flippant, mortifying Beatrice with his obvious impatience to be alone with her. She had barely raised the hot brew to her lips before he was putting her teacup on the table and insisting she must take a tour of the house.

"As Mrs. Wallace can attest from intimate firsthand knowledge, Kesgrave House is tediously large, with dozens and dozens of rooms," he had said, standing with such grace and purpose, Bea felt her stomach flutter in anticipation. "My forbearers were a pompous lot who sought to cow their detractors with an overwrought display of abundance. A deplorable practice, I assure you, for the brighter the plumage, the slighter the bird. Therefore, I am now burdened with an exceptionally large house with an excessive number of rooms, and if we have any hope of concluding our tour before nightfall, we must begin now. I am sure Mrs. Wallace understands."

Oh, yes, Mrs. Wallace had understood. Her visage revealed not a hint of comprehension, but she perceived exactly the reason for his haste, and Bea's cheeks turned a seething shade of scarlet in response.

'Twas excruciating, having the servants know her business, and somehow the housekeeper's studied blandness was more painful than the meaningful look Lady Abercrombie had darted in her direction when Kesgrave announced their intention to leave the luncheon the dowager had laid immediately following the toast to their happiness.

Her eyes firmly fixed to the floor, Bea allowed the duke to lead her from the room.

True to his word, Kesgrave had provided her with a cursory tour of her new home, drawing her attention to noteworthy rooms ("My study, of course, with its generous use of mahogany to spur deep thinking") and notable artworks ("*The Origin of the Milky Way,* one of three paintings Correggio did based on the myth of Hercules, which my grandfather acquired on his grand tour").

She was still challenging his claim that the third duke had smuggled the large Grecian urn in the second-floor hallway out of the Palais des Tuileries by requiring his footman to impersonate a hunchback ("Naturally, I would not expect the Duc d'Orléans's valet to have seen a man with a hump before but presumably he was familiar with the porcelain vase that occupied the lintel in the drawing room") when Kesgrave paused beside the open door to his bedchamber.

"And now, my love," he said on a sigh of deep satisfaction as he pressed his lips softly against her forehead, then her cheek. "And now I promise you will have no cause to take issue with my propensity to be slightly too thorough."

Although her heart tripped in excitement, she managed to say with arch condescension, "Slightly, your grace?" before murmuring in the wrong order the names of three warships that had appeared in the Battle of the Nile.

For once, he had made no effort to correct her.

Having delivered her to the marital bed, the tour had served its function well, but that was where its practical usefulness ended, for as she stepped into the corridor now, she realized she had no idea where to go. She remembered a grand staircase, elegant white marble lined with a delicately carved balustrade, but did not know if it lay to the left or the right.

She could not even recall where the Grecian urn was.

Near the Gainsborough landscape of the cows drinking from a pond. What had Kesgrave called it? *The Watering Place.*

Very good, your grace, she thought in mild contempt, for knowing the name of the painting in no way helped her locate it.

As one direction seemed as good as the other, Bea decided to turn to the left and was rewarded almost immediately with a staircase. It was not, however, the one she had climbed the night before, for although it served the same function of returning her to the first floor, it deposited her in an entirely different part of the house. Taking a wild guess, she went to the right. One long corridor led to a slightly shorter one, which brought her to a charming music room with pale yellow wallpaper and a daunting number of percussion instruments. A stroll down another hallway took her past the work by Correggio—finally, a landmark she recognized— and she realized she was not very far from Kesgrave's study.

It would be so very easy to abandon her plan to win over Mrs. Wallace and instead visit the duke. He would be happy to see her, she knew, and was most likely feeling as bereft in her absence as she felt in his.

But he was bracketed with Mr. Stephens, addressing the many estate matters he had let slip during the past week whilst he was dancing attendance upon her.

To be fair, identifying the man who murdered Mr. Hobson was not a trivial occupation, but just because he had been engaged in one worthwhile pursuit did not mean he could ignore all the others that demanded his attention. Fulfilling his obligations now meant he could devote himself exclusively to her later—a goal to which Bea heartily subscribed and the main reason why she did not wish to interrupt his meeting with the steward.

Well, that *and* the appalling cowardice reversing course would imply.

Staunchly, she turned in the opposite direction of the study and walked briskly past several tempting rooms, including a skylighted rotunda and a conservatory brimming with pink, purple and yellow flowers. The latter, in particular, caught her interest and she longed to inspect it further, both because it looked like a delightful place to read for a few hours and because close examination would postpone the inevitable.

No, you must earn it as a reward, she told herself, resolving to seek out the room again just as soon as she gained the housekeeper's support with a promise to defer to her on all domestic matters.

I am not here, she would insist with all honesty, to upset your orderly routines or create chaos. All I want to do is ensure the continuation of the duke's comfort, which you seem to have well in hand. Please let me know what I can do to assist you.

'Twould be easy enough to endear herself.

Oh, but would it really? she thought, her gait faltering as a new horrifying concern struck her. Mrs. Wallace oversaw not just any house but one of the grandest in London and she was employed by a notoriously high stickler. Possibly, those things were a source of great pride for the woman, who might hold in contempt a duchess who failed to display an equal fastidiousness. Rather than earning her respect, a pledge to cede control might secure her disgust.

Perhaps the better approach was to represent herself as a demanding mistress and make a series of outrageous requests such as...such as...

Alas, Bea was far too rational a creature to come up with

an outrageous request on a moment's notice. If she took some time to think about it, maybe in the lovely conservatory...

Before the appealing thought had an opportunity to take hold, she found herself standing at the top of a staircase leading down.

Very well, she thought, her right foot falling lightly on the first step as she began her descent. Her progress was steady, if a little slow, and although she moved with the sluggish pace of a turtle, she reached the bottom soon enough.

Anxiously, she examined her surroundings. The corridor was narrow and bright, with sunlight shining through the windows. She caught the wafting scent of baking bread, and it was an indication of her apprehension that it did not tempt her at all. In actuality, the familiar smell had the opposite effect, causing her stomach to lurch at the foolhardiness of her scheme.

Every gently reared woman in the kingdom knew the basement was emphatically the servants' domain, and it was an unseemly imposition for the new duchess to wander its halls.

Months ago, in the Lake District, she had dared to visit the kitchens during the course of her investigation into Mr. Otley's death, which had properly horrified the maids. At that time, she had been naught but an insignificant houseguest and still the women had trembled as if she were Queen Charlotte herself.

Wryly, she reminded herself she had wanted to come up with an outrageous request and it appeared she had stumbled upon the most shocking one of all: the insistence that Mrs. Wallace meet with the Duchess of Kesgrave in the housekeeper's office. Naturally, the only proper way to conduct a conversation with the servant was to summon her to the drawing room. The courtesy was not only what her rank required but also what the gracious home itself commanded.

Standing there, at the bottom of the staircase, a beam of sunshine warming her hair, Bea felt an intense desire to yield to the dictates of status and architecture. Would it really be so terrible to submit to forces so much stronger than she? She would merely be dipping her head in respect, not raising her hands in surrender.

Truly, there was no need to turn a simple discussion with a subordinate into a tug-of-war for her soul.

But Bea was too clever to sway herself with a rhetoric appeal.

The situation might seem trivial, but it was in fact hugely significant, for the choices she made now would reverberate long after the moment had passed. She had to establish the tone she wanted at the beginning of her tenure, for only a naïve fool would believe her confidence would grow the longer she occupied the position. If anything, greater exposure to Kesgrave's magnificence—the innumerable estates and pineries—would cause whatever shred of assurance she had to shrivel entirely. Indeed, the Matlock family tree was so tall and illustrious, with its lords privy seal and chief justices of the king's bench, she already felt her shoulders bowing under the weight of its many branches.

If Mrs. Wallace objected to Bea's lack of regard for the dignity of the duke's staff, she would have to take up the matter with Kesgrave himself, as the unfortunate situation was all his doing. He'd had more than a decade to make the correct decision by selecting an elegant bride, a pattern card of respectability and restraint who had been raised since childhood to sit serenely on silk settees and pull bell cords with polite consideration.

Instead, he had chosen her.

Mrs. Wallace and the other occupants of the Berkeley

Square residence would simply have to adjust their expectations accordingly.

Brave words, Bea thought drolly.

Regardless of how very uncourageous she felt, she could not linger at the bottom of the staircase indefinitely, for someone would surely stride by and notice her standing there stupidly. Roused to movement by the prospect, she followed the smell of baking bread and turned left when she arrived at the end of the hallway. Here, the passageway narrowed and she walked past several familiar rooms, including the scullery, meat larder and vegetable stores. The layout of the basement was quite different from the one at Portman Square—larger, of course, for that house could fit inside this one several times over, but also more commodious, with additional spaces for storage and preparation.

Like the conservatory, several of the rooms caught her attention, and if it were not for the chatter of voices—a low hum indistinguishable in both number and gender—wafting from the kitchen or perhaps the servants' hall, she would have paused to examine their contents. The stillroom in particular, with its pretty bottles and overflowing canisters, captured her interest, but she did not dally. In Portman Square, the stillroom was next to the housekeeper's, which meant she was very likely near her destination.

Bea's heartbeat rose sharply.

It was absurd to feel so much anxiety about a single conversation. Stridently, she reminded herself she was a duchess. Kesgrave House was her home now, and she was free to roam its halls without limitations. 'Twas not a castle in a gothic novel with mysterious locked doors and ominous black veils scattered about. Poor Theodore was not trapped in a high tower somewhere desperately trying to gain his freedom and rescue Isabella from the evil clutches of her dead fiancé's father. If she desired, she could inspect every nook and cranny. Certainly, she was allowed to be in the passageway outside the housekeeper's room, and flush with purpose, she took a step forward.

But her defiance, so seemingly sharp and immutable, disappeared in an instant. All it took was one voice to rise above the others—oh, yes, just that one lone voice—and she dissolved into a frightened mouse trembling before a lion.

It was Marlow!

Marlow!

The duke's terrifying butler!

How imposing he was, with his barrel chest and thick black brows that pulsed with disdain, and he already despised her for ruthlessly overriding his authority a few days ago.

Would she have rather stood under the graceful portico and meekly begged entrance to Kesgrave House?

Well, yes, of course, for she had never elbowed her way into any house before, let alone one so overwhelmingly large it cast a shadow on the square opposite for much of the day, and had found the experience to be deeply uncomfortable.

More discomfiting, however, was the dead body of the actor hired by a nefarious villain to ruin her reputation and end her engagement to the duke. Making her betrothed aware of the shocking and unsettling development had taken precedent over appeasing Marlow's vanity with a show of deference.

But that was days and days ago, and now she was the Duchess of Kesgrave in fact, not supposition, and although her position was firmer, it felt more precarious. What would he do if he found her there, wandering the halls like a child lost in a forest?

Treat her with impeccable courtesy, of course. He was butler to the finest home in London save Carlton House and would never debase either himself or his office by acting with anything save the utmost decorum.

But that would just be for appearance's sake and inwardly, silently, he would loathe her for being an inconsequential nobody whose education was so lacking she meandered through the kitchens as if to fetch a light meal for herself.

Did she really care about the opinion of a servant?

Verily, she should not.

And yet she had been Beatrice Hyde-Clare much longer than she had been the Duchess of Kesgrave, and the former could not bear the thought of her own butler harboring a secret disgust of her. 'Twould be another thing entirely if he were honest about it such as her aunt Vera or the vicious Miss Brougham, whose scorn had derailed Bea's first season.

Marlow's voice grew louder, and Bea, panicked at the thought of starting off her tenure with a humiliating faux pas, scurried into the stillroom to hide. Swiftly she closed the door behind her, pressed her back against it and sighed.

She was safe.

Only it was not the stillroom.

No, this room did not have shelves lined with herbs and infusions but rather cabinets, which were filled with plates and glasses of all types. Next to the cupboard along the far wall was a safe, and beside the safe was a desk with an unadorned wooden chair.

Swiftly, her mind took in the scene—plates, safe, desk— and she realized with dawning horror that she had taken refuge in the butler's pantry. The stillroom was to the left, not the right.

Curse it!

Her face turned purple at the thought of discovery, and her heart pounded with such raucous cacophony it was almost the only thing she could hear. Faintly, though, through the door, she heard Marlow's determined rumble. The words themselves were faint, but the disapproving tone came through clearly.

Horribly, the disapprobation stopped in front of the door.

Dear God, he was about to come in.

Hide!

Frantically, her eyes darted around the room, searching... searching for a space in which to conceal herself.

Not the cupboard. Too small.

Maybe under the desk? No, the area was too exposed.

What about drapes? Could she hide behind the drapes? They barely covered the window, which was narrow to begin with.

The door!

Yes, yes, the door, she thought, running toward it with so much force she practically threw herself across the room. Obviously, the only place to hide was in the adjacent room. Gratefully, she turned the knob just as the door to the pantry creaked.

"...a suggestion so catastrophically inane I would assume you had downed an entire bottle of his grace's best claret if I did not know such a sacrilege to be impossible," Marlow said reproachfully.

As gently as she could, Bea closed the door and examined her surroundings: bed, clothespress, shelves.

By all that was holy, she was in his bedroom.

What a humiliating turn!

Truly, she could not imagine anything in the world more devastating than being found in Marlow's bedchamber on her very first morning as the Duchess of Kesgrave. What explanation could she possibly give for the outlandish behavior? What justification could she conceivably provide for the appalling invasion of privacy? If the butler's own sleeping quarters were not inviolate, then nothing sacred remained.

In one fell swoop she would lose the staff's trust and all hope of earning their respect. At once, she would become a source of amusement, an object of mockery. To her face, of course, they would display the same untrammeled deference as if she had not been discovered in Marlow's room, but behind her back they would ridicule and laugh.

Bea could not blame them. She wanted to laugh herself.

Yes, but that was because she was overwrought.

She had to calm down, think rationally, respond sensibly. Panicking had done nothing to help the situation, and reacting without consideration again would only worsen it.

Like hiding under the bed, for instance. Seeking concealment beneath it might seem like the best option in a room with few alternatives, but it would be disastrous if Marlow found her cowering under his mattress. How easily she could imagine the terrifying moment of discovery as the large man sank to his knees and lowered his contemptuous gaze until it was level with hers.

'Twas a scene so horrific not even Mr. Walpole could have conceived it.

Better, she decided, to remain upright and stand behind the sweep of the door. Even if he had reason to enter the room, it was unlikely he would close the door behind him in the middle of the day, particularly while he was chastising a subordinate for performing his duties while inebriated or something equally transgressive. If necessary, she could stand on tiptoes and press her back against the wall just like—

Abruptly, she dropped to her heels as a fragment of their conversation penetrated her frenzy.

Had someone just said the Particular?

Impossible, she thought. He had used the word as an adjective, not a proper noun—to wit: "the particular ninny with whom the duke has saddled us for all eternity."

The butler and his associate would have no reason to talk about the theater on the Strand where Kesgrave and she had concluded an investigation only the day before.

And yet Marlow added, "I cannot believe any investigation of that nature was conducted at some ha'penny theater on the Strand. It is rank gossip of the most scurrilous kind, and I will thank you not to repeat it to anyone, especially the maids, who are susceptible to wild speculation with their impressionable minds. That being said, if such an event did occur, which of course it did not, I'm sure it was his grace's ingenuity that carried the day, not the duchess's. Granted, she is brazen enough to believe she could investigate a murder, but she is a woman and subject to the limitations of her sex, which include routinely overestimating her abilities."

"Explain the Stirling ball, then," the other man insisted.

"I beg your pardon," Marlow said with faint contempt, as if insulted to be called upon to explain anything.

His associate continued undaunted. "She confronted the Earl of Wem at Lord Stirling's ball and persuaded him to confess to killing her parents. You know it. I know it. Everyone on staff knows it. It is all we've talked about for days."

"*You* may have talked about it, Joseph," Marlow said with formidable censure, "but I have not. And now that I know the deplorable tone of the conversation in the servants' hall, I will make every effort to remedy it."

"That is not an answer," Joseph said. "If her grace is incapable of investigating a murder because she is a woman, then how do you explain the way she persuaded the Earl of Wem to confess to killing her parents in a ballroom full of guests?"

"A stroke of luck," Marlow replied.

Joseph's unrestrained laughter was almost immediately transformed into a troublesome cough that he had a difficult time suppressing. He apologized for the outburst and asked what function luck had played at the Larkwells' ball.

"If you are referring to the vulgar display on the terrace with Lord Taunton that resulted in his lordship's hair catching fire," Marlow answered dampeningly, "I can only say it was the inevitable debacle caused by a brash and assertive woman straining above her station."

"They said his grace summoned the Runners to apprehend Taunton," Joseph said. "He would not have done that without cause. You know he is a cautious man who never acts rashly."

"Never?" Marlow asked with so much pointed emphasis Beatrice's cheeks turned bright red. "You have made your argument, Joseph, and although I found your proposal the single most preposterous thing I have ever heard, I paid you the courtesy of listening. Now *you* will pay *me* the same courtesy. You may not under any circumstance ask her grace to look into the matter of Monsieur Alphonse's unfortunate demise. I understand that what happened to him is very upsetting to you—"

"His head was sliced clean from his body!" Joseph interjected, clearly aghast at the understatement.

"—but we cannot allow it to disrupt our day. Now please return to your duties," Marlow said, "and let me never hear another word about it. I, for one, plan to never speak of it again. Have I made myself clear, Joseph?"

Joseph muttered yes, but that was not sufficient for the butler, who insisted the other man speak in full sentences.

"Yes, you have made yourself clear," Joseph said.

"I am gratified to hear it," Marlow said.

His tone was smug, for he obviously enjoyed browbeating his subordinates into acquiescence, but Bea could not picture the intimidating butler with a smile on his face, even one swathed in self-satisfaction.

With his request roundly denied, Joseph saw no reason to remain and immediately quit the room to trim the lamps. Bea closed her eyes and prayed that Marlow would soon follow or at the very least stay in the pantry. The scraping of the chair against the floor indicated an intention to sit down, a development that at once relieved and horrified Bea. As long as he remained at the desk, she was safe from discovery but for how long? Sooner or later, her presence would be missed and she feared what would happen then. Kesgrave would question the servants, and ascertaining that she had not left the house, they would mount a search. Finding no satisfying answers upstairs, they would devote their full attention to the basement and there they would find her, flush to the wall behind the door in Marlow's room.

You are being needlessly negative, Bea told herself as she strained to hear Marlow's movements. There was always the remote possibility Kesgrave would assume she had found marriage to him not to her liking and fled the house in secret. Even now, he could be knocking at 19 Portman Square to inquire about his errant bride.

How easily she could picture the look on Aunt Vera's face as Kesgrave explained that he seemed to have misplaced his duchess. It would be a comical mix of concern and confusion, for as much as she would desire her niece's safety, she would never quite understand why he would wish for her return. Bea had to swallow a giggle as she imagined her relative assuring him it was for the best and perhaps he had escaped a—

The scrape again!

Bea froze as Marlow pushed back the chair.

Was he standing?

Was he leaving?

Please leave, she pleaded silently. Please, please leave.

To her relief, she heard footsteps, but the respite was short-lived because they moved in the wrong direction, toward the bedroom, not out into the hallway. The knob turned and fear caught in her throat as the door opened... opened...opened...and stopped a mere fraction of an inch from her nose. Letting out the breath slowly, she closed her eyes and pressed herself against the wall with every fiber of her being.

And waited.

She didn't think he would linger long. It was the middle of the day, and he had too many responsibilities to absent himself for an extended period of time. No doubt he was merely taking a moment to ensure that his appearance was sufficiently intimidating, a supposition that was affirmed when she heard a drawer open. An unsettling silence followed as he made whatever adjustment he'd deemed necessary, and Bea squeezed her eyes tighter, determined not to witness the utter shock on his face should the horrifying moment of discovery occur.

But it did not.

Marlow completed his business in the bedroom and exited at once, leaving the door open so that Bea could observe him through the crack beside the frame. He returned to his desk but, fortunately, did not sit down. Instead, he straightened the stacks of paper resting on the surface even though they were already pristine and orderly. He pushed his chair in, carefully aligning the slatted back with the edge of the desk and quickly confirmed that the safe was securely fastened. Satisfied with the arrangement, he left.

Intensely relieved to be alone once again, Bea nevertheless held her position, fearful that he would return immediately to finish tidying up the space—smoothing the blanket on the bed, perhaps, or straightening the wall clock, which was slightly askew.

Tarry too long, however, and she would be back amid the brambles, a prospect so awful to contemplate she felt her bones turn to ice. Purposely, she counted to ten, then back down to zero, and screwing her courage to the sticking place, slid out from behind the door. With a calm that was at once deliberate and hard won, she walked through the pantry and felt the unbearable pitch of her anxiety subside the second she stepped into the corridor.

It was empty. Nobody saw her.

Whatever happened now, whatever disaster befell her, she could bear it with equanimity because it would be a million times less horrible than being found tucked behind the door in his bedroom. If Marlow himself appeared, rounding the corner, say, on his way to the kitchen, she would suffer no response at all. Her heart would not pound; her pulse would not quicken.

The awe she had felt upon first enduring the disdain of his thick black brows was gone, swept away by the bracing clarity of truth. Discovering his actual opinion of her liberated Bea from having to worry about it. She was relieved to know with unequivocal certainty exactly where she stood.

Obviously, she could not *remain* in that place. Marlow was welcome to despise her and all women—she was not *so* brash and assertive that she would deny any man his right to cling to small-minded prejudices—but he was not allowed to scorn her aptitude for identifying murderers. Six years of social obscurity and failure had left her with few vanities, and she would permit no one to deride the one thing at which she excelled.

Thinking she overestimated her abilities!

She would show him who had an excessive valuation of their own skills.

How precisely she would do that, she could not say, but as soon as she was safely out of the basement, she would figure it out and then *he* would be in awe of *her*.

Chapter Three

aying that Bea decided in a fit of pique to identify the villain who had chopped off the poor neighbor's head was vastly understating the case.

Oh, no. It was nothing so tidy or tiny as a *fit.*

'Twas more like an orgy of pique or a massive bout of pique or even a gargantuan mountain of pique so commodious a village of trolls could live in its crevasses along with the four princesses they kidnapped from the nearby castle to mend their stockings.

It was an ever-expanding thing—the magnitude of her pique—and by the time Beatrice, Duchess of Kesgrave, sat down on the silk settee and pulled the bell cord in the drawing room, she felt consumed by it.

Curiously, she had not started off that way.

Climbing the stairs to return to the first floor, she had calmly and coolly reviewed the conversation between Marlow and the man he called Joseph. Well aware of the truism about eavesdroppers and kind words, she was determined not to take offense at slights offered in an exchange she had no business hearing.

It had been easy enough at first.

Marlow's casual remark rejecting her investigative skill, for example, was in every way unexceptional. All men, even the most enlightened ones, assumed women to be inferior in some significant way—too weak, too emotional, too silly, too vain, too bookish, too selfish, too ugly, too capable—and she could hardly resent a Berkeley Square butler for holding the same opinion as every Bond Street beau who perused the wares on offer at the Western Exchange.

Likewise, his attribution of her deductive accomplishments to Kesgrave. As a longstanding member of the household, Marlow could not be expected to retain the youthful cynicism of a newly hired footman. A dozen years or so into his service, he subscribed wholly to the doctrine of the duke's perfection, which, to be fair, was the only appropriate response to a coronet and a five-hundred-year-old name. After all, what was the purpose of the lavish munificence of the Matlock family tree if not to overwhelm the servants?

In the same vein, his observation about the Earl of Wem had only made her laugh. To describe eliciting a confession of murder as a stroke of luck—as if his lordship had been an apple that happened to fall while Bea was standing underneath the branch—required mental contortions so great she was surprised Marlow did not suffer spasms of pain from the effort.

Yes, Bea had remained calm and cool as she replayed the conversation in her head, but then she arrived at his description of the events on the terrace at Lord Larkwell's ball and her composure deserted her. Hearing those words again almost stopped her heart. Her cheeks turned first to fire and then to ice. And her breath—it seemed to expel itself from her lungs all at once, making it impossible to breathe.

At the top of the staircase, her hand clutching the railing, Bea had feared she was about to faint.

What an extravagant reaction!

So much fuss over a minor thing, she had thought in disgust. All of London believed she had trapped the duke into marriage, her family included. Aunt Vera had been more delicate in her judgment, refraining from using harsh terms such as *vulgar display* and *inevitable debacle*, but the implication was exactly the same: A woman of Bea's indifferent attributes could nab a man of Kesgrave's only through trickery and deceit.

A widely held notion and yet somehow it had brought her to the brink of a swoon. That was troubling.

The heavy black brows were part of it. Aunt Vera's countenance could express disapproval in myriad ways, but her eyebrows were thin and brown and rarely pulsated. Nor could she sneer convincingly. Her condemnation took the form of petty slights endlessly applied, like pinpricks to one's soul.

But Marlow's disgust was more like an arrow, sharp and true, and it struck her deeply. Like the lion with the thorn in his paw, she could not simply tug it out and nor could she ask Kesgrave to remove it. Appealing to her husband to soothe her hurt feelings was not only intolerable but impractical as well. He was already weighed down by responsibilities—his name, his coronet—and she would not add chastising the servants to appease his wife's ego to the list.

Ah, but it wasn't just vanity, Bea had thought. It was household management and domestic tranquility and her entire future. Securing the esteem of the staff was vital to her career as a duchess, for no woman who failed at home could have any hope of succeeding in society. Marlow, she knew from painful firsthand experience, was determined to undermine her. One by one, yes, she had been able to dismiss the harm of his statements, but taken together they represented a stunning lack of respect for her authority.

It would be one thing if he had kept his views to himself.

Bea had no interest in regulating the thoughts and feelings of the people in her employ. But he had not held his own counsel. No, he had openly expressed his contempt, caring nothing for her dignity ("brash and assertive") and for the position she was struggling to occupy with grace ("straining above her station"). And then he shared it with an underling, which made the offense all the more flagrant. Joseph was under his management, which meant he was subject to his influence and would no doubt be inclined to adopt his opinions.

The situation could not stand.

Clearly, it could not, for Marlow must not be allowed to infect the entire staff with his deleterious judgments.

As it was, she could not hear the perfectly anodyne *your grace* without flinching. How much worse would her twitching problem be when those words were tinged with scorn? Would her entire body convulse?

Even if she was not addressed with derision on a single occasion, the result would be the same because it was what she *believed* was happening that shaped her reality, not the events themselves.

This fact she also knew from painful firsthand experience because she had suffered a horrendous slight soon after her come-out and had allowed it to ruin the rest of the season. Then she had allowed it to ruin the next season and the next until her aspirations were a hollow echo too faint for even her to hear.

Could it happen again?

Oh, yes, she thought, so very easily. Kesgrave House had an excellent library in which she could happily bury herself for decades.

But she did not want to let the mistakes of the past repeat themselves. Last time, she had fallen silent, sanctioning her own exile and withering on the edges of society. By not defending herself, she had created her own terrible consequences.

Here, however, Bea had to pause and, recalling the duke's ministrations yesterday, last night and that morning as well as the lovely conservatory with the pink, purple and yellow flowers, conceded that perhaps *terrible* was not the most accurate description of the consequences she had been forced to endure.

Even so, she had learned her lesson well from Miss Brougham: Allow an imposing creature to define the terms of your existence and six or seven years later she will lead you to your destruction like a lamb to the slaughter.

Patently, Marlow would never stoop to conspiring with Lord Tavistock, as Bea's archnemesis had, but it was impossible to say what other form his spite might take. And if he was turning the servants against her one by one...

No, she thought furiously, the matter had to be dealt with swiftly and firmly, and resenting the obligation, she had tugged the bell cord.

A footman entered almost immediately, a courtesy that disconcerted her slightly, for at Portman Square one usually had to wait a minute or two for a servant to appear and Kesgrave House was so much larger. Plainly, she stated her request and was further disconcerted when she was informed that Joseph was already present.

"I am Joseph, your grace," he explained.

"Ah, yes, of course you are," she said, regretting Mrs. Wallace's thwarted assemblage of the staff more than ever. Formal introductions would not have necessarily solved the problem, for footmen were inevitably a matched set and therefore hard to distinguish even after being made individually known, but at the very least she would have been aware of the function Joseph served within the household. "Then just Marlow, please. Thank you."

As Bea waited for Joseph to return with the butler, she was pleasantly surprised to find herself utterly calm at the prospect of the confrontation. She took a breath and discovered that it was not at all constrained by the wild beating of her heart. Her heartbeat, moreover, was barely discernable.

She ascribed her strange composure to her eagerness to perform the task at hand—no, not deflating the pretensions of a portentous butler, for that aspect of the encounter properly terrified her. Rather, she was excited to probe the mystery of Monsieur Alphonse's grisly death. She might have no idea how to be a duchess, but she certainly knew a thing or two about being an investigator and the sense of familiarity and competence she felt was all she needed to breathe easily. Here, finally, was solid ground.

Terra firma, she thought in homage to her cousin Russell's inadequate Latin.

Kesgrave would be appalled, of course, but even the prospect of his strenuous objection felt wonderfully familiar. He would argue that she was breaking her word, and she would counter that any promise made under duress was not binding. Then she would add that this particular situation did not meet the terms of their agreement because the neighbor's body had not fallen in her path. In fact, she had no clue *where* his body had fallen. Then he would remind her of the spirit of her vow, and she would point out that she made no vow at all, thanks to Mr. Bertram's offended sensibilities. ("I will not condone the denigration and mockery of the sacred institution of marriage with the introduction of gruesome and violent imagery. If that is what you require, you must seek it elsewhere.")

Oh, yes, Bea was eager to begin and could feel no sense of guilt or impropriety at the thought of investigating a murder from the high perch of a duchy. She had done everything correctly, even agreeing to adjust her vows, and still the decapitated corpse of Monsieur Alphonse had been delivered to her feet. She would never presume to know the strange workings of Providence or fate, but it did seem pretty clear to her that some higher power desired her assistance.

It would be discourteous to withhold it.

The door to the drawing room opened, and Marlow's intimidating form entered, followed by Joseph. The two men were of the same height, but whereas the footman was lithe and narrow, the butler was thick and wide, with shoulders that seemed to stretch from one bank of the Thames to the other. It was the stoutness of his form, the way he stood as resolute as an oak tree, that made him so menacing.

His disdainful black brows were merely a bonus—gilding, for example, on a lily.

Examining his blank expression, Bea detected no emotion at all, and although she had not expected to see a hint of shame at the deplorable things he had said about his new mistress, she had thought curiosity or interest would not be out of line. As far as he knew, she had just emerged from her bedchamber and requesting his presence was among her first formal actions as a duchess. Surely, he found that intriguing.

Joseph's visage, however, was equally bereft of emotion, which was, she supposed, a testament to the quality of servant a ducal home retained.

Patiently, Bea waited until the two men were standing in front of her before explaining why she had summoned them. "It has come to my attention that an associate of Joseph's has suffered an untimely death and he—Joseph, not his associate," she said in an unnecessary clarification that indicated she felt more anxiety than she had realized, "would like to consult with me on the matter. I am prepared to offer my assistance now, provided Marlow approves. I am new to this household and have nothing but respect for the orderly workings of its management. I trust you will let me know if you have any objections?"

As Bea had no intention of deferring to Marlow on the matter, she was being deliberately provoking in hopes of eliciting a reaction. The butler did not oblige, keeping his expression entirely empty. Not by a single twitch of a muscle did he reveal that the information he had just heard was shocking to him in any way. His eyes remained focused, his forehead smooth, his shoulders still. To any observer witnessing the exchange, he would appear to be hearing something commonplace that everyone already knew, such as the sun set in the west or grass was green.

Ah, but Joseph...

Baffled by the information, he gawked in astonishment, jaw dropping open and his eyes seeming to pop out of his head. Staring at her in confusion, he tried to comprehend what had just happened. How did she know?

He glanced quickly at Marlow, and finding no edification there, returned his attention to Bea. "But how...?" he asked, trailing off as he struggled to formulate the question. "I don't...I...I mean, how...?"

And still Marlow's demeanor remained unaltered.

It was an impressive achievement by any measure, and although Bea heartily resented his attitude toward her, she could not help admiring his self-control. Perceiving it, she regretted just a tiny bit that the scene in the bedchamber had not descended into full-fledged farce, with Marlow getting down on his hands and knees to find the new Duchess of Kesgrave trembling under his bed. Surely, the surprise of *that* development would have been too much for even the resolute butler. He would have been compelled to reveal some sort of response, even if it was just distress at the unsightly accumulation of dust beneath his mattress.

But of course, there would not be thick layers of dust

under the beds in the servants' quarters. Kesgrave House was too well run for such slipshod housekeeping.

Bea wondered how Marlow would react if she were to repeat his own words back to him. That, she felt confident, would unsettle him enough to cause him to draw his lips together in a slight frown.

But verbatim repetition would also expose her methods, and that was the last thing she wanted. It was far more satisfying to appear slightly omniscient or as if in the short time she had been in the house, she had acquired an efficient network of spies.

To bolster that image, Bea said in response to Joseph's question, "I am a skilled investigator and make a practice of knowing things. That is why you sought my expertise, is it not?"

Dumbfounded, the footman nodded. Then, horrified by the informality of the response, he straightened his shoulders and said, "Yes, your grace."

Happily, Bea did not flinch.

Progress, she thought, before turning to Marlow and inviting him to stay. "I fear the events Joseph is about to relate will be terribly upsetting, and I suspect he will need your support. But you must not feel compelled to remain if you have other, more pressing matters to which to attend. I trust you to determine how best to allocate your time."

He dipped his head.

At last, a response!

Then he spoke: "If it meets with your grace's approval, I will remain."

As Bea had hoped he would remain for the entire interview, she made no objection. "Very good," she said. "Let us begin, then. Tell me about Monsieur Alphonse, Joseph."

The footman darted his eyes at his superior, as if seeking his consent. Bea detected no movement, but Joseph, satisfied by what he found, explained that the deceased servant was the chef at number forty-four. "It is the house just around the bend of the square. Mr. Mayhew hired him two years ago, during a trip to Calais, where Monsieur Alphonse owned a little patisserie. He made extraordinary cakes that looked like the pyramids of Egypt or Roman temples. He could make a cake that looked like anything, just anything at all. But he made other things as well such as these wonderful crispy, caramel biscuits he called *croquantes*. Last week he brought a box of almond ones when he came to visit Mrs. Wallace, and they were splendid. He called on Mrs. Wallace often because he was sweet on her," he said, before hastily adding with a defensive look at Marlow, "Mrs. Wallace herself said that, so it is not gossip."

Bea was astonished by this information. If he had said that Napoleon Bonaparte himself lived next door she could not have been more shocked. "Monsieur Alphonse was Auguste Alphonse Réjane?"

As she had already established herself as slightly all-knowing with the footman, he displayed no surprise at her question, merely tilting his head to the side and asking if she knew him as well. "He was very popular in the square because he was so good-natured and generous. Mrs. Wallace says that French chefs are usually demanding and unpleasant to work with, but Monsieur Alphonse was nothing like that. He was always smiling, even though he didn't like working for Mr. Mayhew. He thought he was—"

Whatever opinion the deceased chef held of his employer, Bea would not discover, for Joseph broke off his speech abruptly and immediately apologized for indulging in vulgar gossip. "Marlow has a very strict rule against gossip, which he finds reprehensible and unbefitting a great house such as this one. It is unacceptable behavior, your grace, and I am very sorry to have forgotten myself so fully."

Naturally, Bea found it noteworthy that the butler who had dismissed her as a brash and assertive schemer enforced an injunction against the very activity in which he himself indulged, but she was too interested in the information to broach the hypocrisy. That the most celebrated chef in Europe had lived around the bend in Berkeley Square was astounding. That he had been brutally murdered was heartbreaking.

"I never had the pleasure of meeting Monsieur Alphonse, as you called him," Bea said now in response to Joseph's question. "But he is discussed in several books I have read about a new style of cooking called *la grande cuisine,* and he wrote a memoir about his experiences cooking for Talleyrand, Napoleon and Czar Alexander of Russia."

Clearly taken aback, Joseph stared at her as if she had announced that she was actually sitting on a tiger, not a settee. "He always said he was a shopkeeper. Something would happen that didn't make sense to him and he would shrug his shoulders and say, 'What do I know? I am just a shopkeeper.' He never once said anything about cooking for Napoleon—at least not while I was around. I asked him once why he left France because he did not seem to like the English. He thought we were staid and predictable."

Well, yes, that was true, Bea thought, recalling the chef had used a variation of that description in his memoir. In fact, the exact phrase was "staid, predictable, unimaginative and banal."

"How did he respond?" she asked.

"Mr. Mayhew's generosity was irresistible," he replied, darting another glace at the butler as if to make sure this statement did not violate the prohibition.

"Was he satisfied with the bargain?" she asked.

Demurring, the footman insisted he could not say.

His tone was firm, but Bea suspected he could actually say

quite a lot if allowed to speak freely. Instead, he refused to utter any word even vaguely scurrilous out of respect for the greatness of the house and the rules that governed its occupants. She wanted to applaud his scruples, but the truth was his integrity left her with a troublesome quandary. Given her own proclivities, it was entirely in her best interest to discourage gossip among the staff, and yet she would discover nothing about Mr. Réjane's demise if none of the servants would provide her with information. Additionally, she did not want to undermine the butler's authority by overturning his injunction against the practice but nor did she desire to weaken her own by deferring on a matter of some importance.

Thoughtfully, she settled on a collaborative approach. "Marlow, I am grateful you have remained in the room because I would appreciate your opinion on the matter. I wholeheartedly agree that gossip is something to be discouraged, and I would be terribly aggrieved to learn the servants were speculating about the duke or myself or exchanging stories about us. But as distasteful as gossip is, I wonder if perhaps something about it isn't essential to the process of detection. If murderers spoke freely about their actions and motives, then there would be no need to investigate them. What are your thoughts on the matter?"

Marlow claimed to have no thoughts that did not mirror her own.

It was a decorous answer and the only one a butler in a ducal residence could give to his mistress, and while Bea appreciated his concurrence, she wondered if he thought she had been brash and assertive in attaining it.

Aware that the situation was not helped by nurturing the wound to her vanity, she returned her attention to Joseph and asked him what Monsieur Alphonse thought of his employer.

Cautiously, as if suspecting an invisible trap, Joseph replied, "He called him a *petit bourgeois*."

Unfamiliar with the phrase, Bea could not believe it denoted anything positive, for even without the belittling adjective diminishing it further, the word *bourgeois* carried the negative connotations of mediocrity and excessive interest in material gain.

"And that is a bad thing to be?" she asked.

Joseph nodded solemnly. "It is the very worst."

"How did this *petit bourgeois* aspect manifest itself?" Bea asked.

"Mr. Mayhew had what Monsieur Alphonse described as a small-minded palate," Joseph said with another worrying glance at the butler. It was one thing to discuss the neighbor's horribly butchered servant and quite another to talk about his inadequate sense of taste.

One did not have to be familiar with Mr. Réjane's philosophy to recognize the phrase as the pejorative it clearly was. "Mr. Mayhew is averse to new flavors?"

"He wanted Monsieur Alphonse to make only the same dozen meals for him and Mrs. Mayhew," Joseph promptly explained, "and when he had a dinner party, he always insisted on the same quail dish over and over again. Anytime Monsieur Alphonse tried to make something new, Mr. Mayhew complained that it was too foreign or too elaborate. He wanted only familiar foods."

It was a staggering notion to Bea—hiring the most inventive chef in the world and leashing him to a narrow rotation of dishes—and she stared at Joseph for several long moments as she tried to digest the absurdity. If all Mr. Mayhew required was technical proficiency, he could have engaged any number of well-respected French chefs and quite a few English cooks.

But of course he had not employed the chef for his skills

but rather his name, which carried with it the luster of emperors and czars.

"Was Monsieur Alphonse bored in his position?" Bea asked, unable to conceive how he could be anything else.

Joseph pursed his lips for a thoughtful moment and said, "If he abided by the limitations set by Mr. Mayhew, then I think he would have been bored to flinders. But he ignored them entirely and made whatever he wanted, whenever he wanted. He stopped *serving* new dishes to the Mayhews, but he certainly did not stop *creating* them. The servants in the house ate better than some lords, your grace. He'd bring us samples too, to get our opinions on new dishes. He always sought as many opinions as possible. And the things he made were wonderful. Mrs. Blewitt, the housekeeper at forty-four, was told explicitly by Mr. Mayhew to supply Monsieur Alphonse with whatever ingredients he required so he had access to everything. He seemed very comfortable there, so I was surprised he had decided to leave."

"He was leaving?" Bea asked, leaning forward in her chair, as any change in the victim's status was noteworthy. "When did he give his notice?"

"Yesterday," Joseph replied. "And no amount of money Mr. Mayhew offered him could induce him to change his mind, so perhaps he *was* bored to flinders."

It was quite startling, Bea thought, that the footman of a neighboring property would be privy to so much private information. "You are very well informed."

A light flush colored his cheeks at the observation, but he kept his eyes steady as he explained that he had overheard Monsieur Alphonse telling Mrs. Wallace his plans. "But I wasn't eavesdropping," he said, rushing to deny the accusation before it might be lodged. "I would never stoop to such shameful behavior. I just happened to be in the stillroom cleaning the bottles when he came to talk to her and he was excited and spoke so loudly I could not help but overhear. He said he was going to Paris to open a patisserie, and that it didn't matter how much money Mr. Mayhew offered him to remain, he would not stay. He was leaving in a few days and wanted Mrs. Wallace to come with him."

Suddenly and strangely, Marlow squeaked.

Chapter Four

✦❧✦

In the amount of time it took for Bea to look from Joseph to Marlow, she constructed and dismantled an overwrought three-act tragedy around the brief, jarring sound: Secret love! Thwarted passion! Seething jealousy!

Afraid of rejection and desperate to maintain domestic tranquility, the butler had managed to successfully repress his feelings—until the day Mrs. Wallace received a proposal of marriage from an upstart Frenchmen who would dare install her in a patisserie. For her to go from keeping house in the finest establishment in all of London to serving cakes to *petit bourgeois* in Paris was an intolerable relegation, and he could not allow it.

No, honor demanded a response, and determined to save the love of his life from the wanton self-destruction of foreign commerce, he raced across the square, wielding a...wielding a...

But here Bea's imagination failed her because she had no idea what weapon Marlow would wield to vanquish a romantic rival, and even if she could figure out the implement (something silver, she concluded, and polished to a high shine, the better to see the spark of righteous indignation in his eyes), she simply could not picture him swinging it with furious abandon until the illustrious chef's head was removed from his body.

The difficulty was not that he lacked the strength to sunder a neck completely, nor that he was deficient in the strong emotions necessary for a violent response, as he had clearly spent years stifling his passions. No, the issue was she simply could not reconcile the indignity of the carnage with the butler's exalted demeanor. The sheer untidiness of decapitation would offend him—all that blood spurting in all those directions! Surely, *he* could not be expected to mop up the mess?

More likely, the sound he'd expelled was the result of the mundane considerations of staffing. The prospect of having to accustom himself to a new housekeeper, perhaps one not as capable or receptive to his guidance as Mrs. Wallace, was no doubt an unpleasant one. Or maybe the explanation was even simpler still: He was alarmed to discover his management was so lax he failed to notice a romance flourishing directly under his nose.

That would be a gross oversight for a butler as profoundly formidable as Marlow.

Examining him now for some indication that she had not imagined the noise, she found his expression as impassive as ever. Joseph's visage was equally bland, but she refused to let that sway her.

Marlow had undeniably made a peep.

Ruminating on it further, however, felt like a distraction from the more pressing issue, and she returned her attention to Joseph to ask how the housekeeper responded to the proposal.

"She refused," he said, pausing slightly as if allowing the butler a moment to digest the information. Then he added,

"But she assured him it wasn't because she did not enjoy his company. She was very clear that her refusal to go had nothing to do with her feelings for him. It was simply that Paris was so full of French people and very far away from her mother, and besides, she had never really wanted to travel anywhere but to Dorset because she loved being near the sea."

Although Mrs. Wallace could not be faulted for her logic, as Paris did indeed contain quite a great many people of Gallic extraction, Bea rather thought her decision had a *little* something to do with her feelings for the chef. If they had been warm enough, then she would have been inclined to put up with a host of inconveniences, including fewer visits with her mother.

"How did Monsieur Alphonse react to her rejection?" she asked. She titled her eyes slightly to the left to observe Marlow's response but had little hope of noting anything of interest. Having allowed one revealing squeak to escape, he was unlikely to permit another.

"He *claimed* to feel great despair," Joseph replied with pointed emphasis.

The implication was impossible to miss, and Bea asked why the footman doubted the sincerity of the statement.

"Well, he did not seem particularly despairing, did he?" Joseph said. "In his voice, I mean. I was in the next room so I couldn't see his face—maybe he *looked* despairing—but his tone was not anguished at all. He said that he wished there was something he could do to change her mind and that he was beyond himself with disappointment, but then he asked Mrs. Wallace where in Dorset she would like to go and she said Poole and he said he had once visited Bournemouth with Mr. Mayhew. Then they discussed the unreliable pleasures of the beach for a few minutes before Monsieur Alphonse announced that he had to go. Mr. Mayhew was hosting a small dinner party and he had left the quails roasting. Then he promised to call again before he departed London and returned to forty-four."

Bea agreed that the chef's behavior did not appear to match his sentiment, but she allowed for the possibility that he had sought to hide the depth of his disappointment by engaging in polite conversation. She herself had done it on more than one occasion when she'd believed Kesgrave indifferent to her appeal.

"And how did Mrs. Wallace seem?" Bea asked, wondering if the housekeeper's behavior could have been spurred by something more sinister than a general disgust of foreign travel. Had she known of a threat to Monsieur Alphonse and sought to keep him safe by turning down his proposal, effectively renouncing him for his own good?

If that was the case, then she had failed spectacularly in her purpose.

Or perhaps the explanation was far more innocuous, and she simply could not bear the thought of leaving Kesgrave's service.

Regardless of the cause itself, if Mrs. Wallace had rejected him for any reason other than a lack of affection, then she would have been sad or forlorn.

"It is impossible to say," Joseph replied.

Bea nodded, not at all surprised by this response. "Because she maintained the inscrutable air of good humor one expects from an experienced housekeeper?"

"No," he said sharply, "because James came running into the room with the news that the duke had just brought his bride home and that threw her into a state of extreme agitation. For a few minutes she paced back and forth in the scullery, folding all the drying cloths and scrubbing rags as if the first place the new duchess would visit was the kitchens. Then she ordered Cook to make fresh tea cakes and told me to clean the mirrors, which was odd soup because I had already cleaned them earlier in the day. I tried to point this out, but she was too agitated to listen. So I came upstairs and cleaned them again."

Ending his answer on a disgruntled note, Joseph realized with belated insight that his description reflected poorly on the housekeeper and he immediately sought to amend the account. "That is to say, Mrs. Wallace had been anticipating the arrival of the new duchess for more than a week and had everything so well prepared there was nothing left for her to do but straighten the towels in the scullery," he said, then looked at the butler again, as if seeking his approval.

Bea, who was impressed by the clever reframing, hoped Marlow bestowed it, although how the footman would ever know escaped her.

"So the conversation between Mrs. Wallace and Monsieur Alphonse happened yesterday?" she asked, drawing attention away from the sensitive subject of her own arrival. She was no more comfortable hearing about it than Joseph was describing it.

"It did, yes, your grace," he said, "at approximately three-thirty in the afternoon."

"Three-thirty," she repeated thoughtfully. "And you said he was in the middle of preparing food for a small dinner party?"

He replied promptly in the affirmative.

"Did Monsieur Alphonse happen to mention how small?" Bea asked.

"Eight guests to dine in addition to Mrs. Mayhew and himself," Joseph said, proving himself to be a very helpful bystander.

As she had yet to be a duchess for a full day and her family rarely extended invitations to dine, Bea truly could not say if the chef's behavior was strange or not. But it struck her as quite odd to leave the kitchen whilst preparing for a large—in no universe would she allow the prospect of hosting eight for dinner to be considered *small*—party to pay a romantical call on a neighbor. Mrs. Wallace had turned down his kind offer, but what if she had consented to be his wife? They would have in effect become betrothed, and she had a difficult time imagining a newly engaged man ceasing his expressions of joy to check on the progress of the quails.

Would not the more practical plan have been to wait until the next morning to make his proposal, when there would be fewer demands on his time? As he had already handed in his notice, he would be free from commitments and welcome to press his suit at leisure.

Ah, but what lovesick swain ever paused to contemplate the pragmatism of his actions? If the idea to make an offer had come upon him in a burst of excitement, then he might have been no more able to restrain himself than he could hold water in his hands.

And yet, Bea thought, the two pieces didn't quite fit together—the spontaneous proposal and the patisserie in Paris. If he had known for a while that he was leaving, then why dash out in the middle of dinner preparations to make an offer? Had it truly not occurred to him earlier that he might want her to accompany him on his new venture?

Yes, it definitely seemed strange to her that a man who had decided to establish a business in a foreign country hadn't realized until less than a week before he left that he might want the woman he loved to come with him.

If nothing else, it was egregiously poor planning on his part.

Maybe she was examining the question from the wrong perspective, she thought and considered the possibility that something happened to alter his plans. Conceivably, an event of some significance might have made him discover he could not live without her or it could have caused him to change his departure date, forcing him to return to Paris earlier than he'd intended.

In both instances, a hurried, impulsive proposal was not entirely out of order.

But what could that event be, she wondered.

Decidedly, the list could not be very long, for the most accomplished chef in all of Europe was not subject to the same vagaries of fate as an ordinary servant. He would never be turned out for squabbling with the other members of the household because he was thoroughly irreplaceable while footmen and scullery maids were interchangeable. Even his employers had to earn his approval: The quality of James Van der Straeten's kitchen had been so underwhelming, Mr. Réjane left the well-known banker's service without preparing a single meal—and then included a lengthy description of the inferiority of the gentleman's Castrol stove in his memoir.

Only something deeply significant or hugely troubling could have changed his plans.

A decisive quarrel, Bea thought, and one that occurred during the preparations for the dinner party. Tempers were frequently frayed by the anticipation of guests, and if Mr. Mayhew had made an outlandish request while Mr. Réjane was struggling to create the perfect meal, the chef might have responded without restraint. A vicious row ensued, ending with Mr. Réjane's resolution to leave.

The fact that Mr. Mayhew had made increasingly generous offers to convince him to stay suggested that the gentleman had realized his misstep at once and sought to fix it.

How had he felt when his attempts at reconciliation were roundly rebuffed? An intractable servant might be infuriating to a man accustomed to a pliant domestic staff.

It was true, Bea thought, and yet she could not imagine

the gentleman chopping off the head of his chef in a surge of fury simply because the man refused to remain in his employ.

At the same time, she could not dismiss it either, for she knew nothing of Mr. Mayhew's *petit bourgeois* character and couldn't say how he would react when thwarted by an upstart Frenchman with ideas beneath his station. That Mr. Réjane could actually prefer drudging in a sweltering kitchen in a benighted Parisian alleyway to working in the gracious splendor of Berkeley Square might have been an insult beyond bearing.

All things considered, it was a minor offense and hardly the sort of thing that should drive a gentleman to strike, let alone kill, one of his subordinates. But Bea did not consider it within her purview as an investigator to make sense of her suspects' motivations. It was her task to discover whether they had the opportunity and wherewithal to commit the crime.

Could Mr. Mayhew have sliced Monsieur Alphonse's neck in half?

To make that determination, she would have to meet him. Without question, how he handled her interest would provide meaningful insight into his disposition, for he could not relish being interrogated by a random stranger, but it was not only intangibles that interested her. The death had been a physically violent one, and possibly Mr. Mayhew lacked the strength to sever a head.

The answer would depend, she supposed, on the type and condition of the weapon used. If its blade was unduly sharp, then the job might be done neatly and quickly.

"Regarding the cut that ended Monsieur Alphonse's life," she said matter-of-factly, "was it done in one masterful stroke or did it require quite a lot of hacking?"

The color drained from Joseph's face, and Bea immediately remembered Mrs. Norton's expression when she had insisted on examining the corpse of Mr. Hobson. Without pausing to consider her words, she had once again revealed her ghoulish soul by not acting with appropriate squeamishness. How appalled the society matron had been at Bea's cool appraisal of the slain actor's wounds, the bloody hole violently gashed into his stomach by fireplace tongs.

A lady of proper feeling would have turned away in horror!

Given that her archnemesis had been party to arranging the terrible scene, Bea cared nothing of her opinion, good or otherwise, but Joseph was a different matter. He was a member of the duke's household, which meant he was a member of her household now, and she would have liked to have made a slightly better impression than appearing coldly indifferent to the lurid details of a decapitation.

Fleetingly, she recalled wondering only a short time ago what kind of duchess the staff would prefer to serve and realized it was too late to worry about the answer. Her true nature had been exposed in a moment of unvarnished honesty, and there was no point in wringing her hands over it now.

It was actually for the best, she decided, for it spared her the obligation of trying to meet their expectations, an effort that would have inevitably ended in failure. Unlike the many young ladies with whom she'd shared a first season—and five unsuccessful subsequent ones—she had not been raised from infancy to bear the weight of a duchy. No one had anticipated anything grander for Beatrice Hyde-Clare than a second or a third son, a clergyman, perhaps, with a rectory where she would comfort the parishioners with tepid tea and familiar platitudes such as "Good things come to those who wait" and "Everything happens for a reason."

Whatever heights of gracious dignity she might have

aspired to—or even briefly achieved—it was all a matter of hopeless speculation now.

Her disgrace assured, Bea did nothing to mitigate it, choosing instead to apologize to Joseph for speaking so plainly. "I should have shown more consideration for your sensibilities," she said, stopping just short of begging his forgiveness, for that, too, would have displayed an unacceptable lack of decorum. "Just because I am accustomed to the ghastliness that accompanies brutal death does not mean everyone else is. But do please tell me what you know about"—she paused momentarily as she tried to think of a gentler description and settled on euphemism—"how Monsieur Alphonse met his unfortunate end. Maybe you can start with the implement that was used. Was it sharp? Very heavy? Perhaps you can describe how large it was."

Although his cheeks were still pale, the footman spoke calmly, displaying no anxiety as he explained that he could tell her nothing in particular about the instrument, as he had never seen the *le peu guillotine*.

As Beatrice herself was unfamiliar with a device called the little guillotine and she had read several compendiums on cooking, she could not fault his ignorance. "*Le peu guillotine?*"

"An invention of Monsieur Alphonse," Joseph explained, "to make chopping meat and vegetables more efficient. As I understand it, it worked like the original it was modeled after, with a blade that dropped a goodly distance to create a clean cut. But of course the *le peu* is much smaller."

With this description it was easy enough to picture the device, to visualize a diminutive version of the apparatus that had stood in the Place de la Revolution and dealt death to thousands, and Bea felt a shiver pass through her at the thought of Europe's greatest chef meeting his end like a joint of mutton.

Ah, so she was not so ghoulish after all.

"How little is it?" she asked.

"I cannot say," Joseph replied, reminding her that he possessed no direct knowledge of the instrument. "But based on the description I was given, I did not imagine it was large enough to fit a human head."

Although Bea appreciated the specificity of his answer, for it anticipated her next question, Marlow found it in bad taste and drew his brows closer together. The footman, shrinking under the glare of his disapproval, apologized to the duchess for speaking so freely.

As she was the one who had used the word *hacking* only a few minutes ago, she thought this display of sensibility was both highly unnecessary and faintly ridiculous. Nevertheless, she thanked Joseph for his consideration and observed that the machine was clearly larger than its name indicated. "If it could chop off a human head, then it cannot differ greatly from its template. What a very distressing thing to keep in the middle of one's kitchen."

Joseph agreed. "Parsons said the truly shocking thing is that nobody had hurt themselves on it before."

"Parsons?" Bea asked.

"The butler at number forty-four," the footman replied. "It was he who told us about the accident. He call on us this morning, very distressed about the whole thing. He is usually quiet and rarely says a word, but this morning he was talkative."

Although a chatty butler was in itself a novelty worthy of further exploration, the fact that he claimed the decapitation was an accident interested her more. "That was how he described the incident? As an accident?"

"Yes," Joseph said firmly, his whole demeanor changing as he darted a look at Marlow that was equal parts smug and relieved as the comment seemed to validate his concern. "He said it was an accident. He said that Monsieur Alphonse must have been fiddling with the blade, which sometimes becomes stuck on its hinge, and it came loose at an inopportune moment and sliced off his...that is, sliced forcefully."

Bea could not tell if the amendment was for her benefit or his own. Despite demonstrating a convincing lack of sensibility, she was nevertheless a female of high rank and required a delicate touch. "But you don't think that's what happened."

Joseph's expression turned doubtful as he explained that he didn't know what to think. "I suppose it is possible. From its description, I know the device has a sharp blade and can do significant damage to a cut of meat. But it was Monsieur Alphonse's own invention and he had been using it for years. It just seems to me that he would know how it works. If it got stuck frequently, as Parsons said, then Monsieur Alphonse would know how to repair it without endangering himself."

It was, Bea thought, a reasonable argument and one she herself would have made if prompted. "And that is why you sought my assistance?"

Joseph nodded. "It's just that the matter was settled so quickly. Parsons discovered the body and decided it was an accident. Mr. Mayhew accepted his explanation and called the constable, who also agreed. That was the extent of the investigation, and I think it's horribly unfair not to at least consider the possibility that he didn't cause his own death in such a clownish way."

Naturally, yes, the greatest chef of Europe deserved a little consideration before being dismissed as a buffoon, and she wondered why the butler would be determined to deny it to him. The obvious answer, of course, was that he was hiding his own guilt. "As far as you are aware, did Parsons have a reason to wish Monsieur Alphonse ill?"

Perceiving the implication at once, for the question was hardly subtle, the footman shook his head emphatically and said he knew of no resentments against him. "As I said, he loved to experiment with new dishes, so he kept the staff at forty-four very well fed. Honestly, your grace, I think Mayhew's servants eat better than the prince regent. And he was amiable and good-natured and rarely took a pet about anything. I remember once he brought us wonderful little rolls shaped like crescents, and Cook was critical of them. She said it was the crumbliest *kipferl* she had ever had because a bit of pastry fell into her lap when she took a bite. Monsieur Alphonse was quite disdainful of her opinion and said she did not understand pastries or dough. And, furthermore, it wasn't *kipferl* at all, but a *variation* on the Viennese classic. He went on for quite a while, scorning all of Cook's opinions, but then he asked for her own *kipferl* recipe and left eager to give it a try, and all was forgotten."

Having read the victim's memoir, *Un Humble Chef Confie Ses Trésors au Monde et Partage Ses Expériences avec les Grandes Maisons d'Europe,* Bea was not surprised by this description of affable good humor, for it perfectly matched the tone of his book. Whereas for many cooks, the tyranny of unreliable outcomes—will the bread rise, will the roux thicken—and the need to perform with precision upon command justified a tyrannical temperament, Mr. Réjane considered the unpredictability of his avocation to be part of its appeal. It was a game to him, never quite knowing if his soufflé would maintain its height or fall.

It was strange, she thought, to contemplate how close she had come to living so near to the distinguished chef whose work she had admired from afar for years. She would have very much liked to have tried his flaky *kipferl* and his *croquantes* and any of the dozens of superb dishes he chronicled in his tome.

'Twas a shame, a very great shame, that such a talent was gone from the world.

Sighing lightly, she returned to the matter of Parsons and asked what other details he had supplied.

"He revealed nothing else of note," Joseph replied. "The exchange we had was hurried and disjointed. He had come to our door looking for smelling salts, you see, for Mrs. Mayhew had fainted dead away when she heard that Monsieur Alphonse's head was lying in a different room from his body and the maid could find none among her mistress's things. Parsons came dashing over here to borrow ours, but I think he really just wanted an excuse to be away from the house for a few minutes. He said several times the accident was horrible, but it was only when he was leaving—after Mrs. Wallace had given him her own smelling salts—that he actually said what happened. It was all so distressing, and not just because Monsieur Alphonse's head had been decapitated, although that is too horrifying to contemplate. But also because the thing was deemed an accident. I tried to ask Parsons how they could be so sure, but he insisted it was the only possible explanation. Then he raised the salts to his own nose because he must have felt a little faint himself and left."

By any account, it was deeply suspicious behavior, the man who had found the body insisting that his explanation was the only viable one. "What time did Parsons call?"

"A little after ten," he said. "I was returning the breakfast tray to the kitchen when he arrived at the door. Dolly immediately went to look for smelling salts, and I stood with him in the entryway, tray in hand, while he waited. He was quiet at first, but then he started talking and he couldn't seem to stop. That was when Mr. Marlow invited him to sit down, but he refused. He said he could not stay that long."

That the butler had also heard the tale firsthand came as a surprise to Bea, who had assumed from his stony silence that he had been in a different part of the house. "Tell me, Marlow, does Parsons's story sound plausible to you? Do you think it is possible that Monsieur Alphonse inadvertently sliced off his own head with his chopping implement?"

Although she readily recalled the contempt with which Marlow had ordered his underling never to speak of the death again, Bea did not ask the question out of an impulse to embarrass him in front of a subordinate by requiring him to violate his own rule. The anger that had spurred the discussion had long since been supplanted by a desire to do right by the talented chef. The murder of any man was a tragedy, to be sure, but there was something about cutting *this* man down in his prime that felt especially calamitous to her.

Marlow's reply was simple. "No, your grace, I do not."

Bea nodded solemnly and considered the next step in her investigation—a deliberation that was not at all necessary, as there was only one reasonable prospect and that was to interview Mrs. Wallace.

Obviously, she did not relish the task, for interrogating the housekeeper on a deeply personal matter was not among the options she had considered when she had sought the woman out for their first discussion earlier that morning. Her plan to be either ingratiatingly deferential or offputtingly demanding was for naught, and as much as she would have preferred to delay the awkward scene, she had too much pride in her proficiency as an investigator to allow mortification to affect her inquiry.

She would conduct the difficult interview before visiting number forty-four to speak to Mr. Mayhew's staff.

Although resolute, she could not quite smother the sigh that rose to her lips and to cover it, she assured Joseph that the matter was under her control now. If something nefarious had happened to the famous chef, he could trust her to bring it to light.

The relief that briefly overtook his expression was gratifying, even if Marlow's visage remained impassive. To the butler, she requested that Mrs. Wallace be sent to the drawing room, and although it was on the tip of her tongue to ask him not to tell her the subject they would discuss, she realized such a cautionary measure was not necessary. Informing the housekeeper that her mistress wished to interrogate her on her flirtation with a servant from a neighboring house who had just been beheaded was not a duty any butler would voluntarily perform.

Mrs. Wallace, therefore, had no idea of the topic of conversation and entered the drawing room with a compact little book in her hands for taking notes. Naturally, she assumed she had been summoned to confer on various domestic matters, such as menus for the week or the new duchess's preferred level of firmness in a pillow, and appeared eager to do so. Whatever grief she felt on the horrendous death of her beau was carefully concealed, and the only emotion Bea could discern on her lightly wrinkled face was curiosity. A petite woman with a slight frame, she wore a dark brown dress that could indicate mourning, but as it bore a marked resemblance to the gown she had worn the day before Bea concluded it was her uniform.

Apprehensive but determined, Bea began by offering her condolences to the housekeeper and insisting she take all the time she needed to recover from her loss. Recalling her comments to Mr. Réjane as relayed by Joseph, she suggested perhaps a visit to her mother.

Mrs. Wallace's lips tightened at these words, and she clasped her hands together as she stared at Bea from underneath her mob cap, which seemed to engulf her small head. Quietly, she asked, "Are you dismissing me, your grace?"

Horrified, Bea sputtered, "No, no, of course not." The last thing she wanted to do was unintentionally fire a longstanding member of the duke's staff! "I am grateful for your efficiency and skill and would never dream of replacing you. If my words or actions have led you to think otherwise, I am sorry."

The housekeeper nodded with visible relief and opened her notebook to a fresh page. Her respite was short-lived, however, for a moment later Bea asked about Monsieur Alphonse's proposal and her shoulders stiffened again. A furrow formed between her brows as she repeated the question with an air of disbelief, "Had I expected Monsieur Alphonse to propose?"

Observing the simmering umbrage, Bea wanted to pretend she had not posed the query and put her off with a ruse—to raise her eyebrow archly, for example, and ask with haughty indifference what interest she could possibly have in the romantic dealings of a pair of servants. As absurd as such a ploy would be, it would carry the day easily, for she was mistress of the house now and her whims would be catered to. Furthermore, Mrs. Wallace could not like the topic any more than she and would gratefully follow her lead.

But Bea had asked the question and, refusing to succumb to her embarrassment, staunchly held the course. "Yes, had you realized his feelings for you had advanced to the point of marriage?"

If the housekeeper was outraged, embarrassed or deeply insulted by the question, she gave no hint of it as she replied no, she had not anticipated a proposal from the French chef.

Bea waited for her to say more, perhaps to articulate her surprise at receiving the offer, but Mrs. Wallace restricted herself to answering only the question itself. As the silence stretched to a full minute, Bea grudgingly conceded she would have to ask her why she thought the chef had decided to propose.

Alas, speculating about the motives of anyone, even a former suitor, was a presumption the housekeeper would not dare. "I can only speak to my own behavior."

As it was a reasonable policy, Bea could not quarrel with her stance, and yet she could not allow the other woman's scruples to impede her search for Mr. Réjane's killer. Firmly, she pressed on. "Did it not strike you as a little strange that he would take time away from preparing for a large dinner party to propose marriage?"

Now, for the first time, Mrs. Wallace's face showed emotion and she said with some alacrity, "It was not a *large* dinner party."

Bea could not comprehend the relevance. "Excuse me?"

"Only eight people were expected," Mrs. Wallace explained, "so one could not describe the dinner party as large. Be that as it may, I cannot say it struck me as strange that he would take time away from preparing for a small dinner party to propose marriage because Monsieur Alphonse made a habit of doing things when he wanted, not when it was deemed appropriate. As Mr. Mayhew's chef, he had a fair amount of freedom."

"Did the other servants in the house begrudge him this privilege?" Bea asked, knowing how easy it was to resent another person for having something you lacked. In the past few months, she had often yearned for more liberty in her ability to move around London.

Mrs. Wallace found the question outrageous—as if she had ever given any thought to the resentments of the other servants who lived in the square. She huffed in offense, then realized her faux pas and immediately apologized for forgetting herself. "I am sorry, but I simply cannot see what the thoughts and opinions of the neighbors have to do with me, your grace."

As her confusion appeared genuine, Bea did not hesitate to explain that she was gathering information to discover who had murdered Monsieur Alphonse. "The more I learn about the situation, the more quickly I will discover the truth."

But the housekeeper refused to entertain the notion that the French chef had been anything other than a victim of misfortune. "The constable has declared it an accident, and I must abide by his decision."

Beatrice, of course, was under no obligation and continued to ask questions in hopes of discovering something useful, but having declared her allegiance to the law, Mrs. Wallace declined to be of further help. She was happy to stay as long as the duchess required, however, for although she had other matters to see to, attending to her mistress's needs was foremost among her responsibilities. "I am sure the shopping can wait indefinitely."

Patently, it could not.

The shopping, the accounts, the linens—all these tasks were clearly more important to the housekeeper, who could not understand why she had been called away from them to surmise wildly about the neighbors. Her expression remained placid, but Bea could detect annoyance simmering beneath the surface, and although she conceded that it was perfectly justified, she could not allow that to sway her from her course.

Determinedly, she persisted in her questions.

Ultimately, it was to no avail, for the housekeeper's insistence that she had no light to shed on the topic proved remarkably accurate. She knew nothing of the machinations at number forty-four and appeared to have less insight into her own proposal than the footman who overheard it from the stillroom.

"Was he truly in despair?" Mrs. Wallace repeated quietly. "That is not a determination I can make. All I can do is refer you to his words, and he said he was in despair at my refusal."

"Yes, of course," Bea murmured soothingly, for there was no reason to reveal her frustration. She had already made an unfavorable impression on the housekeeper by plaguing her with queries and heedlessly ignoring the ruling of an official constable. No doubt she considered Kesgrave House's new mistress to be intolerably brash and assertive as well.

Intolerably, Bea thought wryly, as if there were some measure of brashness and assertiveness that *was* tolerable.

Deciding she had mortified them both enough, Bea thanked Mrs. Wallace for her time and assistance. "You have been very helpful."

"My pleasure, your grace," she said, tapping the little notebook with her finger before asking if the duchess had any thoughts regarding the management of the house. "Perhaps you would like to discuss menus now?"

Bea, who had assumed she could do nothing worse than interrogate the servant about her relationship with a decapitated French chef, felt herself sink lower in the other woman's estimation as she admitted to having no thoughts regarding the planning of that week's meals.

Mrs. Wallace, seemingly incapable of grasping this concept, said with baffled incredulity, "None at all?"

In the housekeeper's bewilderment, Bea felt her inadequacy keenly, for a real duchess would have dozens if not hundreds of thoughts on that week's menus, and scrambling to come up with a single thing, she recalled her determination to make an outrageous demand.

Oh, but if outrageous demands were difficult to think of while wandering the passageways of the servants' quarters by oneself, they were impossible to produce while sitting in the drawing room in the company of one's housekeeper. Wretchedly, she stared at Mrs. Wallace with a vacant expression and tried to come up with a lovely indulgence that her exalted status suddenly made available to her. Surely, there was something she had craved during her years of deprivation with her aunt and uncle. Unfortunately, just thinking of her aunt reminded her of everything that was intimidating about

Kesgrave's position: the eight footmen, the litany of maids, the pinery.

Of course, yes, the pinery!

Knowing little about the process of growing a tropical fruit in the chilly British climate, she could only feel awe at its production and unable to conceive of anything more decadent or absurd, she apologized for misspeaking and requested that a plate of fresh pineapple slices be served every morning with her toast.

Chapter Five

I*n seeking out Kesgrave* in his study, Bea had intended only to inform him of her immediate plans. She had not meant to stand in the doorway like a lovestruck school-girl sighing over her handsome dancing master—and yet that was exactly what she did. As soon as she arrived at the room, she could not help but pause on the threshold to gape at the golden brilliance of his locks.

How luminously they glowed in the light from the window.

She was spared the further indignity of staring dreamily at the elegant line of his nose or the appealing curve of his jaw by the tilt of his head. If he had not been bent over a ledger, there was no telling how deeply she might have descended into besotted appreciation.

Would she have spent the rest of the day gazing in awe at her beautiful husband and marveling at the utter inexplica-bility of desire—the way satiating it had somehow made it stronger?

Mr. Stephens coughed, alerting the duke to her presence, and rose to his feet. "I see the tea has grown cold. I will fetch us a fresh pot from the kitchen. If you will excuse me, your grace," he said with a polite nod at Beatrice.

"You were perfectly correct to fire Mr. Wright," she said in mocking reference to the identity she had briefly assumed in order to gain entry to a victim's house during an earlier investigation. "Mr. Stephens is a far better steward. Mr. Wright would never have thought to discreetly absent himself, preferring instead to gawk at the new mistress of the house with her oddly elaborate curls."

Kesgrave smiled as he stood and pushed his chair away from the desk. "Why oddly? Are they arranged in the Waterfall or the Mathematical?"

"An excellent point, your grace, and I happily concede it," she said, crossing the threshold and closing the door behind her. "I should have said excessively elaborate, although then you would have compared it to the Infinitesimal."

"Such a cravat style does not exist," he said.

"Then you would have invented it to suit your needs," she replied.

He shook his head as he strode across the room to her. "I would never play fast and loose with the truth. Do you not know me at all?"

She drew her brows together as she examined him in a quizzical manner. "Are you not Mr. Theodore Davies, lowly law clerk and dashing figment of my imagination?"

His grin widened as he stopped a mere inch from her and said with amusement, "I am no figment."

No, he was not, she thought, gazing into the spectacular blue of his eyes and feeling lodged there.

Terra firma.

When she made no reply, he lowered his head and murmured, "Hello, my love," before capturing her lips with his own.

'Twas splendid indeed, the sensations he created with his

touch—his lips, his hands, both gently searching—and she could scarcely comprehend how it was possible to feel suddenly as if she were floating when seconds ago the ground had been so solidly beneath her.

"He is not coming back," Kesgrave said softly as he pressed a kiss to her neck.

"All right," she said, reassured by the comment without properly understanding it. "Who?"

Delighted by her confusion, he laughed lightly and said, "Stephens. He will wait to be summoned. Another way in which he is vastly superior to Mr. Wright."

Heat suffused her body at this statement, but it was not embarrassment at the thought of the steward patiently cooling his heels belowstairs while they satisfied their desire. No, it was lust, hot and sweet.

But this was not why she had come to the study, she thought vaguely, nor was it the reason he was there. "What about the tenants?" she asked despite the wild pounding of her heart.

"Flood," he whispered, trailing his lips against her ear, "fire, famine."

Although the words were said with tender pliancy, she felt their rigidity and pulled away. "The tenants."

Kesgrave sighed and rested his forehead against hers. "The tenants."

"I'm sure it's not at all bad as that," she said reasonably.

"We have not yet arrived at famine," he conceded, "but if we do not repair the damage caused by the first two conditions, then the crops might begin to fail."

"It will not come to that," Bea said resolutely, "for Mr. Stephens is far too capable a steward to allow you to succumb to base desires while the tenants wring their hands in despair. Even now, I am willing to wager, he is standing on the other side of this door, waiting to return after what he considers to be a reasonable interlude for a recently wedded couple to have a brief midday conference. Ready? He will knock in three...two...one..."

She paused as if genuinely expecting a rap upon the door.

The duke laughed. "I fear it is time for yet another lecture on my importance."

"Oh, no, your grace," she said, taking a step backward and grinning with impish impertinence. "If the tenants cannot wait for you to satisfy your base desires, then they certainly cannot spare the time it would take you to convince me of your consequence—and I say that knowing full well the languid thoroughness with which you do the former."

Kesgrave's eyes ignited—there was simply no other way to describe the fire that seemed to flair in their cerulean depths. "Mr. Stephens has assured me that if we resolve all the issues this afternoon, he will require nothing of me for a full week. And if he is indeed standing on the other side of the door," he added, his voice growing louder as if addressing an unseen listener, "his understanding of the situation had better be accurate or he will be turned out without notice."

Although her association with the steward had been short, she had little doubt the man was smart enough either to resolve all the issues with Kesgrave now or deal with the balance on his own later. Only a truly foolhardy man would detain a newly married duke in his study for more than a day.

Offering consolation, she said, "It is for the best because I am myself otherwise occupied at the moment."

"Ah," he said with satisfaction, "so you have found the library, have you?"

"Actually, I have not because your tour of the house was singularly lacking in specificity," she said. "I recall a lot of things being pointed at from far away."

"The topic of my base desires has already been addressed in this conversation, but I am happy to defend in great detail a bridegroom's impatience to bed his wife," he said, lips quivering with familiar mirth.

That would never do, no, for she found his pedantry far too appealing to resist and if he launched into a dissertation poor Mr. Stephens would be perched on the other side of the door until dinner.

As much as for her own sake as for his, she said rousingly, "The tenants!"

"The tenants," Kesgrave agreed with a dip of his head. "And while I am ordering thatch for the farmers' roofs, what will you be doing?"

Ah, yes, indeed!

Since her purpose in interrupting was to provide this very answer, she said easily, "Establishing myself with the staff."

'Twas vague, to be sure, and if one chose to be fussy about it, misleading, but it was also the unvarnished truth. She *was* establishing herself with the staff, although she withheld the method by which she would achieve that objective out of fear that Kesgrave would undermine it. It was a daunting task—indeed, she had failed so spectacularly with Mrs. Wallace, she had in fact lost some vital ground there—and if he insisted that they call in the Runners to handle the matter, she had a terrible fear she would concede just to save herself further humiliation.

But that was actually her secondary concern.

The more likely outcome was that he would insert himself into her investigation, and while she adored working in tandem with the duke, whose respect for her skills was as sincere as it was surprising, it was vital to her standing within the household that she accomplish this feat on her own. Marlow's unequivocal dismissal in regard to the Particular investigation still rang in her ears: *I'm sure it was his grace's ingenuity that carried the day, not the duchess's.*

If she accepted Kesgrave's help in pursuing Mr. Réjane's

killer, then this misapprehension would be allowed to persist. Her contribution would be relegated to a mere supporting role, and while she did not doubt that Kesgrave was clever enough to identify a murderer on his own, the fact remained that he had not. That honor belonged to her.

Patently, she felt some regret at excluding him from the case, for it was everything an investigative couple could want: Fame! Decapitation! *Croquantes*!

Nevertheless, it was far more important that she earn the staff's respect—as much as for Kesgrave's sake as for her own. He knew how intimidated she was by the prospect of over-seeing a large household and had assured her that Kesgrave House required no supervision from her. Mrs. Wallace had everything in order, and Bea was required to manage only as much or as little as she desired.

If she so preferred, she could retire to the library and read to her heart's content.

If she so preferred!

Of course she so preferred!

Beatrice Hyde-Clare was a bluestocking through and through, and the thought of having access to the Duke of Kesgrave's magnificent library made her positively giddy with joy. The decades she could pass in happy repose!

Alas, she wasn't an utter peagoose and no amount of biblio-giddiness could allow her to overlook the fact that *retire* was merely just another word for *hide*. Oh, yes, she could *hide* in the library and read to her heart's content.

Even cast in the ugly light of cowardice, the prospect was appealing to Bea, whose courage was not yet an estab-lished fact. She had shown flashes of fearlessness—calling an imperious duke to account in the middle of the Skeffing-tons' drawing room, confronting a murderer on the Lark-wells' terrace during a ball—but only after decades of timidity.

Years versus moments, she thought, unable to know with any reasonable certainty which was the anomaly.

But she had her suspicions, bolstered by six seasons on the fringes of society, spluttering stupidly in response to banal questions and examining her fingers with unwarranted fascination.

It would be so easy—effortless, really—to succumb to her insecurities, to simply sink into them like a rock falling to the bottom of the Thames, and it was the ease itself that terrified her.

She would not cower as a duchess the way she had cowered as a debutante.

No, she would not.

So she would establish herself with the staff in a manner that made her feel competent and capable, ensure the household ran according to her dictates and *then* retire to the library.

It was a simple matter of self-respect.

Kesgrave apparently thought so too because he nodded with approval.

But not only approval, Bea noted with concern. There was a hint of relief in the gesture as well.

Had she really been that transparent in her anxiety? Certainly, she had begun their engagement in a paroxysm of dread over the splendor of his position: the large house, the huge staff, the massive estate, the outsized influence, the vast sway over the fate of thousands. But in the successive week, she had made every effort to appear comfortable with it, smothering—with success, she'd believed—the moments of self-doubt that sprung up at unexpected times, such as when he mentioned with effortless offhandedness possessing a pinery.

Clearly, her efforts had been less than successful. He knew everything.

Well, not quite everything, she thought, resolving never to tell him about her propensity to flinch.

"A worthy goal," Kesgrave said of her plan, "although I don't believe too much exertion will be required. You already have Jenkins's devotion, and Marlow is still too bewildered by your refusal to submit to his withering glare to resist your efforts for long."

His assessment of the current state of affairs was only partially right. Having observed her in a series of outlandish costumes, his groom did indeed appear to favor her. But whatever gains she had made with the butler by arrogantly demanding entrance to the house a few days before had vanished. In the interval since the encounter, his confusion had hardened into dislike. Given the way she had flouted his authority, the transformation was not extraordinary.

"I'm gratified that you agree," Bea said with a deliberately bland smile as she reached for the doorknob. "Shall I send Mr. Stephens in or just assume he knows what my foot on his ear means?"

"Presumably, my steward is lying across the threshold in your scenario because he is prostrate with awe of me?" he asked.

Although he had drawn the correct conclusion, she disavowed it with innocent confusion and insisted the position would improve Mr. Stephens's ability to hear. "The better to respond to your summons promptly, of course," she said.

Kesgrave was not fooled for a moment. "Take precisely that tack with Marlow and you will have him eating oats out of your hand like a newborn foal by dinner."

Bea rather doubted that, but the mention of the evening meal made her aware of the lateness of the hour and all the detecting she had yet to do. "And what time will that be?"

"Not very late. Settling this business should take only a

few more hours," he said, glancing at the wall clock, which read one-thirty. "Perhaps six? I thought we could have an informal meal in our bedchamber—*en famille*, as it were."

Her heart fluttered almost painfully, not in anticipation of the delights of intimacy—although, of course, they held infinite appeal—but in pure pleasure at the description. Not since her parents had died had she felt the lovely warmth of family.

Calmly, as if unaffected by his statement, she agreed to the schedule and stepped out into the hallway to find Mr. Stephens striding toward her with a tray of tea. Although she darted an amused glance at Kesgrave, she managed to restrain her humor enough that she was able to return the steward's murmured greeting with a respectful one of her own. Similarly, she resisted the urge to ask him to pause so that she may press her hand against the teapot to determine how long he had been standing in the corridor waiting for her to emerge.

The door to the study closed, and Bea, slightly daunted by the next step, returned to her bedchamber to fetch a shawl. Finding one suited to the spring weather was not as difficult as she'd expected because Dolly was in her dressing room unpacking her trunks and she located the garment with unnerving efficiency. The maid appeared to know her wardrobe better than she, and Bea felt a sudden burst of gratitude to her cousin Flora, who had recently stolen into her room at Portman Square and taken the suit she typically wore on her investigations. If she had not, Russell's brown topcoat would have joined the pile of chemises and petticoats stacked on the dresser.

Readily, Bea imagined the blank deference with which Dolly would have held out her cousin's old pants and said, "Your breeches, your grace."

It was pure fantasy, and yet still she flinched.

Leaving the house was also easier than she'd anticipated,

for as a duchess she did not have to account for her movements to anyone. Aunt Vera was not there to cluck over the impropriety of an unmarried lady going out on her own. Flora was not a few steps behind to ask what plan was secretly afoot. There was only a single footman dressed in pristine livery who opened the door for her and abstained from asking questions.

Happily, she stepped into the brisk air and thought about the lengths she had to go previously to conduct her investigations. When she had not been outright lying to her relations about her destination, she had been sneaking out of the house through the servants' entrance. Often, she'd adopted various roles to conduct her interviews, and as she strode up the walkway at number forty-four, she thought about how refreshing it was to carry out an investigation as Beatrice Hyde-Clare.

Well, no, not Beatrice Hyde-Clare.

Beatrice, Duchess of Kesgrave.

Was that a twitch? she wondered, feeling a disquieting spasm in her left eye. Had her flinch become an unwelcome convulsion?

Determinedly, she pushed the thought to the corner of her mind, a feat whose futility she realized a moment later when she was compelled to introduce herself. At once, her eyelid began to flutter and she ignored the unsettling contraction of the muscles by sheer force of will.

"Good afternoon, I am the Duchess of Kesgrave," she said.

But the twitch was not the only thing for which she had failed to account. The magnitude of that fateful first utterance had escaped her, and she spoke with a curious breathlessness.

The footman, who could have no awareness of the moment's significance, watched her with steady light brown eyes the same color as his closely cropped hair, waiting, it seemed, for her to say something more.

Belatedly, she realized she had neglected to identify her purpose. "I am here to see Mr. Mayhew."

He accepted her statement with equanimity, then paused in subtle expectation for a brief moment before asking for her card.

Her card!

Good God, yes, her calling card!

What duchess went to visit the neighbors without bringing with her a little packet of embossed cards?

And not just duchesses, she thought contemptuously, any member of society. Placing one's calling card on the salver was the standard protocol for the most basic social interactions.

How could she be so thoughtless?

Poor Aunt Vera, whose only interest in her had been to ensure she behaved with a modicum of propriety!

An uncontrollable urge to laugh threatened to overcome her as she thought about all those years her relative had spent teaching her etiquette.

Her life's work squandered on a wastrel of a niece who was ultimately no better than she ought to be.

Bea's amusement was further spurred by the realization that this was the first time in any of her investigations that someone questioned her identity. Of all the absurd personas she had assumed over the past few months—French maid, law clerk, museum administrator—the hardest one to believe was the only one was that was true.

The reality of her was more difficult to conceive than the fiction.

It was too much for any human being to resist, especially one with such a highly developed sense of the ridiculousness as Bea, and she giggled. Not immoderately. Not excessively. Not even noticeably. It was more like Marlow's odd sound, a peepish squeak so slight the listener could not be sure it had actually been uttered.

But Bea felt it and the familiarity of the sensation soothed her. Her eye stopped twitching, and she smiled so brightly the expression transformed her whole face. "Yes, of course you want my calling card, and I am a dreadful creature for not being able to supply it. What an appalling lack of conduct! The trouble is, my good man," she said, striving for an avuncular tone even though the servant looked to be a few years older than she, "I am just wed and have not had an opportunity to secure them yet. I fear the oversight presents us with quite a quandary, but I am confident that if we put our heads together, we will arrive at an equitable solution. Shall I dash back to Kesgrave House to fetch my marriage lines? I am sure it won't take me more than a dozen minutes."

It was an insincere offer, of course, for she had no idea where the certificate was kept and she certainly was not going to interrupt Kesgrave's business with his steward to ask. She made the proposal only in hopes of embarrassing him with its extravagance.

No footman worthy of his position would allow a duchess to scuttle around Berkeley Square at his bidding.

As if following the script she had supplied, he assured her such lengths were not necessary. Then, however, he diverged from the play by promising to convey her esteem to Mr. Mayhew. "And the next time you pay a call, you may leave your card."

He did not end his short oration by bidding her good day, but the finality was implied.

Contemplating how to respond to the dismissal, Bea decided there was neither need nor cause for subtlety. She could, yes, wriggle her way into the house through sly or deceptive means, but as soon as she gained a foothold, she would have to say the word *decapitation* or the phrase *severed head,* undoing all her fine machinations.

She might as well start as she meant to continue.

To that end, she said with straightforward simplicity, "Your reluctance to admit me is understandable, given the tragic events of early this morning. If you are a sensible person—and by all appearances you are—you are either worried that I am a determined scandalmonger hoping to discover salacious details about Monsieur Alphonse's death or that my delicate sensibilities will be overcome by the horrific nature of it. Please let me ease your mind on both accounts: I find gossiping to be deeply abhorrent, and my sensibilities are of a quite hardy stock. I am here regarding the chef's murder. I am an investigator of some note and have recently solved several murders. Perhaps you are familiar with my *nom de l'en-quêteur,* Beatrice Hyde-Clare. I am happy to supply references if necessary. Simply ask anyone who was at Lord Stirling's ball a week ago about my skill."

The footman tried with admirable determination to keep his expression polite, but her remarkable speech provided too much provocation. The eyes that flickered with mild concern at her first reference to the chef's fate were goggling in baffled astonishment by the time she offered her services.

Well, *offered* was understating her intentions.

Taking advantage of his momentary confusion, she turned sideways and slipped past him into the house. The entry hall was modest and pleasant, with a vase of pink roses resting next to a silver tray on a narrow table. An assortment of elegant calling cards filled the salver, and Bea was able to read the top few names before the footman stepped stiffly in front of her.

"I beg your pardon!" he said forcefully.

His meaning could not have been any clearer, for it was apparent in every rigid line of his body, but Bea chose to misunderstand him and kindly accept his apology. "Your agitation is understandable given the troubling events of this morning. Nobody can rest easily whilst there is a killer afoot, which is precisely why I am here. Now please take me to the room where Monsieur Alphonse was found. I prefer to examine the scene before conducting my interviews."

Bea spoke with pragmatic blandness, shying away from euphemisms like "met his end," to imbue her words with a credible expertise, as if she had a method she traditionally followed and from which she would not allow herself to be diverted.

Her settled approach did little to calm the footman, who was practically trembling at her audacity. "You cannot believe, miss, that I—"

Bea interrupted to do something she never thought she would do in her entire life. "Your grace," she corrected.

His manner altered at once, the anger sweeping from his body with such vigor he seemed almost incapable of standing without it. He tugged his shoulders back, as if to regain his balance, and gracious civility overtook his features. With smooth deference, he said, "Your grace."

The transformation, the heartbeat-quick change, as fleeting as lightning, from outraged to tranquil, was stunning. It would astound anyone, the unqualified affirmation in their superiority, but it had a particularly strong effect on Bea, a drab spinster, a plain wallflower, a poor relation beneath the *ton*'s notice. She could barely breathe from the sense of authority that pulsed through her.

Now, abruptly, unresistingly, the footman stood before her, awaiting her instruction.

It was another jolt, a startlingly sharp one, to discover she could control a person's movements as if he were a puppet in a street performance of Punch and Judy.

No wonder Kesgrave had grown so accustomed to the

sound his own voice—for years, it had been the only one he'd heard. 'Twas not just footmen who fell silent at his command but marquesses and prime ministers as well.

How heady that must be.

Here, she had got a taste, only a very small sample, of the power he had exerted his whole life, and already she could feel its influence. Why bother trying to reason someone into submission when you could simply cow them with your consequence?

It was not a *path* strewn with rose petals but rather rose petals as far as the eye could see in every direction.

The revelation made Kesgrave even more of a remarkable anomaly, for despite the ease and genuflection that permeated every aspect of his life he had somehow acquired the ability to laugh at himself.

She recalled the moment at Lakeview Hall when her heart began its long, slow tumble to his feet. With seeming earnestness, after climbing through her bedchamber window to discuss Mr. Otley's murder, he had drawn attention to a display of humility because he thought she did not credit him with enough modesty. Thoroughly entertained, she'd asked if he was now boasting about *not* boasting.

"It's the depth to which you have driven me, Miss Hyde-Clare," he'd declared.

And it was this response—this easygoing reply that bore no trace of resentment or offense—that actually displayed his modesty. He had been teasing her, yes, by implying that her treatment had eroded his confidence, but also acknowledging an essential truth: He had been brought low by a nonentity at a backwater house party in the Lake District, and he had no quarrel with the situation.

His vanity could withstand the demotion.

Decidedly, Bea resolved to display the same grace and humility even as she used her coronet to browbeat the poor footman who had the misfortune to answer her knock. "To be sure, the circumstance is highly irregular," she said briskly, "but I cannot see how keeping someone of my stature waiting in the hallway will do anything to mitigate it."

Someone of my stature? she thought in astonishment, appalled at how easily the words had come to her but also amused by their tenor, for she sounded like a villain in a Minerva Press novel.

"Do go inform your employer of my presence," she added, with a dismissive flick of her hand. "I trust he is home?"

"Yes, your grace," he said without equivocating.

"Very good. While you're informing Mr. Mayhew that the Duchess of Kesgrave is here—that is, K-E-S-G-R-A-V-E—I will examine the room where Monsieur Alphonse's body was found," she said. "If you would indicate the correct direction?"

It was a tactical mistake, she could see that right away, for a real duchess would demand an escort, not wander around a strange and possibly sinister establishment on her own.

The footman's expression lost some of its awe, replaced by confusion as he struggled to respond to the unusual request. "I don't know..."

Bea allowed him no time to gather his wits. "That's all right, my good man, I do know and very well, for, as I said previously, this is my milieu. You have no reason to be anxious. Mr. Mayhew will be grateful to have the Duchess of Kesgrave's help; I am sure of it. You don't need me to spell my name again, do you? It's so very vexing not having my cards yet."

It was a rhetorical question, but he answered as if she were waiting with bated breath for his response. "No, your grace, that is not necessary."

She dipped her head with the same imperious condescension she had seen Kesgrave employ countless times and said,

"I am ready to go now or do you intend to keep me waiting in this hallway for another fifteen minutes?"

At this question, he jumped slightly.

Oh, yes, the poor footman startled as if stung by a wasp, and Bea felt again the exhilarating thrill of power. In truth, fifteen minutes had not actually passed. It could not have been more than five since she'd stepped into the hallway. But with a single word she had manipulated time to suit her purposes. Effortlessly, she had altered his reality.

It was only a minor modification, she thought, more like the exaggeration of a small child waiting to open a present on Christmas morning than an iniquitous falsification, but she had made a servant recoil and that did not sit comfortably with her. Determinedly, she opened her mouth to offer an apology and immediately found herself at a loss as to what to say. This Beatrice, Duchess of Kesgrave, was not herself. No, she was merely another character she had assumed in the pursuit of an investigation, an autocrat as domineering as Mr. Wright was obsequious, and she did not know her well enough to imagine how she would express contrition.

More likely, she would not.

The footman apparently agreed, for, regaining his composure, he promptly offered his own apology and instructed her to follow him. They had barely taken a dozen steps, however, before a slender man with prominent cheekbones and wide gray eyes stepped forcefully into the corridor and warned them not to take another step forward.

It was Parsons the butler, and he was not pleased by her presence.

Chapter Six

D*espite the aggression* of his pose, Parsons's tone was
conciliatory as he explained that the house was not
accepting callers. "We had a mild domestic disturbance this morning that has created some confusion, and we
are not entertaining visitors at this time."

Although Bea knew few things were worse than suffering
the thorough separation of one's head from one's body, she
thought having such a circumstance reduced to a mild
domestic disturbance was especially demeaning.

Poor Mr. Réjane, victimized again!

Before the footman could explain that the morning's
confusing events were what had brought the visitor to their
door, Bea congratulated Parsons on being exactly the person
she had hoped to see.

He tilted his head down and, as if examining her over the
protuberance of his cheekbones, ignored her statement
entirely. "If you would entrust me with your card, I would
personally ensure that Mr. Mayhew receives it."

How crushingly he spoke, his tone sharp and dismissive
with a hint of impatience as he glared at her with studied

disinterest, as if not entirely sure she was worth the effort of removing from the premises.

Bea marveled at the ease with which London butlers could adopt intimidating poses, helped along, she did not doubt, by their curious physiognomy—Marlow with his pulsating eyebrows and Parsons with his piercing cheekbones.

"The Duchess of Kesgrave does not yet have calling cards as she was only recently wed," the footman explained quickly. "But you must not worry. I refused her marriage lines for obvious reasons."

Upon hearing these words, Parsons inevitably appeared somewhat worried, for neither the introduction of a duchess nor her marriage lines was an auspicious development. Observing the hint of alarm that rose in his gray eyes, Bea wondered what had unsettled him: her reputation as an investigator of suspicious deaths or the general oddness of the footman's declaration.

Despite his discomfort, he remained determined to treat her as any other visitor to the house, with polite interest, and assured her Mr. Mayhew would be honored by the visit. "Is there a particular message you wish me to convey, your grace?"

Bea admired his unwavering commitment to the fiction that she was paying a social call on his employer despite the fact that she'd announced with utter clarity that she was there to speak to him. "There is no particular message I wish *you* to convey, as you will accompany me to the kitchens posthaste to describe the situation in which you found Monsieur Alphonse. But this footman here—" She broke off to ask his name.

"Henry, your grace," he immediately supplied.

"Ah, yes, Henry. *He* may convey to Mr. Mayhew that I am here to investigate the murder of Auguste Alphonse Réjane and look forward to discussing the matter with him as soon as he is ready to accept callers. I am entirely at his disposal," she said, speaking quickly to allow neither man the opportunity to object, although each would be perfectly within his rights. Marching into another person's home and demanding access to his kitchens and staff was a tremendously audacious thing to do, especially for an insignificant spinster who stammered incoherently in response to the most benign social queries.

Oh, but she was not a spinster anymore.

The footman voiced no objection but neither did he jump to do her bidding, standing in the hallway with an expression of stunned indecision on his face as he looked to Parsons for some indication of how he should proceed. The butler appeared to be in the same situation—baffled and uncertain—but having no superior present, he stared at the silver tray on the table next to the door, as if willing her calling card to appear.

"Thank you, Henry, for your prompt delivery of my message," she said firmly, "for I am positive Mr. Mayhew will be very interested in my presence."

As if startled from a reverie, the footman suddenly straightened his shoulders and turned his head toward Bea. "Yes, yes, of course, your grace," he said, then scampered off down the corridor at a slight run.

Parsons opened his mouth to protest but no sound came out, and Bea, realizing her advantage, slipped past his narrow frame. Presumably, she could locate the stairwell to the kitchens easily enough on her own, as all London townhouses had the same general layout with a few modifications. If she just continued down this hallway and looked for a doorway to her right...

Mr. Parsons was appalled by this display of self-sufficiency and trotted after her. "Your grace, I cannot allow you to—"

Without question, he meant that he could not permit her

to sally forth to the servants' quarters and insert herself into the Mayhews' private matters, but Bea intentionally misunderstood him. "No, no, of course you cannot allow the Duchess of Kesgrave to find her own way around the house," she said, interrupting. "Do lead the way."

There, she did it again—stood on her consequence. It was remarkably easy to do when the advantage to be gained was marked so clearly.

As improper as it was to allow a duchess to investigate the horrible death of one's French chef, it was somehow more egregious to stand in the hallway and argue with her about investigating the horrible death of one's French chef. Consequently, Parsons bowed his head and, submitting to what must have felt like an irresistible force, said, "Right this way, your grace."

As she had supposed, the stairs were located at the end of the hallway to the right, in the same general vicinity as in Portman Square, only a few feet farther from the front door.

Taking the first step, Parsons inquired after her comfort and asked if she would perhaps like a cup of tea as she examined the scene of Monsieur Alphonse's horrendous accident.

In fact, she did not require anything other than truthful answers and the freedom to pursue them, but she thought having a task might put the servants at greater ease and acquiesced to his suggestion.

"Very good, your grace," he murmured smoothly, regaining some of his composure with the assumption of a rudimentary chore.

Alas, it slipped again only a few seconds later when they arrived in the kitchen and the protocol for serving tea to a duchess in the servants' quarters escaped him. Fortunately, the slight awkwardness was overcome a moment later when Bea asked him to show her the precise spot where he had discovered the body. His eyes practically popped out of his head at the request.

As she waited for him to regain his poise, she examined the room, which also bore a resemblance to the primary cooking area at Portman Square, with its modest proportions, wooden floor, Rumford stove and long, narrow table scattered with mixing bowls, serving platters and a plate of parsley. Outside, in the courtyard leading to the chicken shed, there was a tidy little garden, which appeared to be in transition, as its assortment of rosebushes had recently been dug up, perhaps due to an infestation of beetles or thrips.

The space varied from the Hyde-Clare kitchen in its ruthless organization, with every pot, pan, bowl, skillet, trivet, kettle, bellows, poker, porringer, roasting rack, pan stand and hook slotted into its proper place. Hanging neatly along the walls were utensils in varying sizes: measuring spoons, grill skewers, knives, ladles, trammels, spatulas, hearth forks, cleavers, skimmers and food choppers.

Mrs. Emerson did not allow Cook to run a chaotic kitchen but neither did she demand such perfection, which was understandable, as food preparation was rarely a tidy pursuit.

At once, Bea wondered if the room always looked like this or if its pristine appearance was an attempt to scrub away the gruesomeness of Mr. Réjane's death. To be sure, the inhabitants of the kitchen were accustomed to blood and viscera, but the head of a fish was a very different matter from the head of a human, particularly one belonging to a French chef you had worked alongside for years.

While she was examining the room, two women entered from the scullery, and Parsons, clearly flummoxed, fell back on the demands of decorum as he understood them and announced with intimidating assurance that the Duchess of Kesgrave required a fresh pot of tea.

Although Bea assumed his intention in speaking with such confidence was to awe the servants into behaving with instinctive propriety, the situation was far too strange for either one to do anything except stare blankly. It seemed inconceivable that the duchess had come belowstairs to fetch her own tea, and yet was that not the implication?

But what else could Parsons do? Presenting her to the kitchen staff was plainly beyond all bounds of decency. As wretched as that morning's discovery had been, its handling had followed established protocols: alert the master, send for the constable, scrub every surface, proceed with life as if nothing untoward had occurred.

Subsequently, Bea had no choice but to step forward and introduce herself. It was, moreover, the most practical option because it allowed her to explain her purpose with clarity and simplicity.

"Good afternoon. As highly unusual as it may seem, I am indeed the Duchess of Kesgrave and I am here to investigate Monsieur Alphonse's death," she said, more than a little astonished that she could utter such an outlandish statement with ease when she had spent six years stuttering her own name with unintelligible confusion. "And to whom do I have the pleasure of speaking?"

The older woman, who was a stout creature with a square face and thin lips that twisted down in the corners, responded for the both of them, dropping a curtsey and identifying herself as Gertrude Vickers. "I am the kitchen maid, your grace. And this"—she gestured to the girl who stood next to her and was, at eighteen or nineteen, more than a dozen years her junior—"is Esther Simon, scullery maid."

Esther, whose blunt features were offset by a willowy frame, looked down at her feet as she mumbled an acknowledgment.

Bea nodded with approval, for she had intended to seek

out the kitchen staff for interrogation. "As you worked closely with Monsieur Alphonse, I am sure you have information vital to my investigation. First, I would like to discover what Parsons knows and to examine the device known as *le peu guillotine* for evidence of what happened."

As she spoke, she looked around the room and realized what she had missed in her initial inspection: the absence of the supposedly lethal apparatus.

"Where is *le peu guillotine*?" Bea said.

Esther kept her gaze studiously focused on the floor while Gertrude looked expectantly at Parsons. The butler coughed slightly and explained that Mr. Mayhew ordered the removal of the instrument. "He thought it was too dangerous to keep on the counter. It is currently in a heap at the bottom of the Thames."

Now that wasn't the last bit suspicious, was it, Bea thought sardonically.

Unable to scrutinize the implement itself, she sought out the space it used to occupy. "Where on the counter did it sit?"

Parsons pointed to a square table beneath a trio of hanging baskets near the arch to the hallway. It was a smallish surface, indicating that it propped up a smallish device.

Addressing the kitchen maid directly, Bea asked how high the machine stood. Gertrude raised a hand to her shoulder.

"That is its elevation when it is on the table?" Bea said to make sure she understood its dimensions.

"Yes, when it is on the table. It was always on that table or the center counter," Gertrude explained.

Noting the size of the table and the height of the machine, Bea thought it was very unlikely that *le peu guillotine* was large enough to remove the head of a grown man. To confirm her suspicion, she asked for a physical description of the victim and discovered he was a man of approximately fifty years of age, possessing modest height and girth.

"He was several inches shorter than Parsons," the kitchen maid said, "and had a narrower frame."

Bea nodded and asked Gertrude to list the items usually inserted into the appliance for dividing.

"Joints of meat mostly," she said. "Onions, bacon, coconuts."

All very modest, Bea thought. "What is the largest thing?"

The other woman's eyes widened in surprise but she other showed no reaction as she said pineapples. "Anything bigger and you have to use a cleaver," she said, nodding to the collection of five heavy, broad blades that hung from the wall. "The *le peu guillotine* made a very precise cut, much neater and cleaner than a food chopper."

She continued to detail the benefits of the apparatus—it was, for example, particularly suited for cutting thin slices of ham—as Bea's gaze lingered on the assortment of cleavers. There was something slightly off in their arrangement, she thought, observing how much larger the first one was than the second. Its blade was almost twice as wide as the one next to it, while the four others decreased gradually in size. It was almost as if one was missing....

Intrigued by the prospect, she walked over to where the kitchen tools dangled from neatly aligned nails and asked where the medium-large cleaver was.

Startled, Gertrude suddenly stopped speaking and shifted her eyes to the wall. At once, she saw it, the same height disparity that Bea had observed, and her eyes narrowed in confusion. Her tone baffled, she admitted she had no idea where it had gone. "It must have been mislaid when we were cleaning up after dinner last night. Things are always chaotic after a dinner party, with so much bustling activity, and that can sometimes happen."

Thoughtfully, Bea examined the room and reconsidered her assumptions about its orderliness. "Is this how the kitchen looked last night?"

"Oh, no, your grace, it was a frightful mess," Gertrude said as the scullery maid nodded in agreement. "We always try to keep the worktables clean but once the guests start to arrive and the food is placed on serving platters, everything becomes a muddled jumble. And there was flour everywhere last night because Thomas—that's the kitchen boy—didn't realize there was a hole in the sack and trailed it everywhere."

"I meant after the party," Bea clarified. "Is this how the room looked when you went to bed?"

"Why, good gracious me, yes, of course," Gertrude said fervently. "Go to sleep with flour all over the floor? And with dirty mixing bowls and egg shells scattered all over the counter? We would be run out of house and home by mice within the week. No matter how long it takes or how late the hour grows, we always restore the kitchen to order before we go to sleep, especially after a party, for that is when things are the messiest. If I myself were not so diligent about cleanliness, Mrs. Blewitt, the housekeeper, would insist on it."

"How late did the hour grow?" Bea asked.

"Around one for me," she said, "a little later for Esther. That is typical for a dinner party of that size because the last course is served around ten and the guests usually leave about an hour later. When I went up to bed Monsieur Alphonse was still in the garden smoking a cheroot. It was his habit to take the air after a long day of cooking."

Bea nodded and looked at the butler. "And what time did you go to sleep?"

"After the last guest left, I oversaw the cleanup of the dining room," he said, "and consulted with Mrs. Blewitt, who was in the pantry checking her stocks, to see if she required my help with anything. That was around midnight. She assured me everything was in order, so I checked that the house was secured, confirmed the cellar door was firmly locked and retired to my room. It was perhaps twelve-thirty by then, maybe twelve forty-five? I know I was in my bed by one o'clock. I, too, saw Monsieur Alphonse in the garden smoking a cheroot."

Taking note of the time, Bea asked him again to show her where exactly the body was when he found it.

His eyes darted to the scullery maid, as if worried about offending her sensibilities with his answer, but he made no protest as he walked toward the small table that usually held *le peu guillotine* and stopped a few feet short. "It was here," he said soberly, his lips compressing tightly as he recalled the horrible event. "It was right here. I found him almost as soon as I entered the room."

Like the rest of the kitchen, the spot where he stood was immaculate. The wood itself showed signs of wear—stains, scratches, gauges—but there was not a hint of the copious amount of blood that must have spilled from the victim.

That could not have been an easy thing to accomplish.

"Who cleaned the floor?" Bea asked.

As innocuous as the question was, it caused Esther to squeal in horror at the grisly allusion and then immediately apologize for displaying inappropriate squeamishness. "I'm sorry, your grace. It's just that it's so..."

But she could not say what exactly it was, for it was too dreadful for words, and Parsons explained that the scullery maid had fainted the moment she grasped fully what had happened to the chef. "She was one of many," he said approvingly, as if swooning was the only proper female response to decapitation. Then he added with a hint of censure, "Gertrude cleaned up the blood with the help of Thomas."

Bea looked at the sturdy kitchen maid. "You did not faint?"

Although her tone had been neutral, Gertrude stiffened with offense. "It was not as if I wasn't deeply distressed by Monsieur Alphonse's death. I worked closely with him for two years and liked him very much. It was a horrible tragedy, what happened. But wringing my hands in distress would not get the floor clean, and Mr. Mayhew was more concerned with disposing of the *le peu* before anyone else got hurt to assign a footman to the task. I was left with the choice of doing it myself or stare at the large puddle of blood."

"Describe it," Bea said.

Uncomprehending, the kitchen maid stared at her. "Pardon me?"

"The puddle," Bea explained, gesturing to the floor as she tried to imagine what it had looked like when Parsons entered the room in the early hours of the morning. She knew nothing about the properties of blood but assumed that it behaved similarly to water in many ways. How far it had spread and how much it had dried would provide her with some useful information. "Describe it."

Gertrude blanched at the request but nodded faintly. "The floor tilts ever so slightly to the east side of the room, so the blood ran toward the fireplace and away from the entrance."

Bea nodded. "And how far did it travel before it started to dry?"

The servant took several steps deeper into the room and stopped about two feet from where Parsons had found the body. "Here. It was hardest to scrub up the blood where it had begun to dry. It made a ring around the edges."

"That could not have been pleasant," Bea observed.

Stoically, the kitchen maid said that it had to be done.

Bea accepted the simple truth of the statement and considered the scene in light of the information she had just discovered. If everything in the kitchen had been washed and returned to its place last night and *le peu* was not substantial enough to accommodate a grown man, then the missing cleaver might in fact be the murder weapon, not Mr. Réjane's invention.

If so, where was it now?

Most likely with the assailant, she thought, for it would have been impossible for Parsons to make an argument for the cutting apparatus with a bloody cleaver lying next to the body.

In that case, a careful inspection of everyone's quarters might reveal the guilty party.

It was equally possible, however, that the killer had left it behind, tossing it onto the floor in a moment of frenzy or panic. If that was true, then the cleaver could very well still be in the room.

But where?

Not in plain sight or Parsons would never have succeeded in convincing Mr. Mayhew and the constable.

Pensively, Bea lowered herself to look under the tables, shelves and cabinets.

At once, the three staff members gasped in collective horror at the sight of the Duchess of Kesgrave on her knees.

Recovering first from his astonishment, Parsons said, "Your grace, you really must not...you must let us...the floor isn't clean...tell us what you are...how can we help..."

Although she was mildly amused by his distress, she conceded that it was probably quite justified and reckoned she was the first peeress to ever drop to her hands and knees in public. Nevertheless, she did not allow their disapproval to sway her from her purpose and, having ruled out the table that supported *le peu*, she lowered her head another inch to look under the cabinet directly to the left of the entry arch. It was the next closest to where Parsons found the body and, sure enough, she spotted something that very possibly met the description of a largish meat cleaver. At the very least, it appeared to have a wooden handle. It was too far away for her to tell for sure, and she tried stretching her arm under the cabinet.

Devil it! It was just beyond her grasp.

She could reach it if she lay flat on the floor, but even she knew that was an indignity too far. Miss Hyde-Clare could have got away with it without raising an eyebrow, but the Duchess of Kesgrave engendered expectations.

Reluctantly, Bea rose to her feet and addressed Parsons. "Beneath the cabinet, about partway to the wall, you will see a device with a wooden handle. Please retrieve it."

The butler was horrified by the request, his face losing some of its color at the prospect of pressing his entire body on kitchen floorboards recently soaked with blood, but he was too well trained to deny her and complied immediately if not enthusiastically.

He was a tall man, however, with longer arms than Beatrice, and could grasp the handle without prostrating himself, which, she thought, was a nicely consoling factor. Judging by the grimace on Parsons's face as he brushed imaginary dust from his knees, he did not agree.

Only when he felt sufficiently self-possessed did the butler hand Bea the item he had retrieved from under the cabinet. As she had suspected, it was the missing cleaver and given the dried blood on the blade, the murder weapon as well.

All three servants comprehended its significance at once, but only Esther, who suffered from an excess of sensibility, promptly dropped to the floor in a faint. Gertrude inspected the scullery maid's head for damage, noted only a small bump and scoffed at the insipid antics.

"Silly thing. It looks no different than after cutting up a side of beef," she muttered.

Parsons, who did not appear to be much more solid on his feet than the scullery maid, said defensively, "It is a little different knowing that the blood is from a human, not a cow."

Out of respect for her superior, Gertrude granted that it might indeed be a little bit different.

Bea, holding the cleaver, noted its weight was quite substantial and its blade was remarkably sharp. It had been honed recently and had probably cut through Mr. Réjane's neck with relative ease.

Oh, but why the neck? There were so many easier ways to kill a man than chopping off his head with a cleaver. Indeed, there were easier ways of killing a man *with* the cleaver—a slice in the gut, for instance, would do the deed very well. It would take a little bit longer for him to die from loss of blood, however, and he would have time to cry out for help.

Was someone nearby to provide assistance?

She turned to Parsons, whose color had yet to return, and asked him what time he had discovered Monsieur Alphonse.

Despite his agitation, he replied calmly. "I woke at five, and the first thing I do every morning after dressing is reignite the fire in the kitchen and put on a pot of water so that when Gertrude wakes up a half hour later, it is already boiling."

Unprompted, the kitchen maid substantiated his claim. "I typically come down at five-thirty and the water is always boiling. Esther keeps the same schedule and will say so when she finishes her faint."

Parsons then added, also without encouragement, that he had not seen the cleaver. "It was dark when I found Monsieur Alphonse—I had only my candle—and it was a very unsettling experience, so I might have overlooked it. But I really didn't see it and have no idea how it got under the cabinet. It's very shocking, your grace, how easily you found it. I cannot believe the murderer counted on such clever thinking. I, for one, really thought it was the *le peu*. The machine had so much potential to do damage."

As she was not privy to his actual emotional state when he'd discovered the body, Bea could not evaluate the truth of this assertion. She could, however, point out that *le peu* had no blood on its blade.

Taken aback by her conviction, he said in amazement, "It did not?"

"It would have been scrubbed clean like everything else in the kitchen before Gertrude went to bed," she explained, "and as it was not the murder weapon, it would have had no opportunity to get dirty."

Defensively, Parsons said, "The murderer might have cleaned it."

Bea allowed that it was possible but thought it made Mr. Mayhew's determination to destroy the device all the more suspicious. Depriving anyone of the chance to examine it ensured that the story of accidental death was more readily believed.

But if Mr. Mayhew had something to do with it, then why had he left the cleaver to be found under the cabinet? Surely, he would be inclined to dispose of it with the same thoroughness as the guillotine?

Alternatively, why not return it clean to its original spot? Then no one would have cause to wonder about it at all.

Possibly, such an activity had not occurred to him—and why would it? He was the owner of a commodious home and a man of considerable material comfort. In all likelihood, he had never washed a kitchen implement in his entire life.

Or maybe it had been tossed under the cabinet in a fit of panic. Could he have still been in the room when Parsons entered the passageway, and hearing him approach, threw it under the cupboard before slipping out through the scullery?

"Was Monsieur Alphonse still warm?" Bea asked.

Parsons's eyes grew impossibly wide and his cheekbones seemed to flare. "Excuse me?"

"When you found his body, was it still warm or had he started to grow cool?" she said. "The body's temperature will provide us with a sense of how long Monsieur Alphonse was dead before he was found."

The rational explanation did little to assuage Parsons's outrage at the assumption that he had *touched* the corpse. "I would never do anything so disrespectful. Monsieur Alphonse deserved to rest in peace even without...even without"—it was difficult for him to get the words out but he persisted —"his head. I had barely understood what I was seeing before Thomas came into the room and started screaming. I calmed him down, then placed a tablecloth over Monsieur Alphonse to ensure his dignity and went to wake up Mr. Mayhew. After that, I did not return to the kitchen until after the constable and his men had left. I believe the same goes for everyone in the house. We allowed Mr. Mayhew and the constable to settle the matter between them."

Gertrude confirmed this, stating that she had not entered the kitchen until after ten o'clock.

"Ten o'clock?" Bea repeated thoughtfully.

That was a full five hours after Parsons discovered the body. What did that tell her about the time Mr. Réjane was killed?

Nothing, she realized.

Accordingly, she turned to the butler and asked him to describe the puddle as he had seen it early in the morning. "Was the blood oozing or had it settled into place? And was it still warm?"

But if the servant had been indignant at the idea of touching the dead chef's skin, he was utterly repulsed at the prospect of soaking his fingers in his blood. Sputtering in horror, he reiterated that it had been too dark to see anything and he would not have looked even if he could. "The man was dead!" he cried when he was capable of complete sentences. "That is all I know, your grace, and I must beg you to apply to Mr. Mayhew for further information regarding Monsieur Alphonse's condition. He talked to the constable at length."

As Bea had every intention of interrogating the master of the house, she nodded smoothly and asked either of them if they knew when Esther had finished in the scullery.

"Not long after me, maybe one-thirty?" Gertrude said. "We share a bed, and I had just fallen asleep when she came in. The door scrapes when you open it. But you will have to confirm the time with her when she awakens. I am sure it won't be long now."

But her tone was satirical, indicating that she thought the very opposite.

"Had Monsieur Alphonse mentioned his plans to leave?" Bea asked.

Gertrude's square face sharpened in response. "Monsieur Alphonse was planning to leave? He said nothing about it to me. Did you know, Mr. Parsons?"

But the butler was already shaking his head vigorously in denial. "I am certain that is not true. He had no reason to leave. His situation here was very comfortable, and Mr. Mayhew endeavored to accommodate him whenever possible. He rarely denied him anything, and Monsieur Alphonse certainly didn't deny himself much."

Although Parsons spoke evenly, without any indication of antipathy or resentment, Bea thought she detected a simmering dislike in his words. Before she could ask him to elaborate, however, Henry appeared to announce that Mr. Mayhew was ready to see her now.

Chapter Seven

H*aving occupied only* the farthest fringe of society for more than half a decade, Bea knew little of the less illustrious members of the *ton*.

Beau Brummell, of course, was well familiar to her, his extravagance, both in personal style and contempt for the regent, having drawn her notice. In the same vein, she had followed the career of Lord Byron, admiring his work (and eagerly awaiting the next canto of *Childe Harold's Pilgrimage* like everyone else) while flinching over the many questionable choices he had made in pursuit of personal satisfaction. She could recognize all the patronesses of Almack's and had even conversed with Lady Cowper at the Leland ball, thanks to Lady Abercrombie's determined efforts to bring her into fashion.

But only the light from the brightest stars in the firmament had managed to penetrate the darkness that surrounded her on the periphery, and as a result, she knew nothing about Mr. Mayhew.

No matter!

He was only too delighted to rectify the situation.

"Our principal seat is Helston Park, which my paternal grandfather, Samuel Mayhew, acquired after its owner defaulted on the mortgage, leaving the stately country estate in abject disrepair. My father, Richard Mayhew, hired Robert Adam to remodel the home, a massive undertaking that in some respects continues today, the efforts of which were more than worth it, as I am sure you will see when you and the duke consent to visit," he said firmly, issuing a summons, not an invitation.

The entire conversation had been conducted thusly, with the banker and member of Parliament from Aylesbury assuring her of one thing or another: She would adore his wife, greatly admire his children, look with awe upon his art collection, highly esteem his business acumen and stare in wonder at his deft command of his horses.

Mayhew and Co.—the banking concern established by his great-grandfather—was equally a bastion of accomplishment: It began distributing banknotes more than eight decades ago and was the very first institution in the world to provide its customers with printed cheques to increase the efficiency of the system.

Knowing nothing of the Mayhew family or the architectural wonders of its family seat, Bea could not judge the accuracy of the vast majority of his claims. It seemed unlikely to her that all the superlatives he used could uniformly apply based simply on the law of averages. Surely, at least one of the portraits in his collection was not quite stellar or his ability to sweep a tight corner with four in hand not entirely the vision of grace and beauty he insisted it was. Nevertheless, she was willing to allow him the benefit of the doubt.

On the history of banking, however, she could extend no such courtesy, as she knew the year the Bank of England issued its first form cheque and it was a full six before Harold Mayhew established his company.

It was, she thought, a reckless boast, for anyone with even a cursory knowledge of financial innovation knew printed cheques were an invention of the Bank of England. Needless to say, Bea's interest in the topic was more than just passing, as she had read all three volumes in Jasper Penwilk's masterful study on European banking systems and the advantages of free competition.

Faintly contemptuous, Bea made no effort to correct Mr. Mayhew's error for the same reason she had made no effort to interrupt his endless pontification: She could perceive no value in alienating Mr. Réjane's employer.

Well, she amended with silent humor, there would be *some* value, for she would enjoy taking the wind out of the insufferable popinjay's sails.

Kesgrave might also be given to ostentatious displays of knowledge, but his information, although frequently as dull, had the advantage of always being accurate.

Additionally, it had less to do with his own personal self-aggrandizement than with particular facts about the world.

As Mr. Mayhew launched into a description of his grandfather's tenure as Lord Mayor of London (1741–44), Bea wondered how much longer she was expected to listen to his speech before she could ask about the destruction of *le peu guillotine,* his conversation with the constable and his feelings on his chef's refusal to remain in his employ. It had already been fifteen...no, she thought, glancing at the clock...twenty minutes, and at some point, her silent submission to his ceaseless prattle would begin to seem insulting. Only a partially insensible woman could listen without protesting.

Five minutes more, she thought, turning away from the sight of Mr. Mayhew in all his splendor—the chartreuse-colored waistcoat, the snug silk breeches, the buckled pumps with a low heel, wide whiskers—to examine the simple plasterwork on the ceiling.

A moment later, however, her eyes were drawn again to the figure sitting across from her in the drawing room, his arms flickering this way and that as he sought to emphasize his point with elaborate hand gestures. By any account, he looked absurd, not because of the wild gesticulations, although, certainly, it did not help that he appeared to be constantly swatting away a fly or trying to push a rhinoceros into a stall, but because the fashion he wore was too youthful for his fifty-something years. It was as if her uncle Horace had decided to adopt the outlandish extremes of dandyism, for the garish silk waistcoat would not have been out of place in late Earl of Fazeley's extensive wardrobe. The foppish earl, however, had not needed to use a corset to restrain a bulky paunch as Mr. Mayhew tried to do. His flailing gestures also revealed thick shoulder pads under his lime-and-salmon-striped coat, and his hair was an incongruous brassy color that made it almost indistinguishable from a wig.

She was, Bea discovered, a little embarrassed on his behalf.

Deciding enough was enough, she straightened her shoulders and resolved to interrupt her host. Assuaging his vanity was all well and good, but only hours before a man's head had been detached from his body and at some point that terrible event had to take precedence. After she had identified the man or woman who had killed Auguste Alphonse Réjane, the greatest chef in Europe, they could adjourn to the drawing room, where Mr. Mayhew could resume glorifying his family name to his heart's content.

Before Bea could insist on turning the conversation to the more pressing topic, her host finished his tediously long speech with a brisk conclusion: "And that, your grace, is everything you get when you conduct business with the Mayhew family. I felt it was necessary to explain it in details so that you may be pleased with the transaction. I trust you are?"

Having absolutely no idea what her host was talking about, Bea feared that she had in fact become unconscious for some portion of his dissertation.

Misinterpreting the look on her face, he waved his hands with approval and said, "Of course, of course. You are overwhelmed. It is entirely understandable. All this grandeur is new to you, the impressive family lines and the great wealth. You require a moment to gather your thoughts, I understand. But you mustn't be too modest, your grace, as you also bring something meaningful to the agreement."

"Mr. Mayhew, I do not know what your footman told you, but I am not here to negotiate a transaction of some sort," she said plainly. "I am here to investigate the murder of your chef. This story you and the constable settled on regarding Monsieur Alphonse's cutting apparatus is highly implausible and cannot be allowed to stand. He was decapitated with a cleaver from your own kitchen."

The banker nodded vigorously, by all indications delighted by her statement. "Yes, yes, precisely, and it is beyond all things wonderful."

His idiotic response to her disquieting news caused her to wonder if she was talking to a man with a mental deficiency. She had entered the room convinced that he had something to hide, for there was no other explanation for why he would dispose of the supposed murder weapon so quickly and thoroughly, but now she wondered if he was simply too dullwitted to behave logically.

To wit, his observation that Mr. Réjane's passing was wonderful.

Demonstrating that he was not entirely lost to sense, the banker rushed to clarify his meaning, insisting that the death of the great chef was a deep and abiding tragedy. "He and his stunning creations will be sorely missed by myself and Mrs. Mayhew. Just last night he made *potage anglaise de poisson à Lady Payton,* which has been described as the most difficult soup in the world, and it was glorious. The expression on Mr. Carmichael's face as he had his first taste made Monsieur Alphonse worth every shilling he soaked me for. But no, I was referring to your murder investigation, for that is what is wonderful. I have long wished to align myself with a duke."

Although she had briefly understood her host, for the soup Mr. Réjane had devised in honor of the well-known Irish writer had indeed been hailed as one of most complicated dishes ever assembled, Bea once again found herself bewildered. "A duke?" she echoed.

"How right you are, your grace," he said with sly appreciation. "I misspoke. *The* duke."

And still comprehension eluded her.

He took no note of her confusion and added with relish, "The Duke of Kesgrave, the most elusive peer of the realm. I have tried for years to capture his interest or seek his favor, but he has always brushed me off. I am beneath his notice, which I cannot resent given the disparity in our situations. But that is all in the past because now I have the ideal opportunity to earn his support and finally gain a foothold in the highest echelon of society. And that, your grace, is truly wonderful. But you must not think you are getting the worst end of the staff, for the Mayhews deserve nobody's scorn, as I have already explained. Our history might not reach back five hundred years, but our past century is impressive and certainly more illustrious than the Hyde-Clares."

Bea heard the disparagement of her family. Oh, yes, she perceived with perfect clarity the disdain for their mediocrity and inconsequentiality, and she was not immune to its effect, for she already felt deeply discomfited by the social imbalance between her and the duke. But as disturbing as his casual denigration was, it was nothing compared with the way he looked at her now with avarice and greed, a gleaming rapaciousness glinting in his eyes as if her very person had been supplanted by something he could use—a tool, perhaps, like a dibble to firmly plant his ambition or a rope to pull himself up.

Bearing the weight of his avidity, she felt nothing like herself, neither the familiar person she had been yesterday afternoon before her wedding to Kesgrave nor the vague stranger who had shrunk in mortification when the maids addressed her with excruciating deference that morning.

She was wholly unknown.

Mr. Mayhew continued. "Specifically, here is what I expect in exchange for my cooperation, all commencing one week from today and extending over a six-month period: two invitations to dine at Kesgrave House, two outings to the duke's box at Covent Garden for plays of Mrs. Mayhew's selection, one dinner at my London house, one weekend stay at Helston Park, one invitation to a house party at the duke's ancestral estate. And, of course, he will move a portion of his deposits from Coutts to Mayhew and Co. As for the actual percentage of his account, I will leave that to his grace to decide."

"How very gracious," she said satirically.

Perceiving a compliment, he dipped his head and fluttered his left hand through the air.

Calmly, as if she did not find him repellent in every way, Bea reviewed the terms of the agreement in order to make sure she understood them correctly. "To be clear, you will allow me to investigate the brutal murder of a member of your own staff if I agree to confer my and the duke's friendship to increase your status among the *beau monde*? Is my understanding of the compact accurate?"

"Yes, your grace," he said, smiling widely. "Entirely correct."

She nodded thoughtfully. "Are the terms of the agreement set or may I negotiate the specifics?"

The glow in his eyes changed, from avarice to anticipation, as he leaned forward in his chair and rubbed his hands together. "Oh, yes, you may indeed. Tell me, your grace, what you have in mind."

What she actually had in mind was some version of a grand exit, with her unceremoniously dumping the pot of tea on his head, calling him a repugnant mushroom with more hair than wit and marching forcefully out of the room.

'Twould be an utter delight, to see him gasping in indignation as Bohea dripped from his ridiculous whiskers onto his absurd silk-clad thighs, his hands flying haphazardly through the air, as if seeking purchase.

But she was not there to satisfy her temper or give leave to her outrage; she was there to find justice for Auguste Alphonse Réjane.

Firmly and fully, she believed that no man, not even the most intemperate monster, deserved decapitation, to have his head in one spot and his body in another. And yet it still seemed worse that it was this man, this rare genius of sugar, flour and butter, who suffered such a horrific fate.

"I would like to propose a few amendments," she said with deceptive smoothness. "Some minor alterations, if you will."

Mr. Mayhew nodded eagerly. "Of course, of course. You wouldn't be the woman you are if you blithely accepted my offer."

"We forego your six-point plan for social advancement and instead call the constable to the house so that we may have a fruitful discussion about Monsieur Alphonse's murder," she said. "I have already gathered information that will be useful to him in his investigation."

A broad grin spread across his face as he lauded her strong opening position and launched into a lecture on the uselessness of her discovery of the murder weapon, for the constable already believed the death to be a tragic accident. "And he is not likely to change his mind."

Bea knew well the incompetence of constables, for the one in the Lake District had been persuaded that Mr. Otley had struck the back of his own head with a candlestick, but she found it inconceivable one would be so apathetic as to hold to the explanation of inadvertent decapitation when convincing evidence of murder was produced.

"I think he will," she said firmly.

"In 1667, my great-grandfather George Richard Mayhew established himself as a goldsmith," he said, beginning his litany of familiar achievements all over again. "The business thrived, and in 1673 he was appointed jeweler in ordinary to King William III."

Exasperated by his buffoonery, she asked testily, "What are you doing?"

"Explaining my importance, as you seem to have forgotten it," he replied. "I assure you, the constable has not."

Ah, so that was how he had got the ruling he had desired, by exerting either his money or his influence. She was just as capable of playing that game as well—indeed, she had the advantage.

"In 1381," she said, "John Matlock helped King Richard quell the Peasants Revolt when he crushed the rebels led by Litster in East Anglia, earning a knighthood."

Anger flashed in the banker's eyes as he sat forward in his chair. "I will not be mocked!"

Well, she thought, someone was not quite as secure in his position as he claimed.

"Mock you?" Bea said, twisting her lips sardonically. "I would never mock a man of your high status and inveterate morality. No, my good sir, I am doing the very opposite of mocking you by paying you the respect of abiding by your rules. Are we not trying to cow each other with our impressive lineages? I thought influence and consequence were the currency with which this agreement would be negotiated, and I feel confident mine trumps yours."

Bea expected him to respond with more anger, for her tone was openly derisive, but he leaned back into his chair, mollified by either her words or her attitude. Lightly, his fingers tapped the arms of the bergère. "You must forgive me, your grace, for forgetting what kind of woman you are. Of course you understand the play. I am merely doing what you yourself did so expertly in pursuit of the duke."

As he spoke, Bea noted the light in his eyes had changed yet again, this time flashing with respect, and although she told herself it was better to be seen as an equal than an object to be manipulated, she felt only repugnance at his esteem.

It was no achievement to earn his admiration.

Indeed, it was more like a failure.

Abhorrent man, she thought, reminding herself that his repulsiveness did not make him guilty of murder.

No, but it did not exonerate him either.

Of all the people she had interviewed so far, he was the most likely suspect, for he had already revealed himself to be deeply immoral and devious.

Coolly, she said, "As we both know, Mr. Mayhew, my lineage trumps yours, so I see no reason to continue this discussion. Kesgrave will clarify the situation with the constable, and I will consult directly with him on my investigation."

As it was not an idle threat, she leaned forward to rise to her feet but her movements were forestalled by Mr. Mayhew's riotous laughter.

"I would hate to have to tell a newly married woman that she doesn't know her husband, but you do not know your husband, my dear," he said with indulgent condescension. "It is understandable given the length of your courtship, which was necessarily brief. You had to snap the parson's mouse trap closed before your quarry could wrangle free. No, please, your grace, do not get all tight in the shoulders as if I am criticizing you. I am not, for I possess a great appreciation for expedience. I do not know how you managed to compromise the duke on the terrace during Lord Larkwell's ball, but I can only assume you were in league with Taunton. Perhaps you promised to use your settlement to pay his gambling debts?"

He paused here as if in expectation of her confirmation, and Bea, her back indeed rigid, struggled to keep her features neutral as he doled out insult after insult. Save for the introduction of the murderous marquess as her conspirator, he said nothing she had not heard a dozen times before. Her own aunt had expressed a similar understanding of the situation and remained baffled still by Kesgrave's disinclination to save himself from her clutches.

When she had first discovered that most of society shared this view of her engagement, she'd been deeply mortified and imagined tongues wagging everywhere she went: at the theater, at dinner parties, at routs, balls and musicales. She could almost hear them whispering behind her back about the dowdy spinster who nabbed the *ton*'s most glittering prize through hideously deceitful means.

Her fears, however, proved unfounded, for everyone stated it plainly to her face: Mrs. Norton, Lord Tavistock, Lord Wem.

Mr. Mayhew, she thought, in amusement.

Realizing that his guest would not honor him with a confession, Mr. Mayhew continued, "Regardless, let me do you the invaluable service of explaining your husband to you.

He is sneering, contemptuous, arrogant, imperious, chilly, snide and generally indifferent to the opinions of others. He is interested in only his own comfort and will not bestir himself to satisfy the whim of anyone, let alone the insignificant nobody who ensnared him in a marriage he neither wanted nor sought. Now I understand that you are trying to style yourself as a lady Runner to create something distinctive about yourself, which I agree is necessary as you are extraordinarily unremarkable otherwise, and I am more than happy to assist you in that endeavor by allowing you access to my staff and home. But I have made my terms clear and am unwilling to compromise. Do we have an agreement?"

"You forgot pedantic," Bea said.

"Excuse me?" he asked jeeringly, clearly peeved by the implication that he had overlooked anything.

"My husband is pedantic," she explained matter-of-factly. "He is sneering, contemptuous, arrogant, imperious, chilly, snide, generally indifferent to the opinions of others *and* pedantic. If you are going to comprehensively list his character traits, then you cannot leave off his most enduring one."

Mr. Mayhew's color rose sharply as he stared at Beatrice, his fingers dancing across the chair's arms with increasing speed and vigor.

Determinedly, he tried to make sense of her unanticipated response and decided that his insightful understanding of her husband's character had unsettled her.

"Oh, yes, I have quite unnerved you," he said smugly. "By revealing to you the truth about your own husband I have forced you to come to terms to the limitations of your own ingenuity. You thought you were so very clever, and now you realize you're not shrewd enough to outmaneuver me. You are trying to brazen it out with empty threats so I won't realize the truth, which is that you have no position from which to negotiate. I am a banker, you see, and understand exactly what you are doing. Next, you will stand up stiffly and announce it is time you returned to Kesgrave House. You will say something to the effect of: My husband will notice I am gone soon and wonder where I am."

The flush in his cheeks subsided as he grew increasingly confident in his understanding of the situation. His lips pursed, he rubbed the generous whiskers lining his jaw with his left hand and considered her silently for several moments. "I find I am reluctant to allow that. Having come closer than I ever thought possible to attaining a long-sought goal, I cannot let you to leave without making another attempt to arrive at a satisfying bargain. Although I vowed not to compromise, I will demonstrate how reasonable I am by offering to eliminate the weekend in the country at Helston Park. Furthermore, you do not have to convince the duke to move any portion of his deposits to Mayhew & Co., only the money he settled upon you for your marriage. A husband cannot object if a wife takes an interest in her own investments, can he? You see how fair-minded I am being? Now come, your grace, agree to meet me in the middle, and we may settle this transaction amicably. To be candid, you have no other option than to accede to my requests if you are to have any hope of scrutinizing Monsieur Alphonse's death. But if you would rather leave than grace us with your presence...."

He trailed off enticingly, entirely convinced in the strength of his argument and his ability to overcome her resistance.

As amused as she was by the confidence of his pose, Bea could not fathom its source, for it bore no resemblance to reality. Although he had convinced himself he held all the advantages, he in fact held none and continuing to believe he did in the face of contrary evidence indicated a plodding mind incapable of grasping simple facts.

Was he really the head of a successful banking concern?

It seemed inconceivable to her, and even if she were interested in making a bargain with him, she would not agree to deposit any portion of her settlement at Mayhew and Co. because she did not believe it would be secure.

Unlike her host, Bea was aware of the futility of her efforts and decided she had wasted enough time talking to him. The more efficient course was to return to Kesgrave House and ask Jenkins to drive her to the constable's office. Although she still found it a difficult idea to digest, the truth was she no longer needed to borrow the duke's consequence, for she possessed her own now and if there was any advantage in being the Duchess of Kesgrave, it was the ability to browbeat public servants.

"I will pursue this matter without your assistance," she said, rising from her chair as she thanked her host for his time. "I will tell the duke of your interest to dine at Kesgrave House. I am sure he will be most gratified."

Her confidence seemed to infuriate him, and Mr. Mayhew lunged to his feet, took two swift steps toward her and grabbed her arm by the elbow. "Sit down! I am not done."

Although one did not have to be a duchess to know that his action was a strict violation of all rules governing civility, the breach somehow seemed more striking in light of her new rank. Perhaps it was merely that as the spinsterish Miss Hyde-Clare she had learned not to expect displays of basic courtesies. Or maybe it was because it required more impudence to grab a ducal arm.

Regardless of its cause, she was genuinely shocked to see his tightened fingers grasping her bare flesh.

It is the bank, Bea thought.

Every day Mr. Mayhew went to the bank, where his name was carved in stone above the doorway, and he ordered people about, quelled dissent and had his opinions affirmed.

There could be no other explanation for his inexplicable faith in his own proficiency and his inability to deal with her refusal. Only a sense of entitlement nurtured for generations could produce such overweening incompetence.

He was a fatuous man who deserved none of her attention, and as she stared up at him whilst simultaneously looking down upon him, she wondered if this feeling of exasperated contempt was how Kesgrave felt most of the time. It had to grow exhausting, people always demanding your attention, desiring your largess, attracting your interest any way they could.

Making no move to free her arm from his grasp, Bea said calmly and firmly, almost as if addressing a small child, "You will release me, Mr. Mayhew."

The unearned confidence of privileged sons, however, ran deep. "I will not."

"Oh, but you will," said a voice silkily from the door.

Chapter Eight

Startled by the Duke of Kesgrave's unexpected presence in his drawing room—why hadn't that wretched butler or one of the footmen announced him—Mr. Mayhew convulsed his hand, momentarily tightening his grip on Bea's elbow to a painful degree, before dropping it as if burned and taking several steps backward into his chair.

As her host struggled to regain his equilibrium, she looked at her husband and said, "We were just discussing you, Kesgrave. Mr. Mayhew would like to come to dinner."

"Would he?" he asked with easy curiosity, but his stance was rigid and Bea wondered how long he had been standing outside the door listening. Entrances as perfect as his simply did not just happen; they were contrived.

Mr. Mayhew, perceiving a grievous faux pas, hastily clarified his position by stammering "no" several times in rapid succession.

It was a humiliating display of weakness from a man who had just gone out of his way to demonstrate his strength, Bea thought. "He is also desirous of using your box at Covent Garden. And there was some talk about a weekend stay at your estate in Cambridgeshire and... Oh, dear, there were so many items on his list of demands, I am afraid I simply cannot remember them all. Would you be so kind as to catalogue them for the duke, Mr. Mayhew?"

"No, no, no," he said again, his smile oily as little droplets of sweat began to form at his temples. "You must have misunderstood me, your grace. I made no list of demands. Those were wants...requests...desires, rather."

Bea nodded thoughtfully as she followed the progression. "Ah, so then Mr. Mayhew *desires*—"

Here, she broke off her speech to smile sweetly at the banker and ask if she got it right.

Wiping the perspiration from his forehead with a cream-colored handkerchief, he amended it slightly to *devoutly wishes*.

"Very good. Mr. Mayhew devoutly wishes you to move a portion of your deposits to his bank. He is not pleased with your keeping all your filthy lucre at—"

"I never said *filthy*," Mr. Mayhew protested loudly with an anxious look at the duke, whose expression revealed none of his thoughts.

Bea promptly conceded the point. "I was editorializing. Forgive me. Mr. Mayhew is not pleased with your keeping all your *lovely money*"—another sweet smile, another glance seeking confirmation—"at Coutts. He did not state the nature of his objection, but I can only assume he is disgruntled by the higher quality of the other bank's clientele and seeks to emulate it. More dukes, fewer army agents and Cornish businessmen?"

"We are delighted with the quality of our clientele, and I made the gentle suggestion only out of concern for his grace. Coutts is a large establishment and as such is not quite capable of providing the duke with all the attention he deserves," Mr. Mayhew insisted, twisting the handkerchief between his fingers as his eyes darted from Kesgrave to Beatrice and then Beatrice to Kesgrave, unsure to whom he should give his answer. "Mayhew and Co. employs clerks who work around the clock and are available at any hour to attend to your needs, including Sundays and Christmas."

If Kesgrave had thoughts on the matter, he did not express them, but Bea applauded this coldhearted approach. "A relentless taskmaster is exactly what one looks for in a banker."

A dark flush suffused Mr. Mayhew's cheeks, and unable to stop himself, he looked at Bea with ardent dislike. The extent of his resentment did not surprise her, for he had been thwarted in his plan to increase his social standing and he did not seem like a man accustomed to the experience of being denied something he desired.

That, too, was the consequence of having his name carved in stone on the entrance to the establishment.

Contemplating the banker's well-developed sense of entitlement, Bea had little trouble imagining him chopping Mr. Réjane's head off in a fit of annoyance at the prospect of the French chef leaving his employ a moment before he was ready to release him from it. Then, having made quick work of the head, he tossed the cleaver under the cabinet and toddled off to bed, confident the constable would believe whatever addlewitted story he told him and the staff would clean up the mess.

'Twas not the scheme of a Machiavellian genius, to be sure, but Mr. Mayhew did not strike her as particularly intelligent.

Smoothly, the banker transformed his glare into a smile as he transferred his gaze from Bea to Kesgrave.

"It is not relentless to provide comprehensive services to our clients," Mr. Mayhew said with studied ease, his hands ceasing to tug on the cloth square as he grew comfortable with a subject familiar to him. "It is good business. I myself am available on the weekend for consultations and even visit my office on Sundays from one to three. Of course, I attend the morning church service and urge my clerks to do the same, for there is no material wealth without spiritual wealth. I am a devout believer in divine guidance and frequently consult a spiritual adviser. To be open on Sunday is highly irregular and frowned upon by many, but I think risking public censure to fulfill my customers' requirements demonstrates Mayhew and Co.'s commitment to their satisfaction. And you must not worry about my clerks. They are well compensated for their diligence. They know my success depends on them and are properly grateful for the trust I place in them."

"I find your display of business acumen quite reassuring," Bea announced. "Your determination to coerce my assistance in securing Kesgrave's business made me worry about the inferiority of your bank."

Mr. Mayhew laughed awkwardly, with more vigor than sincerity, and complimented her grace on her sense of humor, which was...ah...unique. "You do enjoy teasing me, don't you? Always making little jokes at my expense. Coerced!" he repeated, shaking his head in wonder, as if incapable of thinking of such witty sallies himself. Then he turned his attention to the duke and his voice grew grave. "But do allow me to be serious for a moment, your grace, for this house has great cause to be somber. Early this morning we suffered an unparalleled tragedy, as my chef was brutally slain. The constable was no help in the matter, as the incompetent man has convinced himself that Monsieur Alphonse accidentally killed himself with his own kitchen device. That is why I was asking—no, imploring—the duchess to look into the matter on my behalf. An unconventional request, I know, but I heard from so many people how handily she extracted a confession from Lord Wem at the Stirling ball and thought she could perform the same service for me. She is a very capable woman, so skillful and clever, and you are to be congratulated on making an excellent choice, your grace. But my ability to think clearly must have been corrupted by shock, for I realize now how untenable the request is. If her interest in my decapitated chef became public knowledge, she would be exposed to the most vicious gossip and at such a delicate time, when the *ton* is still marveling at your unexpected choice. Everyone assumed you would wed Lady Victoria, whose grace and beauty are universally admired, and the last thing I want to do is draw further attention to the differences between the two ladies. It was inexcusably selfish of me to have even entertained the thought, your grace, and I do hope you will forgive me for contemplating for even one moment exposing your wife to mockery and revilement. The idea of anyone thinking your wife morbid or unnatural causes me tremendous pain."

Bea listened to this lengthy speech in fascination, for it was a marvel of opportunism and self-interest, the way he abased himself before the duke while also trying to direct his actions. It had been shrewd to imply society's disapprobation because it made the inevitable outcome of her behavior central to the conversation and represented an essential truth: No man wanted the *ton* examining his wife's conduct and finding it wanting.

It was, she thought, the first sign of intelligence she had seen in him, for if he was indeed guilty, then removing her decisively from the investigation was the best chance he had of keeping the truth from coming to light.

But no. Barely five minutes ago he had been perfectly happy to allow her to proceed as long as he could personally benefit from it.

That opportunity had passed, and yet Mr. Mayhew was

still determined to wrench something for himself from the experience. He had merely adjusted his approach, seeking to earn Kesgrave's goodwill by presenting himself as a partner in a most cherished goal: preserving the duke's good name.

Kesgrave, however, had no concern for the repute of his name, at least not yet, and had little patience for men trying to earn his favor. Bea rather thought the latter would be known to anyone who had made a study of him, as presumably the ambitious Mr. Mayhew had, but perhaps the bright veneer that enfolded a duchy made such things difficult to see.

Either way, the banker's face lost all hint of color when Kesgrave murmured softly, "I am generally indifferent to the opinions of others."

Ah, so he had heard that part.

Mr. Mayhew, despite the limitations imposed on him by generational privilege, arrived at the same conclusion with equal speed and adjusted his tack in an instant. "What a remarkable coincidence, your grace, for I had just said the very same thing to your duchess not ten minutes before. It is such an admirable trait to have. So many of us worry what society will think, and I count myself among that number. That is why your outlook is so refreshing. So...refreshing," he repeated slowly as he came to the end of his steam of flattering prattle and realized he did not know how to proceed.

Amused, Bea watched his eyes flutter erratically as he evaluated the situation, trying to figure out where the duke stood on the matter of his wife's strange proclivities so that he may stand there too. On the face of it, it should have been a simple calculation, for Kesgrave loathed inconvenience and allowing his wife to interfere in another man's household would create endless nuisances.

Clearly, he should hold the line.

And yet the duke was there in Mr. Mayhew's own drawing

room—after two years of invitations!—bestirring himself on behalf of his wife's strange proclivity.

Like a gambler trying to access the strength of another player's hand from the expression on his face, Mr. Mayhew examined Kesgrave's features for a long moment and, detecting nothing useful, made a wild guess.

"And so, even though I know it might present a few challenges, I would be deeply grateful to her grace if she would consent to look into the matter of Monsieur Alphonse for me," the banker said with perhaps a little too much enthusiasm. Having made his decision, he seemed alive to the benefits of allowing a duchess to run tame in his home.

Although the request was made of Bea, the appeal itself was addressed to her husband, who displayed no inclination to reply, causing Mr. Mayhew to clutch the handkerchief so tightly his knuckles turned white. Bea allowed the awkward silence to stretch to a second past intolerable and pronounced herself delighted to offer her expertise.

"Wonderful, simply wonderful," the banker said, his smile as disgruntled as it was relieved. "Do make yourself comfortable, my dear, while I ring for fresh tea and cakes. And for you, your grace, perhaps a glass of port," he said, eagerly tugging the bell pull.

Almost immediately, Henry presented himself at the door, and having arranged for the comfort of his guests, Mr. Mayhew sat down in the chair opposite them on the settee. "I have not congratulated you yet on your good fortune, your grace, which is quite remiss of me. I wish you and the duchess every happiness in your union."

As it was most certainly not a social call, Bea refused to indulge his pretense that it was and asked him what he had hoped to achieve by having *le peu guillotine* destroyed.

It was a simple enough question, but Mr. Mayhew professed himself utterly baffled and repeated it out loud several times with varying emphasis in an effort to improve his understanding. "*What* did I hope to achieve? What did I hope to *achieve?*"

Slowly, the implication of the query seemed to occur to him and his outrage increased by degrees until every part of him was consumed by offense. Jumping to his feet, he launched into a tirade against her extraordinary impudence. "How dare you come into my home and ask me *what I hoped to achieve.* I am not insensible to the insidiousness of your claim. You are implying that *I* had something to do with Monsieur Alphonse's death. It is an act of inconceivable gall, inconceivable gall I tell you, to sit on *my* settee in *my* drawing room and accuse me of something so contemptible as cutting the head off my own chef. I am a gentleman, your grace. A gentleman! I do not settle arguments with kitchen implements. By God, I don't! If violence is necessary, it is pistols at dawn! And you dare to imply that *I* have behaved with murderous intensity. I, the head of Mayhew & Co., a banking institution that dates back over one hundred years. You insult not only me but generations of Mayhews. Generations! I cannot conceive of your insolence."

Pacing the floor, he vented his outrage with no concern for his guests, and Bea, little worried she would miss something important, such as an inadvertent admission of guilt, slid closer to the duke. "Another successful frank conversation," she observed in a low voice. "I cannot thank you enough, your grace, for that helpful suggestion. I have found it to be a very effective technique for gathering information."

As if incapable of resisting the urge to touch her, he ran his fingers lightly down her back and said softly, "I am willing to concede that I might have somewhat of an advantage in initiating frank conversations, as I'm reasonably certain I've never caused anyone to rail at the drapery."

She looked across the room at Mr. Mayhew, who was

demanding an explanation for Bea's impudence from the curtains. "I believe he's in consultation with them. Oh, no, wait, he's raising his fist in anger. *Now* he is railing. I am not sure how to respond to his tantrum. Without question, the more humane reaction would be to interrupt before he collapses in apoplexy or embarrasses himself in front of the servants, for Henry will be back at any moment with the tray. And yet I cannot help but feel it is good for him to rant freely in the presence of a duke, for overcoming his awe of nobility can only improve his character."

Kesgrave's lips twisted cynically. "It is not awe Mayhew feels for nobility but voracity. He would consume the House of Lords whole if he could."

"Is that why you've never had him to dine?" she asked as the banker turned his attention to the escritoire.

"Not at all," he replied, "I respect ambition and would never penalize a man for possessing it. He is tediously dull and pompous, which you no doubt discovered for yourself during your conversation. How long were you bracketed in here with him before I arrived?"

"I cannot say because I do not know when you arrived," she pointed out logically.

"In time to hear you call me pedantic," he replied.

She was instantly contrite. "Oh, dear. I am so very sorry."

He assured her he took no offense. "Naturally, I am accustomed to the charge, for you lodge it against me almost daily."

"I was not expressing sympathy for you, but for the poor tenants with leaky roofs whose repairs will be delayed so much longer because of Mr. Mayhew's penchant for pontification," she explained, then narrowed her eyes in confusion when the man in question began to attack the bergère next to the writing desk. "Goodness gracious, what is he doing now?"

"Overcoming his awe of chairs," Kesgrave said.

In fact, after an extended struggle to extricate the front left leg, which had got snagged by the rug, the banker sat down at the table, extracted a sheet of paper from one of its compartments and dipped a nib in ink. "Oh, I see, he's writing an editorial for the *London Morning Gazette* about the new Duchess of Kesgrave's huge impudence," she said wryly. "I hope you don't mind public ridicule, your grace."

"As long as it's not in the form of a caricature by Rowlandson, I have no objection," he replied.

Since their host seemed to have settled in to pen his missive, she decided to make herself comfortable as well and reached for the pot of tea, which had cooled to tepid while Mr. Mayhew was expounding on his illustrious family's many accomplishments. "I believe that ship sailed long ago, your grace. If Rowlandson wasn't already making my wan cheeks excessively red after the incident at Lord Stirling's ball, he will begin as soon as our episode at the Particular becomes more widely known. Rest assured, the servants are already talking about it," she said, pouring a cup and offering it to the duke, who accepted it with a murmured thank you. "I expect a print of me wearing a comically large pair of spectacles and examining the lint in Prinny's pocket to appear in Hannah Humphries's window by Thursday week, so you must resign yourself to it now or be prepared to give testimony against me in ecclesiastical court later. Concerned more about your dignity than my happiness, Aunt Vera would consider a print shop in St. James sufficient provocation and instigate the proceedings herself."

"You inflate your aunt's excesses. Rather she would take the more practical route of instructing me to buy all the copies and offering to burn them herself. Divorce would shame your family too," he said.

Affecting astonishment, Bea stared at the duke. "Good lord, Kesgrave, I don't know what you have been about these past few weeks if you have failed to learn that my aunt would gladly tarnish her own name to burnish yours. Her awe of nobility might not be as self-serving as Mr. Mayhew's, but it is just as tedious."

Kesgrave, who refused to allow that anyone's awe of nobility could be quite as tedious as Mr. Mayhew's, glanced at the clock and noted the time. "It appears to be a long editorial."

Bea took a sip of tea that had cooled beyond tepid to outright cold. "My impudence is very huge."

He smiled broadly as he raised his own cup to his lips. "To my infinite delight."

As sighing in infatuation could not be deemed an appropriate activity for the drawing room of a tiresome neighbor, she contented herself with a growl of impatience and wondered if she could finish her interview with Parsons while his employer was distracted. Mr. Mayhew was unlikely to notice her absence.

Perhaps that was the sum total of Mr. Mayhew's plan and the reason he was writing furiously at the escritoire. He thought if he ignored the impertinent interloper long enough, she would leave of her own accord.

If that was his scheme, then it was a facile one. Having felt no compunction about elbowing her way into his home to scrutinize the floor under his kitchen cupboards, she would certainly not find a writing desk to be an insurmountable barrier.

Possibly, that was the level to which his scheming rose—simple minded and futile. She had already noted his lack of intelligence and the misplaced confidence he had in his own abilities.

"Three more minutes," she said firmly.

Kesgrave returned his teacup to the table and agreed to

her plan, for three minutes was a sufficient amount of time for Mr. Mayhew to finish his article. "Or is it a novella?"

"Then we storm the escritoire," she said rousingly.

Responding to the slight revolutionary fervor in her tone, he owned himself ready for the battle. "Just hand me my quill."

Bea laughed lightly at the image of the elegant Duke of Kesgrave in his pristine tailoring brandishing a pen against poor Mr. Mayhew in his clashing silks. Calmly, she inquired about his presence at number forty-forty. "I am still not clear why you left Mr. Stephens in a froth over the tenants to pay a call on a neighbor whom you dislike. Your actions defy logic, your grace."

"*My* actions defy logic?" he said softly with pointed emphasis before insisting that *froth* overstated the steward's condition. "Let's call it a fizz. And, yes, Mr. Stephens was in a fizz over the tenants, but he was also understanding of a newly married man's needs."

"To spend time with his wife?" she asked archly, leaning forward to grasp the handle of the teacup and wishing Henry would appear soon with a plate of cakes. His delay was hardly surprising given the fact that the kitchen had just lost its chef. That said, she would happily accept a days-old version of one of Mr. Réjane's flaky *kipferl*.

"To find out what his wife meant by establishing herself with the staff," Kesgrave explained.

Bea drew her brows in confusion. "I would think such a simple concept is self-explanatory."

"Yes, *you* would," he replied, "and I was satisfied with the comment for a good hour and a half. But then as I was reviewing the figures in the accounting ledger, I paused for a moment to consider what it actually meant and felt a cold chill."

"The temerity of Mr. Stephens, opening a window in your

study without securing your permission," she said with light outrage. "I trust he offered you his coat."

"I felt a chill because I knew it could not be as simple as your telling Mrs. Wallace at what hour you would like your morning tray," he said with a hint of impatience.

"Is that all it takes?" she asked mildly.

"Bea!"

"Yes?"

"You vowed," he said vehemently.

"Actually, I did not, no," she said with a firm shake of her head. "I *tried* to vow and was roundly thwarted by the clergyman you yourself selected. Perhaps if you had taken the time to interview each perspective minister and ascertain his stance on alterations to the Solemnization of Matrimony before the ceremony, then I *would* have vowed and your anger would be entirely justified. But you did not consider our nuptials important enough to require that modicum of effort and you cannot hold me accountable for that."

As Beatrice had taken a similar tact during many of their previous disagreements, Kesgrave knew better than to try to dispute her individual points, many of which were purposely absurd. Instead, he pointed out that it was her intention that counted, not her success in achieving it. "If you tried to overturn Mayhew's chair but failed to unseat him because you misjudged your own strength or underestimated his heft, he would still be irate at your attempt to dump him onto the floor. The difference between intention and action is merely a detail, as I am sure Mr. Bertram would agree."

It was a valid argument, Bea thought, and one she herself might have employed if their situations had been reversed. But they were not, so she waved her hand dismissively and affected a pose of abject scorn. "*Merely* a detail. Merely a *detail?* All meaning lies in the details, as I am sure Mr. Bertram's supervisor would agree. Have you not read Leviticus, your grace? 'All flying insects that walk on all fours are to be regarded as unclean by you. There are, however, some flying insects that walk on all fours that you may eat: those that have jointed legs for hopping on the ground.' *Jointed legs,*" she repeated with forceful intensity. "Now there is a superior being who comprehends the importance of details."

It was a measure of either his affection or self-control that he did not pound his fist on the table in frustration but said with only bland vexation, "Very well, brat, and what of your promise not to investigate the horrible murders that cross your path? How are you going to wiggle off that hook?" he asked, his tone more curious than cross.

"Ah, there, we are well in the clear, your grace," she said with reassuring confidence.

His lips twitched. "Are we?"

"Oh, yes, there will be no undignified wiggling today save for Mr. Mayhew's squirmy fingers. I have held tightly to our compact."

Without saying a word, Kesgrave made his differing understanding of the circumstance known by looking around the room with exaggerated interest.

"No, it is true," she insisted earnestly. "In this case, *I* have crossed *its* path. This murder has absolutely nothing to do with me, and I am intruding with great impudence—you see, Mr. Mayhew is correct to compose a novella—on a private matter. Having said that, I must also note that the victim was the most creative and masterful practitioner of the culinary arts of this or any century and his death deprives the entire world of beauty and grace, which makes it, I would argue, the concern of every person of feeling and sensibility."

Kesgrave's opinion of this particularly dizzying piece of sophistry was readily apparent in his expression, which bore an unsettling resemblance to the one he had worn the day before after concluding his tour of the house in his bedchamber, and Bea, whose breath hitched in perceiving it, knew the look was not appropriate for any drawing room, even one that did not contain a banker furiously venting his spleen via pen and paper at the opposite end of the room.

Transfixed, her heart pounding slightly, she stared into his bright blue eyes and wondered why she was there, anywhere, that wasn't alone with her husband.

Seconds passed, perhaps minutes, certainly the time limit she had imposed on Mr. Mayhew, without either of them speaking, but Bea was spared the mortification of discovering just how long she could sit there gazing insensibly at her husband by their host, who observed the tea service with approval.

"Mrs. Blewitt is a treasure," he added fondly, unaware that Henry had yet to return.

Startled, Bea looked up to find a perfectly composed Mr. Mayhew smiling serenely at her. As if nothing extraordinary had happened, he regained the chair that he had summarily vacated in a distempered freak and asked Bea if she would be so kind as to pour.

She was so taken aback by the change in demeanor, she complied. The pot, however, was nearly empty and only a thin stream trickled out before dribbling into drops. She placed the partially filled cup in front of the banker, who lavishly praised her efficiency before thanking her and the duke for responding so quickly to his summons.

His summons, Bea thought, amused by the pompous attempt to impress her with his confidence. Surely, he did not think he could alter her understanding of recent events by simply claiming them to be the opposite of what they actually were.

Alas, it seemed he was going to make a sincere effort to try, for Mr. Mayhew immediately pressed upon them his very great appreciation for their assistance in the matter. "But before we can devote ourselves fully to figuring out who performed this heinous deed, we must first assuage her grace's concerns regarding the disposal of *le peu guillotine,* as they appear to have distracted her from the more pressing issue. Women," he said with fond exasperation to Kesgrave, as if there was nothing to be done but humor their strange fits and starts. "To that end, I have taken the enterprising step of cataloguing every accident involving the device in the past two years. I trust that will appease her and allow us to return at last to my investigation into Monsieur Alphonse's murder."

Having identified Beatrice as the problem, he did not consider her a safe caretaker of his list and handed it to Kesgrave. Then he lifted the cup, and noting the very small amount of liquid it contained, scowled in annoyance at how inadequately Bea had performed the one task he had assigned her. A snappish look appeared in his eye, but he had the sense not to chastise a duchess for failing to serve him well enough and instead smiled sweetly before asking if she or Kesgrave had any objections to his plan.

Oh, yes, Bea had objections.

Chapter Nine

Bea's first issue concerned his estimation of her and Kesgrave's intelligence. Did he really think so little of their mental acuity that he believed they would fall in line with his amended version of history? Was it merely that he assumed everyone was cognitively impaired in comparison to his own brilliance or was he operating under the misapprehension that they had both suffered memory-reducing head injuries in the past ten minutes?

Her second objection related to the unearned confidence of entitled bankers, as did her third and fourth, for only someone accustomed to the habitual capitulation of his underlings would attempt such a blatantly fatuous tactic. Her fifth, however, was purely pragmatic, for she would not be induced to hand over the reins of her investigation to one of its chief suspects.

Surely, even someone with Mr. Mayhew's limited faculties understood that.

He would have to be a complete dunderhead to think his ruse had any hope of prevailing, and he could not be thoroughly without wits, for, entitled heir or not, he ran a large financial institution with reasonable success.

That was right, Bea thought suddenly, he *did* run a large financial institution with reasonable success. His name was over the door, to be sure, but no business of that scope was run without oversight. Mr. Mayhew had to answer to a governing body of some sort, whether it was a group of family members or an assortment of business associates. He was clever enough to earn their esteem and trust while courting new clients and managing a large staff.

Simply put, he could not be a *complete* dunderhead.

Some part of his brain was clearly capable of concise, cogent thought. What was less discernable was the extent of his coherence.

Could he merely be *half* a dunderhead?

Bea considered his sycophancy, which was at once the most repellant and comical aspect of his character. His assiduousness in seeking the duke's approval made him appear foolish, but his behavior did not exist in isolation. No, he was a banker, which meant his livelihood depended on his proximity to power and most of the power in England was held by affluent peers. His toadying was not only the logical conclusion of a mind properly perceiving the demands of its business but also a professional necessity. Securing Kesgrave's favor was central to his success, and if he chose to sacrifice his own self-respect to obtain wealth and security for his family, then he was only making a sound business decision. No doubt he considered it a small price to pay.

If his fawning was the product of cool calculation, perhaps his other fatuous-seeming traits were as well.

Thoughtfully, she contemplated the blundering way he tried to coerce her agreement to benefit his social standing and the bank. The attempt, so mortifyingly graceless, had

LYNN MESSINA

accomplished the very opposite of its aim: Rather than gain
his assistance, she had resolved to forego it.

Had he been more subtle in his manipulations, a little less
grasping and a little more pleasing, he might have achieved
his devoutly wished goal of greater familiarity with the Duke
of Kesgrave.

Ah, but what if his objective had actually been different
from the stated one, she wondered now as she examined the
situation from the opposite point of view. If his intention had
actually been to thwart an investigation into Mr. Réjane's
murder, then his heavy-handed approach had had a much
better chance of succeeding. She had dismissed his attempt
to negotiate access to his staff as an act of impertinence and
idiocy, but it had in fact put her in an untenable situation. She
could not accede to his demands, particularly on behalf of her
husband, but nor could she override his wishes. If she had
been the woman he thought her—a mushroomy nonentity
trying to style herself as a lady Runner to make herself appear
interesting to the *beau monde*—she would have abandoned the
field at once.

But she was not, of course, and had options that far
exceeded his meager resources, and when she'd exerted her
privilege, he had panicked and grabbed her arm.

In that moment he'd comprehended the meaning of her
confidence: that the duke might in fact take some interest in
his wife.

How awful it must have been for him when, only a
moment later, Kesgrave appeared in the room. Now he had
two inquisitive peers with which to contend!

His solution had been to apply social pressure to convince
Kesgrave to prohibit her from continuing her inquiry.

It was, she conceded, a clever tactic, for she herself had
been horrified by the picture he painted of a monstrously
intrusive woman. The assumption was correct, for it would

indeed make a most delicious on-dit, and it was only Kesgrave's refusal to bow to anyone's censure that caused the effort to fail. A more dogmatic husband would have heartily agreed.

When that stratagem foundered, he had taken a moment to reorganize his thoughts under the guise of having a tantrum and settled on yet another tactic. He would make himself integral to her investigation so that he could stay abreast of its developments and manipulate its direction.

Bea did not assume that the banker's machinations meant he was guilty. As his livelihood depended on his status in society, he was particularly vulnerable to the deleterious effects of gossip. Having his prized French chef brutally slain in his own home would set tongues wagging in a way that a precautionary tale about irresponsible device maintenance would not. The fact that he felt compelled to polish his heritage by wrongfully crediting his family with financial innovations indicated that he was not quite delighted with the luster bestowed by his ancestors and felt vulnerable to society's judgments.

It was possible, therefore, that his manipulations stemmed from an instinct to protect his name and business. But it was equally likely they were spurred by a desire to save himself from the hangman's noose.

And if it was the hangman's noose, then what reason did Mr. Mayhew have to kill Mr. Réjane? Previously, she had thought it might have been the audacity of the chef's presumption to leave his employ a moment before he was prepared to release him. But that was the motive of a dunderhead who acted without consideration. The banker had proved himself more thoughtful, and she knew that if he had acted lethally, then he had stronger cause.

Recalling again the victim's strangely timed proposal to Mrs. Wallace, she felt certain Mr. Mayhew's actions, whatever they were, related somehow to Mr. Réjane's determination to leave. Both events had been precipitated by something.

Convinced it could only be an argument, Bea asked him what he and the chef quarreled about the day before.

He started with surprise but recovered quickly, smiling with warmth and condescension. "My dear duchess, I cannot conceive to what you are referring. If we are going to pursue Monsieur Alphonse's killer together, I must insist that you keep to the facts. Your imagination is charming and I look forward to hearing many entertaining tales from you, perhaps over dinner at Kesgrave House, but I believe this moment calls for sober-minded consideration. Inventing quarrels will do nothing to advance our investigation. Now, regarding my decision to get rid of *le peu guillotine,* I think you will see I was well justified. If Monsieur Alphonse did not hurt himself fatally on it, as you contend, it was only a matter of time before one of the servants did. I am to be lauded for taking preemptive action to protect my staff."

To be sure, the quarrel was speculative, but supposition was an entirely different beast from invention. Some event of deep significance had occurred between the chef and his employer to throw the former's trajectory wildly off course. She firmly believed that when Mr. Réjane woke up yesterday morning he'd had no intention of proposing to Mrs. Wallace, and yet several hours later he ruthlessly abandoned the quails to ask her to accompany him to France. Swiftly and abruptly, he had become unmoored from his position.

Obviously, the only thing that could account for such a rapid change in situation was an intense argument with the man who employed him.

Eliding the truth slightly, Bea advised him to think very carefully before denying it again because she had direct knowledge of the dispute. "Your determination to destroy the apparatus originally identified as the murder weapon already makes you appear less than innocent in the affair. Lying now would only deepen my suspicion."

A variety of expressions flitted across his face—confusion, doubt, anger, dislike—and Bea watched as he struggled to settle on a strategy for dealing with her accusation. He wanted to hold to his denial, but not knowing the source of her information, he was obliged to tread carefully. If he continued to refute it and she produced unassailable evidence, he would not only be caught in the middle of a lie but also embarrassed in front of Kesgrave.

Both were equally important to him, she thought with her new understanding of his character: He would do everything he could to frustrate her investigation while still trying to endear himself to the duke.

Finally, Mr. Mayhew nodded as if suddenly comprehending a thorny question. "Oh, I see, you are referring to the minor disagreement Monsieur Alphonse and I had yesterday. It was your description that confused me, for it was nothing so momentous as a quarrel, just a difference of opinion—very mundane. But you need not apologize, for I know how you ladies enjoy your dramatic confrontations."

Bea ignored the slight against her sex and asked about the source of the so-called minor disagreement.

Mr. Mayhew pursed his lips, clearly not delighted with her other female habit of persistence. Determined to make the interview as difficult as possible, he responded succinctly, saying only that it was over an introduction and requiring Bea to press him further. "An introduction to whom?"

Again, he was disinclined to answer helpfully. "A colleague. Nobody you have heard of, your grace, and certainly well beneath your notice."

Bea tilted her head at what she hoped was an imperious angle and thanked the banker to allow her the courtesy of determining who was beneath her notice. The tips of his ears turned faintly pink as he apologized for trying to spare her tedious details.

Stubbornly, she remained focused on the information she sought. "Monsieur Alphonse requested an introduction to someone of little significance and you refused?"

Mr. Mayhew tittered lightly. "There you go again, your grace, using colorful language to make it all sound so dramatic. I did not refuse, no. The person indicated that now was not a propitious time for the introduction to take place and I chose to abide by that. Naturally, Monsieur Alphonse understood my decision not to impose further and was grateful that I had considered the request. Then we briefly discussed the quality of the quails—excellent, as the meal itself attested—and he returned to the kitchen. All very calm and civil. I cannot imagine why the servants would describe it as a quarrel. I suspect they enjoy drama as much as you."

Bea sought to put his mind at ease by assuring him none of the servants described the incident as such, but Mr. Mayhew, taking her statement as confirmation that the servants had chattered freely about private matters, only in slightly different terms, was further agitated by this proof of their perfidy. Morose, he stared abstractedly into his empty teacup.

Although her patience was worn thin, Bea allowed him a moment to sulk over the supposed disloyalty of his staff before interrupting his blue study to inquire after the identity of the person.

Sighing, Mr. Mayhew returned the cup to the table and provided a name.

But only a name, which was also unhelpful.

"And where can Mr. Bayne be found?" she asked.

"Fleet Street," Mayhew replied, "number one."

The address alone conveyed nothing useful to Bea, who knew the banker's curt answers were designed to obfuscate, but Kesgrave recognized it. "One Fleet Street is the site of Mayhew and Co.'s offices."

Startled by his knowledge, Mr. Mayhew grinned broadly and said with a hint of wonder, "Why, yes, it is. Has his grace honored us with a visit? Perhaps you were seeking information about our institution, as Coutts no longer satisfies? Please know, sir, that I am at your disposal for a comprehensive tour of the premises whenever you desire. No time is inconvenient, no time at all." Then he reminded the duke that he himself attended to business on Sunday as well. "From one to three."

As Kesgrave had no complaint with his current financial arrangements, he paid the offer scant heed and asked if Mr. Bayne was a clerk at the bank.

Mr. Mayhew, however, considered the query to be an indication of interest and proffered immediate and generous praise of his employee. "Mr. Bayne is indeed a clerk and an exceptional one at that. He is everything that is amiable and reliable, as well as thorough and discreet. It would be my pleasure to introduce you to him—or to any of the other clerks we employ. They are all exceptional, to a man."

"What if Mr. Bayne does not wish to meet with the Duke of Kesgrave?" Bea asked.

The banker could not conceive the premise of the query and repeated it softly to himself several times as if hearing it in his own voice would somehow make it intelligible. "But he would want to meet with the Duke of Kesgrave!" he exclaimed excitedly before turning to his grace and apologizing for the slight. "I assure you Mr. Bayne bears you nothing but the utmost respect and would gratefully welcome the opportunity to demonstrate that to you personally. You have only to say the word."

It was a remarkable little speech, fawning on behalf of a subordinate who was denied the option of a dignified response, and Bea marveled at the new and endless depths to which the banker would sink in his pursuit of Kesgrave's goodwill.

"Yes, yes, Mr. Bayne is wonderfully eager to abase himself before the duke to secure a portion of his deposits," she said humorously. "That is naturally understood by all. But let's pretend for a moment that he doesn't want to meet with Kesgrave. Would you respect his wishes and allow him to decline?"

His eyes seemed to pop out of their sockets as he goggled at her as if she were a veritable ninny. "Respect his wishes? Allow him to decline? My dear duchess, you seem to have mistaken Mayhew and Co. for an assembly at Almack's. It is not run by an assortment of patronesses all having equal say. I am in charge and keep a firm hand on the tiller. A very firm hand," he repeated for the duke's particular benefit.

"Why did you not want Mr. Réjane to meet with a clerk from your bank?" Bea asked. "What was your objection?"

Mr. Mayhew smiled patronizingly and chastised her for her irrepressibly female habit of puffery. "My goodness, you are determined to transform a molehill into an imposing mountain, are you not, your grace. Already I've explained that I had no quarrel with the introduction. I made the request and Mr. Bayne decided against it for reasons of his own, although he indicated—again, as I previously said—that the timing was not propitious for him."

"I don't know, Mr. Mayhew," she said thoughtfully, shaking her head in mild disapproval, "allowing clerks to determine which meetings they will agree to attend sounds very much to me like a lax hand on the tiller."

It was a credit to the banker that he managed to keep a polite smile firmly affixed to his face, for his eyes glowed hotly with anger as he assured Bea that the subtleties of helming a business were too complicated for her to comprehend. Her husband, he rushed to add, understood them precisely, for he was a formidable man, an estimable man, a great man who had managed his estates with wisdom and efficiency.

As Mr. Mayhew rattled off his list of laudatory adjectives, Bea thought he needed to be more careful, for the excessiveness of the catalogue seemed to veer into parody.

Kesgrave, ignoring the litany of praise, explained that Mr. Mayhew had no intention of approving the loan. "But he could not refuse it outright because that would offend the man who prepared the lavish feasts that drew his new clients, so he created a procedural barrier. Or, rather, obstacle, which is a more precise description. Plainly, Réjane asked Mayhew and Co. to extend him a loan, and Mayhew replied that it would be inappropriate for him to approve the request, given the nature of their relationship, and explained that the decision would be up to his clerk Bayne. He then allowed Bayne to deny the applicant access and threw his hands up into the air, claiming he was powerless to intercede."

As if offering a demonstration, Mr. Mayhew waved his arms before himself in wide, furious arcs and insisted he *had* been powerless. "It is in the bylaws, you see, in a section outlining how loans may be dispersed to intimates and acquaintances of partners in the firm. It was added by my grandfather who worried that the bonds of affection would influence the partners' ability to make rational business decisions."

Urgently, assertively, he launched into an account of the particulars of the clause, but neither Bea nor Kesgrave paid him any attention and slowly he trailed off.

"What objection could he have to lending Mr. Réjane money?" Bea said to the duke, her brows drawn in confusion. "If he intended to establish a new enterprise with the funds, who would deny him the opportunity? His renown was widespread and he had proved himself to royalty. Anything he created would be sure to succeed."

The duke agreed that Mr. Réjane was a reliable investment but noted that the banker's primary concern was not the acquisition of wealth.

Deeply offended, Mr. Mayhew cried out in protest, insisting that he assiduously pursued the acquisition of wealth to the exclusion of all other vices.

It was a bold statement but demonstrably wrong, and Bea chided the banker for his display of false modesty, for he had also managed to cultivate an excess of pride and envy.

Once again, Mr. Mayhew maintained a delighted expression on his face despite his true feelings, and Bea admired how well he kept himself in check. It could not be easy.

Aware he had given offense, Kesgrave apologized to the banker for causing him undue agitation. "It was never my intention to imply you are not avaricious. Please know that I am fully cognizant of your greed and find it quite unseemly. Have no worry on that score. I was merely drawing greater attention to your desire for prestige because it explains your unwillingness to even discuss the matter with Mr. Réjane. Had you not interrupted, I would have cited your excessive fawning and attempt to coerce the duchess's assistance in moving my deposits to your establishment as evidence of your determination to attain a higher quality of client. You would never consent to loan money to a cook, no matter how talented he was or respected, because that is not the quality of client with whom you wish to associate. You are interested only in the nobility and would happily extend credit to a second son with no skills or competencies as long as he had something suitable to offer as collateral. Have I explained your outlook correctly, Mayhew, or would you like to add a few words in support of your fervent devotion to the aristocracy?"

Nothing Mr. Mayhew could have said in his own defense would better illustrate Kesgrave's point than the way the banker bowed his head and congratulated the duke on his understanding of the situation. Then, his impressive control slipping just a little, he darted a spiteful look at Beatrice, as if to imply that these were precisely the sort of subtleties her inadequate female mind could not grasp.

"How did Mr. Réjane respond when you refused to discuss a loan?" she asked.

"Mr. Bayne refused," he corrected.

Bea, whose patience had been greatly restored by Kesgrave's cool display of temper, accepted the amendment with a genial smile. "Thank you, yes, how did Mr. Réjane respond when Mr. Bayne declined to meet with him and you refused to intercede on his behalf?"

"My hands were tied, which he understood," Mr. Mayhew replied. "He was more upset about the quails. One or two were of questionable quality, and he was very distressed at the thought of serving them to my guests."

That was a lie, Bea knew, for it directly contradicted his earlier statement regarding the birds, and recalling his apprehension about his servants' propensity to gossip, she wondered aloud how Parsons would respond when questioned by the duke. "Will he say that Monsieur Alphonse grew heated because the butcher saddled him with a pair of substandard quails or would he relate a fierce argument about your refusal to provide him with a loan? What about Gertrude? Will she confirm that the quails were substandard? And your housekeeper as well? Are you quite sure the staff comprehend the true source of the chef's displeasure?"

The banker, smiling stiffly, allowed for the possibility that one or two of the servants might have thought they heard Monsieur Alphonse directing his anger at him, not the quails. "I did not want to say this because I have so much respect for the chef, but he did not accept Mr. Bayne's decision with any sense of equanimity. Indeed, he raged at me quite viciously. To be completely honest with you, I feared for my own safety."

Patently, that was false, but it was delivered with sufficient distress, and Bea murmured sympathetically. "I am sure it was terrifying. You must have been relieved when he resigned his position on the spot."

Mr. Mayhew was astonished by the statement.

Oh, yes, he was too taken aback by the information to do anything but stare at her in amazement. But he recalled himself quickly and affected mild disappointment at her credulity in believing the idle talk of servants. "For that is where you heard this canard, is it not, from the servants? They have no understanding of what they overheard. Monsieur Alphonse might have declared in a fit of pique he intended to leave my employ at once—truthfully, I cannot recall all that was said between us—but he was merely venting his spleen. I assure you he was far too satisfied in my employ to seek a position elsewhere. I allowed him every indulgence and paid him handsomely. He would get that nowhere else in London."

He spoke confidently, assuredly, as if Mr. Réjane provided an esoteric or arcane service that he alone appreciated. It was, Bea thought, a decidedly strange and inaccurate way to think about one of the most gifted chefs in the world.

As if aware of her thoughts, Mr. Mayhew added, "Naturally, he had offers. Indeed, he had them constantly, for he was very well-known and who in London would not love to have a chef who once cooked for Napoleon? But Monsieur Alphonse was quite particular in his tastes and could not be happy in just anyone's kitchen. James Van der Straeten—he is a banker as well but runs a small branch of his family's concern in Paris—hired him and Monsieur Alphonse left without putting a single saucepan on the fire because he was appalled by his Rumford stove."

"Castrol," said Bea, who had listened in silence as he maligned the Bank of England.

Mr. Mayhew, resenting the interruption, was just confused enough by it to look at her with benign curiosity. "Excuse me, your grace?"

"It was the Castrol stove that he found objectionable, not the Rumford," Bea explained, recalling the description of Mr. Van der Straeten's inadequate kitchens from the chef's memoir. "The Rumford is quite modern and what you your-self have."

Although much could be excused in a duchess's behavior, particularly one who had assumed the mantle only the day before, lecturing a man about the various apparatuses in his own home was not among the allowances and Mr. Mayhew growled irritably at her presumption. Nevertheless, he managed to reply in a smooth tone when he said, "While I have never been in my own kitchen long enough to notice what type of stove I have, let alone become familiar with its name, I am confident Mr. Van der Straeten has a Rumford. Monsieur Alphonse used that term specifically while assuring me of the superiority of all my equipment, and that is why I am certain he had no intention of leaving. He found me to be the ideal employer, for I was not forever at his heels, demanding that he create new, better, more elaborate dishes for my guests. I required him only to make a small variety of delicious and technically difficult meals, which pleased him greatly. I know this because he frequently complimented me on my palate. It was, he said, the most minutely restricted one he had ever met."

If Bea had any doubt that Mr. Mayhew was making a May game of her, it was banished by this observation, for no one could be so lacking in brain power as to miss the implied insult. No, he was merely pretending to be a lackwit to continue to thwart her in the most audacious way possible. If he was too stupid for consideration, he could neither be a suspect in her investigation nor a threat to it.

"But if Monsieur Alphonse *had* intended to leave you for a less restricted palate, you would have no objections?" she asked.

Mr. Mayhew waved his hand in a sweeping arch and assured her he would have none at all. "I will not deny that employing the world's most lauded chef has greatly benefited my business. As his grace kindly noted earlier, I crave both wealth and prestige, and Monsieur Alphonse has helped me attain both. Everyone accepts an invitation to dine at number forty-four, even Prinny"—here, a slight pause to allow for gasps of surprise, which were not forthcoming—"who desired to taste *croquembouche* made by the hand of its creator," he said, then turned to look at the duke with rueful humor. "You are my only failure, your grace."

Kesgrave accepted this communication with a dip of the head and allowed that he had higher standards than the regent.

Mr. Mayhew readily agreed with his assessment and continued, "As valuable as Monsieur Alphonse was to me, I would never begrudge him the opportunity to take another position. I am a man of business, of course, and would try to change his mind through negotiation. But I would never resort to immoderate violence, if that is what you are implying. I am a banker, your grace, and no banker worth his salt would consider decapitation to be a satisfying solution to a problem."

Bea appreciated how principled he made basic human decency sound, as if bankers should be commended for their unwillingness to remove the heads of members of their staffs.

Even so, she was not sure she believed he would accept Mr. Réjane's decision to leave as easily as he claimed. Only a short while ago, Bea had tried to leave his drawing room and he responded by grabbing her arm. There was, to be clear, a significant difference between squeezing someone's elbow and chopping off his head, but it demonstrated that his first instinct was to respond physically. Mr. Mayhew believed that he was owed things—Bea's compliance, Mr. Réjane's loyalty— and he did not respond well when denied them. It was naïve to think he would happily allow the chef to walk out of his home, especially when there was a chance he would walk *into* Thomas Coutts's or one of the other bankers who resided in London.

It would not have happened, of course, for Mr. Réjane had no intention of remaining in England. But Mr. Mayhew did not know that.

Nobody knew except Mrs. Wallace, Joseph and any other servants at Kesgrave House who happened to be in or near Mrs. Wallace's office during their conversation.

Wondering if the victim's plan to open a patisserie was in some way related to his desire for a loan, Bea asked what Monsieur Alphonse had intended to do with the money.

The question elicited a world-weary sigh from Mr. Mayhew, who hung his head as if in shame and admitted that it was for the chef's brother. "*His brother!* It was an act of imprudence so pronounced I could not speak for a full five minutes. To ask Mayhew & Co. to advance funds to an unknown Frenchman who had not even had the pleasure of boiling water for the great Czar Alexander's tea. And he wanted to use my funds to open a shop in Paris. How could I be expected to respond to something as appalling as that? It was immoral of Monsieur Alphonse to even make the request, unreservedly and undeniably immoral, for it put me in an impossible position. I could not say yes but nor could I say no. If I was driven to extreme measures, he had nobody to blame but himself."

For a moment, fleeting and intense, Bea thought he was confessing to the murder and felt that it had to be some trick, another maneuver to lull them. Quickly enough, however, she realized he was still speaking of business matters. "Extreme measures?"

Mr. Mayhew was startled by the query. "Excuse me?"

"You said you were driven to extreme measures," Bea explained. "What extreme measures?"

The banker let out a laugh—it was a little self-conscious and somewhat affected—and insisted he had no idea what she was talking about. "Oh, dear, so much information is being shared you are growing confused."

Although she was tempted to compliment him on the audacity of the ploy, Bea turned to the duke and asked him to speculate as to what measures Mr. Mayhew might have taken if the procedural obstacle he had erected had proved ineffective.

"I am certain Mayhew does not wish to make me exert myself in speculation," Kesgrave said mildly, "and will simply tell us."

It was comical, to be sure, the look of indecision that swept across the banker's face, for his instinct was clearly to submit to the duke and yet some part of him knew he should resist the compulsion. Finally, after several moments of silent and intense struggle, he said, "It is not my fault. I tried to put him off with vague promises to look into the matter, but he refused to accept my answer. I had no choice but to invent a notoriously difficult associate and put him in charge of the request."

Whatever extreme measure for which Bea was prepared, it certainly was not this. "You mean Mr. Bayne does not exist?"

Defiantly, he said, "I had no choice."

"And subsection F, clause one?" she asked.

"The bylaws only go up to E," he confessed with a hint of shame. "I did not mean to mislead him. I just wanted to avoid discussing the topic for as long as possible because refusing a loan is always so awkward. People get very stiff in the spine about it, as if it were personal and not merely a practical business decision."

His defensiveness could, she thought, mean only one thing. "Monsieur Alphonse found out."

Exhaling heavily, Mr. Mayhew bowed his head. "Yesterday morning. He paid a call to the bank himself and insisted on meeting Mr. Bayne. That's when he discovered the truth. He was irate."

"Well, naturally," Bea said.

The banker grimaced at the rebuke but insisted he had done the only thing he could. "I do not wish to cast aspersions on the dead, but it was really most uncharitable of Monsieur Alphonse to ask me in the first place. He must have known the position he was putting me in and did not care. Now of course I did not chop off his head with a skewer—"

"Cleaver," she corrected.

Yet again, Mr. Mayhew appeared confused. "Excuse me?"

"You cannot cut off someone's head with a skewer," she explained.

The minor distinction between kitchen utensils was as inconsequential as the differences between stoves, and he scoffed at the expectation that he able to distinguish between an object that cut and an object that impaled.

"Truly, your grace, your distraction with minor details has made you insensible to the larger repercussions of the event," he said impatiently. "What you seem incapable of properly comprehending is how disastrous this event is to me personally. If word gets out that the famous chef was murdered in my own home, I will be ruined. Nobody will entrust their money with a man who cannot even provide for his employees' safety. I understand, your grace, that you find the *le peu* explanation too implausible to accept and am in full sympathy with your objections. I see now that it might be difficult to insert a human head fully into the apparatus. But perhaps you are amenable to the possibility that an argument got out of hand and when it was over poor Monsieur Alphonse had been most gruesomely sliced apart? In that circumstance his death is still an accident but with a villain to satisfy your requirements."

It was an astounding offer, as insulting as it was ridiculous, but Bea knew better than to take offense. Having prospered little with his last approach, he was merely changing tactics again.

When this new strategy failed to win the approval of his company, he turned his attention to his own suffering, which he believed had been given short shrift. With little doubt, tarnishing Mayhew and Co. was the true motive behind the senselessly violent act. "Someone is attempting to destroy my reputation, and by asking me irrelevant questions, you are allowing it to happen. I beg you, please, turn your attention to who would want to do me harm. That is how you will find the killer."

Amused despite herself by his persistence, she affected effusive concern and urged him to compile a list of persons who he believed might want to hurt him. "You shall pursue that aspect of the investigation while Kesgrave and I pursue another."

Mr. Mayhew did not like that at all, being relegated to his own subordinate task, but before he could protest, Bea asked if they could speak to his wife while he was composing his list. His countenance lightened even as he professed himself unable to comply with her request, for the poor dear was currently indisposed. "She slept quite horribly last night, and her nerves are monstrously unsettled because of these horrendous events. She is not intrepid like you, your grace. She is a delicate female, prone to spells, and the idea of Monsieur Alphonse's head being"—he indicated to a nearby spot with his hand—"there and his body being...uh...well, *there*"—another gesture to an area slightly farther away—"is more than she can bear. I cannot imagine she will be able to leave her dressing room at all today."

One did not have to have a proclivity for detection to perceive his objective, and Bea, deciding not to quibble for the sake of her investigation, allowed herself to be maneuvered into greater intimacy with her neighbor by suggesting they meet with her in her dressing room.

Mr. Mayhew blinked rapidly several times as if taken aback by the proposal and then complimented her grace on the ingenuity of her solution. "Yes, yes, of course, you *must* meet with her in her dressing room. I am sure she will have just enough vigor to entertain you there. You are so clever to have thought of it."

Bea dipped her head in acknowledgment and refrained from seeking out Kesgrave's gaze, for she knew he could not be pleased with the familiarity.

The banker, barely able to contain his enthusiasm, summoned Henry and instructed him to deliver the fresh tray to Mrs. Mayhew's dressing room. Then, bouncing with a sort of suppressed delight, he led them into the hall. As much as he resented her for destroying the comfortable little fiction he had arranged with the constable, he was equally deter-mined to make the most of the situation, and Bea, following him into the corridor, wondered again about the depth of his cool calculation.

Chapter Ten

❧

The fact that Mrs. Mayhew's dressing room could not comfortably accommodate visitors merely underscored the severity of the situation. Only in a circumstance so utterly dire would she consent to allow her husband to lean against the wall for support, as if he were some sort of cleaning implement like a mop or a broom. And for the Duke of Kesgrave to sit on the rickety John Cobb chair—it was a beloved antique, yes, handed down from her mother's mother, but so unreliable! Only the thought of Monsieur Alphonse's desecrated corpse could distract her from the sight of the duke wobbling back and forth on its uneven legs like a ship on a roiling sea.

"I knew it could not have been his chopping device," Mrs. Mayhew said softly, her tone bearing no sense of satisfaction at having her conclusion affirmed. She was a small woman about a decade and a half younger than her husband, with porcelain skin, pale blue eyes and a languid affect, which she attributed to the shock of that morning's events. Ordinarily, she was a far more animated hostess. "It is too dainty, I thought, like a miniature version for a dollhouse, and while

Monsieur Alphonse was not a large man by any measure, he certainly was not the size of a doll. I thought for certain it had to be something else, but I did not say anything to Mr. Mayhew because I hated to upset him further. He was already so distressed by Monsieur Alphonse's death, and devoting all his attention to getting rid of the device appeared to settle his nerves, so I did not interfere."

Although the rebuke was minor, the banker was not immune to its effects and he straightened his shoulders, pulling them slightly away from the narrow slice of teal blue wall that was available to him. The rest of the perimeter was adorned with either paintings of pheasants and cherubic children or furniture required for the presentation of a well-turned-out female, such as a dressing table with a mirror, a dressing screen in the pastoral mode, and a pair of mahogany cabinets. Like the room itself, the dressing table was heaving with necessities: ribbons, brushes, toilet water, dentifrice, perfume, laudanum, vinegar, face powder, soap, a sponge. Above it hung a handsome rosewood clock with mother-of-pearl inlay.

Mr. Mayhew, defending his actions, explained stiffly to his wife that he thought he was destroying a deadly apparatus. "I could not stand by and allow other servants to get hurt."

At once, Mrs. Mayhew's expression turned fond. "You are so good and thoughtful, my dear."

Her husband demurred and insisted that ensuring no other members of their staff suffered fatal injuries in their kitchen was the very least he could do.

But Mrs. Mayhew refused to be swayed and chastised him for being unduly humble. Then she said to Bea, "He is always underestimating his own abilities. It comes, I believe, from having four younger brothers who often question his judgment. Each one would like to be head of the London bank rather than overseeing a subsidiary concern in the provinces."

As Mr. Mayhew had failed to mention any siblings in his lengthy narration of his family's illustrious history, Bea had no idea he had any, let alone so many. In his version of events, he was the lone successor of generations of greatness, and she could not decide if it was vanity or arrogance that allowed for the erasure of the rest of his family.

Now the banker was the one who looked fondly at his spouse as he explained that his wife's affection for him tended to color her perception of reality. "I assure you my brothers are quite satisfied with my leadership and have no interest in assuming control of the bank. They enjoy life in the country and have no desire to move to the capital. Furthermore, they are grateful not to have to worry about business issues all the time."

Mrs. Mayhew shook her head, as if contending with a familiar matter, and announced that she was permitted to deem her husband heroic if it suited her.

The banker, browbeaten into being admired, said meekly, "Yes, of course, my dear."

Although the exchange revealed a good deal about the couple's relationship, it did nothing to move the investigation forward and Bea prodded the interview back to the original topic by asking Mrs. Mayhew about her dealings with the chef. "Were they cordial?"

Sighing deeply, with either exhaustion or regret, she replied, "Oh, yes, they were, quite cordial. But I did not have much cause to associate with him. As having a masterful French chef was an extension of the bank, Mr. Mayhew oversaw most aspects of his employment. Naturally, I would step in from time to time—like Thursday, for example, when he was called away on business, I met with Monsieur Alphonse and Mrs. Blewitt, our housekeeper, to finalize the details of the menu for last night's little gathering. But other than those few occasions, we had little interaction. But he was always so perfectly lovely when we did meet. He had such an unusual temperament for a chef, so composed and amiable. Nothing seemed to ruffle him, not even when a kitchen maid scalded the *velouté* an hour before the regent arrived. By all accounts, he just shrugged, which was so delightfully Gallic of him, and began to make the sauce again."

"I have heard about his calm disposition from several people now," Bea observed.

"He was a tranquil soul, our Monsieur Alphonse," she said warmly. "It was a trifle disconcerting when he first arrived because one expects one's French chef to be demanding and tyrannical, and it seemed like perhaps he was not quite as excellent as he was reported to be, for surely he should lose his temper sometime. Creation is a force, is it not, your grace?"

Bea nodded vaguely and said, "And given his tranquil soul, what do you make of his violent argument with Mr. Mayhew yesterday?"

Her hostess blinked several times, as if not comprehending the query, then turned to her husband and gently upbraided him for provoking the poor chef when his temper was already frayed by dinner preparations. "I know it was only a small party, but your guests were so important," she said before providing Bea with a list of attendees. It was obvious from her air of expectation that she thought the new duchess would be impressed with her connections, but she managed to hide her disappointment when none of the names sparked recognition. "I suppose even someone as evenly tempered as Monsieur Alphonse could not help but lose his patience every once in a while. I am sure Mr. Mayhew did not mean to goad him, did you, my love?"

Emphatically, the banker did not! His entire ruse had

been devised around the purpose of placating the man indefinitely.

Learning now of the ploy, his wife chided him for failing to plan for every contingency. "It was inevitable, I think, that he would decide to pay a call on the bank to meet the man who held sway over his future. I do not blame him at all for getting so wretchedly upset, for it was an unkind trick to play on a beloved member of our household. But recriminations must wait," Mrs. Mayhew said sadly, "for focusing on the mistakes of the past will bring us no closer to discovering who did this unimaginable thing. I trust you will tell me, your grace, how I may be of help. Is there other information I can provide?"

Although Bea agreed wholeheartedly with Mrs. Mayhew's opinion of the long-term prospects of her husband's scheme, she could not overlook the timing of Mr. Réjane's curiosity. As likely as it was that he would eventually desire to meet the banker who would decide his loan, it was still strange that he decided to make the visit on the morning of an important dinner party. What had made the meeting so urgent that it could not wait one more day?

"How did Monsieur Alphonse seem to you when you met to finalize the menu?" Bea asked, trying to identify the moment when something could have gone awry for the chef.

Mrs. Mayhew's brow furrowed in confusion. "The same as always: cheerful, thoughtful, eager to return to the kitchen. For the main course he was making quail *à la Saint-Jacques,* a delightful dish we have served at least a dozen times before so he was confident in its execution. Is that what you mean? I'm not sure I understand the question."

But Bea rather thought she did, for this was exactly the information she sought. As of the time of Mrs. Mayhew's conference with Mr. Réjane and the housekeeper, the chef had appeared untroubled. Whatever spurred his visit to the bank had not yet occurred.

"What time was your meeting?" Bea asked.

Mrs. Mayhew pressed her lips together thoughtfully and said four o'clock. "Or a little after. Maybe a little before? I rarely look at the clock. I am sure Mrs. Blewitt will be able to supply the precise time. Have you spoken to her? If you are going to conduct a thorough investigation, then you must interview all the servants. It is the only way to get a complete picture of the horrible event as it transpired."

Bea agreed that an interrogation of the full staff was required and noted the look of delight that flitted across the other woman's face.

"You must remain as long as necessary to find the villain," Mrs. Mayhew said soberly. "The situation is highly unusual, but we do not mind at all. In truth, we are gratified by your interest, are we not, Mr. Mayhew?"

Her husband concurred, and taking advantage of their willingness to cooperate, Bea asked them both to account for their movements during the night—between one-thirty and five a.m. specifically.

Deeply offended, the banker inhaled sharply and said, "Well, I never!"

But of course he had—and within the past hour, for Bea's earlier interrogation had clearly implied that she considered him among her list of suspects. Possibly, he was insulted on his wife's behalf. Regardless, there was far less space in the modest-size dressing room for bounding around the floor in a temper and he contended himself with huffing repeatedly. His wife, in contrast, recovered just enough vigor to clap her hands together merrily and announce that it was above all good things to be suspected of murder by the Duchess of Kesgrave.

"In all my calculations, it is the one thing I never considered," Mrs. Mayhew admitted freely. "As you are our new neighbor, I've imagined our meeting a dozen different ways. I hope you won't mind if I tell you I was determined to make your acquaintance. I have watched your recent career with much interest, for I knew you would soon be occupying Kesgrave House and I wanted to make sure we had conversation. But discussing my whereabouts at two in the morning?" She trilled in amusement as she shook her head. "No amount of planning could account for that. I was here, actually, in this very room, for I had a terrible nightmare and woke up to discover my maid, Annette, holding my shoulders and trying to shake me free of the horrible dream. I was too unsettled to go back to sleep so I requested that she read to me for a while. I am not sure how long. We can ask her. Eventually I felt calm enough to return to my bed. I did not wake again until half past nine, which is when Annette told me the horrible news." The little burst of high spirits that had carried her through the narration fled as she searched out her husband's eyes and added softly, "From one nightmare to another. I am so relieved the children are away at school and know nothing of this. That would be yet another horror."

Her husband agreed fervently with this statement and took the opportunity to tell the duke about his three highly intelligent boys, who were studying at Eton.

Bea, recognizing it as the delaying tactic it no doubt was, reminded the banker that they were waiting for him to detail his movements.

Churlishly, he said, "My valet can provide you with the precise time I went to bed, but I believe it was around one, and Parsons woke me with the horrific news soon after he discovered the body. I do not have someone to account for my specific movements in the interim, but I trust that is not necessary."

Well, obviously, it was, for that was the exact purpose of

the exercise, removing him from suspicion based on an insur-mountable alibi. Nevertheless, she accepted it without comment because she was grateful he had provided the infor-mation without arguing further.

"What else can we tell you?" Mrs. Mayhew asked eagerly, darting a meaningful look at her husband, whose expression was not nearly as congenial as hers. "We are determined to be of as much assistance as possible in hopes of furthering our association. I want you to find us to be the most helpful suspects you have ever had the pleasure of questioning."

"Yes," Mr. Mayhew said with a tight smile, making, Bea thought, a sincere effort to comply with his spouse's wishes, "the most helpful suspects ever."

Although the wife was as determined to use the dead chef's gruesome murder to satisfy her social ambition as the husband, Bea was far less appalled by her forthright approach than Mr. Mayhew's manipulative one. It was amusing, how frankly she spoke, almost artless and winsome.

Bea glanced at the duke to see how he received Mrs. Mayhew's offer to help and noted he was also diverted by its extravagance. The object of three decades' worth of toadying, he had naturally assumed he had been subjected to every form of sycophancy, and yet there he was, married to Miss Hyde-Clare for a single day, and already he had been intro-duced to a new level of fawning.

As if aware of the tenor of her thoughts, Kesgrave dipped his head in acknowledgment.

Returning her attention to the Mayhews, Bea asked who among the household did they think could be capable of such a crime.

"Nobody!" Mrs. Mayhew said with vehemence. "I cannot imagine a single one of our servants responding to anything with such severe brutality."

Fervently, the banker echoed her sentiment.

"You mentioned the kitchen maid scalding the *velouté* sauce. Was that Gertrude?" Bea asked, recalling the stout woman who had scrubbed the blood off the floor and resisted the urge to faint. She seemed to have both the temperament and strength to chop the head off her superior.

"Yes, that is she. Gertrude is a rough-seeming creature but very capable. I am sure the problem with the birds last night was an aberration and won't happen again," she said firmly, then she pressed her lips together tightly as if struggling to hold in strong emotion. After a long pause, she said, "Forgive me, your grace. I just realized there will not be a next time, for we could not possibly serve quail *à la Saint-Jacques* without our beloved chef."

While his wife collected herself, Bea looked at Mr. Mayhew and asked what the issue was with the quails. "You said previously that they were of excellent quality."

"They *were* of excellent quality before the kitchen maid allowed them to dry out," he replied plaintively.

As Mr. Réjane was the one who abandoned the quails to pay a romantical call on the neighbors, Bea did not think it was entirely fair to hold the kitchen maid responsible. Nevertheless, she was not surprised that the person with the lowest rank had to shoulder the most blame. "How did Gertrude and Monsieur Alphonse get along? Was he frustrated by these mistakes?"

Mrs. Mayhew firmly denied any tension between the associates and insisted they rubbed together well. But then she bowed her head in slight abashment and confessed she was not actually privy to the day-to-day management of the kitchens. "I look in from time to time, of course, to make sure everything is as it should be, but I leave the management to Mrs. Blewitt. That said, I assume there was no discord belowstairs because none has bubbled up and I trust you know as well as I do, your grace, how difficult it is to suppress the grumbling of disaffected servants."

As Bea did in fact know this to be true, she accepted the answer and asked the banker if he had any thoughts to add. "Only to reiterate that I believe you are approaching the problem from the wrong perspective. You are assuming the culprit is within the house, but I propose it was a stranger who stole into the house to punish me by cutting Monsieur Alphonse down. The question you should be asking is who wishes to do me harm."

But Bea shook her head and reminded him that per their prior agreement, *he* should be asking that question, not she. "That particular line of inquiry falls under your purview. Divide and conquer, you recall? I will continue to operate under the assumption that Monsieur Alphonse was the target, as I believe that is more likely the case."

Mr. Mayhew did not like this answer and opened his mouth to counter it, but before he could speak, his wife ardently endorsed the conclusion. Then she turned to her husband with her lips in a sympathetic moue and apologized for not being able to offer her support.

"But I wish to align myself with the Duchess of Kesgrave by agreeing with her," she explained before hastily adding that this new alliance did not indicate anything worrisome in her regard for him. "I am as fond of you as ever, my love."

Her claim to affection did little to mollify the banker, who felt that his concerns were not being taken seriously. Mrs. Mayhew cooed soothingly as Bea asked to speak to her maid.

Roused out of his sulks by the request, Mr. Mayhew protested the insult, for his wife's word was inviolate and required no verification from the servants.

"Of course! You must confirm my story with hers," Mrs. Mayhew said with an approving nod as she applauded the duchess for her thoroughness. "Do wait here while I fetch her."

But that would never not do, for it would give the women an opportunity to align their version of events, and Mrs. Mayhew, realizing it a moment after she made the suggestion, chuckled in embarrassment. Instead, she asked her husband to summon the maid using the bell tug in her bedchamber. He complied at once, providing her with the opportunity to lavish praise on him behind his back.

"I love him dreadfully," she confessed, "but he is so unassuming, which I know you might have a little trouble believing because of how greatly he has botched this tragedy. I think he was just so grateful to have a benign excuse that he grasped onto Parsons's understanding with both hands, and naturally his confidence swayed the constable. It is so awkward, isn't it, having a murder in one's very own home. But obviously we want justice for the poor dear and that is why I am so grateful to you for offering to help us make sense of this tragedy. I just wish I knew what Parsons was about, blaming the chopping device. I am sure, though, that his motives are as innocent as my husband's."

Her tone, however, was dubious, and Bea wondered what the other woman knew about the butler's relationship with Mr. Réjane. Any attempt to extract information, however, was thwarted by a smiling assurance that she knew nothing about the interactions among the staff and repeated exhortations that she should apply to the housekeeper for further details.

"If there is anything to know about Parsons's relationship with Monsieur Alphonse, Mrs. Blewitt will be in full possession of the details," she said positively. "But as I said before, it is impossible to ignore feuding servants, so I am certain there is nothing to know."

As she had indeed said this very thing before, Bea began

to wonder if it was a case of protesting too much. Twice she had obliquely referred to friction between Mr. Réjane and other members of the staff: Gertrude and Parsons. Did she truly believe one of them was responsible for the heinous act or was she simply diverting attention away from her husband?

Mrs. Mayhew was a smart woman and knew how suspicious her husband's behavior in regard to *le peu* appeared. She had remarked upon it twice now.

What did it say about a man's innocence when even his wife feared he might be guilty, Bea wondered.

Before she could arrive at a conclusion, Mayhew came back and a few minutes later his wife's maid rapped lightly on the door. As she entered the room, Kesgrave rose to his feet to give her his seat, but Mrs. Mayhew, unable to bear the thought of a duke *standing* in her dressing room, jumped up and said Annette must use her chair. A second later, however, she realized that meant returning the duke to his rickety seat, which was also untenable, and she directed her maid to take the recently vacated chair, then urged Kesgrave to assume her own.

The banker nodded his approval and seconded the antics by insisting Annette had excellent balance, but his wife, worried the observation implied that the duke's equilibrium was less than exceptional, insisted that Kesgrave return to the wobbly heirloom.

As ingratiating as always, Mr. Mayhew agreed enthusiastically with this revised plan, announcing that his faith in the duke's balance was absolute, and Kesgrave, no doubt as irritated by their fatuousness as by their servility, shuffled the pair out of the room so that he and Bea could have a candid conversation with the maid. As the door closed in her face, Mrs. Mayhew lauded his practical-minded approach ("With a killer afoot, there is no time to dawdle!").

The maid stood silently during the exchange, and Bea,

assuming she felt reluctant to sit in their company, urged her to take the seat.

"We have only a few questions," she explained. "I trust you know why we are here."

Annette—a rail-thin women of modest height, olive skin and a slightly crooked nose—nodded definitively. "Oh, yes, your grace. The whole house knows. Everyone is talking about it."

Bea was tempted to ask what the servants were saying, for the ones who were critical of her interference might have the most reason to resent it, but she did not want to start off the interview by appearing to pry excessively. Her first question, therefore, was simply a request that she describe the events of the night before and early morning.

Concisely, she detailed helping her mistress change into her nightclothes after the party had ended, which was around eleven o'clock. Mrs. Mayhew was in a cheerful mood because of the success of the dinner. Everything had gone according to plan, and their guests had left very well satisfied with the quality of care they had received.

"She was very chatty and wanted to review every moment of the night, which is not unusual," Annette explained. "She is always talkative when things go well. After she changed into her nightclothes, she sat down at the table in her dressing room to record a few thoughts in her notebook, reminders to herself about little things that can be improved next time. Then she drank a glass of warm milk and said she would read for a while in bed. She was far too tired, though, the poor lamb, and fell asleep almost immediately. I blew out her candles, dampened the fire and turned in myself. That was around midnight."

Bea nodded, as this information conformed with what Mrs. Mayhew had said. "And your bedchamber is where?"

"Just there," she said, pointing to a door partially hidden

by the wardrobe. "It's a cozy space. I also perform many of my chores in there. It's close enough that I can hear Mrs. Mayhew call out for me, but there is also a bell. She rarely uses it because I usually hear her."

"Did she use it this morning?" Bea asked with deliberate vagueness.

Emphatically, Annette shook her head. "You mean when she woke up from her nightmare? Oh, no, not at all. She did not have the ability to think that clearly. She was just terrified, shaking and heaving, and her eyes were blind for a moment. I lit the candle and looked straight at her and I swear she couldn't see me. It was so awful. I've never seen her like that."

"Does she have nightmares often?" Bea asked.

"I wouldn't say *often,* but every now and then, yes," the maid replied cautiously. "But it's more like a little upset and she rings for me and I read to her in bed for a short while. Usually, she falls back to sleep within a half hour. But this one was so unsettling she couldn't stay in her bed and requested I read to her in the dressing room with all the candles lit. I think she was afraid if she stayed in bed, she might fall asleep and have the same awful dream. So we remained in the dressing room and I read to her for a couple of hours."

Again, this aligned closely with what the other woman said and allowed Bea to remove both women from her list of possible suspects. "Do you recall the time Mrs. Mayhew woke up and when she was ready to go back to sleep?"

"I do, yes, it was a little after one-thirty when she woke and coming up on four when she felt calm enough to try sleeping again. She was so upset by it all. She hated the fact that we would both lose sleep and kept looking at the clock, as if deeply distressed that it was growing so late. I told her not to worry because she had no reason to get up early in the morning. Of course, we could never have imagined...." She sighed deeply and let the thought trail off. "Then to awaken to the terrible news. It was devastating."

"And what time was that?" Bea asked.

"Eight-thirty. I dressed myself, then pressed Mrs. Mayhew's pistache morning dress. At nine fifteen, I went downstairs to collect her tray and that is when I learned what had happened. I rushed upstairs to tell the mistress. She was so distressed, she fainted at once. I think it was the lack of sleep. She was already so tired. I ran to the dressing room to fetch her smelling salts, but I couldn't find them. I looked everywhere and made such a mess of everything in my frantic search. My wits were a bit scattered by everything, and I flew downstairs in a panic, which upset Mr. Mayhew, who feared his wife might be seriously injured. I told him she had fainted onto the bed, but he was so anxious and I was anxious and it was a relief when Mr. Parsons volunteered to borrow smelling salts from the neighbors. He was a godsend and returned quickly, but the poor lamb…. I am not sure waking her was an act of kindness because she was so deeply disturbed by it all. She cannot believe something so dreadful could happen in her very own home," she said, looking down at her hands, which were clenched now in her lap. Then she added softly, "None of us can. Everyone is so upset, even Mr. Stebbings."

Tilting her head curiously, Bea asked who Mr. Stebbings was and why his distress was noteworthy.

"He's Mr. Mayhew's valet, your grace," Annette replied, "and resented the cheroots."

"The cheroots?" Bea said.

"Every so often, when he was in a particularly generous mood, Mr. Mayhew would give Monsieur Alphonse a cheroot from his personal stock," the maid explained. "It is a token of his appreciation that he has never extended to Mr. Stebbings, which he considers to be a great personal slight. Or so his numerous complaints in recent months have led me to believe."

Bea was not familiar enough with relations with one's valet to know if this was a legitimate grievance or not. In a more traditional arrangement, he would be ranked higher than the cook, but Mr. Réjane could not be described in such pedestrian terms. He was a master of the culinary arts, an innovator of *la grande cuisine* and a vital aspect in Mr. Mayhew's business endeavor. Giving him the odd cheroot did not strike her as outlandish.

Could Stebbings's sense of hierarchy be that severe?

Ah, but to chop off your colleague's head simply because your employer appeared to favor him?

It was a decidedly disproportionate response.

Perhaps seeing doubt on Beatrice's face, the maid added Mr. Stebbings had got into a fierce argument with Monsieur Alphonse the day before. "He could be heard yelling at him in Mr. Mayhew's dressing room."

The location of the quarrel was quite interesting, for what cause could the chef have to be in his master's dressing room. "Was is common for Monsieur Alphonse to be there?"

Annette could not say, as she did not closely monitor the victim's movements. "But I would not be surprised if he had gone in there before to look for a cheroot. He had a habit of doing whatever he wanted. That, too, might have rubbed Mr. Stebbings the wrong way."

Bea, who had already planned on confirming Mr. Mayhew's own account with his valet, thanked Annette for her time and requested that she send for Stebbings. The maid complied at once, rising to her feet and executing a smooth curtsey before striding to the door. Standing on the other side, eager to be of service, were the Mayhews, and although Bea assured the couple they did not require refreshments, the banker pushed his elbow into the opening before Bea could close the door.

"I have an excellent Haut-Brion in the cellar that I have been saving for a special occasion," he added as inducement. "I would be delighted to open the bottle and toast to your happiness while we wait for Stebbings."

Firmly, Bea thanked him for the generous offer but explained that it was essential to their investigation that she and the duke have a moment to confer privately before their next interview. Mr. Mayhew, attempting to insert himself again into the process, responded with his qualifications, for as a banker he was accustomed to private conferences and knew many tactics for conducing successful interviews.

He barely managed to remove his arm before Bea shut the door.

Even so, she could still hear him on the other side cataloguing his skills.

Having never had anyone be overly eager to assist her before, she knew the problem was uniquely the fault of the duke. If he had been a second son—or even a third or fourth or someone wholly unimportant—then she would not have vexatiously obsequious bankers risking damage to their limbs to curry her favor.

"Fie on you, Kesgrave," she said with mild exasperation as she heard Mrs. Mayhew offer muffled consolation to her husband.

The duke, who was accustomed to accepting blame even when he did not know its cause, approached Bea with amusement flickering in his eyes. "Oh, no, brat, not this time. If you have any complaints about your current situation, you must lodge them with yourself, for interviewing servants in the tiny dressing room of the wife of a toadying banker was not on my list of activities for the afternoon. If you recall, I had suggested we have an informal dinner in our bedchamber.

Indeed, according to my itinerary, you should be trembling beneath me right now, not waiting to ask a valet about his tussle with a dead chef."

It hit her hard, the surge of emotion that swept through her at these words, the wave of desire that washed over her. All at once, it was impossible to breathe and difficult to stand and she pressed her back against the frame of the door for additional support.

How casually he said it—*trembling beneath me*—how coolly, as if they were still discussing Mr. Réjane's cheroots.

Was this how it would be going forward, the sublime tossed carelessly into the mundane?

Forcefully, she drew air into her lungs and took two steps away from the door to prove to herself she was sturdy on her own. Then she curled her fingers to resist the compulsion to touch him and, striving to match his nonchalant tone, said, "Although I now have a keen understanding of how a duke may manipulate time, I also have a passing acquaintance with the clock mechanism. There is one on the wall over there, which is how I know that, according to your own schedule, you would still be bracketed in your study with Mr. Stephens discussing the roofs. I would not be trembling beneath you for another one hour and forty-eight minutes."

A light entered his eyes, hot and fierce, and observing it, Bea felt a strange mix of potency and powerlessness. It was, despite the absurdity of their location and the knock on the door signaling the arrival of Stebbings, a welcome sensation because it made her feel giddy and happy to be in the absurd location awaiting her next suspect.

The annoyance she had felt at Mr. Mayhew's enervating neediness lifted as she stepped farther away from the door.

Kesgrave, assuming an air of fresh understanding, announced that he began to perceive at last why she nurtured such a sharp dislike of dukes. "You are under the misapprehension that we possess magical abilities like Merlin or a sorcerer in a fairy story. Rest assured, my dear, I can no more manipulate time than I can control fire. That said, the clock on the wall over there is off by several minutes, for in fact you should be trembling beneath me in one hour and *fifty-one* minutes."

Naturally, she was compelled to point out the pedantry that required him to account for three minutes.

Although he usually submitted meekly to the frequent charge, he caviled now at the allegation, for it was not a fondness for accuracy that motived him. "Rather, when you regret your decision to alter our schedule—and I am confident you will very shortly—I want to make sure you lament *every* minute."

Smothering a grin, Bea opened the door to admit the valet and, realizing she could not bear to listen to Mrs. Mayhew prattle anxiously again about the wobbliness of the John Cobb chair, asked to be conducted to the servants' hall.

Chapter Eleven

Mrs. *Blewitt, in accordance* with the behavior of her fellow servants, was eager to blame another member of the staff for Mr. Réjane's horrendous decapitation. To her credit, however, she managed to patiently answer several of Beatrice's questions before forcefully pointing her finger.

Calmly, she recounted her movements during the relevant interval in helpful detail, explaining that after reviewing all the items in the pantry so that she could replenish the stores the following day, she had inspected the kitchen to make sure it was up to her cleanliness standards. Then she retired to her room, performed her nightly ablutions, said her prayers and climbed into bed. Although she had not checked the clock specifically to see the hour, she felt strongly it was a little after one.

Furthermore, she readily owned to having a longstanding disagreement with Monsieur Alphonse regarding the plants she chose to cultivate in the little courtyard garden. It was a trifle annoying, yes, the way the Frenchman repeatedly derided her rosebushes, but certainly nothing over which she bore him a grudge.

"He would have preferred that I grow onions," she explained, "because he thought you could never have too many of them. I am sure that is true, but my garden is an English one and must contain roses. I told him I was happy to share the plottage so that he may grow his own crops, but he had no interest in doing the work. I think he just enjoyed tweaking me about my roses. I did not mind in the least. It was like a game to him. Monsieur Alphonse did not take many things seriously. I understood that."

As the chef's nonchalant attitude had been mentioned in several interviews, Bea nodded absently at this statement and opened her mouth to question the nature of the disagreement, which had been described to her in considerably harsher terms by the scullery maid.

Before she could utter a word, however, Mrs. Blewitt's placidity broke and she cried plaintively, "But I do not understand why you are asking all these questions about my behavior when you must already know who the killer is. It's Gertrude. Gertrude hated Monsieur Alphonse and everyone knows it. She could not bear how freely he moved about the house, coming and going as often as he pleased. Every time he wandered out of the kitchen to walk around the square or visit Gunter's, she seethed with anger, and he wandered out all the time, whenever the mood struck. It happened just yesterday! In the middle of preparations for the party! He simply disappeared for almost an hour, leaving the pots boiling and the quails roasting and not telling a soul. Gertrude was beside herself. I have never seen anyone so angry. She roamed the kitchen, muttering to herself and brandishing a ladle like it was a club. I really thought she was going to knock him on the head as soon as he returned. I was prepared to intercede before things got out of hand, but eventually she remembered to check on the quails and returned to work. Even so she could not stop muttering. I paid it no heed because she was always fuming about one thing he did or another. Also, the kitchen boy spilled a bowl of cream and that created another uproar. But then this morning...when I saw...when I saw...his body..."

She lowered her head ignominiously and confessed that she had been so distraught to realize what Gertrude had done, she had fainted dead away.

"Never in my life have I behaved with such abandon," she confessed, falling silent again.

A moment later, however, she continued without prompting. "When I saw what had happened to him, I realized that I'd misjudged Gertrude. Her anger had not subsided but had grown worse and terrible. She's the one you are looking for, your grace. It pains me greatly to say it, for I have worked alongside her for four years, but the truth cannot be suppressed: Gertrude Vickers killed Monsieur Alphonse. May God have mercy on her soul."

Curiously, Stebbings, the valet, had said almost the exact same thing about Henry Pearce, the brown-haired footman who had requested Bea's calling card before allowing her to enter the house. He had made the accusation with a hint of outrage in his voice, as if he could not believe he had to defend his own behavior when a man like Henry was allowed to roam freely.

"Did I lose my temper when I saw Monsieur Alphonse standing on Mr. Mayhew's coat—the *silk* weave with the *cerulean* stripes?" the valet had asked, his tone reasonable. "Why, yes, I did, and I defy any man of sense and feeling to act with total equanimity when confronted with wantonly abused silk. Did I wish he had more respect for the fine quality of Mr. Mayhew's wardrobe? Without question, I'd begged him before to take more care when looking for a cheroot. Indeed, I had advised him to stop treating the master's dressing room as his own private tobacconist. Did I slice his head off because of it? Good gracious, no. As beautiful as it is and as flattering to Mr. Mayhew's frame as its tailoring is, it is just a coat, and I have the sense to realize it is just a coat. But I will tell you who doesn't have that sense of proportion: Henry Pearce."

Bolstering his argument, he'd cited the footman's ready temper, which had been frayed by months of little sleep because he shared a wall with the chef, who snored loudly. "He would be up all night long listening to the thunderous noise. Some nights he cannot get a single minute of sleep. I am not surprised he finally reached his limit and snapped. He is, you will notice, disconcertingly robust. He carries wood up to the top floor several times a day, and he can lift the drawing room table all by himself. I can do neither," Stebbings added, "for I would never do anything so uncouth as develop muscles. They ruin the lines of one's jacket. I can barely slice through a joint of mutton without causing a muscle strain."

More curious yet, Henry had described Mr. Laurent, the groom, in similar terms when *he* had identified *him* as the murderer.

"Obviously, you have to look at who among the staff has the ability to do something like this," the footman had pointed out pragmatically. "Mentally, I mean, not just physically, and in that case you must consider Mr. Laurent as a suspect because he has a habit of treating people like horses. I've seen him put down an injured mare without flinching. And he had a terrible row with Monsieur Alphonse yesterday morning because he took one of the horses without asking. He had done it before and Mr. Laurent had warned him that it could not continue, but Monsieur Alphonse ignored him and did it anyway."

In actuality, the similarities in the servants' behavior—Mrs. Blewitt, Henry, Laurent, Stebbings—were not curious at all, for the impulse to drive suspicion away from oneself and toward another was perfectly valid given the circumstance. To know that someone in the house, someone with whom you worked closely, someone with whom you interacted on a daily basis, was capable of cutting off your associate's head with a meat cleaver was a disturbing proposition at best. At worst, it was a truly terrifying notion to consider, an insidious waking nightmare that crept up your spine like a chittering scarab as you pondered who might be next.

It was little wonder the servants were examining one another with well-honed suspicion.

But being the next victim was not the only thing they feared. Weighing more heavily on their minds was Bea herself, the Duchess of Kesgrave, suddenly and inexplicably thrusting her nose into their business. And making such a fuss about it too! Had the matter not been settled hours ago? Did the constable not leave the premises at nine-thirty that morning at peace with his determination of accidental death? Why, then, was there a peeress in their own servants' hall eyeing them all distrustfully?

It was only a game to her, was it not, this playing at being a lady Runner. It was what the gentry did, adopting humble roles for their amusement and then throwing them off just as lightly. Marie Antoinette, most famously, constructed an entire peasant village where she could pretend to be a dairy-maid who milked cows and tended the garden.

Number forty-four was just the Duchess of Kesgrave's Hameau de la Reine. She would ask her questions and point her finger like a spinning top landing at random, and then she would move on to the next consuming interest, gratified by her ingenuity, and they would go to the gallows.

Bea knew the comparison to the former queen of France

was excessive, if for no other reason than the parallel was unlikely to occur to any of Mr. Mayhew's servants, but she felt the argument held. They had no reason to trust her, even if they had heard about her confrontation with Lord Wem, and the consequences for them were dire, particularly now that she had assumed a duchy. Her word would be taken on faith, the evidence she presented accepted as gospel truth, and the person she deemed guilty would be crushed under the wheels of justice.

There would be no genteel exile to the wilds of Italy.

She had not noticed it at first, the way her new status was altering her investigation, pulling it in strange directions so that it did not form a familiar shape. Rather, it produced a line that squiggled from one edge of the paper to the other, haphazardly bouncing in enthusiastic confusion. Unlike the lovely curls Dolly had arranged, the power conferred on her by marriage—the clout she possessed, the influence she wielded—was an intangible thing she could not see when she looked in the mirror. She could only see it now in the eyes of her respondents.

Having Kesgrave beside her, of course, did little to mitigate the problem, for even if the staff somehow managed to forget who she was, he was right there to remind them. Silently, he sat in the room, judging the proceedings and adding to her consequences.

'Twas the very devil!

Marlow, no doubt, would attribute every advance she made in her investigation to the duke's commanding presence.

Even so, she could not resent his company. The transition from spinster to wife had been so jarring—wonderful, to be sure, but also swift and unsettling—that she could feel only relief in the familiarity of the situation. So much had changed in the past twenty-four hours, and yet his belief in her ability remained unaltered.

Whatever happened later, whatever reasonable objection he made to his wife's unusual avocation, she would have the knowledge of his enduring respect.

It would have to be enough.

Mindful of her authority, Bea answered Mrs. Blewitt's accusation with a mild nod. She kept her expression neutral, deliberately bland, because she did not want to encourage the housekeeper to add elaborate details to her narration in order to make her associate appear guilty. At the same time, she did not want to discourage her from providing vital information.

It was, she acknowledged with a faint hint of exhaustion, a difficult fence to straddle, and struggling to maintain her balance, she found herself longing for the nonthreatening drabness of Beatrice Hyde-Clare.

Mrs. Blewitt, however, was disconcerted by the underwhelming reply and asked curtly if Bea had heard her clearly. The servant remembered herself a moment later, lowered her head and mumbled an apology, which she immediately repeated with more coherence.

"Gertrude is the kitchen maid?" Bea asked, recalling that Mrs. Mayhew had mentioned her as well. She had scalded the *velouté*, and Mr. Réjane, according the report, handled the incident with equanimity.

Could his measured approach have had the opposite of its intended effect and somehow created resentment?

"Yes," Mrs. Blewitt said.

"I will make a note of it," Bea said, thanking her for the information and promising to speak with her next. "First I would like to hear more about your argument with Monsieur Alphonse."

"I do not think there is anything else to add," Mrs. Blewitt replied. "We quibbled about the roses as we frequently do, then, as I said, I went to the pantry to assess our needs for the coming week, inspected the kitchen and went to bed. As it was a longstanding disagreement, I do not think you need to put too fine a point on it, your grace. We bickered but bore each other no ill will. Monsieur Alphonse was a fine cook and an excellent card player. On quiet evenings we would play whist for ha'penny a point well into the night."

Bea acknowledged this assertion with another noncommittal nod, for a claim of friendship with the victim was another common feature of her interviews.

By all accounts, the dead chef had rubbed along well with the entire household: Edward Laurent, the groom, a fellow French exile whose shared heritage forged a nigh-on-unbreakable bond; Martin Stebbings, the valet, who considered the victim to be as a father, often seeking his advice on personal matters; and Henry Peace, the footman, whose success at nine pins had increased considerably since the victim had begun instructing him on the game's finer points.

For every tale of Mr. Réjane's selfishness, privilege or general inconsideration she heard, she was treated to three more describing his generosity, thoughtfulness and good humor.

The barrage of stories, the way they seemed to volley from cruel to kind and kind to cruel, further squiggled the shape she was trying to discern. After speaking to almost the entire staff, she still could not identify a single cohesive narrative amid the jumble of noise. It was all clamor—screechy and distorting—and she didn't know what to think.

Indeed, the only thing she knew for certain was that she had failed to eliminate a single suspect from her list, other than Mrs. Mayhew and her maid. Everyone to whom she had spoken had both an opportunity to harm the victim and a reason to wish him ill.

And everyone, just like Mrs. Blewitt, had professed bewilderment when she broached the subject of their disagreement with the renowned chef.

Kindly, Bea said to the housekeeper, "I do not doubt that there was much you admired about Monsieur Alphonse. He seems to have been well liked among the servants. That said, you were seen threatening him with a shovel at one in the morning, which is after the time you claimed to have retired to bed. I trust you perceive why I doubt your statement."

A trapped look entered the housekeeper's eye as she realized she would not be able to brazen out the interview with an audacious lie. Abruptly, she glanced at Kesgrave, then swiftly returned her attention to Bea, and in the brief moment, in that fleeting gaze, the new duchess felt an entire tragedy play out: act one, act two, act three.

Bea wanted to say something to ease Mrs. Blewitt's terror, to assure her that she had nothing to worry about, that she was just gathering information. But knowing nothing of the shape of the crime, Bea could draw no conclusions about the housekeeper's culpability. Any reassurances she offered would be empty.

Breathing heavily, as if struggling for control, Mrs. Blewitt said that she did perceive the problem and apologized for trying to misdirect her grace. "We did have our usual quarrel about the roses—truly, I swear. I noticed that he was standing on one of the branches and I kindly asked him to please tread carefully, for he was always trampling them. He insisted he was not standing *on* the bush, just *next* to it, but I have eyes. I know what I saw. We argued heatedly because he refused to acknowledge that he had done anything wrong. I could tell he was determined to be unreasonable about it so I left in a lather and went to the pantry to assess our supply needs. But before going to bed, I visited the kitchen to make sure everything was in order and I saw him out in the garden smoking a cheroot with two dozen uprooted rosebushes around him. He had dug them up with the shovel," she said, her fury at the vandalism still strong. "He'd rooted them all out and then he said to me with a smirk, '*Now* I've trampled them.' It's true, I was angry. I don't think I've ever been so angry in my whole life so, yes, I raised the shovel over my head and said I would show him trampled." Her eyes were dark brown spots against her white face. "But that's all I did. As soon as I realized how heated I had got, I was horrified by my lack of control. I dropped the shovel, ran out of the garden and into my room, shut the door and sat at my table for several minutes while I struggled to calm down. Then I got ready for bed, prayed for the patience to deal with Monsieur Alphonse's mercurial nature and went to sleep."

Thoughtfully, Bea nodded and asked the woman if she knew Monsieur Alphonse had resigned his position.

Mrs. Blewitt, her hands shaking slightly, said she had heard talk of it today but had no idea of his plans when they had their confrontation the night before. "Do you think that is why he was so cruel? Because he knew he was leaving?"

Obviously, Bea could not ascribe any motive to the dead man, but she thought it was more likely his ordinarily mellow temper had been frayed by the events of a long and disappointing day. Not only did he discover that his employer planned to deceive him indefinitely in order to avoid granting his loan request, he also learned that the woman he loved did not return his regard with enough ardor to justify moving away from her mother. It was little wonder he had released his anger and frustration on the poor rosebushes and Mr. Mayhew's silk waistcoat.

Bea posited that perhaps he was tired, and Mrs. Blewitt nodded sadly.

As deeply ashamed as she was by her unrestrained response, the housekeeper felt it paled in comparison to the kitchen maid's inability to control herself. "I behaved immoderately once, but Gertrude regularly threatened Monsieur Alphonse with whatever she had at hand: a bellows, knife, a spatula, a trivet, a *cleaver*. She was never particular about the item, only about finally giving that Frenchie his comeuppance. And if you had seen the way she'd swung the ladle yesterday, the slash it made in the air as it went back and forth…the crack it would have made if it had smashed into someone's skull, you would have some concerns."

Bea allowed her the flourish and conceded silently that she would have considered a vengeful ladle to be a matter of grave concern if the victim had been battered to death by the kitchen utensil.

Nevertheless, the housekeeper's list of convenient weapons included a cleaver, which Bea could not ignore and she asked the other woman to describe the incident.

Here, Mrs. Blewitt's confidence faltered, for she did not know which incident to relate. "Horrifyingly, there are too many to count. The most recent one was about a month ago, when Monsieur Alphonse decided to take a stroll around the square while he was preparing *espagnole* to go with the lamb. He told Gertrude to simmer the roux but didn't say for how long and of course it burned because she was also chopping carrots and onions for the soup. It caused an awful mess, even smoked up the kitchen, and she made her usual route around the room, muttering angrily and swinging the cleaver. We all know to give her a wide berth when she is in a mood, which is easy enough because she's a little scary when she gets her dander up. I have overlooked it in the past because she is reliable and efficient. Her anger, while intense, is always fleeting, but this time I fear she was unable to let go of her resentment," she said fiercely before tempering her statement with the caveat that she could be wrong. "Truly, I hope I am."

But Bea rather thought she did not, for if someone was

going to hang for the chef's murder, it might as well be the irascible kitchen maid with a habit of threatening his life.

Although Bea had no more questions, Kesgrave leaned forward and asked where the shovel was now. "I did not see it in the courtyard."

Startled, the housekeeper explained that it had been put away. "I do not know by whom."

The duke nodded and asked her to bring the implement to the room so that he could examine it. Mrs. Blewitt blanched visibly at the request but immediately complied.

Once she had left the room, Bea asked, "You think the killer bashed him over the head with the shovel to render him insensible?"

"I am not quite sure what I think," he confessed. "But I cannot conceive of any man losing his head without making a sustained effort to retain it. None of our suspects have injuries that indicate a violent struggle."

Bea, acknowledging it was a reasonable supposition, added that they had little reason to believe the constable ran his fingers along the contour of the skull to look for a bruise or a bump. "I am sure he was too squeamish to even contemplate the idea."

The housekeeper returned a minute later, her breath slightly shallow as she handed the shovel to the duke. Unremarkable in every way, it had a long handle roughened from use and a broad flat blade about a quarter inch thick. Applied to the back of a man's head, it would certainly knock him out —*if* the assailant was able to raise it high enough in the air to put sufficient heft into the swing.

Mrs. Blewitt, by her own account, possessed the strength to wield it effectively.

Had she?

Esther, the scullery maid who had pointed them toward the housekeeper, certainly thought so.

Or, rather, she claimed to think it in order to support her own agenda.

Smothering a sigh, Bea thanked the housekeeper for her time and requested she send in Gertrude next.

At once Mrs. Blewitt's expression lightened, and she left the room in much better spirits than she'd entered it.

Kesgrave handed the shovel to Bea to inspect. "It's heavy but manageable. Stebbings would claim he could not lift it an inch off the ground."

Bea smiled faintly at the cynical assessment of the valet's performance as she clutched the implement in both hands. Examining the blade, she noted that there did not appear to be any blood on it. "But it is difficult to say because it is so dirty."

"It would not have been necessary to break skin to render Réjane unconscious," Kesgrave said. "All the attacker needed to gain the advantage was to stun him momentarily."

A knock sounded on the door, and Bea leaned the shovel against the wall while bidding the servant to enter. Gertrude Vickers, her arms laden with a tea tray, crossed the threshold and placed the salver on the table. Then she stood awkwardly by the table, an apprehensive expression on her face as she examined the hem of her apron. Clearly, she had heard enough accounts of what went on during these private interviews to worry about her associates' depictions of her.

Seeking to ease some of her discomfort, Bea smiled warmly and asked her to be seated.

The kitchen maid started with surprise and might have argued if she had not the sense to reconsider bickering with a duchess. Gingerly, she lowered herself onto a chair.

Timidity from the woman who had scrupulously scrubbed away all traces of Mr. Réjane's blood from the kitchen floor was unexpected, and Bea wondered if it was the product of a guilty conscience or the natural response to being considered for a murder by an exalted peeress of the realm.

Her discomfort was so acute, she protested her innocence before either Bea or the duke could say a word, her voice trembling with fear and passion as she exclaimed, "I would never, never, never harm Monsieur Alphonse. You must believe me. I never wished him ill. Never!"

Although her tone was forceful, the speech had the paradoxical effect of making her seem frail, a significant accomplishment given the sturdiness of her frame. Everything about her was thick—neck, forearms, even her fingers—and yet Bea worried she might shatter in the next moment.

Clasping the edge of the table with her fingers, she acknowledged that she had her issues with Monsieur Alphonse. "I admit it, I did. It would be stupid to deny it. But I defy anyone to work with him and not lose their temper once in a while. He was impossible, wandering away all the time without telling me he was going out, leaving me to figure it out. Figure it out! His recipes are all so complicated, his techniques so intricate, I never knew what to do. Leave the broth to boil? Take it off the fire? Add more carrots? Remove the onion? He would disappear for an hour or two and leave me in such a state. And yesterday, with the quails. Oh, the quails! They were so dry. I was sure that was the end of the road for me, that Mr. Mayhew would send me away. He was furious about the quails. Monsieur Alphonse's reputation as the finest chef in all of London is vital to his business, and last night he had important clients, whom he was determined to impress, to dine."

As overwhelmed as she already was by information, Bea leaned forward at this tidbit, for it was the first time the banker's presence belowstairs had been mentioned.

And an angry outburst—that was interesting.

"Was it usual for Mr. Mayhew to visit the kitchens during a dinner party to express his displeasure?" Bea asked.

The kitchen maid shook her head vehemently. "Oh, no, no. He had never done it before, which shows how very livid he was about the quails. I feared he might overexert his heart."

As she was not the owner of a large financial concern, Bea could not say how destructive the event was to Mr. Mayhew's business prospects. She did, however, know enough about the requirements of civility to realize absenting oneself from company to chastise the servants was not an acceptable way for a host to behave.

She felt confident the banker knew it too, and yet his anger had so consumed him, he had put aside the demands of etiquette to satisfy his temper. Like the victim, his ability to regulate his behavior had been worn thin by the anxieties of the day. Could it have been made so threadbare that he chopped off the head of his intractable French chef?

Possibly, yes.

It was difficult to rule anything out when one was in a lather.

At the same time, the woman before her had shown herself to be an overt threat.

"And you were the target of his anger, not Monsieur Alphonse?" Bea asked.

Gertrude tightened her grip on the table as she admitted there was no point in getting cross with the victim because he rarely reacted with anything but a dismissive shrug. "You could yell so loudly the glass in the windows would shake, and he would just lift his shoulders carelessly and carry on with his task. It was how he responded to everything, both criticism and praise. He knew he was the best chef in all of London and could leave at any moment and land firmly on his feet. It was why he was always wandering off. His position in this household was secure and there was nothing anyone could say to Mr. Mayhew that would change that."

"Whereas your position is tenuous," Bea observed.

The kitchen maid did not deny it. "But it has been more secure, I think, since Monsieur Alphonse arrived because he is such an excellent chef. Mr. Mayhew's satisfaction with his work extended to me as well. He had no cause to upset the apple cart. The opposite is true as well, though, and last night he was very angry about the quails."

Trying to get a better sense of the state of Mr. Mayhew's emotions, she asked the kitchen maid if she thought the problem was truly the quails.

Gertrude tilted her head to the side as she pursed her lips. "I'm not sure I understand the question, your grace."

"You said that Mr. Mayhew had never visited the kitchens before to complain about the meal, so I was wondering if perhaps he was upset about something else and was only *focusing* on the dry quails," she explained.

Perceiving now the distinction, Gertrude refused to speculate as to the cause of Mr. Mayhew's actions. "With all due respect, it is not my place."

Ah, yes, Bea thought peevishly, the circumspection of servants. They were always eager to gossip about their employer except when directly called upon to.

Very well.

"Let us return, then, to your relationship with Monsieur Alphonse, which has been described as volatile," Bea said.

Gertrude flinched at the description but quietly acknowledged its accuracy. Then, as if realizing it was better to admit to her faults herself rather than allow the gossip of her fellow servants to undermine her standing, she admitted to losing her temper quite frequently. "When I am flustered or don't know how to do something, I respond angrily. Like yesterday, when he left me with the quails. I had no idea he was gone because he did not see fit to tell me and I had no idea how long they had been on the fire, so I became cross and threatened to assault him with the ladle. But I would never actually do it. I threatened all the time to clunk him over the head with ladles and roasting pans and, yes, with a cleaver a few times."

Her face grew paler the longer she spoke until it was almost entirely out of color by the time she mentioned the murder weapon. Heartfully, she continued, trying to impress on Bea how much she liked Monsieur Alphonse. "He had such a carefree way about him he was impossible not to like. He was so generous with his cooking, always experimenting with new dishes and sharing the results with us. Before he came, I had to cook all the meals for the staff on top of my other responsibilities, but Monsieur Alphonse *wanted* to prepare them. There was nothing he enjoyed more than creating recipes and trying new combinations of ingredients. He made some wonderful dishes such as *turbot à la hollandaise* and *salmon à la régence*. It took him more than a half dozen tries to get the flavor of his *potage aux champignon* just right, and each time he used Château d'Yquem wine, adjusting its measure a little bit at a time. I am sure Mr. Mayhew would have a fit if ever found out how much money was being spent on the servants' meals. He did not approve of Monsieur Alphonse creating new dishes. He considered the original assortment to be quite adequate to his needs. Now that Monsieur is gone I will be required to do the cooking again, and I am sure my colleagues will not be delighted with my meat pies, as they had an aversion to them before he arrived."

It was a cogent argument, enlightened self-interest, and Bea found it persuasive. If his presence in the house did in fact lighten her load, then chopping off his head would only increase it. Few kitchen maids were inclined to do that, especially at the risk of going to the gallows. Furthermore, she had been dealing with Mr. Réjane's impetuosity for more than two years, and the fact that she was frequently seen swinging one kitchen implement or another threateningly only lessened the likeliness of her guilt, for it begged the question: Why kill him now?

But the query was disingenuous because the answer was obvious: She had been taken to task by her employer for Mr. Réjane's failing. Although it had been his sudden disappearance that had caused the quails to overcook, Gertrude had suffered the humiliating consequences. Irate at the unfairness, she could have lashed out at the person she held responsible.

While Bea considered the merits of her theory, Kesgrave said, "Château d'Yquem is an expensive wine from the Sauternes region. How did Réjane gain access to Mr. Mayhew's cellar without his permission or knowledge?"

As logical as the question was, especially from a gentleman who possessed a very fine cellar as the Duke of Kesgrave most certainly did, the kitchen maid was surprised by it and sat up sharply in her chair. Visibly uncomfortable, she looked down at her fingers grasping the table and said softly, "He stole the key from Parsons."

Beatrice, who had struggled from the beginning of her investigation to find a convincing motive among the petty squabbles over cheroots and roses, thought she had finally stumbled across something that made sense. Preserving the sanctity of the wine cellar was the butler's single most important responsibility. He was the only member of the household staff who was allowed to enter the room, and he controlled every aspect of the wine: He tracked the stock, kept records of purchases and condition, ensured a varied and balanced assortment of vintages, chose wine to pair with each course. His authority was so complete, he even poured the wine during meals.

The rule was inviolate: No one but the butler touched the wine.

To discover that Auguste Alphonse Réjane had not only dared to invade the sacred space but to rummage through it as though it were his own private pantry was shocking.

And yet, Bea thought, not shocking at all, for how could he perfect a mushroom soup that required Château d'Yquem without Château d'Yquem? Naturally, he would have considered it just another ingredient like butter or chicken broth.

How he had contrived it was the more interesting question, for Parsons did not strike her as lax in his management. His severe demeanor and stiff posture indicated that he would be a vigilant guardian of his domain. And Mr. Mayhew was by all appearances a demanding employer who would expect a certain standard of service.

"He stole the key on multiple occasions?" Kesgrave asked.

"Oh, no, not multiple times," Gertrude said quietly. "He stole it once—he made Parsons his favorite stew, which contained a sleeping draught—and took it to a locksmith, who made a copy. It was a violation, a gross violation. Parsons was in a towering rage when he found out."

Bea, darting a look at the duke, who agreed that it was a very gross violation, especially in pursuit of a flawless dish. It would be slightly more understandable, though certainly not forgivable, if something significant was at stake. "When did Parsons find out?"

Her discomfort increasing, the kitchen maid said yesterday morning. "While organizing the wines for the dinner. He was deciding which would go with each course, and he noticed several bottles of the Château d'Yquem were missing. He knew right away the culprit was Monsieur Alphonse because nobody else would have the nerve to steal from the master's collection. He did not deny it. He felt no shame at all and argued it was more sinful to deny an artist the tools he needed to craft his creation. After that, it became a very big row. The yelling and screaming—I've never seen anyone as angry as Parsons."

It required very little imagination for Bea to picture the butler's rage and still less for her to envision him acting on it. Thoughtfully, she asked the inevitable follow-up question. "Angry enough to kill him?"

But Gertrude, who had been so recently on the defensive about her own immoderate temper, refused to go on the offensive about someone else's. "Oh, no, your grace, please, you must not think it. I didn't want to mention it in the first place because I knew that was what you would think."

Even as she shook her head vehemently in denial a thoughtful look came over her face and she conceded it was a serious infraction, for which Parsons, not Monsieur Alphonse, would be held accountable. "There are dozens of butlers in London, aren't there, who could easily do his job. But a masterful chef is irreplaceable. There is not another like him in all of England. The consequences for Parsons would be horrible if Mr. Mayhew found out. He would be sacked at once, which everyone knows, and I wouldn't be surprised if his anger *had* turned violent. But *so* violent he would kill him? Impossible. He couldn't have done it. I'm sure of that. Monsieur Alphonse showed no more respect or consideration for him than he did the rest of us, and Parsons *did* sometimes get riled. But not enough to kill him. Of that, I am sure."

She spoke firmly, and yet with each assurance she gave, the conviction in her tone lessened until the final assertion came out almost as a question.

As far as accusations went, it was an understated one, especially compared with her fellow servants' efforts, which had lacked subtlety. Indeed, it was so restrained, Bea could not be entirely sure she *was* pointing her finger at Parsons.

Oh, but of course she was—and look at how well it had

worked. The interview had begun with the kitchen maid withering under Bea's interest and concluded with Bea's gaze turned toward another suspect. And Parsons was a very promising one indeed, for he had discovered Monsieur Alphonse and insisted against all reason that his death was merely a horrible accident.

A dubious claim from the very beginning, it took on a new complexion with the discovery of a significant and well-justified resentment.

Nevertheless, Bea remained focused on her current interrogation and reviewed with Gertrude her movements the night before. "And when you went up to bed at one, you saw Monsieur Alphonse in the courtyard?"

"Yes, your grace, yes, I did," she said firmly. "He was doing a spot of gardening."

As she was familiar with the chef's thorough destruction of the roses, Bea assumed this was a deliberate understatement and regarded her suspect cynically. "A *spot* of gardening?"

For the first time since she had entered the room, the maid's demeanor lightened and she seemed almost to giggle. "Excuse me, your grace, I should have said a lot of gardening, for he was in the process of digging up Mrs. Blewitt's roses. I know I should not make light of it, for it was very wrong of him to destroy her whole garden, but she is so very possessive of her flowers and treats us all with suspicion any time we get within a foot of them. I can only suppose Monsieur Alphonse decided he'd had enough of her distrust. To be sure, he would have preferred onions, but it was not as if he intended to do the gardening himself," Gertrude said, then, realizing the incongruity of the statement in the face of evidence to the contrary, she added that rooting up the bushes was much easier than planting them.

As Bea agreed with this assessment, she nodded and

seeking to confirm the housekeeper's version of events, asked if Mrs. Blewitt had seen what Monsieur Alphonse had done to the garden when she came in to inspect the kitchen.

"She couldn't have possibly noticed it then," Gertrude said, "because the second she did, she would have put a stop to it."

Bea, unable to argue with the irrefutable logic, thanked the kitchen maid for her time and asked her to summon Parsons. Visibly relieved, the kitchen maid leaped to her feet, murmured a final, "Yes, your grace," and fairly ran to the door.

Chapter Twelve

Parsons cried.

'Twas a disconcerting sight, to be sure—those prominent cheekbones, so judgmental whilst contemplating Beatrice in the corridor, glistening with tears, and his lower lip trembling like that of a naughty child being scolded by his strict governess. And his pointed chin, it bobbed up and down without control as droplets fell freely from his jaw onto the lapel of his jacket, the lines of which were ruined by shoulders rounded with despair.

It had engulfed him so suddenly, the storm of emotion, and Bea wasn't even sure what had sparked it. All she had said to the tall man as he'd entered the room was that he may take a seat.

That was all it had required—a murmured invitation and a slight gesture toward a chair.

Ah, but obviously that was not all, for he, like Gertrude and Annette and everyone else in the house who had gone before him, knew precisely the purpose of her interview and found the prospect of an interrogation deeply distressing.

He had, Bea thought, better cause than most to be apprehensive, for the evidence was surely stacked against him. His claim that the chef had perished in an accident was foolish at best and nefarious at worst, and he had a very strong motive for wishing Mr. Réjane ill. Although the chef had done many things to agitate and annoy his colleagues, only his transgression against Parsons had actually threatened a man's livelihood.

Just because he appeared guilty, however, did not mean he actually was, and Bea considered how best to proceed. In her experience, butlers did not weep—they intimidated and dismissed, yes, but did not crumble into sobbing heaps—and the thought of offering comfort was at once insufficient and patently absurd. Wrapping her arms around an elephant and murmuring soothingly in its humongous ear would be less preposterous than her trying to console Parsons.

An invigorating slap on the cheek, perhaps, would remind him of the situation and help him to regain his composure. Uncle Horace had once performed the service for his steward, who was in a lather because he'd spilled ink all over the month's accounts, rendering them unreadable.

But surely it would never do for the Duchess of Kesgrave to go around striking the neighbor's servant, no matter how positive her intent. And although the slap had returned the steward to his senses, her uncle's hand had left a red mark on the other man's face, which had troubled her relative so much, his own ability to think was undermined.

No accounts were balanced that day.

Maybe a restorative drink, she wondered. A glass of port or madeira?

Undaunted by the display, Kesgrave addressed the butler with brisk authority, assuring him that the situation could not be quite as dismal as his behavior indicated. "Calm yourself please and tell us the cause of your agitation."

Parsons, reminded of his duty by the sternness of the

duke's tone, straightened his shoulders and managed a respectful response that was interrupted only once by a hiccup.

Kesgrave nodded and advised the butler to sit down.

Bea, bracing for another flood, watched in relief as the servant smoothly lowered into the chair and looked at the duke for further instruction. Remnants of his outburst remained on his face, particularly his gray eyes, which were red and damp, but he presented an otherwise composed appearance.

He was mortified by the breach, Bea knew, for he could not quite bring himself to look directly upon her or the duke. But his voice was steady as he apologized for the appalling display and explained its cause. "I am aware of how the situation appears, and in a moment of unrestrained apprehension, I allowed myself to be overcome. It will not happen again, your grace."

Parsons addressed his comment to the duke, but then he tilted his head slightly and spoke directly to Bea, silently acknowledging that it was, first and foremost, her investigation. "Please ask your questions, and I will endeavor to answer them to the best of my ability."

His demeanor was so greatly altered from their interaction earlier in the day, Bea could scarcely believe it was the same person. That murder could chasten a Berkeley Square butler demonstrated its insidiousness and why it must be rooted out and not merely buried. "You said you are aware of how the situation appears. How does the situation appear?"

"I did not like the victim," Parsons admitted matter-of-factly as he began to list the many facts aligned against him. "I had a vicious row with the victim. I have the physical strength to overcome the victim and harm him. No one can attest to where I was during the time of the incident. I discovered the victim's body. I told Mr. Mayhew that the victim's death was an accident. These facts taken together make it appear as if I killed Monsieur Alphonse and then tried to cover it up. I know the staff has informed you of these factors because they resent me for trying to keep the household in order and had a great liking for Monsieur Alphonse, who made them lovely cakes and tarts."

Well, yes, Bea thought, the case against him did seem rather solidly made. Fortunately for the butler, she was dubious of solid cases. "Why did you say it was an accident?"

Although Parsons's shoulders rounded again and he had to take a deep breath before speaking, his composure held. "I was scared, your grace. When I saw him lying there dead, I panicked. I didn't mean to lie. It's just the words came out and I knew what everyone would say so I kept lying. I kept exonerating myself. It was necessary because we'd had an argument the day before, a vicious argument that everyone knew about. I tried to control my temper, I tried very hard, but Monsieur Alphonse's disregard of the danger he had put me in infuriated me and I yelled. Everyone heard me yelling at him. So I knew they would think I did it. That's why I said it was an accident. I don't know if Mr. Mayhew believed me, but he does not like dealing with complications and the murder of his French chef was a very large one. He was grateful, I think, to have an explanation that simplified the situation. The constable was as well. The matter had been resolved, and there seemed like there was no reason to tell the truth."

It was a reasonable answer, and Bea had enough empathy to imagine how terrifying it must be to see a corpse and know you were the one to whom the whole staff would point.

Everyone always cried, "It wasn't me, I didn't do it." But in the end someone had.

"Very well," Bea said with in a hint of weariness in her tone, "let's try this again. Tell me the truth about discovering

Monsieur Alphonse's body, and do not leave out any details this time."

Parsons blanched at the instructions and looked fleetingly at Kesgrave, uncertain if he should really make such a grim description to the duchess. Finding nothing to indicate otherwise, he explained that he had awoken at five as usual. "I performed my customary waking activities, dressed and went into the kitchen to reignite the fire so that I may begin to boil water—all that was true. But it was actually in the passageway that I realized something was wrong. My foot kicked an object, and not thinking very much on the matter, I leaned over with the candle and noticed the thing was hairy. I assumed it was a small animal, but when I touched it, it rolled and I realized it was Monsieur Alphonse's head."

He paused here, as if expecting a reaction from Bea—a cry of alarm, perhaps a mild faint of horror—and when he failed to get anything but an encouraging nod, he continued. "It was horrible, horrifying, terrible. I...I dropped it at once and then leaned against the wall for a dozen seconds, trying to stop my heart from racing. Slowly, it occurred to me that the rest of him had to be somewhere, so I raised the light and looked around. It was not far, the body, perched at the entrance of the kitchen. I must have cried out because as I was standing there trying to gather my wits, Thomas, the kitchen boy, appeared. And he looked at me with such terror, as if *I* had been the one who had done it. I knew then how it would be, the assumptions, the accusations, so I panicked and looked around and saw the *le peu*, just sitting there, and it seemed so plausible in the moment."

Bea, who had only a few days before found herself standing a few feet away from a skewered corpse when the most accomplished gossip in London opened the door and stepped into the hallway, easily imagined the terror he felt. "How did Thomas respond?"

Calmed slightly by the question, for clearly his story was not going to be dismissed out of hand, Parsons said, "He stared at me with his eyes open wide for a long time, and I thought for sure he was going to call me a liar and all at once I saw myself standing on the gallows, my head inches from the noose. But then he nodded and began to scream and run down the passageway to wake up everyone in the rooms above the stables. As soon as he was gone, I ran to the *le peu* and moved it closer to the body so the explanation made more sense. In my haste, I tripped over something and knew it was the real murder weapon. I didn't look, though, I didn't have time. I just kicked it as hard as I could under the cabinet. I swear I had no idea it was a cleaver. Then I put a tablecloth over the body so that I would not have to stare at it. I am quite ashamed to admit I forgot about the head. I left it lying in the corridor and it was kicked several more times by the staff."

It required all her self-control, but Bea managed to not flinch at the image of the head of the greatest chef in all of Europe being knocked around the hallway like a ball in a field. Auguste Alphonse Réjane had been the master of his craft, the creator of an elaborate style of cooking that appealed to bankers and emperors alike, and for what—to suffer a hideous desecration.

As if the death itself weren't ghastly enough in its own right.

Bea was hardly surprised Thomas and the footmen and Mr. Mayhew and subsequently the constable had latched on to the guillotine as a reasonable explanation. In her experience, people who were adjacent to the horrendous crime of murder were always happy to accept the less awful alternative, however improbable it might be.

Given that the cutting instrument was not actually the culprit, Bea sought to get a sense of what the site of the separation looked like by asking him to describe the cut at the neck.

Parsons recoiled at the question, and his pointed chin began to flap as he stuttered inarticulately for several seconds before he fell silent. Then he stared blindly, as if focusing on something only he could see, and admitted that he could not possibly say. "It was dark and I chose not to look. I am sorry if that seems cowardly to you."

But it did not—of course it did not—and Bea rushed to assure him that he had behaved reasonably, especially with the terror of discovery upon him and a fear of being accused.

Nevertheless, knowing nothing about the site of the cut made the investigation several times more difficult, and she again regretted not having the opportunity to examine the corpse.

There was an easy solution to her dilemma, to be sure, and that was to visit the constable and ask to see the body.

How easily she could imagine it: the uproar that would cause, the bewilderment on the constable's face as he tried to figure out if she was sincere in her request or bedeviling him with nonsense.

No, she decided, that was giving the constable too much credit. He would care nothing about her intentions, tossing her forcefully from the premises and warning her harshly of the rough treatment she should expect if she dared to return.

Except he would not do that because she was the Duchess of Kesgrave.

Nobody ejected a duchess.

The constable would permit her to make her examination, either begrudgingly or with obsequious enthusiasm.

But it would not end there, of course it would not. Within hours the story would be bandied about in every drawing room in London, and a scathing scandal would ensue.

It was exactly as Mr. Mayhew had said: The new duchess's

morbid curiosity in decapitated chefs would be mocked and reviled.

Thanks to the scene at Lord Stirling's ball, her proclivity was widely known, but it was one thing to convince an older gentleman possibly teetering on the edge of senility to confess to the murder of one's parents in a crowded ballroom and quite another to deliberately seek out a victim who bore no relation to you. The former could be excused because family matters were frequently messy, and sometimes it was simply impossible to contain them to the confines of one's front parlor. But it was never acceptable to pester one's neighbors, especially during a difficult time, which the violent execution of a masterful French chef surely was.

Bea knew her conduct was so excessively indecorous that even she would be inclined to wonder what could motivate a duchess to behave in such a shockingly ghoulish and inconsiderate manner.

Even if she was inclined to ignore the ridicule and contempt for the sake of the victim (the greatest chef in Europe!), she could not expose Kesgrave to it. The *ton* already thought he was the helpless dupe of her cold-blooded scheme to entrap him in marriage. How much worse the pity would be if they knew he'd been shackled to a bride who chose to examine headless corpses?

In this, Mr. Mayhew had been right.

Of course, Kesgrave had been unwavering in his insistence that he was immune to the slings and arrows of scandal and its purveyors. As the Duke of Kesgrave, he did what he pleased and allowed others to ape his ways. The moment he engaged in a particular activity was the moment that particular activity became the rage.

But what had he ever done that was shocking, she wondered now. He was the consummate nobleman who belonged to the correct clubs and possessed the correct skills and behaved in the correct manner. All his affairs—and she meant that in every sense of the word, even if the thought of his mistresses made her heart tumble, especially now that she knew intimately what that position entailed—were conducted with discretion and aligned with the expectations of the day.

Kesgrave had never veered from the path, not in any significant way. What did it matter if he had, for example, worn unadorned trousers to court, rather than the embroidered breeches of custom?

He was, Bea thought, rather like Job professing his faith in the midst of abundance.

Marrying her was the first time he had stepped off the path, and she feared he could not comprehend the consequences because he had never suffered any before. Briefly, she glanced at him and noted how untroubled he appeared by the disaster she seemed determined to bring to his door. Nothing about this investigation would remain private, and she wondered how firmly he would hold to his faith once it had actually been tested.

To be sure, Bea did not consider herself the embodiment of a curious god's uncertainty or even a May game set into motion by a conniving devil. Nevertheless, she thought it would be prudent to forego paying a visit to the constable.

Instead, she asked Parsons again about the temperature of Monsieur Alphonse's body, a question to which he had taken great offense during their first interview. "Was it still warm to the touch or did it feel a little cooler than usual?"

Appalled anew, he stammered that he had not made contact with the chef's skin. Then he shook his head fiercely and admitted that his finger might have grazed the chef's hand while he was settling the tablecloth over him.

"And how did he feel?" Bea asked, knowing that the answer would provide only minimal insight. She had no idea how quickly a body cooled, but given the time frame she was dealing with—between one-thirty and five—the only useful answer was if Mr. Réjane's temperature had felt normal. That would indicate that the murder had just happened.

Alas, Parsons was unable to answer this question without any equanimity. He babbled that the chef had felt warm but cool and then cool but warm, then coolish and warmish. Then tears flooded his eyes and he cried in earnest for a full minute before composing himself and apologizing quite ardently for his lack of control.

"After I put the tablecloth over him, I banished everyone from the kitchen until Mr. Mayhew came down to take over the matter," he said, quickly adding that he had done that because he thought it was disrespectful for everyone to stand there and gawk, not because he was hiding something. "I instructed everyone to return to their daily chores. The silver needed polishing and the mirrors needed cleaning and the lamps needed trimming and the clocks needed setting."

It was an ambitious list to attempt, Bea thought, with a beheaded servant lying under a cloth in the kitchen. "Did the chores get done?"

Parsons shook his head. "As far as I know, nothing has been done properly today. Earlier, I watched Henry polish the same fork for twenty minutes."

"What happened after Mr. Mayhew took over?" Bea asked.

"He sent Henry to fetch the constable, and then went into his study to wait for him. He did not go down to see the...um, Monsieur Alphonse until after the constable came. They had a long consultation in his study, and then they went down to the kitchen together to examine the scene. After inspecting the evidence, the constable agreed with my assessment and considered the matter resolved. He had just issued instructions to his men for removing the body when Annette came running down the stairs calling for smelling salts. Mrs. Mayhew had fainted, and she couldn't revive her. Mr. Mayhew grew quite distressed, and I volunteered to get smelling salts from the neighbor."

Solemnly, he thanked his grace for the loan.

Kesgrave, unaware of his own generosity, assured him it was no bother.

"And Mrs. Mayhew was still in a faint when you returned?" Bea asked.

"She was, yes, but the smelling salts brought her around immediately," he said. "By then the constable's men had removed the body. As soon as it was gone, Mr. Mayhew ordered Henry to remove the *le peu* so nobody else would get hurt. Everything had sorted itself out nicely until you arrived."

The butler's tone was neutral, but Bea felt the implied criticism and sweetly apologized for undoing all his excellent work in hiding the true cause of Mr. Réjane's death.

Horrified, Parsons sputtered with embarrassment, apologizing profusely and insisting that was not what he had meant. "In truth, your grace, I am very grateful for your interest. My behavior this morning was rash and deplorable, and I am ashamed of it now. If you had not come, my actions would have stood and then we would never discover what had really happened to Monsieur Alphonse. I am not so blinded by personal antipathy that I do not recognize what a tragedy that would have been."

Bea did not know if she should take him at his word, but it was a persuasive speech well delivered. "Tell us about your argument with him regarding the wine cellar."

Although he had known the question was in the offing, Parsons startled as if surprised and blinked several times. "As you've already heard the story, I am not sure what I can add. Monsieur Alphonse defied my authority, arranged my insentience and removed the key to the wine cellar from my person. It was a tremendous betrayal of trust and a thoroughly unethical act, which I discovered only yesterday, when I was assessing the wine needs for the dinner. I confronted him, and he was unrepentant. He actually laughed and said I was getting myself in a lather over nothing, just a few bottles of mediocre wine. Mediocre wine!" he intoned again, unable to suppress the shock in his voice. Then he turned to the duke and implored him to understand the hopelessness of the situation. "Your grace, it was four bottles of Château d'Yquem. If he considered Château d'Yquem mediocre, I cannot begin to fathom what vintage he considered to be excellent."

Kesgrave, perceiving the injustice, murmured consolingly.

Although Bea did not mind the digression, she had no interest in extending it and brought the conversation back to the topic at hand. "If Mr. Mayhew finds out that Monsieur Alphonse not only stole the key to the cellar but availed himself of its stock, you will be fired."

Parsons bowed his head. "Yes."

"You must have been furious over his disregard for your welfare," she said.

He did not try to deny it, which was sensible because even now his fury over the maltreatment was palpable. But he did attempt to claim that it did not matter. "Getting angry at Monsieur Alphonse was futile because he was like an overindulged child. He took responsibility for nothing and did as he pleased regardless of whom it hurt. He was so skilled and talented that he always got his way, and it simply did not occur to him to deny himself, not even out of courtesy to others. That is why he made free use of the wine cellar without caring that Mayhew would cast me out if he discovered the truth. But he was also kind and generous with his skill and talent—like a child as well. He genuinely loved watching people enjoy his food, and it made no difference to him if it was a scullery maid or the prince regent. He just wanted his work to be enjoyed. That is why it was hard for anyone here to bear him true malice, even myself, although I was irate with him yesterday and would still be irate with him today if he hadn't suffered such a grievous fate."

As Bea had heard a variation on the same general idea from several of the other servants, she nodded and reviewed his movements after the party. "You said you last saw him in the garden."

"Yes," the butler promptly replied, "smoking a cheroot, which he frequently did after a dinner party. Sometimes he would sit out there for hours. Mr. Mayhew was aware of the habit and regularly supplied him with cheroots. It was the cause of some resentment in the household."

Although Annette had already mentioned the valet's envy, Bea tilted her head with interest and said mildly, "Resentment?"

"Stebbings felt that the same consideration should be extended to him and was bitter that it never was," he said, then paused as if reluctant to continue. Then he added, "And Mrs. Mayhew did not like it. She feared that showing a marked preference for one servant over the others, even one with such prodigious talents as Monsieur Alphonse, would create tensions among the staff."

As it had plainly done exactly that, Bea thought Mrs. Mayhew had been right to worry. But Monsieur Alphonse was the recipient of so many advantages, one more hardly made a difference. As Parsons had said, the masterful French chef was spoiled.

Having gathered all the information she needed, Bea looked at Kesgrave to see if he had any questions and when he demurred, she thanked the butler for his time. Unnerved by the courtesy, he apologized again for making a mockery of Monsieur Alphonse's death by lying about its cause.

Although it was not Bea's place to absolve him, she offered her understanding and told him it was better to tell the truth later than never at all. "If you recall anything else that might be relevant, however slight, please send a note to Kesgrave House."

The butler agreed at once, opening the door to leave the servants' hall and revealing Henry on the threshold with a hesitant look on his face.

"I did not want to interrupt," he explained as he awkwardly stepped aside to allow the butler to pass, "but I have a missive from Mr. Mayhew that I was instructed to give you right away. He says it's of vital importance and requires your immediate attention. He is awaiting your reply."

Bea accepted the note with great reluctance. "Thank you, Henry."

The footman nodded, visibly relieved to have successfully discharged his duty after an extended delay, and then paused in the doorway uncertainly. Neither the duke nor the duchess seemed inclined to respond to his master's command with anything resembling urgency, and he was not quite sure if he should hover while they read the letter or leave them in peace.

Obviously, it was the latter, Bea thought, wondering if she was allowed in her new position to shoo servants away.

"That will be all," Kesgrave said.

Henry mumbled something unintelligible and closed the door.

Unable to believe the letter contained a single sentence that was genuinely helpful, she handed it to her husband, observing that it was most likely addressed to him anyway.

"Yes, his sycophancy does seem of the particular sort that focuses on me. But do not despair, soon you will have a dozen toadies of your own. You must decide how you will want to handle them. As you know, I find ostentatious displays of knowledge to be diverting for them and satisfying for me," he said, unfolding the note and scanning it quickly. "Ah, he apologizes for the state of the servants' hall. If he had realized we would be using it as our private study, he would have applied a fresh coat of paint."

"How very like him to cut to the heart of the matter," Bea said.

"Mr. Mayhew is eager to update us on the progress of his investigation and to review his list of people who he believes would like to see him suffer," he continued. "It's an exhaustive catalogue containing eighteen names, and he worries that hunger might undermine our ability to think clearly so he suggests we share a light meal before we discuss our findings."

"He's very clever," Bea murmured, unable to determine if his invitation stemmed from a desire to stay abreast of their investigation in order to frustrate its outcome or to exploit its opportunity for greater intimacy with the duke.

When she posed the question to Kesgrave, he firmly stated it was obviously the latter. "If Mayhew had realized that having one of his staff brutally murdered in his own home would bring the Duke of Kesgrave to his doorstep, I am convinced he would have chopped off Réjane's head himself months ago."

Bea smiled faintly and murmured, "Oh, surely not. He would have chosen a significantly less consequential member of his staff to sacrifice."

Kesgrave conceded the point and speculated that the banker would have killed the scullery maid or a stable boy.

Suddenly exhausted, Bea suggested they present themselves to Mr. Mayhew at once so they could refuse his invitation and leave number forty-four.

Emphatically, the duke said no.

"You can't mean to accept!" she cried, aghast.

"Good god, no," he said, appalled at the prospect. "I mean to have no further contact with him today."

Bea applauded the plan and wondered how it might be contrived. "Anticipating our refusal, he is no doubt standing at the top of the staircase waiting to waylay us."

At this prospect, the duke furrowed his brow briefly before announcing a solution. "We will leave by the servants' entrance."

It was a good plan, Bea thought, simple, elegant, practical, and yet it caused her to throw back her head and reel with laughter, for it was funny, so very, very funny, to find herself in the exact spot where she had begun. There she was, a duchess with a house so immense she could wander its halls for days and a staff so large she could not keep count, and she was still sneaking out the servants' entrance like a dreary spinster with no expectations and disapproving relations.

But not alone—oh, no, never alone again—which just made the situation all the more comical, for now she was scurrying through the staff door in the august company of Damien Matlock, sixth Duke of Kesgrave.

His ancestors would be mortified, she knew, by the depths to which she had sunk him. And so quickly too!

They had been married for little more than one full day and already she had brought him low.

No, not already, she realized. *Again.*

Only yesterday she had unwittingly caused him to be entombed in the basement of a modest-size theater on the Strand.

And now she was compounding the indignity by forcing him to creep out of another man's house like a thief.

Was there no end to the humiliation to which she would subject him?

Remarkably, he did not look shamed or demeaned or even

a little bit annoyed. Just the opposite, in fact, for his expression was one of delight and intrigue, as if suddenly awake to the wonderful possibilities of a secret egress.

It was absurd, of course, for he was a man of wealth and privilege and the ability to move freely had always been his own. No rules of propriety had ever constrained his desire to take a turn around the square, and yet she believed he felt something new and reckless there, with her, in Mr. Mayhew's servants' hall.

Abruptly, she stopped laughing, struck by the feeling that seemed to endlessly overtake her—that she somehow loved him more in this moment than she had in the one before.

Against all reasonable expectation, her love continued to grow. Again and again and again, it expanded in directions she could never have conceived—not as a timid wallflower waiting out a ball in a chair by the fig tree in the corner, to be sure, but also last night as a creature of sensation in his arms.

Overwhelmed by the utter incomprehensible beauty of life, she leaned forward and pressed her lips against his. It was gentle and sweet, only a light brushing of gratitude before they made their ignominious exit through the servants' door, but Kesgrave, not realizing her intention, immediately deepened the kiss. His arms pulled her forward while his mouth tilted her head back, and he murmured softly as she fought for breath, "Trembling beneath me."

The air left her lungs, simply whooshed away, as desire, as uncontrollable as wildfire, spiked through her. But even as her body succumbed to his touch, her mind perceived the stark reality of the situation, for the Duke of Kesgrave was now in actual fact seducing his wife in the servants' hall of a Fleet Street banker.

How many generations of Matlocks were turning in their graves?

Dozens, she thought, dozens and dozens stretching all the way back to the Peasants' Revolt.

Overcome with amusement, swept away by happiness, she stepped back, momentarily breaking contact, then threw her arms around his shoulders in an embrace that was as effusive as it was clumsy. "I love you," she said, struggling to regain her equilibrium.

Kesgrave chuckled lightly as he straightened them both and regarded her with unsettling tenderness. "How very fortunate, for I love you, too."

Oh, yes, very unsettling indeed, she thought, staring into the brilliant blue depths of his eyes, for she could easily spend the rest of her life there, right there, oblivious to the requirements of decorum or civility.

But the duke had other plans, trembling plans, and he promptly opened the door and led her out into the passageway, where the servants who had been hovering scattered to various corners and crevices and feigned consuming interest in their dust rags and cuffs. Undaunted by their interest, Kesgrave strolled down the corridor with the blithe indifference of a gentleman sauntering among the shops on Bond Street, and Bea felt an intense urge to giggle.

She did not, of course, for she had no wish to undermine the impressiveness of his achievement, the way he made it seem as though all dukes regularly exited their neighbors' properties through the servants' entrance. She maintained her composure after they were outside and Kesgrave linked his arms through hers and commented mildly on the weather, which was inordinately clement for April. She even kept her poise as they entered Kesgrave House and Marlow's gaze fell upon her with unbridled curiosity. He had questions, so many questions, but propriety prevented him from asking a single one. And duty, of course, for the duke requested that dinner be laid out in his dressing room as previously discussed.

No, with a modesty even her indiscriminately censorious Aunt Vera would admire, Bea held her impish sense of humor in check for a full fifteen minutes and did not allow even one faintly amused chuckle to escape her until they were firmly ensconced in Kesgrave's bedchamber.

Then she laughed and laughed and laughed.

And so did the duke.

Chapter Thirteen

I n a pleasant state of languid satiation, her head resting on Kesgrave's shoulder, the candles burning low, a glass of warming champagne on the night table beside a plate with four biscuits and half a gooseberry tart, Bea said, "What about the severed head? Could there be a particular meaning in the way he was killed, with violent hacks to the neck? We don't know how it was actually managed, but I cannot imagine it is easy to cut through muscle and bone, even with a very sharp cleaver. If ending his life was the intention, then slicing open his gut would have achieved the same end with considerably less effort."

As these observations were preceded by nothing remotely similar, their most recent exchange consisting mostly of delighted sighs mingled with murmurs of endearment, she would not have been offended if he protested the gruesome turn her thoughts had taken. An eyebrow raised archly, perhaps, as he commented on her charming conversation.

But he did not. Rather, he brushed the hair gently from her forehead and allowed that one would not be wrong in drawing certain conclusions from the ferocity of the act. "But I think it would be erroneous to build your argument from there. People behave in incomprehensible ways."

Bea knew it to be true and said with regret, "It is a shame we do not have the body to examine."

"It is?" Kesgrave asked, his amused tone indicating that he thought precisely the opposite.

"Obviously, I am as horrified as anyone by the notion of scrutinizing a severed corpse, but there is much information to be discovered from it," she explained, shifting slightly so she could address him directly. "I believe the roughness of the cut would tell us how the job was managed, which would give us some indication of who could have done it. Or mayhap he died of another wound that was overlooked. Having the body would aid in our investigation."

Smiling, he shook his head slightly and said, "No, I don't think that's true."

Bea considered him with a look of fond condescension and attributed their disparity in their opinions to his lack of experience. "You have not been presented yet with a corpse to know how much information is to be gathered from one."

"No, brat," he said with a pinch on her hip that caused her to squeal and squirm. "I meant I do not believe you are as horrified by the notion as everyone else. I don't think you are horrified at all and instead regret the opportunity to acquire knowledge about the human body and file it away in your remarkable brain for some future use."

He spoke lightly, without resentment or anger, as if making an anodyne observation about the condition of the drapes (quite excellent, as far as she could tell, with no fraying or fading), and yet the topic was not the trifle his tone implied.

Here, now, they had arrived at the heart of it, and she

could not say if he had stumbled ineptly into difficult territory or strode confidently. She had known their brief exchange in Mr. Mayhew's drawing room would not be the end of it, and he had every right to protest her involvement in another murder. The words themselves did not matter—the pledge she made, the vow she did not—because people were governed by expectations, not contracts. She knew what Kesgrave wanted and expected from a wife, and if she'd had no intention of providing it, then she should never have married him.

He would help her carry out this current investigation, of that she had no doubt, for he had demonstrated himself to be reasonable and kind time and again. But it was the future they were discussing now and he would make it clear once and for all that this strange hobby of hers would end here. All he had to do was state it simply, as he was her husband and no longer had to bother with pledges and vows. His word was law, conferred by church and state, and she was bound by the same institutions to follow it.

She had anticipated this moment for over two weeks and yet was startled to discover she was not prepared for it. It was the setting, she told herself, the intimacy of the marriage bed, the lovely lethargy of physical satisfaction, so unfamiliar and unexpected, that made her feel unsettled, as if, vaguely, he was rejecting some part of her. Two things had entered her life during that extraordinary sojourn to the Lake District— Kesgrave and murder—and they felt inexorably entwined. Staring at the duke athwart the cooling corpse of Mr. Otley in the darkened library, she had changed, and as much as she knew that agreeing to halt her investigations would not change her back to the woman she had been before, drab and silent, she could not quite smother the fear.

'Twas wholly irrational because she knew it was not her

pose as an amateur Runner that had secured his affection. It was her wit and intelligence and courage and a sense of humor so impish it actually made her appear beautiful.

Oh, but what part of love was rational, she wondered, feeling as though one of the barriers that kept the old Bea at bay was about to be demolished.

Determined to delay the conversation for a little while longer, she extricated herself from his arms to don the night rail that had been discarded in haste next to the bed. Raising an eyebrow archly, she smiled and said, "You think my brain is remarkable, your grace?"

But the gown wasn't enough. Even with it on, she still felt unduly exposed, so she looked around for a distraction and settled on the glass of champagne. Her hand had just brushed the stem when Kesgrave's arm snaked out and tugged her back toward him, spilling the liquid.

"You will not do that," he said as he settled her against the pillows.

Truly baffled, she said, "If you do not want me to drink champagne, then you should not pour it for me."

He shook his head fiercely and looking at her with glaring disapproval, as if she were being deliberately obtuse. "No, don't pull away from me."

Of course, he had known what she had done—not the physical withdrawal but the mental. Over and over he had displayed a disconcerting omniscience, seeming to know where she was or what she was thinking without any explanation.

She was disquieted by it now, for it made her feel as though she had nothing of her own, not even her thoughts, and although she knew it was a pitiable attempt, she blinked with exaggerated coquettishness, hoping for a comical effect, and said, "Did I do that?"

He would not allow it. "No, Bea, no. We will discuss your investigative habit."

How serious he sounded, she thought, nodding slowly as she shifted her position until her back was upright and her shoulders pressed against the headboard. If she was to be put in her place by her husband, it would not be while she was underneath him. "All right, your grace."

Inexplicably, he began with an observation about himself. "I never expected to feel joy."

It was a perplexing statement, a seeming non sequitur, and although Bea could not fathom what the information had to do with her future, she knew precisely how it applied to her past. For the vast majority of her life, she had felt exactly that way, and if she was startled to discover a duke lived with the same limitations, she was not entirely surprised. "All right," she said again.

"I have been happy," he amended with scrupulous precision, "for my life has been filled with comfort and convenience and I have denied myself little. I will not pretend that a dukedom is an albatross around my neck. But this thing with you, what I feel, what we have...I close my eyes and see such glories, so much joy. It is not what I expected to ever feel. In truth, I would never have even sought it out because it did not seem necessary."

Bea, who had discovered herself in the wake of Mr. Otley's murder to be clever, knew the moment called for some droll remark, some sly comment. Always, she had something to say that would draw attention away from herself or lighten a mood or poke fun at a vanity.

But now she had nothing. All she could do was stare in wonder into his earnest and brilliantly blue eyes.

"I have some concerns for your happiness," he added.

Bea was astonished that he could possibly doubt the joy

she herself felt with him. Close his eyes and see glories? She saw them with her eyes open wide. "Don't," she said.

"Oh, but I do," he insisted gravely.

The solemnity of his tone angered her as much as it caused her to worry that she had somehow done something wrong. "Don't," she said again, catapulting herself into his arms and pressing one soft kiss against his lips, then another and another. "Don't, don't, don't."

Whatever she had failed to do was forgotten as his mouth moved hungrily over her own, his fingers inching under the plain fabric of her night rail and sliding it off her shoulders. But even as she quivered in delight, succumbing to the mind-numbing pleasure of his touch, he pulled back and laying his lips softly on her forehead, said, "I do. A dukedom is not an albatross around my neck, but it is a smaller bird, like a ptarmigan. There is much that is boring and stultifying, and for all the toadying there is thrice as much spitefulness and malice. I can insulate you only so much from the Mrs. Nortons and Lord Tavistocks of the world."

Perceiving now his concern, Bea felt on much steadier ground and insisted she had acquitted herself admirably on both accounts. "Recall, if you will, that I figured out Mrs. Norton's game before she had a chance to make her final move, and I managed to elicit the information I required from Tavistock despite his uncooperative attitude. Have no worry, Damien, I do not need you to insulate me from them."

Kesgrave smiled faintly. "The Marlows, then."

Although her eyes twinkled, she kept her expression serious and said with sober approval, "Ah, well, yes, obviously, I would be grateful for anything you can arrange on that front."

"Obviously," he repeated fondly.

"As you may recall, I recently suggested that you put in a

good word for me and you refused out of hand," she said. "Perhaps that proposal is worthy of a second look."

"I recall, yes, your wanting me to assure him you would make a biddable mistress," he said. "I remain resolute in my refusal to lie to the staff."

"So much for insulating me, your grace," she muttered.

"I want you to be happy as I am," he insisted, "and so—"

"Joyful," she corrected.

He tilted his head slightly. "Excuse me?"

"You said I make you feel joyful," she explained. "Ordinarily, I would not enforce the distinction, but I know how highly you prize precision and seek only to satisfy your own requirements."

Now he laughed. "Yes, brat, you do, and I want you to be joyful too, which is why I have decided not to intercede with your investigative habit if you choose to pursue it. In the interest of fair disclosure, I will admit that I say this fully believing that it's simply too implausible for yet another murder victim to cross your path. You are, after all, a gently bred young lady, and the excess of corpses that have entered your life in recent months strains credulity. But I have believed that from the start and have been proved wrong four times. So, if it should happen for an inconceivable fifth or sixth time, I will do nothing to stand in your way and only ask how I may be of assistance."

For a moment, brief but sharp, Bea believed he was teasing her. The words he said so closely resembled the words she longed for him to say she thought he was uttering them out loud so she could hear the absurdity for herself.

Now she was supposed to laugh at the ridiculousness of her pretentions.

Oh, but he was sincere.

Blue eyes steady, he regarded her thoughtfully, no scorn or amusement on his face, only concern.

Her heart suddenly racing, she found it desperately difficult to take her next breath. He could not know what it
meant, the simple statement, the acceptance it represented,
for if asking her to stop was some sort of rejection of who she
was, then the inverse must be true as well.

On a shallow breath, she said, "We had an agreement,
your grace. You promised to stop making me love you more,
for it is really quite excruciatingly uncomfortable to have a
heart this full."

"I clearly recall refusing to make any such promise," he
said firmly, "and if you had wanted me to vow to treat you
with a little less respect, then you should have taken the time
to interview clergymen until you found one who was receptive to the amendment."

Delighted to have her own words repeated back to her,
Bea asked what had prompted the reassessment. "You were
vehemently opposed yesterday."

"I want you to be happy and for that—" he began.

"Joyful."

"Yes, joyful," he said. "You are a duchess now, and I know
that is not something you desired. I know you would prefer
that I were someone of minor importance, a baronet or a
second son with a very good book collection."

"Actually, I was holding out for a third son with a majestic
library when I deigned to consider your suit," she explained
with an impertinent grin. "That is why I was still unmarried
at the ripe old age of six and twenty."

"A very rare creature indeed," he replied, returning her
smile. "I heard they only go abroad on a full moon, like
vampires."

"You mean werewolves," she said.

He acknowledged the correction and apologized for
confusing his mythical creatures.

She shook her head and made a tsk-tsking sound of hearty

disapproval. "And yet you can list *all* twenty-one ships that engaged in the Battle of the Nile. I fear your education was sadly lacking in practicality."

"There were fifteen ships, and if you persist in mocking my education, I shall list all of them for you in the order in which they appeared in battle," he threatened.

Alas, Bea was far too besotted with his pedantry to find this anything but an inducement, and noting the lascivious glint that entered her eyes, he said, "I know you dread the grandeur of my life—the servants, the houses, the social obligations."

"The pineries," she inserted.

Although this particular anxiety was news to him, he duly added it to the catalogue. "The pineries. Watching you interrogate various suspects today, I realized that investigating murders makes you feel confident. It makes you feel strong. When you thanked Mayhew to allow you the courtesy of determining who was beneath your notice, you seemed impervious, invulnerable. I don't want to take that away from you. Moreover, I cannot. Because I need you to feel strong and confident as the Duchess of Kesgrave or you won't be happy."

She had been teasing before, about the pain of a full heart, but it was in fact quite unbearable and she felt something inside her straining to burst.

Tears, she thought contemptuously.

No, no, she would not mar the perfection of the moment with a maudlin display. She would be irreverent. Yes, irreverent, for that was how she had wooed him. All she had to do was say something clever.

Wit and flippancy, unfortunately, were beyond her meager capabilities, for the emotion that swirled inside her was far too turbulent for the simplicity of words. It raged fiercely, demanding action, and reveling in the strange magic of its power, she pressed herself gently against her husband and spoke softly in his ear.

"Joyful," she said, her voice scarcely more than a whisper as she repeated it along the line of his jaw, then on the side of his neck and at the top of his spine—joyful, joyful, joyful, she intoned, seemingly incapable of stopping herself, for it was indeed utter joy that she felt.

Chapter Fourteen

❦

s her purpose in raising the issue of Mr. Réjane's severed head had been to induce Kesgrave to intercede with the constable on her behalf so that she may examine the body without bestirring the gossips, Bea did not consider the conversation to have been an unqualified success. It had resulted in several other wonderful outcomes, including a satisfying resolution to the thorny issue of her troubling fondness for detection, but as far as furthering her inquiry went, it had been a failure.

Nevertheless, marital accord and the freedom to realize one's full potential added a sort of giddy sprightliness to one's thoughts, and having effectively staved off a bout of weeping in a marvelously gratifying fashion, she was eager to return to the matter at hand.

Slipping back into her night rail, she crossed the room to the chest of drawers to look for a sheet of paper and a quill.

"There is an escritoire in my dressing room," Kesgrave said, observing her movements from the bed with a delighted expression.

She darted quickly into the adjacent room, which was larger than her and Flora's bedchambers in Portman Square combined, and located the writing desk along the far wall under an imposing painting of a turban-topped gentleman sporting a sword and standing on the crest of a hill. She selected a fine sheet of cream-colored paper, a ledger to write against and a pencil.

As she returned to the bedchamber, her stomach rumbled.

"I wonder, your grace, if it's possible to get more of the ham and perhaps some more Wiltshire to go with it?" she asked, selecting one of the biscuits on the plate on the night table as she climbed back onto the bed. "I am feeling a bit peckish."

"Of course," he said, gesturing to the bell pull near the edge of the bed.

She was appalled. "At this hour?"

"What hour is it?" he asked.

Bea had no idea, which indicated, she felt, that it was too late to bother the servants.

Kesgrave held out the candle and noted it was a little past eleven, which meant several servants were still in the kitchen. "Regardless of the time, you cannot expect me to go traipsing around my own larder. I am happy to treat Mayhew's pantry with such disrespect but value the esteem of my own staff much too highly. You shall ring the bell and wait with deferential patience for one of the footmen to present himself at the door."

Thoughtfully, she contemplated him in the candlelight, whose golden glow somehow made his handsome features angelic. "You are scared of them."

He blinked in surprise at the accusation. "Terrified. Have I not been candid about that from the very beginning? It is the servants' house; I merely live in it."

"And this is the strength and confidence you wish me to emulate?" she asked with amusement.

"There is no confidence abroad without comfort at home," he said earnestly, as if quoting scripture.

"Humbug," she dismissed.

And yet Kesgrave remained resolutely ensconced on the other side of the bed, his back against the pillows, his angel face alight with humor.

"Very well," she muttered, pulling the cord, "but when James or Joseph or whoever appears at the door, I am saying that it is you who desires a snack. Knowing your cowardice, they will easily believe you fobbed off an unpleasant task to your new wife. They probably think it's the only reason you married someone as brash and assertive as I. No doubt they regard me with great pity in the servants' quarters."

The duke nodded approvingly. "You see, there are ways of establishing yourself with the staff other than identifying the murderer in the house next door."

Bea expected him then to ask the natural corollary—how was identifying the murderer in the house next door establishing herself with the staff—but to her relief he showed no such curiosity. No matter how joyful he made her, she was never going to relay the tale of hiding behind the door in the butler's bedroom.

It was indeed Joseph who answered the summons and after a lavish description of her husband's inopportune hunger and desire for ham and Wiltshire, she assured him she had made progress in her investigation of Monsieur Alphonse's death.

"Parsons has admitted that he said it was an accident to drive attention away from himself, so you were right to be suspicious," she said, then added that the duke would also enjoy a little more of the foie gras. "With a loaf of bread to go with it as well."

When she closed the door and returned to the bed, Kesgrave said, "It appears I am craving a midnight feast."

"You have had an active evening," she informed him, settling herself against the headboard with the ledger pressed against her raised knees. "Now let us make a list of our suspects. Ordinarily, I would begin by noting everyone's movements in order to exclude those people who could not have been in the room to commit the crime. However, the circumstance makes that impossible, as everyone professes to being in the same place: tucked up warmly in their beds. Likewise, in the usual course of my investigation, I would identify who among the assailants nurtured a particular enmity toward the victim. Here, too, we are in a quandary, for it appears everyone had a quarrel with him. Nevertheless, we must start somewhere so I suggest at the beginning."

"Parsons," he said, easily following her line of thought.

"Parsons," she agreed. "As he himself pointed out, there is plenty of evidence against him. But that is why I don't think he is guilty. From the moment he discovered the dead body, he has done everything wrong. I think if he were actually guilty, he would have made more of an effort to appear innocent."

Kesgrave allowed that her reasoning was sound, but it failed to account for the massive unpredictable factor that had upended the butler's well-conceived scheme. "At no point in the planning of his murder could he have imagined the Duchess of Kesgrave knocking on the door demanding the right to investigate. If you remove that from the equation, he in fact did do everything right. He knew his employer would not want to deal with the wretched inconvenience of having a chef whose head was chopped off. That is why he decapitated him—because he knew the more gruesome the deed, the more eagerly his employer would accept any explanation that made the slightest modicum of sense."

Bea conceded it was a valid point. "He did say everything had worked out nicely until I showed up."

"And he had the strongest motive," he added. "As soon as Mayhew finds out about the pilfered wine, he will be sacked. And I am confident that is only a matter of time."

"It is a strong motive, to be sure," she said thoughtfully. "But he did not point a finger at anyone else. I cannot say that is significant, but he is the only servant we interviewed who did not blame someone else. Stebbings blamed Henry, Henry blamed Laurent, Laurent blamed Esther, Esther blamed Mrs. Blewitt, Mrs. Blewitt blamed Gertrude, Gertrude blamed Parsons. Even Annette, who isn't a suspect, blamed Stebbings. I feel like that should weigh in his favor."

"But only one person among the litany may be guilty," Kesgrave said. "The rest are innocent, which means that innocent people point fingers just as often as the guilty. Or, perhaps in this case, more than."

"All right," Bea said with a sigh as she added Parsons to the sheet of paper. Not at the very top to leave room for other contenders but certainly close to it. As she wrote the butler's name, a sense of familiarity overtook her and she remembered suddenly sitting beside the duke near the fire in her bedchamber at Lakeview Hall composing a list of suspects.

Effortlessly, she recalled the mischief on his face as he explained to her that the list they were composing was merely figurative. "The names," he had said, "aren't actually being compiled on a sheet of paper somewhere."

It had been near midnight on that occasion too, and she'd worn a white night rail markedly similar to the one she'd adorned to confer with Joseph. The sense of congeniality was also the same, that ambience of amiable camaraderie among colleagues but now with a knee-weakening dash of intimacy.

In the Lake District, every rule of etiquette and social

decorum required that she, a spinster with no beauty or prospects, maintain an air of disinterest in the Duke of Kesgrave, and she had behaved with propriety. Never once had she allowed herself to look upon him with anything other than collegial regard.

Struck by the yawning gap between the two situations, she altered her position, shifting a quarter rotation and crossing her legs so that she could admire the fine line of his profile openly.

"It is my turn to identify a suspect," she said thoughtfully. "The kitchen maid, obviously. Her quarrel with Monsieur Alphonse is longstanding, she was taken strongly to task for letting the quails dry out even though it was not her fault, and she frequently threatened him with bodily harm. Did I leave anything out?"

"Only that she is adept at chopping up large joints of meat with cleavers and isn't squeamish," he said.

Although Bea was not either, she flinched at this description. "I am putting her above Parsons because she pointed her finger at him. Now you may pick someone."

"Mrs. Blewitt," he said just as a knock sounded at the door. Although Bea shifted to answer it, he was halfway across the room by the time she had put down the ledger and uncrossed her legs. Easily, he accepted the tray from Joseph and placed it gently in the center of the large bed.

Bea's stomach rumbled again in anticipation, but she waited patiently as the duke spread foie gras on a slice of bread for her.

"Ah, yes," she said with an approving nod. "Driven to murder by the desecration of her beloved rosebushes. I am not a gardener, but I can easily imagine responding with violence if someone treated my books with the same violence. I believe that is the only factor aligned against her or am I forgetting something?"

"The case for her is rather slim," he admitted, "although the roses are more convincing than the silk weave with the cerulean stripes."

"So you do not think the valet murdered him for a puff of his cheroot?" she said taking a bite. Goodness gracious, it was delicious. Midnight snacks at 19 Portman Square had always been thin on the ground and what little there was had never tasted this wonderful.

"Highly unlikely," he said. "I do not necessarily believe he lacks the physical strength to chop off a head, for removing dirt and stains from buckskin requires a fair amount of muscle. But strength of resolve is another matter. I think if he did summon the mettle to strike the first blow, he would recoil in horror and run away."

Bea added Stebbings's name about a quarter of the way from the bottom of the sheet. "We also have Edward Laurent, the groom. He argued with the victim over his taking a horse from the stable without permission. The footman insisted it was a heated argument, but other witnesses said it was a minor tussle. I do not think a minor tussle is sufficient cause for decapitation, so I am putting him beneath the valet. I'm also not convinced that the footman was driven to a murderous rage by lack of sleep. Who does that leave among the servants?"

"The scullery maid," he said.

"Yes, of course, the case of the pernicious pickles," Bea said, recalling the groom's insistence that Esther acted in revenge for the wretched illness she had suffered after eating one of the chef's improperly preserved cucumbers. "I think we can both agree that unintentional food poisoning neither counts as a murder attempt nor requires retribution."

Kesgrave cocked his head to the side. "We can, yes. But you are not allowing for the possibility that the pernicious pickles were Réjane's attempt at eliminating the one person who knows his terrible, dark secret."

Delighted with the duke's sudden gothic turn, Bea murmured bravo before assuring him that terrible, dark secrets were never far from her mind. "Although her motive might be questionable, she had the same opportunity as everyone else, so she must be kept in the mix. Bearing in mind we cannot account for the exigencies of a Mrs. Radcliffe plot or the fact that the suspect under consideration appears unable to contemplate blood without fainting, where would you like me to place her," she asked, holding up her sheet of paper, "for the list we are composing this time is literal."

He cut off a slice of Wiltshire and handed it to her. "Below the footman."

"Very good," she said as she made quick work of the cheese. "As that takes care of the servants, now let us turn our attention to Mr. Mayhew. I will admit that at first, I thought he was a clownish nodcock, but now I see the value to his approach. He only pretends to be a clownish nodcock in order to get away with singular acts of impertinence such as trying to trade social status for access to his staff. I was supposed to find his offer outrageous and refuse it out of hand. He never wanted me to accept it. The question is why, and that, your grace, I will admit I do not know. Either he was hoping to avoid the scandal of a decapitated chef, which Parsons's opinion substantiates, or was trying to thwart my investigation so I cannot uncover his guilt."

Kesgrave smiled and assured her she was giving the matter too much thought. "He is a grasping mushroom—no more, no less."

"That is what he wants you to think," Bea said, selecting a slice of ham and taking a bite.

Amused, he agreed it was possible, for the description did

in fact apply to his destruction of *le peu guillotine*. "Disposing of it was smart, but only someone remarkably stupid could get away with doing it. But what is his motive?"

"Greed," she said.

He rolled his eyes at the simple blatancy of the answer. "Well, yes."

"No, but think about it. Having Auguste Alphonse Réjane in his kitchen was lucrative for him as it advanced his objectives both socially and financially. You heard him—even Prinny has been to dine. He was an irresistible lure, and despite what Mr. Mayhew says, I do not believe he would simply permit him to walk out of his house and into the house of a competitor," she said, examining the tray pensively. Foie gras or more ham? "It is not only that he would lose business opportunities if the great chef went to work for another banker in London. He would see it as a loss of honor as well. He would not allow that Mr. Réjane was acting reasonably because a reasonable person would not have asked for the loan in the first place. Furthermore, Mr. Mayhew feels entitled to things, as if they belong to him. I am sure he considered Mr. Réjane his and his alone, and would be outraged at the idea of his possession exerting its own authority. That's why I believe he could have killed him and why the assault was so violent. Mine, he would think, as he swung the cleaver. Mine, he would think, as he chopped through bone."

Although Kesgrave agreed wholly with her assessment of both Mr. Mayhew's character and conceded that perhaps violence did undergird his resentment, he could not believe that a man of business would act so rashly. "For all his ridiculous fawning and dinner invitations, he is still a banker occupied with practical concerns. What you're suggesting doesn't make pragmatic sense. Réjane planned to return to Paris, not accept a position with Thomas Coutts. Perhaps if he intended to remain in London, Mayhew's sense of entitlement and outrage would be a factor but the chef was leaving the country. I have to assume that as a matter of expediency, Mayhew would allow that resolution to prevail rather than slicing off his head. The latter is simply too messy in every sense of the word."

"Well, yes, that is all true," Bea replied, "but Mr. Mayhew did not know that Mr. Réjane was returning to Paris. Nobody in the house knew."

The duke found this to be a very curious thing and lowered the sliver of Wiltshire he was about to eat to examine her inquisitively. "How are you in possession of information that is unknown to the people with whom he resided?"

"Mrs. Wallace," she said as she spread foie gras on a thick slab of bread.

Having little expectation of his housekeeper's introduction into the conversation, he stared at her in confusion. "Mrs. Wallace?"

Oh, yes, of course, the Duke of Kesgrave knew nothing about the romantical dealings that may or may not flourish among his servants. Why in the world would he? "Mr. Réjane told her because they had a bit of a flirtation."

Although she spoke with conviction, he assumed she was jesting and he laughed for several seconds before breaking off abruptly. "Truly?"

Since Bea herself found the relationship highly perplexing, she was not at all surprised by his attitude. It had progressed to the stage of a marriage proposal, and yet both parties seemed to treat the offer as a matter of blithe consideration.

"Truly," she said, relaying a general summary of the couple's romance as described first by Joseph and then later by the housekeeper. "By all accounts, neither party seemed especially upset by her refusal. Mrs. Wallace, in particular, admits to being a little confused as to why the offer was made in the first place, which I can only assume indicates she had not realized the depth of Mr. Réjane's regard."

But the idea of his brisk, practical-minded housekeeper being courted by an effusive French chef was too far beyond Kesgrave's comprehension for him to entertain theories about the latter's intentions. "I am certain you misunderstand the situation."

"I do not," she said with a hint of amusement. "Mrs. Wallace confirmed the story herself."

"But was it an actual proposal?" he asked, settling into a theory of miscommunication. "It is possible he said something that she mistakenly construed as a proposal?"

The poor dear was grasping at straws, Bea thought, giggling at the outlandish suggestion. "Yes, yes, of course, Damien, you have hit the nail on the head, you clever man. He said, 'Will you carry tea, and she heard, Will you marry me.'"

"That's not quite what I meant," he muttered in a disgruntled tone as he raised to his lips a glass of champagne, recently poured and still deliciously chilled. "Perhaps he was discussing his return to France and said something to the effect of: 'I would love to show you Paris.' And she misinterpreted from there."

Now Bea laughed harder, for the image of the brisk, practical-minded housekeeper creating a romantical proposal out of half cloth was even more entertaining. Restraining her mirth, she conceded that it was an intriguing theory. "Without question, it is. But recall that the original report came from Joseph, who was in the stillroom and overheard the conversation. If Monsieur Alphonse had spoken otherwise or was there for another purpose entirely, then Joseph would have—"

But she was struck by her own words: another purpose.

Another purpose...another purpose...*another purpose.*

Oh, yes, of course!

Squealing with exhilaration, Bea leaped across the bed, upending the tray and tackling her husband without care or consideration for the food on the bed or the drink in his hand. Forcefully, he flew back against the pillow as champagne spilled onto the covers and she landed on top of him.

"You clever man!" she said excitedly, kissing him deeply in appreciation, "you clever, clever man!"

Just as suddenly, she rolled off him, bounding to her feet as she marveled at how obvious it was. Another purpose!

"No, come back here," Kesgrave said, tugging her hand. "I don't feel lauded enough."

Chuckling lightly, she said, "No, I cannot imagine you ever do."

But she allowed herself to be drawn back for another consuming kiss and found herself genuinely tempted by the ardor of his response.

"You clever man," she breathed on a sigh as his fingers tugged her night rail up higher.

With gentle determination, she extricated herself from his embrace and fetched his dressing gown from the chair on which it had been discarded. She tossed it to him. "Come on, let's go."

He sat up—but to straighten the mess she had made on the bed, not to don his robe. Showing only mild curiosity as he returned the loaf of bread to the tray, he asked where they were going.

"To the housekeeper's room," she said impatiently. "Do not worry about the crumbs. We can clean them up later."

Of the two propositions, it was impossible to tell which one horrified him more. Stiffly, he said with some of his old imperiousness, "My dear former Miss Hyde-Clare, you may welcome the advent of vermin into your bedchamber, but I have many reasonable objections that I am happy to list in great detail if you do not find the prospect innately repellant."

"As much as I adore listening to you pontificate interminably on tedious subjects, your grace, I simply do not have the time right now to indulge you," she said. "Come please. We must hurry."

Kesgrave restored the wedge of Wiltshire to its plate and placed both on the tray. "The Black Death, which was spread by rats, killed several million people in the span of only a few years."

"You are stalling," she said.

"I am, yes," he said agreeably, "but I am serious as well. This is an old house and we are constantly fighting pests."

Smothering a sigh, she leaned over the bed and piled the ham slices neatly on the tray, then wiped gently at the faint greasy stain on the bedcover. "There," she said, brushing the last few crumbs into her hand, "now we can return the tray to the kitchen on our way to search Mrs. Wallace's rooms. I applaud your efficiency. Now do let's go."

"Given my stance on traipsing through the servants quarters, I would expect you to anticipate my aversion to searching the housekeeper's rooms," he said.

"We are looking for a murderer, not a rasher of bacon," she countered tartly.

"I don't believe the distinction between the two is as great as you think it is, as both can wait until morning," he said. "Please ring for Joseph to collect the tray and tell me why we are searching Mrs. Wallace's office. As I know establishing yourself with the staff is one of your goals, I am compelled to warn you that rifling through her private possessions in the middle of the night is not the best way to go about it."

Never one to continue the fight after the cause had been

lost, Bea tugged the bell pull and settled herself again on the bed. "In light of your ridiculous theory regarding Mr. Réjane's proposal—and speaking of establishing oneself with the staff, calling your housekeeper a dotty female is also not ideal—I realized that he might have had another purpose in coming to Kesgrave House to speak with her. In that event, the proposal was merely a pretext to gain him entry into her rooms. Why would he want access to her rooms? To hide something in a safe place."

Smiling at her reasoning, he called her conclusion outrageous but conceded it was still more plausible than Monsieur Alphonse's nurturing a hopeless passion for Mrs. Wallace. "What do you supposed he secreted away?"

"Ah, yes, what do *you* suppose, your grace," she asked with pointed annoyance, "for it could be almost an infinite number of things. If only someone would let us investigate the answer right away rather than requiring us to twiddle our thumbs with tedious impatience until respectable calling hours."

But if she had hoped to heighten his interest in the mysterious hidden object, she failed miserably. He displayed no curiosity in the unknown item and only nodded absently as she began to speculate. What her comment did awaken, however, was a sense of challenge, and he was determined to do everything he could to alleviate the tedium of waiting.

"For I cannot allow my wife to expire from boredom," he said softly as he pressed her against the pillows. Carefully, he took the glass of champagne from her grasp and settled it on the night table in noticeable contrast to the heedless way she had knocked his own drink out of his hand.

"Not unless you are lecturing her on the Great Plague," she added as caveat.

She felt his smile on her skin as he pressed kisses against her neck. "Not unless."

Already, she felt her boredom easing. "What about Joseph?"

An inarticulate murmur was his only response.

"He will knock at an inopportune time," she said breathily, her ability to think rationally slipping away as sensation began to overtake her.

"I will leave the tray outside," he said reassuringly, although he demonstrated no indication of doing so. Indeed, he seemed to sink further into her as he raised the hem of her night rail.

"Oh, yes, that will keep the Black Death from your door," she said on a light laugh before succumbing entirely to her husband's attentions.

Chapter Fifteen

enied the opportunity to burst in on Mrs. Wallace in the middle of the night, Bea was reluctant to bother her now that Kesgrave had deemed the hour appropriate for an invasion.

"It is not an invasion," she said sharply as he escorted her down the hallway toward the staircase in the back of the house. "It is a conversation."

"Followed by a frenzied ransacking of her private possessions," he said.

"A thoughtful search," she corrected but knew the distinction was not as clear as her emphatic tone implied. If only they'd made their foray under the cover of darkness with the fire of discovery propelling them forward. Now, in the bright light of day and after several hours of consideration, the hunt for Mr. Réjane's hidden object felt intrusive, almost like the invasion Kesgrave claimed it to be, and like any incursion, it required a careful negotiation of terms. The details would have to be worked out in advance before a single drawer could be inspected.

It was so inefficient, the demands of diplomacy, and yet it

was not the inefficiency of the endeavor that had her taking the stairs more slowly than usual.

No, it was the looming awkwardness of the forthcoming conversation. It was perfectly wretched to have to tell one's housekeeper that her suitor's seemingly earnest proposal of marriage had been naught but a ploy to gain access to her room to use it as a strongbox. If Mrs. Wallace put any stock at all in his offer, then she would find this information to be a cruel betrayal.

Furthermore, the revelation would require her to contemplate just how her employers had arrived at their distressing conclusion. As she was a reasonably intelligent woman, the obvious answer would occur to her quickly enough: Baffled by his offer, they had turned the matter over and over again in their heads until they found an explanation more outlandish than the act itself.

Mrs. Wallace would be mortified to realize she was the target of so much ducal consideration and confusion. The poor woman would probably never be able to raise her head again in the presence of Kesgrave and would be well within her right to hold the new duchess responsible for the humiliation.

So much for establishing herself with the staff, Bea thought wryly.

All this awfulness could have been avoided if Kesgrave had simply allowed her to pursue her supposition the night before. Her plan had not been without its drawbacks, she conceded, but it had had one significant advantage: the disorienting nature of sudden arousal. Awakened from a deep sleep, her wits nicely scattered, Mrs. Wallace would have stood bemusedly by as her things were carelessly rummaged through by the Duke and Duchess of Kesgrave.

Like a horde of locusts clearing a field, they would have been gone before she scarcely knew they had been there.

Quick and clean, all feelings spared!

But no, Kesgrave had to insist on respecting his servant's privacy.

Did he not comprehend what being lord of the manor meant?

As churlish as she was with Kesgrave for creating what she considered to be an intolerable situation, she refused to hand the matter over to him. The notion that Mr. Réjane had hidden something of great value in the housekeeper's rooms was hers, and she would be the one to explain it to Mrs. Wallace, no matter how wildly implausible it sounded.

There was always a chance—slim, she felt, but no less real —that her conclusion entirely missed the mark, and if that was the case, then it would be her name the staff bandied about in the servants' hall, not the duke's.

At the bottom of the staircase they turned right and immediately encountered Joseph, who, spotting the duchess first, smiled in greeting, for her presence belowstairs was already a familiar sight. A moment later, however, his eyes perceived the duke, and he straightened his posture so force-fully Bea feared his spine would crack.

Knowing better than to show concern for his physical well-being, Bea dipped her head in acknowledgment and wished him good morning.

"Good morning, your grace," he said, speaking a little louder than was necessary in his anxiety.

Or perhaps, Bea thought, he was alerting his colleagues to their presence, for the other servant they encountered en route to the housekeeper's rooms already had his eyes tilted down when they passed.

Mrs. Wallace was standing on the threshold of her office and did not appear unduly alarmed by their presence—an impressive accomplishment, Bea decided. Given the subject of their previous discussion and how infrequently Kesgrave visited the lower quarters, the housekeeper must have some inkling of the impropriety or discomfort to come.

Bea greeted her warmly and announced they had a matter they needed to discuss with her right away.

"Of course, your grace," Mrs. Wallace murmured, "please come in."

Although Kesgrave professed to be afraid of earning his staff's disapprobation by invading their private quarters, he displayed no ill ease at being in Mrs. Wallace's small office. Smoothly, he gestured to a chair, encouraging the housekeeper to take a seat, complimented her on the cheerful assortment of yellow roses that sat in a white porcelain vase on her desk, and received her gratitude with a gracious nod. Then he leaned against the door.

Bea, perceiving it was her turn to speak, decided there was no point in gently working her way up to the awkward topic. She would state it simply and without equivocation. "Mrs. Wallace, it has come to my attention that Monsieur Alphonse may have used his visit to you on the day he died as an opportunity to hide something in your office."

The housekeeper was as skilled as the rest of the servants at concealing her emotions, but she could not smother the shock that entered her eyes or resist the urge to look at Kesgrave for confirmation of his wife's statement. Her surprise was fleeting, however, for only a moment later, she returned her gaze to the duchess and announced that she had no recollection of her visitor behaving in a manner that suggested he had a secret object to hide.

"He sat in that chair," she explained, indicating the one Bea currently occupied, "and spoke to me for about thirty minutes."

As much as Bea appreciated Mrs. Wallace's dispassionate response, she could not help being slightly taken aback by it and wondered at the effort it required for her to appear unaffected by the news. Naturally, she did not draw attention to it and surveyed the room from her vantage point. She saw few opportunities for concealment. The desk was simple and solid, with no outfacing drawers or compartments, and the chair was likewise plain and sparse.

Thoughtfully, she considered the shelves along the wall.

Could they be reached from the chair?

Gauging the distance, she imagined her fingers would just touch the edge of the wood. If Mr. Réjane was several inches taller than she, he might have been able to make firm contact....

But that would require quite a lot of conspicuous stretching and Mrs. Wallace claimed to have noticed nothing amiss.

That meant he must have hidden the item while the housekeeper was absent from the room. "Did you leave him alone at any point?"

"No," she said firmly, and then immediately drew her brows together. "Well, yes, I did, but only very briefly and just to go into the other room. He suggested we toast to our futures—his in Paris, mine in London—and I went to get a bottle of cordial my mother sent me. I keep it in a chest at the foot of my bed. It could not have taken me more than half a minute to fetch it. Actually, we needed glasses as well, and those took me a little longer to locate. Perhaps I was gone for one and a half minutes. Is that enough time for him to have hidden something? He certainly did not seem harried or disturbed when I returned, and I took particular note because I wanted to reassure myself that he was not hurt by my refusal. Additionally, nothing was out of place after he left, which I know because I always straighten up every night before I go to bed. If something had been moved, I would have noticed."

"I do not doubt that, Mrs. Wallace, for you are remarkably efficient," Bea said sincerely. Although flattery may be as good as solving a murder for earning a servant's respect, her admiration for the housekeeper was genuine. If only every person she interrogated were as straightforward and informative as she. "With those constraints in mind, where do you think he might have hidden the object?"

Mrs. Wallace pursed her lips and looked around her room consideringly. "It would depend on the object, I suppose. What are you looking for?"

It was a reasonable question, and Bea admitted with some reluctance that she did not actually know. "But bearing in mind what you said earlier about his not appearing to have something to hide, we may assume the item was very small or very slim."

"Like a letter?" Mrs. Wallace said. "Or a piece of jewelry?"

Bea agreed they were both likely prospects.

The housekeeper sighed and admitted with consternation that it could be anywhere then—hidden behind the console, pressed between the pages of a book, tucked discreetly in a drawer. Then she looked at her mistress and asked how she would like her to conduct the search. "I can do it myself or summon one of the footmen to look."

Ah, yes, of course, Bea thought, struck by the trickiness of the situation. She had been so worried about embarrassing Mrs. Wallace with her suitor's true motives, she had failed to consider the specifics of the search itself. Obviously, it would be untenable for the Duke of Kesgrave to rifle through his housekeeper's things—not because she was his housekeeper but because *he* was the *duke*. Peers of the realm did not do their own rifling. They employed servants for that.

She had done it again, she realized with satirical humor, brought Kesgrave to yet another new low. Would there be no end to the depths to which she would consign him? And this time it would somehow be worse because she would be diminishing him in the eyes of his own servant.

Would assuring Mrs. Wallace that she intended to perform the task herself help to improve his standing among the servants?

Probably not, she decided, as marriage to her had already dealt it a decisive blow.

The question was, then, could it do further harm?

She rather thought the answer was no, as Marlow steadfastly believed she was a brazen hussy, an opinion no doubt shared by the rest of the staff. In that case, shamelessly hunting through the housekeeper's possessions was in perfect keeping with their expectation of her and nothing would be lost. If anything, Kesgrave might gain their compassion for having allowed himself to be gulled into a match that was even less advantageous than they had first perceived.

But that was not ideal either, earning the pity of one's retainers.

Then again, really, how much sympathy could a servant truly feel for a duke? She herself loved him quite dreadfully, and she had so little care for his dignity that she'd brought him to his housekeeper's office to comb through her things.

Before Beatrice could reply to Mrs. Wallace, Kesgrave intervened "Did you have those flowers?"

Focused on the pragmatic concerns of the search, Mrs. Wallace was startled by the question and appeared initially incapable of grasping it. "Did I have...." She repeated, trailing off before lapsing into a moment of silence. "Yes, your grace, I did. Mr. Marlow gave them to me from the delivery we received from the florist on Wednesday," she explained as the color rose in her cheeks. Hastily, she added that they were only castoffs. "With sparse blossoms or bruised petals. He did not think they were fit for the drawing room or your bedchamber, so he gave them to me."

At first Bea attributed her blush to the revelation of Marlow's kindness—and recalled suddenly the odd high squeak the butler had made when he learned of Mr. Réjane's proposal—but she quickly realized Kesgrave was the source of her embarrassment. She was horrified by the prospect that he might think that she had appropriated his flowers for her own enjoyment.

Mildly, Kesgrave applauded the practicality of the arrangement and commended the butler for coming up with it, as there was no reason for such lovely roses to go to waste. "But I was thinking rather that the vase might make an excellent hiding place," he said, "as it is in within easy reach of the desk."

The vase!

"Yes, of course," Bea said eagerly, eyeing the vessel, which was slender, to be sure, but not so narrow that an emerald ring or a pearl necklace would not slide easily through the opening. "So not a secret document revealing Mr. Mayhew's true parentage, then."

Kesgrave's lips quirked, indicating that he had not realized they were entertaining that possibility. "Not a secret document, no."

As Mrs. Wallace looked on in bewilderment, Bea lifted the vase and noted its inordinate weight. "That would seem to confirm your supposition. Would you like to do the honors?" she asked, holding out the vase.

He deferred to her and asked Mrs. Wallace to retrieve a glass so they may empty the water neatly. She complied at once, disappearing into the other room and returning with two goblets and a teacup. "I was not sure if one would do," she explained awkwardly.

Bea removed the roses, placed them gently on the desk and tilted the vase. At once she heard the clang of metal and smiled excitedly at Kesgrave. A few moment later, several dozen gold coins clattered onto the surface. "Well done, your grace," she murmured.

Agog, Mrs. Wallace stared at the treasure. "But that is a small fortune in guineas. In my very room. *Under my very nose,*" she said, her tone as amazed as it was dismayed, before fervently apologizing to the duke for her ignorance. "I had no idea. I assure you, your grace, I had no idea at all. I cannot believe Monsieur Alphonse dropped them in there while I was getting the cordial. There are so many. I was gone for only one minute, maybe two, and when I returned, he was sitting in that chair, as calmly as you please, and he had just placed a small fortune in my flower vase. If I had had any suspicion that such a wicked scheme was afoot, I would have reported it to you at once, your grace. Oh, my, and think of the scandal if Dolly had found the money when she came in to change the water. What a horror! If I had had any clue they were there, I would have come to you at once. You must believe me, your grace."

Having accepted her suitor's romantic duplicity with aplomb, the housekeeper seemed thoroughly unnerved by his financial deceit.

"You may calm yourself, Mrs. Wallace," Kesgrave said firmly, "for I have no worry on that head. I am sure you were ignorant of Monsieur Alphonse's dealings, and even if you were not, you have done nothing wrong. We know nothing of the source of the money, and there is no reason to assume the explanation is sinister."

Pausing her count of soggy guineas at twenty-one, Bea glanced at the duke with amusement. "*No* reason?"

Mrs. Wallace shook her head and sank down into her chair on the other side of the desk, as if suddenly too tired to stand. "I cannot imagine what he was about, hiding a small fortune in my office. It is a wonder, your grace, and I am grateful you were so clever as to figure it out now. I keep imagining how horrifying it would have been if in a few days I emptied the vase myself and discovered them."

She spoke with gushing admiration, not only for Kesgrave's ingenuity in identifying where the treasure was hidden but also for his shrewdness in recognizing a threat to her and taking steps to remove it. Hearing it, Bea grinned in delight, for far from bringing him low, she had raised him in his housekeeper's esteem.

That she had managed to further establish her husband with his own staff was an irony not lost on her.

Bea finished her count at thirty-seven while the duke poured the water from the glasses back into the small vase against Mrs. Wallace's protest that she would be happy to do that.

"Nonsense," he said, returning the tidy bouquet to the vessel, "it is done."

Mrs. Wallace thanked him with a hint of worship in her tone, and Bea perceived again the great advantage of being a duke, for performing even the most insignificant task was seen as a tremendous accomplishment. She herself had arranged hundreds, if not thousands, of flowers in vases and had never once got so much as a grateful smile from her family.

Bea gathered the guineas into a neat pile, and Mrs. Wallace, as if suddenly recalling her presence, insisted on getting a small bag so the duke may carry them easily. She refused to listen to his contention that he could simply slide the coins into his pockets.

"And ruin the impeccable line of your coat, your grace?" she scoffed dismissively as she darted into the other room. A moment later she reappeared with an olive-green purse. "I am sure such an extreme sacrifice is not required."

She held the small bag open as Bea scooped the coins inside.

"Ah, that is perfect," Kesgrave said, nodding with approval.

"Yes, thank you," Bea said as she tugged the two pink ribbons to close the purse. "We are very grateful for your help."

Indeed, what Bea was truly grateful for was the housekeeper's pragmaticism. With her sensible outlook, the only mortifying thing about the exchange was her adoration of her employer, a discovery Bea wasted no time in mentioning to Kesgrave.

"I cannot imagine why that is a revelation to you," he observed, following her into the drawing room to discuss the next phase of their investigation. He closed the door and joined her on the settee. "I have repeatedly explained how scrupulously I follow their rules. All you have to do to earn the esteem of the staff is allow them to go about their business with no interference. It's really very simple, Bea, and hardly requires the effort of solving a murder."

As Bea already knew there were two sets of rules—one for him and one for everyone else—she saw no point in responding to his comment. Instead, she turned her attention to their puzzling discovery. Naturally, when she had realized that Monsieur Alphonse had secreted away a mysterious item in Mrs. Wallace's office, she had not actually believed it was a slip of paper that revealed the name of his murderer.

But she had not completely rejected it either.

And now she had thirty-seven guineas.

As Mrs. Wallace had said on multiple occasions, it was a small fortune, and the most logical and obvious conclusion was that it had originally belonged to someone else—someone who had perhaps tried to regain it and killed the chef in the process.

Or maybe merely sought revenge for the theft.

Kesgrave, however, took issue with her deduction and

pointed out that the money might have belonged to Réjane. "Given that his head was ultimately removed from his body, it is not unreasonable to assume he felt some concern for his personal safety. Perhaps he was in the process of removing his possessions by degrees so as not to call attention to his plan to leave the establishment under the cover of darkness. He might have been planning to join his brother in Paris all along."

Although Bea appreciated any scheme that included a midnight escape, she felt the size of the fortune precluded such a benign explanation. "No, it must be in some way tied to his fate. If we discover the source of the funds, we might discover the identity of the killer."

But Kesgrave was not convinced, for the amount was not so great as to incite murder. "As you yourself said, the method of decapitation indicates a tremendous amount of anger toward the victim. Would the theft of such a paltry sum really provoke so much wrath?"

Ah, but it was not a paltry sum, Bea thought, so astonished by the duke's perspective that she stared at him as if he had just announced the Earth was flat. "Are you truly ignorant of how little money your servants make? Thirty-seven guineas is four years' worth of wages for Joseph."

"It is actually three years' worth for Joseph," Kesgrave said smoothly. "It is *four* years' worth for Helen in the scullery and fourteen years' worth for Silas the kitchen boy, but he is only twelve and will see reasonable increases as he ages. It is twice what Mrs. Wallace makes per annum, one and a half times what Marlow earns and eight pounds more than what Jenkins receives. I give these figures to demonstrate that I know precisely how little money my servants make and would counter that the word *little* is inaccurate, as I provide salaries that are well above the average for a London household. I may jest about treading carefully among my staff to retain their goodwill, but the truth is, I compensate them well and they know it. That is why Mrs. Wallace adores me."

He spoke softly, mildly, his tone almost conversational, but Bea detected the thread of irritation just beneath the surface and realized she had given offense without intending to. It was a surprise, to be sure, for she considered her observation to be entirely innocuous, for only someone who was insulated from the vagaries of fate would consider thirty-seven guineas to be an insignificant sum. Men were murdered for far less in the noisome alleyways of St. Giles.

As Bea had not intended to provoke a response from her husband, she was not quite sure how she did it. Was it the implication that he did not know something that pertained specifically to the management of his estate? He was, after all, a man who prided himself on knowing the particulars of a great many things, and the amount of money he paid his servants was not a minor detail. Even Aunt Vera could rattle off the list of salaries for 19 Portman Square, although she always did it in a peevishly helpless tone, as if at once baffled and annoyed by the fact that one had to pay one's staff at all. Perhaps knowing the servants' wages was a basic requirement of household management, and she had insulted him by implying he fell short of the minimum standard.

That was certainly in keeping with the duke's perception of himself.

Or she was giving the matter too much thought and the problem was simply that he resented being accused of naiveté?

Possibly, he was embarrassed by the charge.

No doubt he considered himself hugely cynical, for he was endlessly sought after for the things he could provide—comfort, stature, consequence—and had learned to distrust the motives of the vast majority of the *ton*.

If that was the case, she thought, calling attention to his

response would only make the situation worse, would it not, for there was nothing more embarrassing than having one's embarrassment remarked upon. Likely, he would grow even more defensive and list the salaries of every member of Haverill Hall.

They would remain in the drawing room for hours and grow no closer to identifying the person who chopped the head off the greatest chef in Europe.

For Mr. Réjane's sake, then, Bea decided to evade the issue entirely by changing the subject. Thoughtfully, she drew her eyebrows together and observed that the reason his housekeeper worshipped him—"Note, I never said anything as insipid as *adore*"—was he'd noticed the flowers. "It is your eye for minutia that makes you so popular with your staff and is one of the reasons why you are so well suited to be an investigative assistant."

Kesgrave regarded her silently for several long moments before saying with amusement, "Investigative assistant, brat? Previously, I was your partner. How did I merit the demotion?"

"You did not get a demotion, your grace, so much as I earned a promotion," she explained helpfully. "But you must not despair that you will remain in the subordinate position indefinitely, for you show great promise. Figuring out where Mr. Réjane had hidden his treasure was a particularly clever stroke. If you continue to display such ingenuity, you will be a senior investigative assistant in no time."

She expected him to laugh, for he usually took her nonsensical condescension in the ridiculous spirit it was intended, but instead he stood up, took several steps and said with ardent disapproval, "You are appeasing me."

Although she was taken aback by the accusation, she made no effort to deny it. Having been disconcerted by his umbrage and lacking a full understanding of it, she had indeed taken the easiest path. Nevertheless, she did not think his description was entirely accurate. "On the contrary, I am placating you. To appease you, I would have to accede to your demands, of which you have made none. Rather, I am trying to make you less severe by introducing a new topic. I would have thought the matter of your demotion would have been sufficiently insulting to your ego to distract you from your ill humor."

Even as his lips remained tightly pressed together, Bea thought she could detect a lightening of his expression. "And now you are trying to cajole me," he said.

Again, she was compelled to disagree. "I believe the term you want in this instance is *tease,* for I have made no effort to flatter you. Far be it from me to lecture you on the differences between words, for you are the pedant in the family, but you seem to be having trouble today grasping the subtle distinctions in meaning. But you must not worry. I am here and have ready access to a dictionary to ensure your diction is as precise as always. And now you might think I am coaxing you out of your bad temper, but I am in fact *still* teasing you."

Kesgrave laughed, and returning to the settee in three easy steps, took her hands into his own. "Calling thirty-seven guineas a paltry sum was ill-considered, which I knew the moment I said it, and yet I took a pet when you very reasonably pointed it out. Please forgive me."

Bea observed that obviously there was nothing to forgive, because people were allowed to have bouts of churlishness if they so desired—to which Kesgrave promptly responded that he had been surly. "Churlish implies a sort of mean-spiritedness and I was merely bad-tempered."

Delighted by his return to form, Bea provoked him further by defending her term ("I meant it in the sense of a lack of civility or graciousness"), and the exchange devolved in a display of affection that was directly at odds with the goal of attaining justice for the slain Frenchman.

Aware of the disservice, Bea struggled to put some distance between her and the duke, an act made more difficult by the fact that she lay beneath him on the settee. In a matter-of-fact tone that belied the way her blood was pounding, she said, "Regarding the thirty-seven guineas."

Kesgrave, perceiving her intention, immediately altered his position so that she could rise into a sitting position with a modicum of dignity. Then he laughed softly and said, "I knew it was a demotion."

Bea took a steadying breath and marveled again that she could still feel so much for him. She would have thought that the consummation of their relationship would have in some way tempered her desire. Instead, it appeared to have intensified it. "Your inability to grasp the urgency of the investigation puts you at a disadvantage with the murderer, who did not consult the patronesses of Almack's regarding the proper hour for decapitation."

"Surely, three a.m. *is* the proper hour for decapitation," he murmured.

Allowing for the accuracy of the remark, Bea replied, "Nevertheless, your refusal to invade Mrs. Wallace's room until proper visiting hours is the one deficiency that stands against you. But your superiors are confident you can learn from your mistakes and quickly recover your position."

"Ah, so you admit it was an invasion," Kesgrave said with air of vindication.

"And your frivolousness," she added, "so that's actually two deficiencies. Nonetheless, we are partners, though not what you would call equal ones, and we must devote some attention to discovering the source of Mr. Réjane's small fortune. It is possible, yes, that the money was his own savings, accumulated over a period of several years, but given the fact that he required a bank loan to help his brother, I think it's far more likely that it belonged to someone else. I think the obvious person in this situation is Mr. Mayhew himself."

Kesgrave nodded firmly. "As you pointed out, few of the servants would be in the position to accumulate so much wealth and if they did it would have taken them several years. None of the younger members of the staff could ever hope to save that much money."

"You think the butler could have," Bea said, following his line of thought.

"His salary over several years would make it possible, and if Réjane stole his life savings after endangering his position, an enraged Parsons might have struck back. It would explain the violence of the assault."

Bea agreed with his assessment and added that the groom could have also amassed the tidy sum over the course of years. "Or Mrs. Blewitt. Any of the upper servants could have saved thirty-seven guineas if their salaries were commensurate with their position. But it seems likelier that the source of the money is the Mayhews, either master or mistress. I lean toward the former because of the timing of his call to Mrs. Wallace, which followed a trip to the Mayhew & Co. offices to inquire about his bank loan only to discover that he had been fobbed off with a lie. We knew he was irate and probably felt he was owed compensation by—"

She broke off with a gasp as another idea occurred to her.

Excitedly, she said, "Kesgrave, he was *in the bank*."

At first, he did not comprehend the meaning behind her emphasis and looked at her with confusion, but he quickly grasped her intention. "You think he took the money from the bank?"

"Is it so implausible?" she asked, anticipating his rejection of her theory. "As I said, the timing hits the target in the center and explains why he felt compelled to leave the house in the middle of preparations for a large dinner party. Having stolen the money from Mayhew & Co., he had to remove it from the house at once. And if we are looking for a source of a sizable collection of coins, I hardly think we can do better than a bank."

"On the face of it, yes, a bank is an excellent place from which to steal a small fortune, for that is where fortunes of all sizes reside, but in actuality the money at a bank is well guarded and secure. If Réjane had a talent for picking locks, he might have made a go of it after several days of research to discover where the money was stored and learn the guards' schedules. And then he would have to move at night, at a quiet hour when the bank was all but deserted and even then, at least one guard would remain on duty. Also, Mayhew intimated that some of his clerks remain in the building overnight. Possibly, he could arrange the thing for during open hours, but that, too, would require a fair amount of research. Furthermore, his best chance would be to assume a disguise and pretend to be a large depositor and fling around great amounts of money to disconcert and lull the clerk into providing you with the opportunity to act," he said thoughtfully. "But what you are suggesting—an impromptu theft conceived and executed on a whim—is impossible."

It might have indeed been beyond the chef's capabilities, but Bea thought that Kesgrave, who possessed the required lock-picking skills and, apparently, a wily and devious mind, could accomplish the task with aplomb. She could not say why she found the prospect of the duke being capable of great feats of larceny so appealing and yet, for some reason, she did. Contemplating it, she was almost inclined to reinstate his position as full partner on the spot. "Very well, let's say he did not get the money from the bank."

"He did not," Kesgrave interrupted, objecting to her speculative tone.

Bea eyed him balefully. "Didn't I just say that, your grace?"

"No, you did not."

Having owned herself deeply enamored with his pedantry, she could hardly quibble about it now. "Very well. As Mr. Réjane could not possibly have got the money from the bank —there, I trust that is unequivocal enough for even you—let us consider from where else he might have stolen it. From a reserve Mr. Mayhew keeps on hand to pay for minor expenses, one supposes. Tell me, Kesgrave, where do you keep your pin money?"

Even before the duke could protest the description of his cache as something so delicate as "pin money," she realized her error. "Good God, Beatrice, you are a dunderhead!" she cried in disgust as she leaped to her feet, suddenly too filled with energy to sit still. "Stebbings all but told you where Réjane got the money."

She did not have to elaborate, for Kesgrave was only a step behind. "Mr. Mayhew's coat."

"The silk weave with the cerulean stripes," she added as she strode toward the ornate fireplace, with its lavish bouquet of roses spilling out of a glass vase.

"I do not doubt his dressing room is exactly where Mayhew keeps his coins and banknotes," the duke said. "It is not an uncommon spot for such storage. Unless Mayhew is particularly careful with his things, the valet would know precisely where the cache is. If he did not discover the victim with the coins in his hand, then he must have suspected what he was about."

"We must interview him again," Bea said tersely. Clearly, Stebbings knew a lot more information than he had revealed the day before.

Kesgrave agreed at once.

Gratified, she announced she would fetch her pelisse from upstairs and be ready to leave in five minutes.

But the duke had another idea. "No, let us stay here and I will send a footman to bring him to Kesgrave House."

Although her instinct was to object to the delay—would he never grasp the importance of urgency?—she quickly perceived the advantages of the alteration, for they were all around her in the gilded ceiling and the marble hearth and the Aubusson rug, which was still pristine despite years of abuse. "Oh, yes, that is an excellent plan. We shall intimidate him with the opulence of your drawing room and he will tell us everything we want to know, perhaps even confess to the crime," she said, regarding him with sincere admiration. "I must commend you, your grace, on possessing such a wily and devious mind."

His lips quivered as the duke shook his head. "As much as I desire your approval, Bea, I had nothing conniving in mind. I simply have no inclination to return to Mayhew's home, for in doing so I would be forced to converse with him again and I will not do that for anyone, not even you, my love."

But Bea, who was determined to see him as a diabolical genius, rolled her eyes at this demurral and grinned.

Chapter Sixteen

Bea knew that the next time Marlow grumbled to his fellow servants about their brash and assertive mistress he would start with the unutterable vulgarity of her inviting the neighbor's valet to enter Kesgrave House through the front door.

The front door!

If the butler had possessed a string of pearls, he would have clutched them in dismay until his knuckles turned white.

Lacking the adornment as well as the freedom to express his outrage, he nodded slightly and murmured, "Very good, your grace."

As he left the room, Bea shook her head sadly and said with pursed lips, "You have offended the butler with your cunning scheme to intimidate Stebbings."

"It was not a scheme," Kesgrave said again. "I was simply desiring my own comfort."

"There is no need for false modesty, for Marlow is gone," Bea insisted as she stuck her head out of the door to confirm his absence, "and cannot be convinced."

Kesgrave pulled her away from the door and into his arms. "Brat," he said fondly before indulging in a delightfully luxurious kiss that ended far too soon with the appearance of Mrs. Wallace bearing a tea tray.

Silently, he watched as the housekeeper placed the silver salver on the table and neatly arranged its contents, including a plate piled high with tea cakes. When she left, he said, "Tea? We are now serving tea to Mayhew's valet?"

"I simply desire your comfort, your grace," Bea explained as she took a cake off the top of the stack and tore off a small bite. As always, the baked goods Mrs. Wallace managed to supply on a regular basis were delicious.

"I believe we've switched to considering your comfort now," he said.

Bea's response was forestalled by the arrival of Marlow, who announced the presence of the valet in a begrudging yet imperious tone. Then he immediately closed the door, as if unable to look upon the scene unfolding before him—first the front door, now the heirloom china.

'Twas all too much to bear.

Amused, Bea turned her attention to Stebbings and noted that he appeared to be in little better condition than the butler, his face pale, his eyes fluttering, his hands fisted in discomfort as he apologized for interrupting.

"Y...you are...are having tea, your grace," he sputtered. "I am happy to stand in the hallway while you finish."

Bea waved breezily and bid him to come farther into the room as she and the duke settled onto the settee. "There is no need to wait. Please, come sit down."

This seemingly harmless request put the valet in a terrible fix—for he could not possibly take a seat in the Duke of Kesgrave's drawing room like a proper guest but nor could he defy the duchess's order—and he looked around desperately as if seeking a third option, like a bed of nails or something equally uncomfortable.

Find nothing to suit his needs, he settled for the hardest chair in the room and lowered himself gingerly. Then he bowed his head and grasped the wooden seat.

Bea lifted the plate of tea cakes off the tray and offered him one. "I'm sure they are not as good as Monsieur Alphonse's delightful creations, but they are rather tasty."

Stebbings squarish face lost its last bit of color as he raised his head to look at her in the eye. He seemed determined to hold himself together, his grip tightening as if in physical exertion, but something in Bea's curious gaze shattered his resolve and he shrieked in protest. "I didn't do it! I didn't! I swear! You must believe me! I never touched him, not even when I saw all those guineas in his hand! Never, never, never," he chanted frantically, "never, never, never."

Even as Bea leaned forward to seize on his statement regarding the coins, Kesgrave, demonstrating yet again a lack of urgency, ordered Stebbings to calm himself. The command was issued in the same matter-of-fact tone the duke used to request tea and had the desired effect. The valet's shallow breaths slowly gave way to normal inhalations.

When he was satisfied with the other man's control of himself, Kesgrave said, "Now, without getting worked up again, please tell us about your encounter with Monsieur Alphonse in Mayhew's dressing room. I believe you just mentioned something about coins? Do tell us about those."

Although the valet looked as though he was seconds away from succumbing to another fear-induced convulsion, his voice was even as he apologized for his intemperate response. "I did not anticipate a summons to Kesgrave House, and having received one I expected to be accused of murder. Everyone knows what you did at the Stirling ball," he said, speaking to Beatrice now, his focus directly on her as his voice grew stronger, "how you coerced Lord Wem into confessing, and I was terrified you brought me here to trick me to confess, just like Wem. But I am innocent and Wem was guilty—I have to keep reminding myself of that: Wem was guilty and I am innocent. I have faith in you, your grace. I have faith that you compelled Wem to confess because he had done something terrible to your parents. I have faith that you won't compel an innocent man to confess to a crime he did not commit. So, please, ask your questions. And if I may, yes, I would like a tea cake, thank you."

As she held the plate out again for his perusal, she noted that despite the smoothness of his tone, his hand shook slightly as he selected a pastry. He was frightened.

"I believe his grace has already posed it," she said gently as she returned the plate to the table. "Tell us about the coins."

"Right, yes," Stebbings said, gripping the tea cake a little too tightly as crumbs fell into his lap, creating a small mess that he was too distressed to notice. "Mr. Mayhew keeps a collection of coins in a box in the clothespress. It is not a very great amount of coins, usually around fifty guineas, so that he may take a few when he is going to his club or to church. Monsieur Alphonse was angry with Mr. Mayhew on Friday for lying to him about the bank loan for his brother. I do not know the details, but Monsieur Alphonse felt grievously mistreated and was determined to take what he felt he was owed from Mr. Mayhew. He found the box with the coins and stuffed every last guinea into his pockets. That is when I discovered him."

Bea nodded, for what he had said aligned with her own conclusions. "And what did you do?"

"I told him if he put the money back, I would not say anything about it to Mr. Mayhew," Stebbings explained.

"But he did not put the money back," she said.

His gaze remained steady at he answered the implied

question. "No. I begged him to return the coins but he refused. Then I told him that if he did not return the money, I would tell Mr. Mayhew at once what had happened."

"And that is when the exchange grew heated?" she asked, recalling Annette's description of their argument.

His faith in her wavered—just a little bit but enough for her to see the doubt creep into his eyes—and he took a deep breath before responding. "No, it grew heated when he threatened me in return. I had been stealing from Mr. Mayhew for years, which Monsieur Alphonse knew because he had once observed me pocketing a few coins while he was waiting for an opportunity to sneak a cheroot. I did not take a lot, I swear, just a coin here and there every few weeks. Mr. Mayhew never noticed because he did not keep careful count and he did not realize I knew the box was there. Monsieur Alphonse said that if I told Mr. Mayhew about his thievery, he would tell him about mine, and of the two of us who would be turned over to the magistrate for our crimes, I was the only one who would suffer the consequences, for he was the most famous chef in the world and I was nobody in particular. He said all he would have to do is bake a few *croquantes* for the magistrate and—poof—the charges would be gone. I trust you see now, your grace, why I must have faith in your decency and wisdom. I have confessed to a crime, and you could have me sent to Newgate if that is your desire. I humbly submit to your wisdom."

As much as Bea wanted to dismiss his statement as extravagant toadying to her new title, she realized the submission was actually made to Miss Hyde-Clare. The faith he professed to have was in the woman who had confronted Lord Wem, not the one who married Kesgrave.

With that consideration in mind, she told him that her interest in the matter extended only to discovering who killed Monsieur Alphonse. "If you are not the one who removed his head from his shoulders, then the business between us is concluded. Although I would advise you going forward not to steal money from your employer, as that is an excellent way to see your own head removed from your shoulders."

This sobering piece of advice did little to temper his relief at her statement, and his entire body seemed to exhale with the deep breath he let out. "That is precisely what you will discover because I had nothing to do with it. After Monsieur Alphonse issued his threat, I withdrew mine and begged him to take only a few coins at a time because Mr. Mayhew would notice if they all disappeared at once."

"And you would be blamed," Bea observed, silently noting that he had a far better motive than she had ever imagined. The theft of thirty-seven guineas was grand larceny. If the jurors found him guilty, he would be hanged.

"I would be blamed, yes, of course. The dressing room is my domain, and I know it intimately."

"And you had taken money from him before," Bea pointed out. "If he sometimes wondered why it seemed as though he had fewer coins in his box than he'd thought, those suspicions would solidify and he would realize you had been stealing from him for years."

Stebbings lowered his head in shame. "Yes."

Was fear of the gallows enough to drive the valet to murder?

It was certainly an inducement, she thought, looking at his pale face. If the chef was dead, he could neither assert his innocence nor proclaim Stebbings's guilt. He would be blamed for the theft, and the valet would slip the noose.

As always, she was struck by the brutality of the assault and wondered why Stebbings would choose such a violent and difficult method. Possibly, it was necessary for the story he had planned to tell in the morning about ruthless thieves or evil-minded associates who had broken into the house and murdered the victim. Whatever tale he had contrived became unnecessary the moment Parsons told his own fiction.

How relieved he must have been when the butler announced it was an accident.

Having devised a damning scenario for the valet, Bea wondered if it was likely.

The fact that he had stolen from his employer for years indicated a conscience somewhat in repose, but decapitation was many miles removed from judicious thievery. And Stebbings had been quite judicious in his thievery, skimming just enough coins to line his pockets and evade suspicion. That was the act of a prudent man who understood consequences, valued patience and possessed the self-control to keep his greed in check.

It was these character traits, Bea thought, that argued in favor of his innocence. Chopping the head off the chef to solve a problem simply seemed too immoderate and extreme for a man with his fortitude and foresight.

"Am I correct in assuming Mr. Mayhew hasn't noticed yet that the money is gone?" Bea asked.

Stebbings, his gaze firmly focused on the lovely Aubusson rug, admitted that he had not. "He has been too distracted."

But he did not say the incriminatory part out loud: that Mr. Mayhew's distraction and Mr. Réjane's death all but ensured he would escape prosecution.

Perhaps aware of where his interlocutor's thoughts had gone, he added that he hoped his freely given confession would weigh in his favor.

Bea, however, was not convinced that *freely* was the accurate description, for as soon as he received the summons to Kesgrave House he realized something quite inauspicious was afoot. He might not have been certain the duchess knew about the guineas, but he had enough cause to suspect it. In that case, revealing the truth before she asked was his only recourse, for it gave his admission the patina of honesty when it actually bore the luster of desperation.

When Bea failed to congratulate him on his candor or agree with his assessment, Stebbings raised his eyes to meet hers and pleaded for understanding. "I was angry and terrified, I admit it. We did not rub together very well, Monsieur Alphonse and I. For all his generosity, I found him to be a very selfish man. I know the staff thinks I am inordinately focused on this business with the cheroots, but I believe it sums up the whole issue. He had an abundance of cheroots. Mr. Mayhew gave him cheroots, and he took them periodically from the dressing room. Yesterday, I saw even Mrs. Mayhew slip him two. He had all the cheroots he could desire and still he never shared a single one with me. He was miserly when it counted, and I did not like him. But I did not kill him," he said earnestly. "No matter how much I disliked him, I would never have killed him or anyone. I hope you can believe that, your grace. But even if you cannot, I have faith that your sense of fairness and justice will not allow doubt to guide your behavior and you will continue to investigate the crime until you have found the true perpetrator."

Although she knew he was trying to manipulate her, she could not resent the effort, for regardless of his status—guilty or innocent—he had every right to try to save himself by employing whatever means were at his disposal.

And like every other member of the staff, he had pointed the finger elsewhere.

Recalling their previous interview, she asked if he still thought Henry was responsible.

Blushing brightly, he shook his head and said that the footmen would never have killed Monsieur Alphonse over a little snoring.

"A little snoring?" Bea repeated wryly. "Last time we spoke

you said it sounded like a dozen horses thundering down the lane."

Stebbings lowered his eyes again to the carpet and muttered something about the effectiveness of a well-placed pillow over a fellow's ears. Then he mumbled an apology for attempting to mislead her and the duke. "I knew with our argument in the dressing room that I appeared guilty and I wanted to supply a better suspect. It is a measure of my desperation that the only name I could come up with was Henry. He could never have done it, for he is quite mild-mannered and gentle for all his strength. If I had been thinking clearly, I would have said someone more notoriously volatile like Gertrude in the kitchen. She has a terrible temper and little control over it. Everyone has witnessed it, even Mrs. Mayhew," he said offhandedly, then he stiffened in his chair as a thought struck him. "Yes, *even* Mrs. Mayhew. She was meeting with Mrs. Blewitt in her office one morning when Gertrude had a most alarming tantrum. And it was particularly egregious because that was the time Gertrude threatened to assault Monsieur Alphonse with a clever. You must ask...I mean, you *should* ask Mrs. Mayhew about the incident. I think you will find it speaks to Gertrude's lack of control. Even with the mistress in the room she could not restrain her anger."

He was doing it again, Bea thought, supplying another suspect, a better one who, he must know, had already been brought to her notice.

And yet she could not entirely dismiss the information, for his observation was accurate. Even with the lax supervision at 19 Portman Square the staff knew better than to lose their tempers in the presence of the family. Once, when she was sneaking out of the house through the servants' entrance, she heard Dawson upbraiding Harris sharply for spilling milk into the eggs after assuring him with soothing calm in the breakfast room that it was no bother. That the kitchen maid could not show the same restraint was very damning indeed and allowed for the possibility that she had lashed out at Mr. Réjane later for the drubbing she had suffered at Mr. Mayhew's hands during the dinner.

Revealing nothing of her thoughts, Bea thanked him for sharing his opinion and looked at Kesgrave to see if he had any questions. Assured he had none, she announced to the valet that their business was concluded at that time.

His color still high, Stebbings nodded profusely and owned himself to be deeply grateful for her consideration. "I promise everything I have told you is the truth. I will not lie to you again, your grace."

As soon as Marlow had shown the valet out, Bea turned to the duke and said, "We seem to be acquiring new suspects, rather than culling them."

Kesgrave dipped his head in acknowledgment and added that Stebbings's motive was particularly strong—stronger, to be sure, than the kitchen maid's. "It was clever of him to make it a matter of temperament."

"Yes, and he does have a point. Having had the self-control to implement a yearslong scheme to steal money from his employer, he hardly seems likely to act with such immoderation or abandon," she said, then sighed deeply and leaned her head against the back of the settee. "He has put us in a devil of a fix."

Kesgrave, who was sitting in the wooden chair Stebbings had recently vacated, stretched out his long legs and crossed them at the ankles. "How so?"

"Mrs. Mayhew," she said.

He raised an eyebrow, still not comprehending her meaning.

"We are obligated now to ask her about the incident between the kitchen maid and Mr. Réjane," she explained.

Readily he agreed. "And?"

"*And* we decided earlier that we would not return to number forty-four, and we cannot invite her here, for being invited to Kesgrave House is one of Mr. Mayhew's chief desires. If you will recall, it was on his original list of demands. I simply cannot abide the prospect of giving him anything he wants. Perhaps we can meet her in the square," she said thoughtfully, standing to look out the window at the verdant lawn across the way. "I can post a watch in front of her house, and when she goes outside, we can bump into her as if by accident."

"Now who is displaying a lack of urgency?" he asked, clearly entertained by her proposal.

To be sure, he was only teasing her, but his point was well taken. Waiting for Mrs. Mayhew to appear was a time-consuming and unreliable approach, and remaining on hand to hold the supposedly impromptu conversation would mean she could not pursue other lines of inquiry.

It was not a viable option.

"You are right, Kesgrave," she admitted with a faint air of defeat, "we must strengthen our spines and invite her here. But we will remove the cakes so that she cannot claim we had her here to dine. I'll write the note while you ring for the footman to take the tray away."

The duke cheerfully did as instructed and found himself summoned only a moment later by his steward, who hoped to take advantage of his presence to address further issues involving the roofs.

Bea kept the missive curt and to the point, making it clear that she had a few more questions to ask regarding Monsieur Alphonse's death and that Mrs. Mayhew would find only glancing hospitality: "As you are far too busy to linger."

When Mrs. Mayhew arrived a half hour later, however, she announced that she had rescheduled all her commitments for the entire afternoon so that Mrs. Mayhew could remain as long as the duchess required. "I could not bear it you had felt rushed on my account, your grace. You must give me no consideration at all. My goodness, this is a lovely room," she said, her head tipped back as she admired the frescoes on the ceiling. "So very grand. I have told Mr. Mayhew on more than one occasion that our home requires more ornamentation, for our drawing room is really quite plain, but he cannot be swayed by my appeals. He likes his creature comforts and cannot tolerate the thought of craftsmen in and out of the house for months. But if he could see the beauty of your drawing room, I am sure he would change his mind."

It was a plea, of course, for the duchess to invite her husband to visit so that he may inspect the grandeur of Kesgrave House for himself. "I have far too much respect for Mr. Mayhew to doubt the firmness of his convictions," Bea said.

Mrs. Mayhew laughed lightly at this statement, indicating that she perceived its undertone, and allowed that the esteem was earned, as her husband could be quite stubborn. "But even he could not resist such splendor. I feel certain he would modify his position just upon entering this room," she said, coughing lightly and immediately apologizing for the inter-ruption. "It is merely that I am parched." Pause. "So very parched."

"You must not think that I mind your little cough," Bea assured her before she could make some endearingly depre-cating comment about how she was feigning thirst to wrangle tea. "My aunt had a dreadfully persistent one last winter and I grew quite accustomed to ignoring it. Now then, taking you at your word to show you no consideration, I shall cut right to the heart of the matter and ask about an incident you witnessed in the kitchens involving Gertrude and Monsieur Alphonse."

Mrs. Mayhew, reaffirming her pledge to be the most helpful suspect the duchess had ever interviewed, immediately apologized for not being able to help. "I cannot recall any incidents involving Gertrude and Monsieur Alphonse. I can describe several interactions between Mr. Mayhew and Monsieur Alphonse," she said, as if offering a consolation prize, "for I was a party to several of their menu discussions, and I can speak in great detail of the conversations Monsieur Alphonse and I had, for I was known to seek him out upon occasion to request a particular dish. But I am afraid I cannot provide information about interactions between staff members. If you would like, I can arrange an interview with Mrs. Blewitt, who will no doubt know exactly which incident you are interested in."

Bea thanked Mrs. Mayhew for her offer but assured her that this incident did indeed involve her. "It occurred while you were belowstairs."

Mrs. Mayhew's expression, alas, remained an unhelpful mix of incomprehension and confusion. "I am still not quite sure what that has to do with me."

"You were in the housekeeper's office," Bea added.

Now the banker's wife perked up. "Ah, there, you see! Mrs. Blewitt is precisely to whom you should talk. Shall we interview her together? I think she will find my presence reassuring."

If Beatrice decided to interview the housekeeper again, she would certainly not do so in the presence of her mistress. "Let us approach the matter from a different direction. Mrs. Mayhew, when were you last in Mrs. Blewitt's office?"

"Thursday," she said promptly, an eager smile spreading across her face as she leaned forward, delighted to finally be of help. "I met with Mrs. Blewitt to finalize the menu for Friday's dinner party. Mr. Mayhew usually takes care of such matters, but he was called away at the last minute and I was required to step in. It was so very inconvenient because I was on the way to the milliner to buy a new hat."

"And while you were finalizing the menu for the party, did an incident occur between Gertrude and Monsieur Alphonse?" Bea asked.

"No," she said with firm resolve.

"Are you sure?"

Mrs. Mayhew trilled with amusement. "Am I sure? My dear duchess, Monsieur Alphonse sat next to me the entire time and I am sure the kitchen maid did not enter the room once."

"And before that, when were you in Mrs. Blewitt's office?"

"Good gracious, the time before that..." she murmured, her nose scrunching in thought as she considered the question. "The time before Thursday...the time before....perhaps early March? I do recall that it was quite chilly in her office because her fire had run out of coals, but maybe it was late February? It's dreadful, your grace, because it's so difficult to recall and yet I do so want to impress you with my memory. I must confess that I have an intense compulsion to make something up just to appear useful. Now let me think..."

Mrs. Mayhew closed her eyes as if concentrating very hard and remained silent for a full minute. "My visits to her office are infrequent because it's far easier to summon her to the drawing room. But I do like to pop belowstairs without notice every so often because it keeps everyone on their toes. That is a management tip I would give if I presumed to give management tips to duchesses. Like on Thursday, when Mr. Mayhew was called away to meet with his new investor, Mr. Bayne, and I had to step in to discuss the menu, I could have done it in the comfort of the drawing room, but I realized it had been quite a while since I had looked in on the servants unexpectedly. And of course everything was running smoothly, just as I anticipated—as you yourself have no doubt observed, having spent some time down there yourself. It's such a strange idea to contemplate, the Duke and Duchess of Kesgrave in one's very own servants' hall. I do not recall when that humble room has been so honored before. Of course, Mr. Mayhew and I would be deeply grateful for the opportunity to entertain you in slightly more splendor. You must not worry that my husband will pester you with talk of the bank, for it would be a purely social occasion. Mr. Mayhew can be a tiny bit single-minded in the pursuit of new business—it comes, I think, from being the eldest of so many brothers and wanting to prove himself capable—and some people might find that intensity a little off-putting, but that is why he has me. I am the civilizing force in his life, reminding him that most people do not want to be regarded only as potential depositors."

Mrs. Mayhew continued to prattle, apologizing for her husband's enthusiasms while lauding his many triumphs and deploring the pressures to succeed in a family business, but Bea had stopped listening. As soon as she had heard the name of the new investor, her mind began to assemble puzzle pieces, for it seemed too coincidental that the fictional clerk to whom Mr. Mayhew referred Mr. Réjane's business shared a name with a new investor.

No, the more likely explanation was the banker had been lying again and, lacking the ingenuity to invent a new name, defaulted to one he had already used.

As Mrs. Mayhew appeared to be no closer to the end of her monologue, Bea was compelled to interject.

Her guest, afraid that she had rattled on too long, apologized with a hint of mortification and said that she may have allowed her determination to be helpful get the better of her. "I wanted to give you every detail I remember in case I know something important. I will try to be more judicial in the future."

Bea thanked her for both her enthusiasm and restraint before following up on the piece of information that interested her. "Mr. Mayhew did not consult with Mrs. Blewitt on Thursday to finalize the menu because he had a meeting with Mr. Bayne, an investor?"

"Yes, yes, he did, but that is not at all unusual. He meets with investors frequently."

"And are they all named Mr. Bayne?" Bea asked.

Disconcerted by the question, for she had not missed the satirical note in the duchess's tone, Mrs. Mayhew laughed awkwardly and said with hesitance, "Well, no, they have names particular to their families. Mr. Illing is called Mr. Illing, and Mr. Scott is called Mr. Scott. I am sure the other members of Mr. Bayne's family are also called Bayne, although having met none of them, not even Mr. Bayne himself, I cannot swear to it."

As Bea was increasingly convinced the investor called Mr. Bayne was no less a figment of Mr. Mayhew's imagination than the bank clerk of the same name, Bea was hardly surprised she had yet to meet him. "And Monsieur Alphonse was at this meeting?"

Now the banker's wife was completely mystified and stared at her host in utter befuddlement. "Monsieur Alphonse? Attend a meeting with an investor? It would be highly unconventional for Mr. Mayhew, of the estimable Mayhew & Co., to bring his chef to a meeting with an investor. I suppose if the meeting was to discuss funding a joint venture with Monsieur Alphonse, it would not be so strange. I do recall Monsieur Alphonse being quite determined to help his brother establish a patisserie, but I do not believe he was seeking investors. It is possible I am wrong, as Mr. Mayhew does not discuss the particulars of bank business with me."

"I did not mean the investor meeting," Bea struggled to

clarify. "I meant the meeting with Mrs. Blewitt to discuss the menu for the dinner party on Friday."

"Oh, *that* meeting?" she said, giggling self-consciously at the misunderstanding. "Of course, that was what you meant. Good gracious, you must think I am a silly goose to make such a muddle of it. I came here so determined to help and now I am wasting your time! Yes, Monsieur Alphonse was there. After all, we were discussing the menus and reviewing what was available at the market because having the right ingredients is vital to a meal's preparation. You cannot make duck *à l'orange* without duck or *l'orange,* although Monsieur Alphonse would never have made anything with citrus because Mr. Mayhew detests the flavor. Too strong. Oh, dear, I cannot imagine what we are going to do without him." As if struck anew by the consequences of his death, she paused to sigh sadly and shake her head with mournful regret. But then her features brightened as she lifted her gaze. "I cannot tell you, your grace, how grateful I am for your interest. The situation was being handled in the most rag-mannered fashion until you stepped in. Blaming that idiotic device! Truly, I do not know what that constable was about, allowing Mr. Mayhew to sway his opinion, although perhaps it is not his fault as my husband can be very convincing. I do hope when this terrible episode is behind us, you will allow me to thank you and the duke for your kindness by hosting you properly."

To be sure, Bea would permit no such thing, and ignoring the second invitation to dine just as assiduously as she had ignored the first, she sought to confirm that Monsieur Alphonse was present when Mrs. Mayhew announced why she was stepping in for her husband at the meeting. It was, however, a futile endeavor, for her guest claimed to have no recollection of any particulars that did not pertain specifically to the menu, and as if sensing the duchess's disappointment, proceeded to relate every detail she could recall. As she listed the several dozen ingredients that went into all seven layers of the *gâteau à la mousse,* Bea began to suspect something slightly nefarious was afoot, and she went to the window to make sure Mrs. Crackenthorpe of *The Tatler* was not hovering in the square noting the number of minutes the banker's wife remained inside Kesgrave House.

Bea would not put such a maneuver past either of the residents of number forty-four.

Even so, she saw only a maroon landau with a pair of bays drive by.

If Mrs. Mayhew was employing an extreme dilatory tactic to puff up her own importance, it was for nobody's benefit but her own.

The idea amused Bea, for she had spent countless hours in drawing rooms with Aunt Vera and Flora, and neither one had ever felt gratified by the experience.

Ah, but she was a duchess now.

Bea returned to the settee and sat down as Mrs. Mayhew lamented the challenges of finding strawberries at Christmas.

Christmas? Bea thought, surprised to discover Mrs. Mayhew had rambled as far back as December while she was examining the square for interlopers. It was unacceptable, traveling backward in time, and she decided she had to end the session immediately or listen to another year's worth of menus.

Interrupting curtly, she said, "I must bring this interview to an end now, Mrs. Mayhew, as I am in the middle of an investigation and do not have time for a social call."

Although Bea's intent had been to be abrupt and a little rude, her guest took no exception to her words, smiling brightly and murmuring, "Social call, yes, of course. I apologize for allowing our *social call* to run on a little too long. It was merely that I was overtaken by the comfort of Kesgrave House. Such a pleasure to see that its interior matches the gracious perfection of its exterior. I have often wondered, walking by it daily. But do allow me to leave you now in peace. I am grateful for your hospitality, your grace, and hope that I may be able to repay the kindness in the near future if you are amenable. But, of course, I understand if you are not. You only have to say, for I am as determined to be as good a friend to you as you require."

Once again, Bea found herself almost charmed by Mrs. Mayhew's sycophancy, which possessed an appealing guileless-ness. By openly stating her intention to be as ingratiating as possible she eliminated much of the heavy maneuvering that usually undergirded excessive flattery.

The lightness of her touch contrasted sharply with her husband's oozingly aggressive approach, which, Bea realized now, assumed a sort of unqualified success and blamed its target when it fell short. It was this sense of entitlement that gave Bea her most enduring disgust of Mr. Mayhew and the reason she could not eliminate him from her list of suspects even though more likely ones had recently emerged.

To that end, she resigned herself to summoning yet another servant to Kesgrave House.

Chapter Seventeen

The duke appeared in the drawing room just as Joseph was setting a new tea tray on the low table next to the settee, and examining its contents, Bea tilted her head thoughtfully. It seemed to her that the pile of tea cakes could be higher. Mrs. Blewitt was a housekeeper, after all, and would not be as easy to impress as Stebbings.

"Do see if we have more tea cakes in the kitchen, for I want the plate to create a sense of abundance," Bea said to the footman, "and let's use the more impressive teapot."

Although clearly confused by her request, Joseph nodded firmly and promised to return with the items posthaste.

Kesgrave, amused by her description, asked if she imagined a shelf with teapots arranged in order of impressiveness.

In fact, this was exactly what Bea saw when she pictured the copious storage in the butler's pantry, with its lavish collections and neat assortments. "Given your aversion to the servants quarters, your grace, I do not know how you can be convinced they are not. Regardless, Joseph understood my request perfectly."

"I suspect you mean *adequately*," he said.

"Either way, Mrs. Blewitt will be impressed," she said, before inquiring, as always, about the roofs.

"They will hold for another day," he said vaguely, leaving his wife to wonder if he meant the inconvenience of dealing with them or the structures themselves. "And your conversation with Mrs. Mayhew? I trust it was productive?"

"Mrs. Mayhew certainly found it so, for she effortlessly accomplished her goal of sitting in the drawing room of Kesgrave House for a full forty-five minutes," she said wryly. "If I had not interrupted a lamentation on the difficulty of finding strawberries in December, she would no doubt be here still, prattling cheerfully about the scarcity of grouse in July."

Kesgrave looked at her as if she had said something at once shocking and amusing. "Why a grouse shortage in the summer? Did they all decide to fly north to the Arctic in search of cooler weather?"

Bea, who had only intended to make a point about Mrs. Mayhew's loquaciousness, not to accurately represent hunting conditions in the British Isles, observed that it was awfully clever of the duke to have suffered a roof emergency just as their neighbor was due to arrive.

"I cannot apologize for the vastness of my estate," he said softly, sitting on the settee and pulling her down next to him so that he could lay a delicate kiss on her lips.

"You can but you won't," she pointed out.

He acknowledged this as true but remained adamantly convinced that she would eventually find something to appreciate in his situation. "Even if it is only my library."

"Which I have still yet to visit," she said, sounding genuinely surprised by that development. There was, mistress of Kesgrave House for almost forty-eight hours and she had yet to hide herself away.

"We must rectify that immediately," he said, "for I have an absurd desire to see you trembling there."

And now she blushed, for she had failed to realize not only the various locations in which one could conduct marital relations but also that he had been considering them so thoroughly.

Obviously, a newly married man could not be expected to resist so charming a response in his bride and the second delicate kiss quickly turned passionate.

But even as Bea began to contemplate the advantages of the settee, Kesgrave drew back, shifted uncomfortably and moved several inches away from her on the cushion.

"Mrs. Mayhew," he said.

Her thoughts still muddled, she stared at him in confusion.

"You said she found the meeting productive," he explained, a pleased smile hovering on his lips. "Did you as well?"

Oh, he liked that, didn't he, corrupting her ability to think clearly. "Yes and no. She had no recollection whatsoever of Gertrude Vickers threatening Monsieur Alphonse with a cleaver, which is why I have summoned Mrs. Blewitt to confirm it. However, she did provide one vital piece of information. The reason she met with Mrs. Blewitt and Mr. Réjane to finalize the menu on Thursday was her husband was called away at the last minute for a meeting with a new investor called Mr. Bayne."

Kesgrave raised an eyebrow in a particularly refined manner. "Oh, did he?"

"Indeed, yes," she replied firmly.

"And I trust she explained to the company why her husband was absent from the meeting," he said.

"I think we may safely assume she did," Bea confirmed, "which is why Mr. Réjane went haring off to the bank the next morning to meet with his own Mr. Bayne and discovered promptly enough that the clerk did not exist. He then returned to Berkeley Square and confronted Mr. Mayhew, who admitted that he never had any intention of providing the loan. In response, he resigned his post and rifled through his employer's dressing room until he found something of value to compensate him for what he felt he was owed."

The duke regarded her thoughtfully for a long moment and then said, "It is, I agree, an important piece of information, but I am not sure it adds anything to the case against Mayhew. Knowing why Réjane chose to go to the bank on the morning of the dinner party doesn't incriminate him further."

Bea knew this was true: Just because every one of Mr. Réjane's actions on the last day of his life traced back to his visit to the bank did not mean his murderer's did as well. The chef's anger had cascading effects. His outrage over Mr. Mayhew's lies, for example, led to his searching his employer's dressing room and the vicious argument with Stebbings. In the same way, his theft of the coins led to his visit to Mrs. Wallace, which caused the quails to dry out and Gertrude's public drubbing at the hands of her employer.

These resentments were engendered by the visit to the bank but not directly caused by it.

Cascading effects, she thought again.

But as plausible as these sequences of events were, they felt slightly too tortuous to Bea, as if she were rummaging around for a more complicated solution when a simple one was right before her. If the bank was somehow central to the explanation, then surely Mr. Mayhew himself was central to the explanation. He was, after all, the one who had grasped on to the butler's benign explanation and ordered the immediate destruction of the evidence. And he had tried to coolly manipulate her every movement from the moment she'd stepped into his drawing room.

There was a cold-blooded shrewdness about Mr. Mayhew she simply could not dismiss, which she tried to explain to the duke by citing the example of the skewer.

"The skewer?" he said.

"Yes," she affirmed, "the skewer. Subtly, he indicated that he did not know what a cleaver was by calling it a skewer. It is that clear-headed attention to detail that makes him dangerous. He's awake to the game and playing it at all times."

Kesgrave looked doubtful, and before he could make a counterargument, she allowed that it was all a bit of a speculative stretch.

"Obviously, Gertrude Vickers's immoderate temperament makes her a much better suspect, which is why we are waiting on Mrs. Blewitt's pleasure," she said.

Joseph returned then with additional tea cakes for the plate and a silver teapot that gleamed brightly in the light.

"Perfect," Bea said happily as he rearranged the tray. "Mrs. Blewitt will be so overwhelmed by the magnificence she will immediately tell us everything we wish to know."

But Mr. Mayhew's housekeeper was definitely not as easily intimidated as his valet, and she stood stiffly near the doorway, refusing either to take a seat or accept a refreshment.

"Mr. and Mrs. Mayhew are my employers," she said with rigid determination, "and they have treated me with respect and consideration for more than a dozen years. I will not say one word against them. I am sorry if that creates a problem for you, your grace, but I must abide by my conscience."

Bea darted a look at the duke, for it was unexpected that the unsavory banker had managed to inspire loyalty in at least one member of his staff, then returned her gaze to Mrs. Blewitt and assured her she had no desire to make her violate any of her principles. "Indeed, I did not invite you here to discuss your employers. I had a question about Gertrude Vickers."

At once, Mrs. Blewitt's posture relaxed and she repeated the name in surprised relief. "Oh, yes, I see, *Gertrude*. Well, that's all right, then. What would you like to know about her?"

Bea marveled at the change in her demeanor. "We are trying to assess her ability to control her temper. You have talked previously about her many outbursts, but we are interested in one in particular."

This information confused the housekeeper, and she regarded Bea cautiously. "Of course, your grace. I will do my best to recall the specific incident."

"It is in regards to Mrs. Mayhew," Bea said.

At once Mrs. Blewitt shook her head. "Gertrude has a fierce and unregulated temper, but she would never lose it with Mrs. Mayhew. She has full respect for her authority and desires to keep her position. She knows which side her bread is buttered, even with all her problems with Monsieur Alphonse."

"Of course," Bea replied, for she had not imagined the kitchen maid losing her temper with her mistress. "Rather, I was wondering if Gertrude had one of her episodes in front of Mrs. Mayhew."

Once again, the housekeeper fiercely denied it. "Oh, no, never!" she said. "She is not lost to all reason. In their presence she is as respectful and deferential as anyone would want."

As Stebbings himself had freely admitted that he had cast around somehow desperately for someone else to blame, Bea was only mildly surprised to hear his account contested by the housekeeper. Increasingly, it appeared that the spinning top pointed firmly at Stebbings.

"What about near them?" Kesgrave asked, drawing attention to himself for the first time. "Has Gertrude lost her temper when Mrs. Mayhew was belowstairs? Perhaps she did not realize she was there?"

"Oh, that, yes," Mrs. Blewitt said with an easy smile. "She has done that on at least two occasions that I can recall or maybe three. She doesn't realize how her voice travels from the kitchen when she yells, even though I have told her repeatedly that I can hear every word in my office and still-room. I am sure it is the same in the butler's pantry. One time she threatened to burn Monsieur Alphonse's ear off while Mrs. Mayhew and I were discussing the sugar budget. It was very embarrassing for me because it looked as though I have poor control of the staff. It would have been in her rights to criticize me, but even though the yelling made our conversation difficult, she spoke as if nothing was amiss in the kitchen and we never discussed it. She is very gracious like that, always worrying about everyone else's comfort. Another time the hubbub was so loud she had no choice to interrupt our meeting and investigate."

"And what did she find?" Bea asked.

"Gertrude pacing the kitchen floor and yelling about Monsieur Alphonse's inconsideration. Four pots boiling and he walked out! He wanted a muscadine ice from Gunter's so he left to get one in the middle of dinner preparations. She was irate."

Now that sounded more like the scene Stebbings had described, Bea thought. "Was she wielding a tool as she paced and yelled?"

"An implement?" she repeated pensively, then shook her head. "I cannot recall any one in particular, but she must have had something because Gertrude is always clasping a poker or tongs or whatnot."

Vague though it was, the answer still substantiated the valet's version of events. "And did she cease pacing and yelling when she saw Mrs. Mayhew?"

Mrs. Blewitt laughed wryly. "Gertrude stop in the middle of a tantrum? Never! She continues to wail and scream until she wears herself out, usually after three or four minutes. Then she calms down and acts as though nothing remarkable has happened. I have never heard her apologize or even acknowledge that her response might not have been appropriate, especially when she is wrong. On that occasion the four boiling pots were actually simmering broths, so there was nothing to be done but wait."

It seemed to Bea that the woman she was describing—hot-headed, impetuousness, irrational—could easily swing the meat clever she happened to be holding in her hand and make several deep cuts in her victim's neck before she even realized what she was doing. Red-hot rage was swept along by its own momentum, like a wave crashing on the seashore, but it needed a push to begin its wild descent. It required provocation.

The question, then, was: Did Mr. Réjane provide it?

Given what they knew about his actions on the night of the murder, it did not seem impossible. He had torn up Mrs. Blewitt's roses in a fit of pique because his temper had been worn thin by his confrontation with Mr. Mayhew and he was tired of her accusations. In a similar mood, he could have decided to take out his churlishness on the kitchen maid for past offenses.

"How did Monsieur Alphonse respond to Gertrude's outbursts?" Bea asked.

Mrs. Blewitt furrowed her brow. "I'm not sure I understand what you mean, your grace."

"What did he do while Gertrude was pacing the kitchen with a poker or tongs and yelling invectives?" Bea clarified.

"Oh, I see. He had no response because he was never around. Gertrude always lost her temper *after* he left the room," she explained.

"So he bore her no resentment in return?" Bea asked.

Smiling faintly, Mrs. Blewitt said, "He bore no resentment against any person, just my roses. He was remarkably even-tempered for a chef, especially one who worked in the finest kitchens in Europe. I am not saying he didn't have his moments because he did, but most of the time he was pleasant and calm. He seemed to truly enjoy cooking and creating things and he was always happy to teach Thomas how to do something better, like slicing onions. I think the most impassioned I've ever seen him was on Friday morning, when he returned from an errand in a lather about something, and then all he intended to do was write a sternly worded letter."

Well, it was not *all* he'd intended to do, Bea thought, for only a little while later, he was ransacking his employer's personal possessions and stealing a small fortune that he promptly hid away in a neighbor's house. Nevertheless, the mention of a letter was interesting and she pressed the housekeeper for more information.

Offended by the implication that she would read a fellow servant's private correspondence, Mrs. Blewitt insisted she could relate no details about the missive. "And of course I did not ask. I would never pry. All I know is that he was extremely unhappy with the level of service he had received at the establishment and was determined to make sure the owners knew it."

The owners, Bea thought, meaning the four younger Mayhew siblings.

She darted a glance at Kesgrave, who also considered the information significant, and asked if Mr. Mayhew knew about the letter.

Mrs. Blewitt's eyebrows flew up to her hairline. "I should think not! Monsieur Alphonse was unconventional in many ways, but even he was not so freakish as to seek out the master of the house and tell him about an unsatisfactory shopping experience."

But what if Mr. Réjane mentioned the letter to him during their quarrel? Perhaps Mr. Mayhew had reason to fear his brothers' showing interest in his management of the bank.

Could he be hiding something?

Having extracted all the information she required from Mrs. Blewitt, Bea asked her husband if there was anything further he would like to know, and receiving a negative response, thanked the housekeeper for her time.

Clearly relieved to be dismissed, Mrs. Blewitt lowered into an awkward curtsey and bid them good day. Then she all but ran from the room.

As soon as she was gone, Bea turned to Kesgrave and said with barely suppressed excitement, "You know what we must do now."

Smiling faintly, he said, "I know what we *should* do, which is question Mr. Mayhew about the letter to judge if it caused him concern, but I fear you are going to say something utterly foolish like break into Mayhew & Co."

She beamed at him with approval. "Yes. We must break into Mayhew & Co."

His shake of the head was swift and emphatic. "No."

"Oh, but we must, for we cannot proceed in our investigation until we know what the victim knew," she explained sensibly. "If he discovered something truly reprehensible about Mr. Mayhew while he was at the bank, then Mr. Mayhew would have cause to kill him before he could reveal the truth to his brothers. Perhaps he stood to lose everything. As you yourself have pointed out several times, Mr. Mayhew's motive is weak. But money is a strong motive. If Mr. Réjane discovered something while he was at the bank, we must discover it too. It is imperative!"

Again, more calmly this time, he said no.

But a one-word answer wasn't a reasonable argument, and she knew the duke would not expect her to abide by it. That he had a sincere respect for her intellectual abilities had been made abundantly clear on several occasions, and if he truly wanted her to agree with him, he would make an effort to apply logic to the situation. The fact that he did not indicated more than anything that he agreed with her.

"As you proposed two methods earlier, I will leave it to you to decide which is the more suitable approach," she said graciously, "although personally I prefer the late-night option, for I find your ability to open any lock inexplicably stirring and relish the prospect of skulking in dark corners with you."

"No," he said tersely.

Oh, but his resolve was slipping.

Bea drew several steps closer to him. "Although most people bow eagerly to your coronet, there are limits to its influence, your grace, and I am certain convincing a man to admit to incriminating evidence is an inevitable boundary. It is up to us to uncover the truth, and the only way we can do that is to break into the bank and examine its operation for ourselves. Given your vast knowledge of financial matters and the deft way you handle your own accounts, I am sure you will spot the impropriety in a matter of minutes."

"Now you are trying to flatter me," he said accusingly.

She made no effort to deny it. "But only because you make it easy by excelling at so many things. If you weren't quite so impressive, your grace, I would be reduced to less dignified methods."

Curiously, he tilted his head and asked what could be less dignified than blatant flummery.

"Salaciously insinuating that the sooner we identify Mr. Réjane's killer, the sooner we may resume our tour of the house, starting with the library," she said mildly. "Fortunately, your excess of accomplishments spares me the necessity such debased innuendo."

But Kesgrave, whose eyes sparked with heat at the mention of the library, observed that his own opinion of himself had taken a sharp tumble recently. "For one thing, I am far too easily manipulated by my wife."

Because it was all still just a little too difficult to fully comprehend—dull Beatrice Hyde-Clare ensnaring the impossibly handsome and excessively imperious Duke of Kesgrave —she assured him he need only wait a short interval and the weakness would pass. But Kesgrave, clearly convinced the affliction was permanent, sighed with a hint of weariness and said with firm decisiveness that it would not.

Chapter Eighteen

❧

A s the *Harpers had* made the strategic mistake of locating their fictional theater in a well-populated city in reasonable proximity to London, Bea suggested that the Erskines reside much farther afield—in the upper-north corner of Scotland.

"The county of Caithness has two municipalities of significant size, Wick and Thurso," she explained, their coach lurching slightly to the left as they turned onto Catherine Street en route to Mayhew & Co. "The former has a thriving herring industry, so I suggest we hail from the latter. We are far less likely to meet anyone who grew up in Thurso. Now do let me hear your Scottish brogue, Kesgrave, bearing in mind, of course, that the Highlands dialect is slightly different from the Lowlands' because it is more phonologically informed by a Gaelic substratum."

Kesgrave, his lips twitching with familiar amusement, reminded his wife that there was no need for them to assume false identities. "We will stride into the bank as the Duke and Duchess of Kesgrave and announce that we would like to deposit funds in a new account."

Bea, whose opinion of his plan had not improved upon repetition, pointed out yet again how foolish it was to act with such blatancy. "The clerk will know at once something havey-cavey is going on when two such august personages purport to step into their bank on a Sunday afternoon to personally open an account."

"You must not worry: Our forthright manner will disconcert them," he said definitively.

Not worry about marching into enemy territory without an assumed identity! 'Twas madness. "I cannot comprehend how you can say that with such certainty."

"Because all these months later I am still disconcerted by yours," he explained, teasingly.

"Now *you* are trying to flatter *me*," she muttered, "but I am not as susceptible to blandishments. If you cannot do a Scottish brogue, let us try Welsh, which is perhaps a little less of a challenge, as it is phonetically similar to the English spoken in Bristol, although it is non-rhotic."

But rather than speak with a melodic lilt or make any attempt to lengthen his vowels, the duke slipped forward on the bench, brushed a wisp of hair gently back from her forehead and took possession of her lips. Startled, she protested briefly, then succumbed to its effects, for it was intoxicating and sweet, and made her heart thump with happiness and need.

It ended as abruptly as it began, with Kesgrave sliding back in his seat.

Bea curled her fingers under the cushion to ensure her balance, which felt a little unreliable, and stared blankly for a moment, taking the time to gather her wits.

No doubt that had been precisely his intention.

"Really, Kesgrave, you should have a little self-respect," she said satirically, "for you are not wholly without rhetorical gifts. Before attempting to seduce me into agreement, you owe it to yourself to at least try to make a persuasive argument."

Naturally, he did not own the tactic, insisting the display of affection was an earnest gesture, not a calculated maneuver. "You are genuinely irresistible, brat."

Bea did not doubt his sincerity, for the Duke of Kesgrave had long revealed himself to be a man of unusual tastes, and as gratified as she was by his lack of resistance, she did not allow it to alter her purpose.

Acknowledging the compliment with a brisk nod, she wondered if perhaps he would not do better with an accent from another region altogether. "What if we go farther southward and try Cornish? The language itself is derived from the Brythonic branch of Celtic, and lenition occurs in the *f, s,* and *th* sounds."

Aghast at the information, Kesgrave said, "How on earth did you acquire such an arcane assortment of dialectical minutia?"

Bea was vaguely shocked by the question, for the answer should have been readily apparent to him. "*Wattlesworth's History of Languages and Their Improving Effects on Civilization from the 15th Century through the 18th Century with a Brief Sojourn to 13th-Century Salisbury.*"

"What is a Wattlesworth, I wonder," he murmured.

"Although I applaud the effort, your grace, your attempt to distract me will bear no fruit," Bea said matter-of-factly, her grip on the cushion loosening as she grew more confident in her stability. "That said, a Wattlesworth is Lester J. Wattlesworth, a don of comparative philology at Oxford, and I am happy to lend you his compendium if your own library does not already contain it. Now please, if you will, demonstrate your proficiency in your preferred dialect and we shall construct our identity from there."

"I cannot decide if I am gratified by your assumption that

my education was so comprehensive as to include lessons in thespianism or insulted that you'd think a peer of my standing would require them," he replied.

"Ah, so you are lacking the skill entirely," she said with a hint of disappointment. "You must not feel bad, your grace. I did not think to ask you which accents you were capable of before we wed, and that oversight is mine. No matter. I will do the talking once we arrive. Are you content to be the Erskines from Thurso or do you have some objection?"

Refusing to be provoked, Kesgrave announced that his family name would stand them in excellent stead, especially if Mr. Mayhew was present.

To be sure, this was a wrinkle Bea had failed to consider, for she could not imagine any gentleman returning to his post only a day after a member of his staff had been ruthlessly decapitated. Even if he cared little for the chef's death, having contrived it personally himself, she thought it behooved him to at least appear too distraught to take up his responsibilities.

Pointing this fact out to the duke, Bea was irritated by his insistence that it made no difference either way to the success of their scheme and mumbling softly under her breath, lamented the vexatious assurance of overly confident men. It was, she knew, an unfair charge, for no matter how much the duke's unshakable certainty might frustrate her, it bore no resemblance to Mr. Mayhew's unearned entitlement.

Unaware of the company to which she had silently consigned him, Kesgrave chuckled and promised her his confidence was always perfectly calibrated to the situation.

At this statement, which seemed to prove her point, Bea wanted to screech, but she was denied the opportunity by their arrival at the bank.

Blast it!

They had still yet to settle on an approach.

As if suddenly aware that her anxiety was genuine, the duke took her hand in his and said solemnly, "Trust me, my dear, you have no cause for concern. I have the matter firmly in hand. I have followed you into plenty of scrapes. This time you must follow me."

"A scrape?" she repeated, thoroughly unsettled by his understanding of their purpose. "You are leading me into a scrape? This was supposed to be a well-executed scheme, not a scrape. I wonder at your ability to inspire your followers, your grace, for that was hardly the rousing St. Crispin's Day speech one hopes for before battle. Perhaps we should review Mr. Erskine's history before we leave the carriage. The family seat is situated on a lovely park near the river and you come from a family of avid..."

But Kesgrave, adopting one of Bea's favorite maneuvers, left the carriage while she was still talking. He was at a slight disadvantage though, for rather than walk into the bank and assume she would follow, he was obligated to help her climb down from the conveyance. As soon as her feet were on the pavement, however, he continued to the entrance, and allowing her no time to admire the building's classic architecture, held out the door for her.

Succumbing to his determination, Bea entered the bank's bright rotunda, with its high arching windows, and murmured to the duke, "I hope I will have no cause to regret this."

"Your faith in me is humbling, my love," he replied softly, before stepping farther into the elaborately designed interior, complete with coved ceilings, plaster pediments, and an assortment of Greek goddesses in an alcove to the left. One carried a bow and quiver of arrows, and Bea wondered what Diana had to do with banking. Perhaps the Mayhews hunted down clients who stood in default.

Bea had little time to consider it because her husband had

marched up to a clerk in a forest green waistcoat and declared himself to be the Duke of Kesgrave.

Oh, but how he said it—in stentorian tones, yes, so that everyone in the vicinity could hear, but also with pride and conceit, as if his presence should have been eagerly anticipated.

The clerk, whose tag identified him as Mr. Squires, responded to it at once, bowing deeply as if in the presence of royalty, although surely, he had been trained better than that, and pledging to be of service.

And the look Kesgrave gave him in response, barely moving his head at all, as if somehow flicking away a fly with his glance.

It was magnificent, Bea thought.

Everyone else in the establishment thought so too, for slowly a hush fell over the room, which was large and ornate, with a row of desks along the eastern end and a kiosk with a gleaming copper roof in the middle. A high wooden structure topped by glass and divided by partitions was occupied by a quartet of clerks, who ceased what they were doing to watch the owner of the company fly across the floor to welcome the duke.

Ah, so Kesgrave had been right about that as well— despite the brutal death that darkened his home, the banker was eagerly overseeing his business as usual.

"Your grace!" Mr. Mayhew said, his breath hitching slightly from the physical exertion. His delight, however, was unmarred by surprise or confusion.

Barely acknowledging the greeting, Kesgrave said, "I am here."

And the timber of his voice—it conveyed so much at once: impatience, importance, boredom. It was, she thought, a dialect all its own.

Little wonder he had no use for a Wattlesworth.

Mr. Mayhew, perceiving the meaning of the seemingly gratuitous statement, requested with overweening obsequiousness that Kesgrave follow him to his office. Then, as if noticing Bea for the first time, he acknowledged her with an absent salutation, then returned to smiling deferentially at the duke.

The bank owner's office was gracious and comfortable, with deep-red walls, gold-colored fixtures, and a table between two low cabinets for the storage of files. Three chairs surrounded the table, which was topped with blotting paper and a bottle of ink, but he led them to a seating area near the bookshelves.

"Please sit down, your grace, and make yourself comfortable," he said with ingratiating zeal, displaying no concern or confusion over their sudden appearance as he gestured to the largest chair, which, with its boxy shape, bore an unsettling resemblance to King George's throne.

Forcefully, Bea smothered a giggle as Kesgrave majestically sat down. Lacking an equally extravagant option, Bea made do with a midnight-blue armchair. Mr. Mayhew, literally lowering himself before greatness, assumed a bergère that was a few inches shorter than was customary for such a seat.

A brief moment of silence followed as Mr. Mayhew waited for the duke to speak first. When he did not, the banker jumped into the fray. "This is the greatest pleasure—"

Kesgrave, timing it perfectly, began to speak at the exact same moment, leaving Bea to wonder how he had arranged the thing. Perhaps he had observed the inhalation of breath that denoted speech.

Of course, Mr. Mayhew apologized at once for talking over the duke, which required him to talk further over the duke, a consequence that led to another apology and the awkward realization that he had done it yet again. Baffled, he fell silent.

Kesgrave ignored it all and announced they were there to make amends.

To his credit, Mr. Mayhew showed no reaction at all to this remarkable statement. His face impassive, he said with oily smoothness, "I am sure that is not necessary."

"You dare contradict me?" Kesgrave asked imperiously.

Mr. Mayhew withered slightly but managed to keep his shoulders straight. "No, no, your grace."

"Yesterday, on the urging of the duchess, I devoted my time and energy to investigating the death of Auguste Alphonse Réjane, who you said was killed in an accident involving *le peu guillotine*. As my wife was insistent that something sinister had happened, I had no choice but to give the matter my full attention. I have done that now to my great discomfort and decided your original assessment of the situation was accurate," he announced.

The banker could not have been more surprised if Bea had tipped him out of the chair onto the rug. "It was?"

"It was death by misadventure, an unfortunate development, which I suspected from the very beginning," Kesgrave said.

"You did?" Mr. Mayhew replied in wonder.

"Nevertheless, I was compelled to make a thorough inspection of the situation out of deference to my wife," he explained. "I am sure you know how women are, Mayhew, impetuous, irrational, histrionic and emotional. Having committed myself to one, I was obligated to allow her her lead, especially because she considers herself to be something of an expert."

"Some men find a confident female appealing," Mr. Mayhew murmured generously.

"It was, on the whole, a waste of time," Kesgrave continued, "but I am a man in the first flush of marriage and can allow the indulgence. Your constraints, however, are not as fluid, and I wasted your time yesterday. That is why I am here to make amends. I will deposit fifty thousand pounds with your bank. Does that suffice?"

Did it suffice?

Did it suffice!

The expression of utter astonishment on Mr. Mayhew's face clearly stated that the question did not need to be asked.

Of course it sufficed.

A fraction would have.

A mere tenth!

Before Mr. Mayhew could gather his wits enough to express his approval of the plan, a knock sounded on the door and a dark-haired clerk entered with a tray. Gratefully, as if requiring a distraction, the banker jumped to his feet and accepted the tray. "Very good, Herbert. Your timing is ideal. Please place it on the small table and bring me the monthly register from the safe. Thank you."

Bea, whose appreciation for the duke's acting skills had risen sharply as she listened to him convincingly dismiss both her and her sex in a single sweeping stroke, was further impressed by his ability to affect scorn for the perfectly benign tea Mr. Mayhew offered.

"Is this an example of how you conduct your business, Mayhew, failing to consult your client on his preference?" he asked contemptuously. "Am I to find my money invested in a joint-stock company of which I've never heard?"

"Of course not, your grace," the banker said with soothing calm, as if trying to pacify a wild animal. "Your sanction is essential at Mayhew & Co. Please tell me how I may please you."

"Arrack," he said.

Some of Mr. Mayhew's assuredness slipped. "Arrack."

"Yes, I would like a glass of Batavia arrack."

As the fermented sugarcane drink from Asia was something of an unusual request—not entirely obscure but also not commonly found in even the most well-stocked pantry of a Fleet Street bank—Mr. Mayhew wanted to suggest a more reasonable alternative such as claret or port. But he could not, for Kesgrave had boxed him in nicely.

His shoulders sagging slightly in defeat, Mr. Mayhew opened the door and called back the clerk to make the specific request. Kesgrave, however, forestalled him with his ardent disapproval of managers who do not personally attend to matters for their most important clients. "Am I depositing fifty thousand pounds in your clerk's bank, Mayhew, or yours?" he asked with a faint sneer. "If it is the former, then allow me to be introduced to Herbert, for he and I have much to discuss."

Laughing awkwardly, Mr. Mayhew insisted that Kesgrave had misunderstood. He had been inviting his colleague in to entertain the duke and his wife while he fetched the arrack.

"Entertain me?" Kesgrave asked with vigorous disdain. "Am I a small child in need of diversion? Will he perform a puppet show?"

"No, no, of course not," the banker said, warding off the clerk with a frantic wave of his hand. "I was just teasing. Obviously, you will be fine on your own. I will be back in just a moment and then we may proceed with your deposit. I have a few papers for you to fill out. Or"—his features lightened as another, arrack-free option occurred him—"shall I send them directly to your steward or solicitor for perusal? In which case, you may return to Berkeley Square immediately and not linger here."

"Am I to understand, Mayhew, that you would rather deal with my steward than me?" Kesgrave asked superciliously.

His face pinched with anxiety, the banker rushed to assure him he would like nothing less than to be deprived of the pleasure of attending to the duke's needs. "I am determined to offer satisfaction. You only have to tell me how I may."

"Arrack," Kesgrave said tersely.

"Yes, your grace, directly," Mr. Mayhew said, sweeping out of the door to locate the hard-to-find alcohol.

But Kesgrave was not done with him yet. "And ask the duchess what she would like. I do not believe she was consulted either on her preference."

"The tea is delightful, thank you," Bea said and noted the banker's relief, which lasted only long enough for her to add that she had a particular craving for macarons.

Having already been tormented by the duke, Mr. Mayhew knew better than to protest. "My pleasure," he said with a stiff smile and promised to return with the items presently. Then he walked out of the room and left them alone in his office with all his ledgers, documents and files.

As the door clicked shut, Kesgrave leaned back in his thronelike chair and smiled smugly. "Does Mrs. Erskine want to apologize for her lack of faith now or later? It is all the same to me."

Bea, who would never be so petty-minded as to deny a wronged party the satisfaction of gloating, promptly acknowledged her miscalculation and vowed not to underestimate him again. "But," she added as she tried to open the cabinet to the left of the table and discovered it to be locked, "I could not have known that your money makes people stupid."

Kesgrave smiled faintly as he began to apply a small device to the cabinet's lock. "Yes, you could."

As she had observed the effect his wealth and title had on people on more than one occasion, she conceded the truth of the remark. Then she tried the second cabinet and found to her relief it opened easily. Its two sections were divided by a shelf; on the top were folders filled with loose sheets of papers.

Contracts, she wondered as she began to peruse them.

"How long before he returns?" Bea asked, briefly lifting her gaze to observe his brows drawn in concentration. Suddenly they lightened and the door to the second cabinet gave way.

"Ten minutes," he said tersely, pulling out a ledger. "It could be as many as fifteen, as Herbert will have to go slightly farther afield to find a tavern that is open on Sunday. Regardless, Mayhew will feel compelled to update us on his progress, so let us assume ten. I urge you to look quickly even though I am not sure what we are looking for."

"Anything irregular," she said as she flipped through one file after the other. They were all loan requests that had been denied by the bank. "I am confident we will know it when we see it. Something is off here and we will find it."

Kesgrave laid a book on the table and said, "Well, it is not in here. This book contains a list of all the bank's depositors and their assets."

"I have loan applications," she replied, thrusting the folders back into the cabinet and pulling out a ledger. She opened it to the first page and examined it in silence for several seconds before announcing she'd found the expense account for office supplies and sundry requirements. "He spent four pounds on paper last month, and two crowns on sugar. No, wait, that was aggregate. Each clerk had to contribute a shilling and there are...one, three...six...eight...ten...ten clerks, so he actually pays half that. Ah, and he reimburses himself the price of membership fees at Brooks and Whites, which seems a trifle corrupt."

"Actually, I imagine he picks up a good deal of business by advancing gamblers the blunt to settle their debts," Kesgrave said.

"Well, then, that is a dead end, is it not."

Bea continued to look through the book but found nothing else of interest.

"I have the account ledger," he announced, "with the running balances of all the depositors. It appears to be in order. I recognize a few names, which seems like an unacceptable breach in courtesy."

She put the book of expenses back into the cabinet and, turning her attention to the bottom shelf, withdrew a folder. It contained loan applications that had been approved. "How much time is left?"

"Four minutes, three to be safe," he said.

"If he returns sooner, you can stare down your nose at him and announce that you will take your fifty thousand pounds to a bank that allows you to peruse its private documents," she said.

"I suspect even Mayhew's sycophancy has its limits," Kesgrave said, laughing. "I have one more book here and another stack of documents."

"Very good," she said and instantly reconsidered when she realized they had few chances left to find something genuinely incriminating. Other than overcharging his own clerks for sugar, Mr. Mayhew seemed to run a circumspect business. She opened the last ledger and noted it was a record of his employees. Reading through the first column on the opening page, she immediately noticed something amiss.

"Mr. Réjane is here," she said softly.

Not comprehending, Kesgrave darted a confused glance up.

"His salary," she explained, "is included in the employee ledger. I think Mr. Mayhew paid him with the bank's money. It is irregular, is it not?"

Again, the duke could not agree. He owned it was not ideal, but as with the membership to the gentlemen's clubs, it could reasonably be described as a business expense. "He uses exquisite dinners to draw in new clients."

Bea thought that if she were one of Mr. Mayhew's brothers, she would object to his drawing from the bank's account to bear the expense of his servants, but it was not the sort of revelation one slew another man to conceal.

Disappointed, Bea turned the page, quickly skimming the names. There was Herbert, who had brought the tea, and Squires, the clerk who had greeted them as soon they had entered.

Now this is interesting, she thought, encountering Parsons's name. She allowed that Mr. Réjane could be categorized as a business expense in a roundabout way, but making the same argument for the butler would require far too many contortions. And he was compensated at a markedly smaller rate than the grand chef. Was the butler aware of the pay disparity? If he was, he must have found it so insufferably intolerable that this man who had endangered his own livelihood drew such a comfortable living he did not have to worry about insecurity himself.

Insufferable enough for murder?

She flipped the page.

"We must put everything back," Kesgrave said. "Ten minutes have passed and I am sure he will return presently."

Bea agreed, for it felt to her as if she had been rummaging through the cabinet for considerably longer than a mere ten minutes, but she nevertheless lingered over the employer ledger. It was the most promising document she had examined all afternoon.

Kesgrave closed the cabinet door and began fiddling with the latch to lock it again. "Bea!" he said somewhat more forcefully.

"Yes, yes," she said, her eyes racing down the page as she read name after name. It was surprising to her how many men it took to run a banking concern. And so many clerks: George Anson, William Hawes, Michael Parnell, Alan Bayne, Charles Watson.

Hold on a moment: Alan Bayne?

"*Bea!*" Kesgrave breathed urgently.

With no time left, she tore the page out of the book, folded it haphazardly and, having no other recourse, thrust it into her bodice. Then she shoved the ledger back into the cabinet and tossed the pile of documents, now chaotically disordered, on top. She slammed the cabinet door shut and with Kesgrave nipping at her heels, dashed back to her chair.

They had barely regained their seats when the door opened and Mr. Mayhew entered followed by Herbert with a silver tray bearing the requested items. Carefully, he settled the salver on the table, lifted the plate piled with macarons and held it out for Bea's selection. Although she'd asked for the pastry only out of expedience, she found herself genuinely hungry after the harried search and chose the top two. Next Herbert handed a glass filled with a rich, burnished copper liquid to Kesgrave, bowed slightly and left the room.

Mr. Mayhew, having satisfied his clients' demands, grinned broadly and announced the preliminary papers arranging for the deposit were in order as well and the duke may begin filling out the documents.

"I have changed my mind," Kesgrave said as he stood up.

At this communication, the banker's smile dimmed and he regarded the duke with apprehension. "You would like something else to drink? A glass of madeira, perhaps? I find arrack is a trifle strong when not made into a punch. Herbert could fetch brandy. Or maybe an ale?"

"I have no inclination to linger further," Kesgrave explained, "so you may send the documents to my steward for perusal. Mr. Stephens is knowledgeable and efficient and will handle the matter. Thank you for your time."

"Oh, but you can't..." Mr. Mayhew began but trailed off as he realized it was not in his best interest to tell the Duke of Kesgrave what he could or could not do. He bowed his head deferentially and conceded it was the far more practical plan. "I should have proposed it myself, your grace."

In point of fact, he had, and it was, Bea thought, a rather damning indictment of the nobility that he knew neither guest would correct him. Every peer no doubt believed that all the best ideas where his.

As the duke walked to the door, Bea scooped up the remaining macarons—there were four left—and cradled them delicately in her gloved hands. "Yes, Mayhew, thank you for your time, and I do hope you accept my apology for causing you so much inconvenience."

"It is my pleasure to be inconvenienced by you, your grace," he said smoothly before urging her to do so at any time.

Bea smiled blandly.

Inevitably, he insisted on escorting them to their carriage and highlighting the building's important architectural features, such as the James Payne rotunda, which could not be built today, for its construction was far too complicated and expensive. "It required several hundred men," he explained.

Although Bea knew the claim immediately to be false, for she had read several books on architecture, including Colin Campbell's *Vitruvius Britannicus, or The British Architect: Containing the Plan, Elevations, and Section of the Regular Buildings, Both Publick and Private, in Great Britain, with Variety of New Design,* she expressed amazement at the towering achievement.

Mr. Mayhew simpered in delight.

Delivered to their carriage, they were received by Jenkins,

who had accompanied Miss Hyde-Clare on enough outings to know they were rarely innocuous errands.

"'Tis good to see you unharmed, your grace," the coachman said cheerfully.

All it had taken to establish herself with Kesgrave's groom was getting ruthlessly pummeled in the middle of the Strand, a process she (unfortunately!) could not repeat with the rest of the staff.

Climbing into the conveyance, she assured him it was good to be unharmed. Then she settled herself comfortably on the cushion and turned her attention to the macarons. When Kesgrave sat on the bench beside her, she held out her hand to offer him one, but he boldly plunged his hand down the front of her dress.

"In broad daylight, your grace..." she murmured chidingly.

Undaunted, he smoothly extracted the torn ledger sheet and examined it to see what she'd found so interesting. While she waited for him to spot the anomaly, she nibbled on the pastry.

It did not take long.

"He lied about Mr. Bayne," he said, looking up from the page.

Bea nodded. "He lied about Mr. Bayne, who is in fact employed by Mayhew & Co., so he also lied about lying, which, while somewhat confusing, is also extremely suspicious and indicates that there is a terrible, dark secret here after all. Our next step is obvious: We must locate and interview Mr. Bayne to discover why Mr. Mayhew is determined to hide him. If he won't tell us the truth, then we will coerce it from Mr. Bayne's associates. Naturally, we will have to return to the bank to conduct the inquiry. As the Duke and Duchess of Kesgrave were quite blatant in their identities, they can neither return so quickly nor show inexplicable interest in a lowly clerk. Mr. and Mrs. Erskine, however, may do so without raising an eyebrow. Do let me hear your Scottish brogue so that I may make suggestions for how to improve it."

But he was still examining the sheet and paid her no heed. "Bayne is drawing a very comfortable salary," he observed. "At two hundred and forty pounds per annum, he can well afford to pay Mayhew's sugar supplement."

Bea nodded because the statement was accurate. Compared with the amount of money some of the other clerks at the bank made, it was an exceedingly generous income and Bayne could easily manage small luxuries like sweetener. But because she had a knack for remembering everything she read, she called up the ledger detailing the bank's various expenditures and realized Mr. Bayne had not been included among the list of employees who paid the surcharge.

That list had contained only ten names.

Possibly, that was because the fourteen out of the twenty-four clerks employed by Mr. Mayhew refused on principle to pay for sugar at their place of work or preferred their tea plain or forewent the pleasure of tea or coffee entirely. It was certainly not unheard of for a man to have ale with breakfast.

But it was strange, Bea thought, that none of the generously compensated clerks like Bayne stood the lavish expense of the supplement. It was only the ones with parsimonious salaries who contributed: Herbert, for example, who earned just sixty pounds per year. Surely, if anyone was going to forego an indulgence it would be he?

Considering the great disparity in pay, she leaned over so that she could examine the page her husband held. It was so very curious that only the clerks with the smallest salaries were standing the expense of sugar.

Too curious.

"Kesgrave," she said thoughtfully, "what is the likelihood

that not a single one of the fourteen employees who could easily afford the sugar supplement enjoys sugar in his tea?"

He glanced at her inquisitively, then back down at the sheet of paper as if looking for something in particular. "Highly improbable."

"I agree, and yet that it precisely what has happened here," she said, explaining the discrepancy she had observed. "I cannot believe the figures are legitimate. Something is being misrepresented here."

Kesgrave agreed. "Mr. Bayne is in fact fictional."

"As are Mr. Keel, Mr. Dore, Mr. Munyard, Mr. Tablin, and the rest of their so-called colleagues," she said, reading from the list of names. "Mr. Mayhew has invented an entire staff of well-paid clerks and is defrauding the bank for three thousand three hundred and sixty pounds per annum. There it is, your grace, the perfectly reasonable motive we have been looking for. Mr. Réjane's murder was not any of the things we thought: petty, irrational, spontaneous, revengeful. It was an act carefully planned by a man who knew his livelihood was at stake. If his angry chef managed to send a letter of complaint off to his brothers about a fictional clerk, they would have investigated and almost certainly discovered Bayne in the ledger. His scheme would unravel almost at once. We found it after a haphazard ten-minute search."

Although her voice lilted in disgust, she was actually relieved to have discovered a motive that was commensurate with the profound loss of the gifted chef's talents. At least he had been slain to preserve an avaricious man's wealth and status, not just his vanity.

But it had all been for naught, for his brothers would learn the truth anyway.

"We must go back," Bea said insistently. "We must confront him with his perfidy at once. There is no time to waste."

But Kesgrave disagreed. "At the risk of earning your further contempt for my lack of urgency, I think we should devise a more nuanced plan than barging into his office and hurling accusations at him."

As much as she wanted to give a full-throttle defense of her own proposal, she realized the response lacked refinement and decided to hear him out. "Continue."

"Knowing why he did it does not prove the case," he said reasonably. "Cause does not equal guilt, and even if it did, it doesn't *prove* it. Mayhew seeks my favor, but he won't confess to murder to earn it."

Having witnessed the banker's recent obsequious display, Bea was tempted to disagree with that assessment. If some beneficial bargain could be arranged to ensure deposits and status from a cell in Newgate....

But obviously, no.

Always delighted to entertain a scheme, she asked him what he had in mind. "Given your recent descent into gothic-style thinking, I have great hopes for something at once byzantine and lurid."

He laughed and assured her he was about to disappoint her, then.

"Not possible!" she said with sincerity—which turned out to be true, for his proposal entailed using the information about Mr. Bayne to trick Mr. Mayhew into confessing. "If hiring an actor to play the clerk did not remind me of Tavistock, I would insist we drive to the Particular at once and enlist Mr. Steagle."

"Fortunately, I do not think we will have to go to such lengths," Kesgrave said. "The specter of him should be sufficient. As loath as you are to bestow your attention on Mayhew, I trust you will make an exception, as I think we will have a greater success if we confront him in his own home."

"A drawing room vignette!" she said with deep appreciation for his sense of drama.

"Precisely."

"Very well," she said, giving her approval of the plan, "but if we are to put on a show, we must invite Marlow, for all of this was done for his benefit."

His grace refused to discuss it.

Chapter Nineteen

As *much as Beatrice* wanted to ask the Mayhews to dinner and coerce the banker into revealing his guilt over syllabub, she decided such a course was a little too vindictive. Receiving an invitation to dine at Kesgrave House was among the mushroomy couple's most ardent desires, and allowing them to believe they had reached the summit of their social ambition mere seconds before pushing them off the peak had an unwanted air of poignancy.

She could not bring herself to condone the arrangement even though it would have provided Marlow with an opportunity to observe her investigative acumen firsthand.

Her original plan of bringing the butler with them to number forty-four had also not prospered. Its failure wasn't due to Kesgrave's insistence that taking one's butler on social calls was entirely beyond the pale, even for her. She had heard the argument frequently enough from Aunt Vera—decorum, decorum, decorum—to ignore it easily now. The fact that decapitation was somehow not further beyond the pale denoted the limitations of propriety itself.

No, what had caused her to change her mind was the realization of how the invitation to the neighbors' house would appear to Marlow.

What she had told Kesgrave the day before was true: Her intention in identifying Mr. Réjane's murderer was to establish herself with the staff. Marlow, casually dismissing her success and skills, had left her no option other than to prove herself.

He could not know that, of course, and Bea wanted to keep it that way. Insisting he accompany her and the duke to the Mayhews would reveal how much she desired his good opinion.

Surely, there was no faster way to lose a butler's esteem than making an effort to acquire it.

Hours later, while listening to her hostess discuss her and her husband's imminent plan to visit Paris, Bea thought again of Marlow and smiled as she imagined him trying to maintain that calculatingly bland expression in the face of such tedium.

"It is de rigueur to proclaim oneself averse to foreign travel, for it involves foreigners, whom are so easy to deplore, but I am more enlightened than most. I love seeing new places and acquainting myself with new types of people," she said, having exhausted the topic of the duchess's visit to her husband's banking establishment. Astonishingly, it had taken a full fifteen minutes for her to ascertain her guest's full opinion of the experience, desiring to hear every thought Bea had ever had about the majestic rotunda, regal statues, noble pediments, stately kiosk, gracious desks.

And the chair!

Why, yes, it *had* been modeled after the throne at Westminster—the very one the king used for his coronation. ("We had tried several other chairs, but with Mr. Mayhew's regal bearing, nothing else would do. It is, I will admit, a little mortifying to have a husband who is so monarchical.")

'Twas not a direct replica, of course, for that would be sacrilege, but rather a facsimile in the general style.

"And France is such an interesting country, do you not think?" Mrs. Mayhew asked before eagerly providing the correct answer. "But of course you do, for you are well educated, your grace. Other women might censure your blue-stocking behavior, but I think it is wonderful to know things like the height of Canterbury Cathedral and the year the Parthenon was built. Ah, you are wondering if I am interested in classical architecture, and the answer is yes, I will visit Les Invalides and the Hôtel de Sully. But you must not fret that I will be distracted from our purpose, which is to hire a new chef. We will never find anyone as talented as Monsieur Alphonse, but that does not excuse us from making an effort."

Naturally, Bea was not at all worried that Mrs. Mayhew would allow herself to be diverted from her objective by the pleasures of Paris, as she knew the woman would not be visiting the city anytime soon—at least not in the company of her husband.

That Mrs. Mayhew's spirits had been dulled by the specter of murder that had hung over the house was apparent by how buoyant they were now that it had been removed.

Well, that and Kesgrave's deposit of fifty thousand pounds.

Those twin good fortunes had made her almost light-headed with happiness. Knowing how fond Bea was of macarons, she held out a plate spilling with them at regular intervals, and she kept offering to refill the duke's glass of arrack even though he had barely taken two sips of the liqueur.

Although Mrs. Mayhew was grateful for Kesgrave's vindication, she remained convinced that Beatrice had been correct in her actions and opinions. Even if *le peu guillotine* was responsible for Monsieur Alphonse's death, the duchess's suspicions were entirely justified. "And I'm not just saying that because I shared them too," she had said graciously before turning the conversation to a less chastening topic such as her trip to France.

"I am sure you are wondering how one finds a new chef in the vast city of Paris," Mrs. Mayhew continued, "and you are right to ask. Mr. Mayhew will begin by consulting with his friend Mr. Rothschild, who also oversees a large financial concern."

As she suspected that this was another topic on which the banker's wife could expound endlessly, Bea decided she had indulged the Mayhews in enough benign conversation. Launching into their scheme, she timorously interrupted her hostess to ask if she may have her help in a troubling matter. Then she looked at Mr. Mayhew and said that she would need his assistance as well. "If you would deign to give it."

"Of course, of course, your grace," he replied robustly. "You need only ask."

"It is a sensitive subject and one my husband does not want to hear another word about," Bea said, casting a brief, defiant look at Kesgrave, whose expression remained inscrutably blank at this statement. "He is, you see, still displeased with my misunderstanding of Monsieur Alphonse's death and wants me to avoid awkward questions, as he is determined to make amends for intruding on what was a tragic episode for your household."

Mrs. Mayhew, drawing her brows together sympathetically, murmured soothingly, "You poor dear, I can positively feel your anxiety from where I am sitting. You are new to marriage and not used to husbands, so let me be the first to assure you they are often churlish. You must pay it no mind and do what you think is best according to your own conscience. Now how may we help you?"

Although the other woman's voice was even and gentle, Bea could detect her excitement beneath the surface. Even if she didn't say another word, the Duchess of Kesgrave had already revealed several uncomfortable things about her marriage—an indication that Mrs. Mayhew had indeed managed to forge an intimate relationship with the new peer.

"You are so kind," Bea said, then pulled the ledger sheet from her pocket and held it up. "You see, the problem is this."

Mr. Mayhew, unable to recognize his own handwriting from several feet away, furrowed his forehead. "What is that?"

But his wife, who was only one chair over, gasped in recognition.

"It is a page from your ledger recording your employees' salaries," Bea said simply. "Mrs. Wallace had it."

Mr. Mayhew's utter bewilderment would have been funny if the situation itself were not so serious. "Mrs. Wallace? I don't know any Mrs. Wallaces."

"Mrs. Wallace is our housekeeper at Kesgrave House," Bea said.

Alas, the information only baffled him further, and he stared at her with a distracted air, as if trying to work out a very complicated equation in his head. "Your housekeeper was at my bank?" he said.

As he seemed to find the prospect of Mrs. Wallace among the regal statues and noble pediments of Mayhew & Co. to be particularly upsetting, Bea rushed to assure him that his understanding of the situation was wrong. "She did not travel to One Fleet Street. She and Monsieur Alphonse had a little romance, of which you are perfectly ignorant, for why would you know about a flirtation among the servants? When he decided to leave your employ and return to France, he asked Mrs. Wallace to accompany him as his wife. She declined the honor. At that time, he concealed this sheet from your bank ledger in her office. It was hidden under a vase whose water she changed earlier today. She had no idea it was there, so imagine her surprise when she found this list of names."

Bea paused to allow her listener to do just that, and it appeared to her that Mr. Mayhew actually made an effort to visualize the expression on the unknown woman's face.

"She could not conceive what it meant," Bea added, "so she gave it to me. Naturally, I was perplexed as well because it is a very strange thing for one's housekeeper to find under her flower vase. I could not figure out its meaning until I came across a familiar name. I trust you know which one I mean."

Alas, he did not. "A familiar name?"

"Mr. Bayne," she said.

Comprehension, finally!

But even as awareness glinted in his eyes, his demeanor remained calm as he said without a hint of self-consciousness, "Oh, I see, you found the list of my employees' salaries."

His placidity was, she believed, further proof of his cunning nature. A less sly creature would have revealed a measure of apprehension at learning that his elaborate scheme to defraud his brothers out of thousands of pounds per annum had been discovered. But by all indicators, Mr. Mayhew minded it not one wit, and realizing that, she decided to alter their plan slightly in hopes of disorienting him in another way.

"As soon as I read the name, I perceived the truth," she said. "Mr. Bayne killed Monsieur Alphonse at your behest."

As the statement was patently absurd, she was hardly surprised when Mr. Mayhew responded with amusement, first gurgling gently and then guffawing riotously. Doubling over, he clutched his stomach as if trying to contain his humor, then recovered his sense to look at Kesgrave. His voice brimming with compassion, he said, "Women indeed, your grace! You warned me of your wife's flights of fancy, and yet I was still unprepared for her outlandish conclusion. My dear duchess, I fear you are wildly off the mark. Mr. Bayne could not have possibly killed Monsieur Alphonse at my behest for the very simple reason that Mr. Bayne does not exist. I am sure I told you this already."

"That is a lie!" Bea declared hotly. "You are lying about Mr. Bayne to hide your guilt. If I cannot interview him, I cannot discover the truth. You are determined to block my investigation."

Again, he regarded Kesgrave sympathetically and shook his head, deeply saddened by the display. "To what investigation do you refer? The one your husband apologized for this afternoon? My dear duchess, you are mortifying yourself with these outrageous accusations. Come, let us have no more talk of it. Mrs. Mayhew and I are planning a trip to Paris to find a new chef. I am sure a man of your distinction, Kesgrave, is well traveled. What do you advise for first-time visitors to the city?"

"Yes," Mrs. Mayhew said, joining the conversation, for she was as eager as her husband to smooth ducal feathers, "do give us advice, your grace, for we are eager to take instruction. Being without the comforts of home can be challenging. How do you mitigate that influence?"

"No, no, no," Bea cried angrily, stamping her feet in excessive frustration because she believed that was what the banker believed silly women did. "Mr. Bayne has to exist. He draws a salary from your bank. I *demand* to be introduced to him at once."

"I must ask you to calm yourself, your grace," Mr. Mayhew said harshly, then immediately apologized to Kesgrave for his presumption. "Of course it is not my place to admonish the duchess, but getting worked up over a fictitious character is not how we behave in the best drawing rooms."

Graciously supplying the banker with the length of cord

he required to hang himself, Kesgrave assured him that it presented no problem for him. "You must act according to your conscience."

Fervently, Mr. Mayhew agreed. "I must."

"If Mr. Bayne does not exist, how can he be on a list of employers who get paid regularly?" Bea asked, her tone piercing and shrill. "I'll tell you the answer. He cannot. It is impossible. A phantom cannot draw a salary!"

"It is simple, your grace," he said calmly. "*I* draw Mr. Bayne's salary."

It was a measure of his ingenuity that he could own his guilt whilst smiling innocently.

His wife, who did not possess her husband's steely nerves, leaped anxiously into the conversation to ask the duke about the Luxembourg Gardens. "Tell me, your grace, is the Medici fountain worth a visit? I have heard conflicting reports. Apparently, it fell into disrepair, but Napoleon diverted some funds to restoring it?"

But the mention of diverted funds was not quite the sweeping subject change Mrs. Mayhew had hoped for, and she fell silent, pressing her lips together almost painfully.

Bea ignored her entirely and looked accusingly at the banker. "You drew the salary? But that is theft!"

"My dear girl, I *own* the bank. I cannot steal from myself," he explained with a look of amused condescension that he directed at the duke. "I am not surprised you cannot understand that. You are female, after all, and limited in your ability to think through complicated matters. It is not your fault that numbers confuse you. Nevertheless, I would beg you to cease humiliating your husband."

Ah, yes, her husband.

Did Mr. Mayhew not find it curious that the duke had yet to intercede?

Surely, if he was embarrassed by his wife's intractability, he would put an end to it. He had certainly proved himself autocratic enough.

Bea continued to argue. "You are stealing from the bank's other owners, your own brothers!"

Somehow, he managed to retain his calm, dismissing this charge as easily as the others. "My brothers draw a nice living from Mayhew & Co. and have no cause to complain."

How confidently he spoke! How assured! How secure!

But Bea couldn't believe it.

No, she could not. It simply wasn't possible that four members of the same family—brothers, no less, with all the attendant rivalries and jealousies that relationship entailed—would blithely shrug off the theft of thousands of pounds per annum.

"Oh, but would your brothers agree?" Bea asked, making her last play, determined to pierce his mask of cool indifference. He exuded calm composure, but surely inside he was trembling with apprehension at the revelation of a scheme so nefarious he had killed to keep it secret. "Would they really believe they have got their fair share and to begrudge you a little extra would be churlish? I don't think so, Mr. Mayhew. I don't think so at all. I think they would be irate and remove you from your position at once. Would they take criminal action against you? I don't know. That would depend on their appetite for scandal. But I do know whatever measures they took would be devastating to your comfort. You would lose your house, your staff, your horses and memberships. You would lose everything, and that is why you killed Monsieur Alphonse. Because he was about to send a letter to your brothers alerting them to your mismanagement and you were terrified of losing everything."

Mr. Mayhew laughed.

Delighted with her tirade, utterly gleeful, he laughed and laughed, and Bea, observing the seeming sincerity of his amusement, decided he was the most diabolical villain she had ever encountered. She did not expect all murderers to crumble like Wem at Lord Stirling's ball, to admit what they did while reverting to some childlike state, but nor did she anticipate a wall of obfuscation so immense she could not scale it.

Eventually, after a great long while during which his wife glared at him with impatience, Mr. Mayhew gained control of his amusement and turned to Kesgrave with a gleam in his eyes.

And it was such a gleam—such a bright, eager, voracious, predatory glow—that it caused everything in the room to shift. Like a portrait slightly askew, the view had been tilted for a long time and now suddenly it was straight and she could see the image for what it was.

Bea inhaled sharply and felt the pervasive relief that came with clarity.

Triumphant in his good fortune, Mr. Mayhew said to the duke, "Your wife is accusing me, your grace. I cannot imagine what kind of amends that will require."

But in fact he could, for if the investigation itself had warranted a deposit of fifty thousand pounds, then a charge of murder in his very own home had to be worth double that.

No, triple.

Maybe quadruple.

On and on the numbers spun in his head, growing impossibly higher as he contemplated the duchess's folly, and Bea could not understand how she had considered him a viable suspect for so long. The face he presented to the world—slack, leaden-eyed, uncomprehending—was the only face he had. There was no Machiavellian schemer plotting in secret behind the dull facade. No, it was dullness all the way through.

That was why he had no reaction to the threat of

Monsieur Alphonse's letter—he genuinely lacked the intelligence to imagine how a report detailing his managerial malfeasance might negatively affect him.

It was horrifying now to see how she had altered reality to make it align with her assumptions. Over and over again she had contorted the truth to squeeze it into a box labeled "genius," like when she had assumed he misidentified the use of a cleaver to throw off suspicion.

But why would he know cleavers and skewers—that one chops, the other pokes and neither pinches? The minutia of the kitchens was entirely irrelevant to his existence. He never even went belowstairs. All meetings with Mr. Réjane were conducted in his study.

Mrs. Mayhew, keenly aware that another Parisian landmark would not alleviate the awkward vulgarity of her husband's display, tried a more forthright approach. "Darling, one does not receive reparations by seeking them," she chided gently with a contrite smile at Kesgrave.

Her husband, instantly alive to her game, all but winked at her as he apologized to Kesgrave for his faux pas. "Of course I would never expect you to increase your deposits just because your wife accused me of murder in my own drawing room. That would be dreadfully gauche. But if you do decide to make an alteration, Mayhew & Co. would have no objection."

It was comical, Bea decided, the disparity in the two spouses, for even though they both liked to blather, Mrs. Mayhew perceived the undercurrents of a conversation as well as their implications.

She would have no difficulty in recognizing the problem a letter from Monsieur Alphonse would present.

No, she would not, Bea realized pensively, her gaze sliding to the banker's wife to also consider her in a new light. To be sure, she had a firm alibi in her lady's maid, but what if she did not? What if Annette had been compelled to lie or was deceived in some way by her mistress? The perpetrator of the last murder she investigated had also appeared free from suspicion, and he turned out to be a villain through and through.

Mrs. Mayhew's motive was just as strong as her husband's —stronger, actually, because she understood the problem in a way her plodding spouse did not. For one thing, she realized his brothers were not satisfied with the "nice living" they drew from Mayhew & Co., for she made several comments about their competitiveness. The more likely situation was that each brother was on the constant lookout for an opportunity to overcome the advantages of primogeniture and seize control of the London bank. Nobody was ever satisfied with running a modest provincial concern when there was an influential establishment in the capital to oversee.

Furthermore, Mrs. Mayhew, who made a habit of visiting belowstairs whereas her husband did not, had witnessed one of the kitchen maid's outbursts. Unaware of her illustrious audience, Gertrude had stomped angrily around the kitchen wielding a cleaver threateningly.

If she wanted to implicate someone else in her crime, Mrs. Mayhew could not have found a better sacrificial lamb than Gertrude Vickers. Regularly, as if by clockwork, she provided fresh fodder for any Machiavellian schemer determined to cast suspicion in a different direction. Of course Monsieur Alphonse was viciously beheaded by the kitchen maid—she had been telling you of her intentions for months!

And how had she described her?

Bea briefly closed her eyes to recall: *Gertrude is a rough-seeming creature but very capable.*

Did that, finally, explain the wrenching brutality of the murder? Because Mrs. Mayhew believed that was the way a rough-seeming kitchen maid would end a life?

'Twas a horrifying thought.

But if that was the way of it, how had the banker's wife managed it?

Mr. Réjane was no hulking giant, but nor was he an unusually small man. Subduing him would require strength Mrs. Mayhew decidedly did not possess.

She would have had to incapacitate him first.

How?

With the shovel, she wondered, recalling the way Mrs. Blewitt had brandished it threateningly. It had been conveniently left in the courtyard, and someone *had* put it away.

Could Mrs. Mayhew have knocked Mr. Réjane over the head with it?

It was possible, yes, but given its heft and Mrs. Mayhew's slight frame, it would have required all her effort. If she had to struggle unduly with the implement, Mr. Réjane would have time to notice the attack and disarm her.

Why take that risk?

Better to employ a method that did not rely on strength.

A drug of some sort?

Bea herself had spotted laudanum on Mrs. Mayhew's vanity. Could she have used a tincture of laudanum to render him unconscious?

Possibly.

But how would she have convinced him to ingest the drug? She could not simply adulterate a glass of wine and serve it to him. As the lady of the house there would be no precedent for sharing a drink with one of the servants.

The cheroots on the other hand...

Yes, she thought, sitting up straighter in her chair. Mr. Mayhew furnished his chef with them regularly, and his wife, who reportedly did not approve of the practice, was spotted giving Mr. Réjane a pair of cheroots on the day of the dinner party.

Clearly, yes, that was how she did it, and once he was insensible, it would have been easy enough to slice his head off—physically, she thought, recalling the distinction Henry had made, not mentally.

Mentally, it had to have been horrifically difficult.

But if she had that within her, the ability to make the cut, whether unflinchingly or with great revulsion, the question was how she could have done it while also being in the presence of her maid.

Whatever her talents, Mrs. Mayhew could not be in two places at once.

Had Annette lied to protect her mistress?

It was possible, of course, for servants told untruths at the direction of their employers all the time. But collaborating Mrs. Mayhew's story about a nightmare was not a harmless white lie; it was helping a murderess get away with her crime. Surely, Annette did not value her position so highly that she would run the risk of being hanged alongside her mistress?

And to hold to that lie when questioned by the Duke and Duchess of Kesgrave—Bea could not believe the lady's maid had enough spine to withstand that kind of pressure without revealing anxiety.

No, Bea assumed Annette was telling the truth, which meant Mrs. Mayhew had enacted her deception via another method.

Scrutinize the variation, she told herself, reviewing the suspect's story. The intensity of the nightmare was unusual, even if she sometimes had bad dreams. Ordinarily, she summoned her maid to her bedside to read her a comforting story for a short time. But on the night of the murder her dreams were so terrifying she could not bear to stay in her bed and insisted they retire to the dressing room for several hours.

The variations: a different room and a longer time period.

What, then, did the dressing room offer that the bedchamber did not?

Considering the unusual length of the interval, Bea immediately thought of the clock—the one that was prominently displayed above the vanity. She had noticed it almost as soon as she had entered the room and consulted it herself whilst teasing Kesgrave about their plan to have an informal dinner in the bedchamber.

At that time, she had rattled off how many hours and minutes until they would be alone together, and Kesgrave, marvelous pedant as he was, corrected her assessment.

What had he said?

The clock on the wall over there is off by several minutes, for in fact you should be trembling beneath me in one hour and fifty-one minutes.

Oh, but the clock *should not* have been wrong. According to Parsons, setting the clocks was among the duties performed daily by the staff. The only way the time could be off by so many minutes was if someone had moved the hands recently.

Not just recently, Bea realized, but since the morning of the party. The butler himself had said it: None of the chores had been performed properly the day before because the servants were too distressed by the murder. That meant the clock in Mrs. Mayhew's dressing room had not been reset as per usual, which was why the time was still off when Bea consulted it yesterday a little after four.

Could Mrs. Mayhew really have been so devious as to—quickly, Bea did the calculation—push back the hands by an hour to make it appear as though she had been in the dressing room during the interval of the murder? If she had killed the chef after everyone had retired—likely around two o'clock, for the last person to go to sleep had been Mrs. Blewitt at one-thirty—then she could have returned to her room, cleaned up, changed the clock, climbed into bed and promptly affected a terrifying nightmare. Hours later, when the maid thought she was going to sleep at four, she was really going to sleep later, around five o'clock or so.

It was an elaborate scheme and very difficult to prove. But there must be evidence somewhere in the house: a bloody glove, a poisoned cheroot.

Bea's stare as she considered Mrs. Mayhew's guilt must have been quite intense for Mr. Mayhew, who was not known for his observational skills, noticed her interest and jubilantly remarked on it.

"The duchess is going to accuse you next!" he exclaimed, practically bouncing with excitement as he gestured to his wife. "By the time she is done making her way through the entire household, Kesgrave will have committed his whole fortune to Mayhew & Co."

He spoke with such casual contempt for her deductive skills, Bea could not help but turn lightly pink at his observation. She tilted her eyes briefly down, and when she raised them again, she found the duke studiously examining her.

"Are you certain?" he asked softly.

She nodded.

"I suppose I am not fully surprised," he admitted.

Mr. Mayhew, not appreciating the sotto voce exchange between the spouses, complained that he could not hear a word the duke was saying.

"La, they are probably discussing the best way to extricate themselves from our presence," Mrs. Mayhew said with an almost aggressive vivacity, "for you are making them extremely uncomfortable with your talk of deposits."

Reminded again of his manners, Mayhew brazened out the blunder by insisting he was considering only the duke's convenience, for it was far easier to stay abreast of one's investments when they were in a single place.

"You mean his steward's convenience," his wife corrected sharply, "for it is he who keeps abreast, not Kesgrave himself."

As Mrs. Mayhew strove to appear delighted with her husband, Bea realized the woman had actually done him a favor by unceremoniously chopping off the head of his prized chef, for if she had not behaved so immoderately now, she would have inevitably behaved immoderately in the future— with him as her victim.

"He is right, Mrs. Mayhew," she said, taken aback by her own strange reluctance to say the words forthrightly. Only minutes ago, she had laid the same charge at the banker's feet and experienced not a hint of self-consciousness. Was it because Mrs. Mayhew was a woman or because she had not irritated Bea with the same vigor? She had felt repelled by Mr. Mayhew from the moment he'd started to detail his pedigree. "I am going to accuse you next."

Having his supposition confirmed delighted Mr. Mayhew, who clapped his hands exuberantly, but his wife stared silently for several long seconds. Then said somberly, "Please don't. It is not funny anymore."

Bea rather thought it had never been funny: the greatest chef in the world cut down in his prime. All the wonders that would never exist.

"I have not worked out all the details," she said, "but to start, I know you changed the clock in your dressing room to make it appear as though you were there between the hours of two and four when you were actually in the kitchen killing Mr. Réjane around two. I also know you administered laudanum to him so he would not struggle while you removed his head with a meat cleaver. You administered the drug via the two cheroots you gave him that afternoon. You used a cleaver because you had heard the kitchen maid threaten his life with it and you wanted suspicion to fall on her. You chopped off his head because you assumed that is how she

339

would have done it. You murdered him because you feared your husband's elaborate fraud would unravel if Mr. Réjane had been allowed to send a letter complaining about your husband's mistreatment of him to the Mayhew brothers."

The lady turned ashen. Her lips remained pulled in a friendly arch, as if she were contemplating a pleasant thought, but their red was the only hint of color on her face. Her eyelids blinked furiously, and Bea felt she could see the cogs in her brain turning as she tried to decide how to respond to such a thorough charge.

Bea thought her best strategy was to deny it categorically, to insist that her guest was confused or bore her some grudge or simply lacked the mental acuity of a man to understand the matter properly. The groundwork for the latter approach had already been neatly laid by Kesgrave, and all she had to do was build on its very sound foundation. Female inadequacy could always be relied on to invalidate a very good theory, and here it was only her word against Mrs. Mayhew's. Her case could not be proved so much as robustly argued.

Ah, but she *was* a duchess now, which meant any argument she made would be more solemnly considered. That was why the servants had so eagerly blamed each other for the vicious crime. They knew a peeress's interest made them more vulnerable to a miscarriage of justice.

Nevertheless, Bea did not believe Mrs. Mayhew could be condemned on her word alone. She would have to figure out some way to maneuver her into admitting the deed. Or perhaps she could gain access to the private quarters of the house to find incriminating evidence, although it seemed unlikely that a woman who had planned a murder to such coolly brilliant detail had left a bloody night rail laying around.

Bea, however, was spared the necessity of doing anything more by Mr. Mayhew, who inhaled sharply and screeched,

"You harridan! You fishwife! How could you behave so reck-lessly! Slaughtering our golden goose! Are you mad?"

Displaying none of the cold calculation with which Bea credited her, Mrs. Mayhew narrowed her eyes with fury as color flooded her cheeks. "Me! Me! *Me!* You are blaming *me* for this disaster! None of this would have happened if you weren't such a hen-witted clodpole that you cannot come up with one other name when inventing excuses to meet with your mistress. The second I mentioned you had an appointment with an investor called Bayne I knew what you had done because Monsieur Alphonse stared at me so intently!"

Indignant, Mr. Mayhew jumped to his feet, his cheeks turning an unnatural shade of red. "Good God, you dimwitted harpy, she is *not* my mistress. She is my spiritual adviser and I cannot palm her off when she has vital informa-tion about our future to impart!"

Mrs. Mayhew leaped up as well and marched toward him until her nose was but a few inches from his. "You fool! The only thing she has to impart is a bill for her services, which you pay month after month without any consideration of our finances. And she *is* your mistress, you insufferable buffoon. Just because she reads the tarot while you are having relations does not mean it isn't intercourse!"

"She has a harelip, for god's sake," he shrieked, as if that put an end to the notion of anything inappropriate about their conduct. "And I only compensate her generously because her advice helps the business."

Mrs. Mayhew found this statement so maddening, she actually screamed. "*I* help the business by providing you with a gracious home and a serene hostess at your table!"

The banker cackled in contempt, a harsh and unsettling sound. "*You* gracious and serene? You are a shrew, a vile virago I have had to put up with all these years. And now you've ruined everything. Everything! And for what? For why? A wild misconception based on female intuition."

His wife leaned forward until her nose was actually pressing against his and yelled at the top of her lungs, "He was going to send a *letter*."

"Good God, yes, let's hack up the cook because he was going to put pen to paper. What a very great horror!" he shouted with sarcastic fervor. "Get it through your head, you abhorrent termagant: *My brothers would not have cared.* They wouldn't even have noticed a letter from a disgruntled chef. And if they did—so what? Not a single one of them would begrudge me a stipend for all my hard work."

"A stipend?" she squealed with disdain. "A stipend! It's not a stipend, you bacon-brained rattleplate! It's thievery plain and simple."

"*You* were the one who called it a stipend," he spat.

"*I* was trying to help you appease your conscience because you are a sniveling twit," she sneered.

Around and around they went, a swirling whirlwind of hatred, contempt and anger, and Bea, suddenly weary of it all, turned to the duke. But she was flummoxed by the display of untethered viciousness and realized she had no clear thought to impart. She desired the scene to be over but wanted no part in the ending of it, and could not imagine either possibility. Consequently, when she looked at Kesgrave she was at a loss for words and when she did finally speak, it was more of a plea than a rational request for help: "Your grace."

Kesgrave, as if he had been waiting for just such a cue, nodded abruptly and asked her to wait there for a moment. Then he crossed swiftly to the doorway and disappeared into the hall. Mrs. Mayhew howled savagely at the mention of a scarlet gown and shrieked that if anything had led them into penury it was his Arabian stallion.

"I ride Caesar daily," he bellowed in outrage. "You wore that dress once!"

"To dine with *Brummell*," she sputtered.

Only a minute later the duke returned with—inconceivably—Marlow at his heels. In the hallway, just outside the room, Parsons hovered with an appalled expression on his face, which contrasted sharply with the other butler's bland impassivity.

"A Runner has been sent for," Kesgrave explained mildly, "and Marlow is going to monitor the situation until he arrives. We may go."

Although the butler's presence in the house was wholly inexplicable, Bea was not entirely surprised by it. She did not believe, no, that the duke had anticipated the horrible scene unfolding in the drawing room, but he'd had enough concern about the confrontation that he had stationed Marlow nearby: outside the door, on the pavement in front, in the square across the road.

Heartfully, gratefully, she said, "Thank you, Marlow."

As stoic as ever, the butler acknowledged the deeply felt sentiment with a barely perceptible nod, then winced uncontrollably when Mrs. Mayhew hurled a string of invectives at her husband over a certain gilded high-perch phaeton he lacked the skill to drive. "Thank *you,* your grace," he said with unprecedented emphasis. "It appears Monsieur Alphonse did not suffer an accident after all."

'Twas an admission—a quiet one, to be sure, dignified, understated, butler-ish, but an admission nonetheless—and Bea felt the respect it conveyed. "It appears not."

"You insufferable gorgon!" Mr. Mayhew cried. "You *dare* mock my imbalance condition when you are utterly useless with an embroidery needle?"

"You know I suffered a terrible injury to my thumb as a small child!"

Kesgrave murmured further instructions to Marlow, then escorted his wife from the room just as a porcelain vase slammed against the wall. Parsons shuddered in alarm, and the duke placed a firm, comforting hand on the man's shoulder and assured him Marlow had the matter under control. Although the butler's expression plainly indicated he did not think it was true, he expressed profound gratitude for their assistance.

Outside, the air was crisp and Bea sighed with deep relief to be away from the stultifying atmosphere of the drawing room. Although the decay of the Mayhews' relationship was particularly their own, something about it felt oddly similar to the deterioration of the Skeffingtons'. Both enterprises, presumably optimistic at the onset, had ended in murder and enmity, which Bea, scarcely two days into her own union, found almost too dispiriting to contemplate.

And yet she seemed unable to think of anything else, the two awful scenes appearing to play concurrently in her head, Lady Skeffington's cool indifference, Mrs. Mayhew's blistering rage. So much contempt and hatred.

Thoughtfully, as if genuinely considering a problem, Kesgrave said, "Obviously, I cannot deposit my money with Mayhew & Co. now."

Bea smiled faintly at this comment, for she had a deep appreciation for the value of well-conceived understatement, and agreed that his current situation was largely superior. "Unless Coutts's management has its own secret corruption scheme. I will look into it at once."

But the attempt at humor fell flat, for it only made her feel somehow complicit in the Mayhews' tragedy, as if it were her investigation that had created its conditions. It was absurd, she knew, for the wounds had already been festering, and if Parsons's version of events had been allowed to stand, something else would have brought the putrefaction to light.

Malevolence oozed.

It was an exceptionally dismal thought—ah, yes, the dreary Miss Hyde-Clare—and she smothered a sigh.

Or rather, she thought she had smothered it, but a moment later Kesgrave took her hand in his own. It was a mundane gesture, yes, and yet wildly shocking because dukes did not show their affection publicly, certainly not to their wives, and there were quite a few passersby to witness the outrageous deed. Indeed, Bea thought for certain she had noticed Mrs. Ralston's intrusive nose among the observers, and the prospect of London's most zealous gossip haunting Berkeley Square in hopes of catching sight of just such an exhibition almost made her grin.

Clutching Kesgrave's hand gratefully, Bea marveled at how he continually revealed himself to be more than she expected —more, of course, than the pedantic bore whom she longed to pelt with fillets of salmon in the dining room at Lakeview Hall, but also more than the thoughtful, open-minded, deprecating soul she had discovered him to be.

It was the opposite, she supposed, that caused gnawing resentment, the bitter revelation that the person you married was somehow and substantially less than you had believed.

"If you deem it necessary to inspect Coutts's books," the duke said as they turned up the path to Kesgrave House, "then I must insist on a full week to examine the situation before we make the attempt. As it is accustomed to a higher quality of client than Mayhew & Co., we cannot expect them to genuflect quite so deeply before my title."

Naturally, Bea scoffed at the display of modesty, for having seen him don his full consequence she felt confident he could cower anyone, especially the proprietors of an esteemed institution devoted to the acquisition and consolidation of wealth. In fact, she believed so fully in his ability to puff himself up to a monstrous size, she insisted they visit

Coutts on the morrow so that her thesis could be proved correct.

Firmly rejecting the proposal, Kesgrave announced that while he was happy to be bear-led to his ruin by his wife, he required a more compelling reason than to satisfy her curiosity.

Beatrice lamented his lack of inquisitiveness and asked where the world would be if, observing the apple that had clonked him on the head, Newton had shrugged his shoulders indifferently and returned to his book.

Kesgrave replied that his humiliating himself at a banking establishment was not equal to the discovery of gravity.

Once again, his wife tsked disapprovingly and noted that his humility was getting excessively out of hand.

And, quarreling ardently with her husband, the Duchess of Kesgrave entered her home.

About the Author

Lynn Messina is the author of more than a dozen novels, including the Beatrice Hyde-Clare mysteries, a series of cozies set in Regency-era England. Her first novel, *Fashionistas,* has been translated into sixteen languages and was briefly slated to be a movie starring Lindsay Lohan. Her essays have appeared in *Self, American Baby* and *the New York Times* Modern Love column, and she's a regular contributor to the *Times* parenting blog. She lives in New York City with her sons.

More Mystery!

Some Romance!

Anything can happen in Regency London, as five headstrong and passionate women defy propriety and find love with powerful lords as determined as they are.

Love Takes Root series

Book One: The Harlow Hoyden

Book Two: The Other Harlow Girl

Book Three: The Fellingham Minx

Book Four: The Bolingbroke Chit

Book Five: The Impertinent Miss Templeton